"How come the device speaks English, though?" Grant asked

"You sure don't. And you can't tell me anybody else out here does, either."

"Oh, but one does," Pine said. "As I told you, we learned from Gil Bates."

Everybody got real silent and still. She had said that right off, Kane remembered. He caught himself with his hand formed up in a half fist. In the corner of his eye he caught Grant deliberately opening his own right hand.

"So was it you who negotiated with Gil Bates?" Brigid asked, suddenly in the studiedly neutral tones of a lifelong Archivist. "Your people?"

Before Pine could respond, a retina-searing light beam speared a blazing yellow transverse down the sky. A tall figure striding past not twenty meters from Kane emitted a terrible shriek and fell to the ground with its robes blazing blue.

Other titles in this series:

James Axler
Outlanders®

CLOSING THE
COSMIC EYE

A GOLD EAGLE BOOK FROM
WORLDWIDE®

TORONTO • NEW YORK • LONDON
AMSTERDAM • PARIS • SYDNEY • HAMBURG
STOCKHOLM • ATHENS • TOKYO • MILAN
MADRID • WARSAW • BUDAPEST • AUCKLAND

For Scott Cline,
who isn't expecting it....

First edition February 2007

ISBN-13: 978-0-373-63853-6
ISBN-10:   0-373-63853-1

CLOSING THE COSMIC EYE

Special thanks to Victor Milán for his contribution to this work.

Copyright © 2007 by Worldwide Library.

"Think again of those astronomers who beamed radio signals into space from Arecibo, describing Earth's location and its inhabitants. In its suicidal folly that act rivalled the folly of the last Inca emperor, Atahuallpa, who described to his gold-crazy Spanish captors the wealth of his capital and provided them with guides for the journey. If there really are any radio civilizations within listening distance of us, then for heaven's sake let's turn off our own transmitters and try to escape detection, or we are doomed."
—Jared Diamond, author of
The Rise and Fall of the Third Chimpanzee

The Road to Outlands—
From Secret Government Files to the Future

Almost two hundred years after the global holocaust, Kane, a former Magistrate of Cobaltville, often thought the world had been lucky to survive at all after a nuclear device detonated in the Russian embassy in Washington, D.C. The aftermath— forever known as skydark—reshaped continents and turned civilization into ashes.

Nearly depopulated, America became the Deathlands— poisoned by radiation, home to chaos and mutated life forms. Feudal rule reappeared in the form of baronies, while remote outposts clung to a brutish existence.

What eventually helped shape this wasteland were the redoubts, the secret preholocaust military installations with stores of weapons, and the home of gateways, the locational matter-transfer facilities. Some of the redoubts hid clues that had once fed wild theories of government cover-ups and alien visitations.

Rearmed from redoubt stockpiles, the barons consolidated their power and reclaimed technology for the villes. Their power, supported by some invisible authority, extended beyond their fortified walls to what was now called the Outlands. It was here that the rootstock of humanity survived, living with hellzones and chemical storms, hounded by Magistrates.

In the villes, rigid laws were enforced—to atone for the sins of the past and prepare the way for a better future. That was the barons' public credo and their right-to-rule.

Kane, along with friend and fellow Magistrate Grant, had upheld that claim until a fateful Outlands expedition. A displaced piece of technology…a question to a keeper of the archives…a vague clue about alien masters—and their world shifted radically. Suddenly, Brigid Baptiste, the archivist, faced summary execution, and Grant a quick termination. For

Kane there was forgiveness if he pledged his unquestioning allegiance to Baron Cobalt and his unknown masters and abandoned his friends.

But that allegiance would make him support a mysterious and alien power and deny loyalty and friends. Then what else was there?

Kane had been brought up solely to serve the ville. Brigid's only link with her family was her mother's red-gold hair, green eyes and supple form. Grant's clues to his lineage were his ebony skin and powerful physique. But Domi, she of the white hair, was an Outlander pressed into sexual servitude in Cobaltville. She at least knew her roots and was a reminder to the exiles that the outcasts belonged in the human family.

Parents, friends, community—the very rootedness of humanity was denied. With no continuity, there was no forward momentum to the future. And that was the crux—when Kane began to wonder if there *was* a future.

For Kane, it wouldn't do. So the only way was out—way, way out.

After their escape, they found shelter at the forgotten Cerberus redoubt headed by Lakesh, a scientist, Cobaltville's head archivist, and secret opponent of the barons.

With their past turned into a lie, their future threatened, only one thing was left to give meaning to the outcasts. The hunger for freedom, the will to resist the hostile influences. And perhaps, by opposing, end them.

Prologue

The moons Somar, pink, and Nivatra, blue, hung low in the eastern sky, above a distant range of mountains scarcely visible in the darkness. Two figures wrapped in hooded robes against chill wind stood on a rounded slab of sandstone, trusting that the desert day's heat radiating from the surrounding rock, and the properties of the robes themselves, would mask their bodies' heat.

Below and before them, the desert's mauve sand glowed with a glare that had nothing to do with moons. The pale purple glare, with a core of eye-searing white, left yellow blobs of afterimage in the eye, like lightning. The light came from a giant amethyst, or so it seemed, descending from the black sky to touch the sand.

"The Kh'hisst," the smaller of the pair said. Her vocal apparatus made light of the guttural and glottal stop, but lisped slightly at the sibilant. Her taller companion shivered. "Virulent as a plague. Where they go, their masters—the Paa—come soon behind."

"What can they want, Elder?" the second figure said. This taller entity was clearly of a different species from the first.

The lesser form shrugged. "Perhaps our Groks will tell us. They whine when we make them try to read the Kh'hisst, but when needs must, the Devil drives."

A wind whistled up from the desert below, singing softly and discordantly among the rocks, smelling of sand and ozone. To the taller figure's exposed cheek its touch felt warmer than might be expected. Perhaps it was residual heat of a full day of fierce, ultraviolet-rich sunlight. Perhaps it was something else.

The crystal ship hovered. It was modest by the standards of the major Grand Council races, a mere five hundred yards, perhaps, from tip to tip, standing edgewise as it was. A lander, perhaps, or frigate. The taller being was no expert on spacecraft, having lived her whole life here, on this world of Sidra. She expected to die here, as well.

The thought made her shiver. Though clearly the giant vessel did not seek them—the Kh'hisst would make nothing of scorching this stretch of backwater world horizon to horizon with their chained lightnings—it brought to her the jarring realization that death could come at any time.

My brother, she thought. I wonder—

She felt the dry grasp of the other's hand on hers. For a moment she wondered; no other species could read the thoughts or feelings of her kind, not directly, the way the Grok, for example, could for all other sophont races in the Far Arm. But no—the one she named Elder, though by genes and biochemistry no more similar to her than she was to slime mold, and scarcely more than either was to the rock beneath their feet, was empathetic in a more conservative sense. And very, very little escaped her hidden eyes.

The smaller being squeezed her hand briefly and let it go. It was ever her way to offer support in such a way as not to encourage dependency. For that weakened, and the coalition races could not afford more weakness than they suffered already. That went especially for the taller and younger of the pair: for of all sapient races, few were more despised.

If any.

Overhead a patch of sky flared white. From the cliff tops above rose voices calling out in alarm.

"Elder!" called one down through cupped hands. "Come off the ledge! A storm comes."

"Haven't you got eyes?" the mother snapped. It was a rhetorical question, though it need not have been: not all known races of the Far Arm did have eyes, although everyone in this small resistance band happened to possess them. "There are no clouds above. See the stars?"

Her companion looked up. She saw stars in fact, with not the slightest wisp of cloud to screen them.

And she saw more: a line of dazzle that faded almost at once but left a pinkish pulsation in the eye that only reluctantly vanished. A swarm of yellow motes, blinking quickly out. A sudden yellow globe, which darkened to rose, to red, then assumed an angry ember hint.

She gasped. "Yes, a storm has come," said the shrouded Elder. "But not within our atmosphere. Yet."

"So it is the end," the taller figure said brokenly.

The smaller's laugh rasped like a file on granite. "Only by accident. We're far too insignificant to attract such attention. And far too weak, especially in this region of space, to effect such a spectacular display."

The great violet ship began to ascend. A cloud of dust swirled from below, looking as if each mote glowed with its own blue-white light. High above it another new star appeared, as red as an inflamed eye. It grew, and as it did so a heart of intense yellow could be seen. Its outlines seemed to waver.

Soundless still, the amethyst ship slid sideways above the flat desert floor, still rising. Its ascent seemed to lack urgency, its lateral movement apparently precautionary.

The star became a shape: a great ship, miles long, stricken, shattered, ablaze as it suffered catastrophic reentry. As the crystal ship, now clearly out of its descent path, commenced again its perfect vertical rise, the doomed leviathan streaked overhead in a glory of trailing flames. It was so huge and terrible that the taller being ducked, though even she knew the vessel had to still be in the stratosphere or above.

"Our enemies fight our enemies," commented the Elder, who stood slight but unbowed beneath the psychic weight of the monstrous hurtling machine. "It's an ill wind that blows no good." She was fond of using bromides and shopworn catchphrases, the resistance leader, as if daring others to disrespect her for it.

A shattering crack fell upon them then. The taller creature pressed her pale, soft-skinned hands to the sides of her head to shield her ears. The noise of the burning hulk's hypersonic passing made the sandstone shake beneath their feet, and beat from the stone surfaces like furnace heat.

The doomed monster careened on into the west, drawing a rose-and-blue-white ghost trail of ionized air behind it, as if it had snagged one of the planet's spectacular auroras and was unraveling it behind. The comet head vanished over the mountains behind the small party.

A white flash lit the sky beyond the peaks, turning them to black silhouettes. The taller figure whipped her head aside and threw up a hand to shield her eyes.

For a time she and her companion stood, scarcely remembering or daring to breathe as the dome rose up to become a sphere, still bright but dimming, swarming with colors and patterns like an oil droplet on a pool of water.

"Brace yourselves," called out the Elder briskly.

Another crack came, deeper and immeasurably vaster than the sonic boom of moments before. And it went on and on. This time the earth shook more authoritatively. The taller creature watched warily as head-sized stones bounced down the slope above them. Their companions, up on top of the mesa, cried out in dismay as the rolling shock wave tumbled them like toys. Fortunately, all had had sense enough to move far enough from the edge that none took a header. Down in the blast shadow of the hill, the taller being felt the shock wave as no more than a quick, faint blow to her face.

"One hundred miles away," someone called down from above.

"So much the worse for Wunlei town," another voice called.

"I grieve for them," the Elder said matter-of-factly. "Yet I'll make bold enough to say this may go well for us, those of us who survive."

She turned back to the desert below. Her acolyte turned with her. The desert lay like a calm lake before them, the sand faintly aglow with the light of the setting moons. Of the amethyst ship the taller creature could see no sign, although the battle in orbit still flashed and flared and shimmered overhead. More spots glowed, in various colors.

Each pretty shiny cloud, she thought, means the death of hundreds of sophonts. Thousands. She shivered again.

"But then," the Elder said, so softly those above could not have heard her even if their ears weren't still ringing, "I've always been an optimist...."

Chapter 1

"Bingo," Larry Robison said over the team push. "Head shot. Sometimes you scare me, Iron Man."

"Part of the service," a voice said in his head. "Moving to Position Gabriel, over."

Robison shook his head. I didn't see that, he thought, lowering his binoculars as somewhere hundreds of yards behind him Joe "Iron Man" Weaver hefted his heavy sniper rifle and shifted it to a new location selected in advance.

What Robison had seen, or imagined he had seen, through the glasses was a wisp of blue luminescence wafting upward from the spurting, headless neck stump. Like a soul departing a freshly killed body.

I have to be hallucinating. I'd rather face that than the implications.

"Move it along, Phone Man," a far too familiar voice rasped in his skull, courtesy of the bone-conduction speaker taped to the mastoid process behind his ear. "Or are you waiting for a written invitation?"

"Engraved," he said, rising from behind the moss-covered log. The night ahead was shades of gray and black amid a dense smell of green. Though he wore night-vision goggles, he kept them pushed up top of his Kevlar boonie hat. His biggest enemy right then wasn't fauna, whether four-legged, two-legged or sporting no fauna at all. Rather it was flora.

Up here in the Andes foothills of what had been Peru, the Río Marañón basin was neither as stupefyingly humid-hot as the lower Amazon it flowed to join, nor as thickly vegetated. Where he was there was no canopy to speak of, though the trees rose dizzyingly tall against a sky showing stars through high clouds. But there was more ground cover, more midlevel brush that offered nasty places where an incautious intruder, even moving slowly, could twist an ankle or take a spill down a hidden gully onto rocks that could bust a leg despite the special-weave cloth of Team Phoenix's camou uniforms and upper-body armor.

Variations in vegetation and land conformation showed up poorly on the night-vision goggles' ambient-light enhancers, and not at all on infrared. So instead of goggles they relied on good old-fashioned eyeballs tonight. When they needed special vision they would use the scopes mounted on their longblasters.

Though the team's erstwhile special-operations troopers were well-versed in using the coolest high-tech gear—including stuff not even available back in the day before they were laid down in suspended animation for their two-century-long nuclear winter nap—they had all bashed about bush in the world's bad places to have a healthy skepticism of technology. They could roll both ways, as brash former Delta operator Sean Reichert, the team's youngest, now out about thirty yards away on point to Robison's left, might say.

Of course, the fact that environmental hazards were most immediate in the current situation did *not* imply that

predators weren't a threat. Particularly the bipedal brand.
But the brutal fact was that, while their opposition weren't
the total masters of stealth in this terrain that some of the
local inhabitants were, the brush was dense enough to
cover a multitude of sins, even from the laser-sharp eyes
and ears and noses of the Team Phoenix operatives.

Fortunately, they didn't have to rely on their senses alone.

"Magic Voice," Hays subvocalized for the benefit of
the flesh-colored patch taped to his Adam's apple. In full
daylight it was almost invisible. "What's our sitch, over?"

"Phone Man," came a voice that, to a guy with his ass
in the grass deep in bandit country, sounded magical indeed—young, feminine, touched with both Spanish and
Indian accents. "I see negative response to the Angel
shot, over."

Larry "Phone Man" Robison nodded. He wasn't forgetting that the speaker, sitting miles away in the concrete-
and-steel redoubt the team had dubbed the Fortress of
Solecism, in honor of its former proprietor—and their
former employer—wouldn't be looking his way.

That the downriver raiders hadn't noticed anything unusual wasn't particularly surprising. Though Little Willi,
the sniper rifle, spoke with a voice uncommonly loud,
from over a mile away with lots of moist, sound-deadening vegetation, its report had been impossible to distinguish
from the thunder muttering off to the north beyond the hills
that defined the river valley, and Robison had known it was
coming. Besides, the team's surveillance had reported the
man was alone, watching his buddies' back trail while they
crept on their objective, an unsuspecting Atshuara village
five hundred farther on.

"PBIs, Eye in the Sky shows your route clear to your objectives, over." As "Angel" was code name for their sniper watching over his mates with his monstrous 20 mm rifle, so "PBI" meant the other three out with their boots on the ground—World War I slang for "Poor Bloody Infantry."

"Suave," Reichert said over the same net. Magic Voice was always in the comm circuit when the team was on the ground. Anything else would obviate the whole point of having an all-seeing combat director on-line.

It was also a rude way to treat a fourteen-year-old orphan with genius IQ who had been saved from slavery in a team raid six months earlier.

"Thanks, Magic Voice," Major Mike Hays said. "Now clamp the pieholes and save your gas for serious humping, Phoenix. We got miles to go before we sleep."

"You forgot 'promises to keep,'" Robison said, slipping forward through the brush with his suppressed machine pistol cradled before his chest.

"Fuck that," Reichert said. "I ain't no Promise Keeper."

Major Mike's laughter rumbled in Robison's ears. It was a small joke, and a lame one. But it was also a precious reminder of a chronological home no man would ever see again—a home two centuries dead, and so different from the world they now inhabited as to be functionally another planet.

"WHAT IS THE MEANING of this?"

A few heads mounted above the shoulders packed in solid around the perimeter of the gymnasium where Grant and Kane were wrestling turned at the sharp, imperious voice. Most didn't. Although the audience consisted almost entirely of refugees from the Manitius Moon base, relative newcomers to the Cerberus redoubt buried beneath the Bitterroot mountains of what had once been Montana, all had long since heard enough of Dr. Mohandas Lakesh Singh's command voice to be pretty well immunized by now.

"Sport," Domi said sullenly. She shot a glance at the stocky, light-skinned black woman who stood next to her, shifting her weight from side to side, craning her cornrowed head and generally looking stressed out. "*Her* idea."

In the middle of the gym the clinch continued. Lakesh turned a fearsome glare upon the redoubt's medic.

"Reba," he said, "I trust you have some explanation for this."

"Yeah," Reba DeFore said. "They're fused out. This was the exact sort of thing I was trying to forestall, damnit!"

"You're doing a bloody great job of it," growled one of the Manitius émigrés standing next to Lakesh.

"Sod off," another said. "*I'm* enjoying the show." Some of the refugees from the Manitius base felt gratitude to Kane and Grant for liberating them from alien oppression and near certain death. Others resented them. The audience for the afternoon's athletic event—afternoon by the clocks, since the sun never penetrated the redoubt's vanadium-steel bowels—belonged pretty solidly to the latter faction. Except for the two women, one sturdy and bronze, the other slight, snow-white and ruby eyed as an albino ferret, who stood at the rear of the mob.

Lakesh was an East Indian man, apparently in his late forties or early fifties. The gaze he turned on the speakers was incongruously deep blue. And righteously pissed.

"How did this happen?" asked the woman who accompanied him. She stood almost as tall as him, with wide shoulders held in a manner that did nothing to discourage her full breasts from pushing out the front of her white jumpsuit. Nothing conscious lay behind that: even after spending several years free of the spavined life of a senior archivist in Cobaltville, Brigid Baptiste had no real emotional grasp of the fact she was a strikingly beautiful woman. Even though the hair falling around her shoulders was the hue of Hawaiian fast-flow lava and her eyes had the color of cut and polished emeralds.

Reba DeFore's sturdy shoulders rose and fell in a sigh. "I thought our personnel—especially you field operators— needed some normal activity for a change. You know, something that doesn't involve breaking people and killing things. Or getting and staying ready to do so. Anyway, I had the gym cleared out of the stuff stored here so it could be used for what the builders intended. And then—" she waved a weary hand at the floor where Kane and Grant were battling "—*this* happened."

"Darlingest Domi," Lakesh asked the small albino, "*how* did it happen?"

Domi didn't reply, but shrugged a shoulder. She was wearing a T-shirt, once red and now faded by sun to a splotchy pink, cut middie length with the short sleeves ripped off. Below it she wore denim cutoffs and a pair of red stand-up stockings. A well-weathered pair of Converse All-Stars completed the ensemble.

"Absurd," Lakesh said to himself. "Ladies, gentlemen, please let me past. We must put a stop to it at once."

"Why?" said a woman with wild black hair, showing bare-scalp patches in evidence of fairly advanced female alopecia. "Let the stiff-necked bastards take some starch out of each other, say I." Her comrades grumbled agreement.

Lakesh raised his voice as he addressed Grant and Kane. "Gentlemen," he called, "if I may intrude…"

Grant and Kane froze at the sound of Lakesh's voice, then picked themselves cautiously up off the floor.

"It doesn't look as if the silly protracted adolescents did each other any permanent harm," Brigid said waspishly.

DeFore grinned. "You say so, Brigid. If she's wrong, Lakesh—they know where to find me." She went out the door.

Kane and Grant now stood, unconsciously shoulder to shoulder, glaring defiantly at Lakesh. "What?" Grant demanded.

"I need to talk to you gentlemen immediately," Lakesh said.

"We were just having some nice, healthy exercise," Kane said. "Just like Reba wanted."

"Be glad she's not here to hear that, Kane," Brigid said. "She tells me she's keeping a stainless-steel enema syringe in the meat freezer for the next time she loses patience with you."

"Her and what army? The Millennium Consortium's Chinese—"

"Gentlemen, ladies," Lakesh said, his usual calm quite ruffled. "We must consult. *Now*."

"What's the flap this time, Lakesh?" Grant said, drying himself with a towel he'd picked up off the hardwood floor. "The end of the world as we know it?"

"Yes," Lakesh said. "Quite conceivably. Or more precisely, the end of the universe as we know it."

Chapter 2

Larry Robison felt it when it all went to worms. Long before his conscious mind had sorted out the sensory inputs, he knew.

"Wait one." The feminine voice, formerly so reassuring, rang in his skull like a harbinger of doom. "I get more heat signatures. Two, four, five—it's as if they're coming out of the earth!"

"They are," Hays's voice said. "Where?"

A bullet gouged a splinter from a tree trunk two yards over Robison's head and tumbled moaning into the darkness. He dived from crouching behind a tree into a waist-high clump of scrub. The shot crack told him the answer a millisecond before he heard "Behind you!"

Doing business as Magic Voice, the girl named Marina had talked them right up onto the tails of the raiding party bound for the village: twenty soldiers from La República del Río Marañón, the very nation in which she had been held captive since her capture in childhood from a ville her Atshuara people. The Fortress of Solecism had been tracking them since satellite imaging, courtesy of Cerberus, had picked up their power launch coming north on the river the afternoon before.

But only a limited number of surveillance satellites still

survived, more than two centuries after the nukecaust. And the team's allies in North America could only spare a limited proportion of such assets, especially given their continuing struggle with the overlords.

But the four-man team did not depend on orbital birds for overhead assistance. The secret subterranean base they had taken over, with Cerberus's help, from their erstwhile employer Gilgamesh Bates, had been designed and built for the War on Drugs. It came equipped with a number of useful assets of its own, including remotely piloted Unmanned Aerial Vehicles for reconnaissance.

Fifteen miles behind them Marina piloted a West-German-made UAV with the aplomb of a twentieth-century teen raised playing video games. The craft was the size of a large radio-controlled hobby plane, sporting an eight-foot wingspan and loaded with microminiaturized sensors. Its electric motor, powered by a stack of compact lithium polymer batteries, made no noise perceptible more than a hundred yards off. And right now her infrared monitors was showing her—

"Behind you," Magic Voice said.

She sounded perfectly calm. After what she had endured, sitting in the climate-controlled comfort of the redoubt playing eye in the sky was a piece of cake. Even though the lives of the men who had made themselves her foster brothers and fathers relied upon her.

"Iron Man," Robison heard Hays rasp over the comm circuit, "can you clear our back trail?"

Writhing deeper into brush that he hoped would screen him from observation from the rear, as well as in front, Robison heard a sharp crack overhead, followed by a hard, heavy thud. Which meant one of their ambushers had departed the planet without ceremony, courtesy of a solid slug from Little Willi.

"Mechanic, I'll do what I can," Weaver imperturbable voice came back. "But there're a lot of them, and I can't see through trees." His current sniper position lay atop a ridge barely two hundred yards behind them. The thought of Weaver up there all alone made Robison's skin crawl: folks played for high stakes hereabouts. There were reasons snipers were inevitably deployed in two- or even three-man teams. When you were pouring every joule of concentration through the glass, you couldn't spare any attention to covering your own ass.

Speaking of which, the ex-SEAL thought as another burst of gunfire ripped out from somewhere to the rear. This one didn't come anywhere near. He heard voices calling softly in a language that was neither English nor Spanish. His heart did a nosedive, but later there would be time to deal with the ramifications. If later happened at all…

He turned his suppressed .40-caliber MP-5 back the way he and his three teammates had come and peered over the top of the night scope mounted on its receiver. He wanted to absorb as much detail as he could before losing most resolution by diving into his own glass.

Then he hunkered down to put eye to lens. Something moved, no more than twenty yards back, at the verge of a tiny clearing he'd skirted just moments before. He drew a deep breath and held it as a yellow blob appeared against a dark green background. He sighted in on the reticule on the featureless protrusion that was the head and pulsed out a neat 2-round burst.

The Heckler & Koch thumped and its bolt clacked as it reciprocated. In the general commotion of shooting and shouts and crashing brush the sounds would be lost. The figure dropped.

"Phone Man, Loverboy," Hays said, "what's your sitch?"

"Trouble ahead, trouble behind," Sean "Loverboy" Reichert replied. "We got Atshuara coming out of spider holes all around, and they don't seem well disposed toward us."

"I think our indig friends have decided to switch sides," Robison said. Bursts of full-auto ripped out farther back. Presumably from the gang of Río Marañón troopies they'd been about to land on.

Another yellow blur showed in his scope. It moved slowly left to right. He gave it a double tap in the center of mass. It fell without a sound.

"Super," Hays said. "Here's the deal—we're gonna get the bastards crossfiring each other, then run an end-around and de-ass the area."

"What about the village?" Weaver asked.

"It's bait," Robison said, surprised at the bitterness in his own voice. *What was I expecting, gratitude?* "The ville isn't the target. It's been us all along."

"Roger that," Hays said. "Prep two flash-bangs each. Then on my call pitch one backward toward the *maricones*, then one forward toward our new former friends. Got that?"

Maricones was the slang term the team and its native allies had adopted for soldiers from the republic, themselves once allies, now enemies. It meant "eunuchs."

Robison acknowledged, already acting, leaving the MP-5 on the ground momentarily.

"Roger dodger, you old codger," Reichert replied.

"You'll pay for that later, Loverboy. Ready? One, two, *three*."

Pushing himself on his left arm and twisting his torso, Robison threw one canister back behind him, making sure not to bounce it off the tree trunk he'd been hiding behind. Then he simply switched arms and tossed the other gren the other way. Then he buried his face in the loose soil.

The bombs lit the night with huge blue-white hemispheres of light and split it with cracks that felt like nails being driven into his brain. The flash-bangs were also called stun grenades, meant to disorient a foe at close quarters by overloading his visual and aural senses.

They were also great gaudy fireworks. Instantly gunfire exploded from both directions. To Robison's momentary astonishment orange lines zipped through the trees from the rear like laser beams: the Río Marañón troops had actually loaded tracers in their magazines. As a raid or ambush tactic it was on a par with lighting off a flare and sticking it in your rucksack: Here I am! Come kill me!

As he began to crawl with great dispatch on belly and elbows to what was now his left, the surprise faded quickly. The Spanish-speaking invaders from downriver possessed apparently bottomless wells of stupidity, which was why Team Phoenix and its head-hunting Atshuara allies had been able to stand them off successfully in a constant low-level guerrilla campaign—in spite of the fact that one of their star players had switched teams.

Meanwhile the firefight between the downriver troopies and the attackers who'd popped out of spider holes around Team Phoenix was still raging. The *maricones'*

AKMs made heavy, relatively slow thuds; the newcomers' weapons either boomed out like shotguns or rang out with the louder reports of FN FALs, which fired full-length 7.62 mm cartridges, unlike AKs, which fired a shortened and less powerful assault rifle round. The FNs were blazing off full-auto, which meant their more potent bullets weren't likely hitting anything. The recoil was just too great even for very good spray shooting.

The shots from the Team Phoenix's back trail confirmed Robison's fears: some of their own tribal allies had turned on them. Team Phoenix itself had provided the Belgian-made rifles to the locals from the giant, well-stuffed arsenal within the Fortress of Solecism. The Atshuara loved the weps, even though they were almost as long as the tribals themselves. And they'd never admit they couldn't control them on full-automatic, either.

Team Phoenix had also taught them the trick of masking their body-heat signatures from overhead thermal surveillance by digging spider holes and topping them off with wood and woven-mat lids covered with vegetation carefully dug out still living.

"I'm coming up behind you, Phone Man," Hays called. "Don't light me up. Sean's headed the other way." Which made sense. They had been spread out line abreast as they crept up to take on the Marañón raiders. Hays had been in the middle.

"We might just pull this one off, Mechanic," Robison said to Hays as he fast-crawled across an open space. Muzzles-flames blossomed to his right. Shots cracked over his head, each mini-sonic boom as loud as a pistol report.

The former SEAL twisted, fired his MP-5. He aimed for

the muzzle-flares using the iron combat sights; the light would wash out his infrared.

Screams replied. One muzzle-flash strobed skyward as the man behind it fell backward with his finger locked on the trigger of the big longblaster.

I'm hanging in the breeze, here, Robison thought. His machine pistol ran dry. As he came up off the ground, he let the blast drop to the extent of the sling around his neck. He had magazines in a chest pack for quick reload, but the H&K was meant for covert murder, not full-dress firefights. A suppresser-shrouded barrel would quickly burn out under rapid fire, and the MP-5 fired from a closed bolt, meaning that while it was far more accurate than a shit-for-blowback machine pistol, its receiver tended to overheat and lock up, too. And he had brought along something even better for dancing real close....

Launching himself into a crouched-over sprint for the cover of a trio of trees standing with their big boles almost touching, seven or eight yards ahead, he reached over his back and closed his fingers on the pistol grip of the weapon slung barrel-down over his ruck. Grinning ferally, he pulled the Saiga autoloading shotgun free and fired from the hip one-handed.

Back in the day, when they were choosing their weapons as loyal employees of computer supermogul Gilgamesh Bates, Major Mike Hays had disparaged Robison's preference for 20-gauge. Until Robison had proved that he could get more metal on target in the same amount of time with his twenty than anyone in Bates's whole vast UR Software security corps could with the heavier charge of a 12-gauge. A 20-gauge gave three-quarters the killing power of a 12-gauge for two-thirds the recoil, Robison liked to point out.

The ex-SEAL had no way of knowing whether his scattergun charges actually hit anything. Most likely they didn't, even though the heavy Russian autoloader with its modified AK action was not at all troublesome to shoot one-handed. But the big full-throat booming and giant flame were intimidating. The men charging quit shooting at him, probably because they were hugging the earth.

Robison could sense shots coming in from other directions, though. A tracer zipped right in front of his face, leaving green afterimage splitting his vision in two. He launched himself in a full-on dive for the shelter of the three trees.

He landed, rolled, came out in a prone position with the shotgun up. Shots still thumped into the trees a yard or two above his head, but he couldn't see any flashes in his field of vision. "Mechanic, move on up," he called, "I'll cover—"

He heard a splitting sound behind him and snapped his head around.

In time to see the central tree of the trio topple toward him.

Chapter 3

Giant pulsating yellow-white flame lit the small clearing. Shattering noise sent roosting birds flapping up into the night, their piping cries audible between bursts. Major Mike Hays was coming to rescue his man down.

His body was twisted to the right as he ran, leaping over a low hummock of ground. He was a sturdily built man of medium height with a bit more gut than he cared to see in the mirror, silver-white hair and mustache, and startling blue eyes. He carried his modified MAG-58 machine gun by its pistol grips fore and aft, firing it like a giant 7.62 mm Tommy gun as if to hold off the ambushing tribals by force of will and noise and fire.

To his left a grenade cracked off in the woods. From concealment behind his chief, Reichert was dropping down covering fire, 40 mm grenades launched from his pistol-style H&K with the retractable stock.

Unseen by Hays as he sprinted toward where Larry Robison lay pinned beneath a fallen tree, a man rose from a patch of scrub, wearing the camou blouse and floppy boonie hat of a Río Marañón soldier and bringing a Roman-nosed AKM to his shoulder. The soldier drew a bead on the running badger-shaped man, leading his target as if he actually knew what he was doing.

A white flash, then a ripping crack. As the soldier's head snapped back, the garish limelight illuminated yellowish teeth bared by the peeling away of his lips by a blast wave. The head went back and back, then disappeared completely. A 20 mm explosive projectile had struck the top of his longblaster's receiver at over 700 meters a second and detonated, shattering hands and chest and face and tearing his head right off his neck. Geysering blood from the stump of his neck, he crumpled.

Hays knelt by Robison. The tall, burly ex-SEAL lay twisted with his Smith & Wesson Classic 610 revolver in his hand and his round, handsome, bearded face rigid. The tree that lay across his hips and the small of his back was better than a foot thick.

"Deadfall," Robison grunted as Hays slammed open the tray of his MG, tossed away the tag end of a mostly spent ammo belt and yanked the beginning of a new one out of his rucksack. He laid it in the receiver and slammed the cover shut; it would unreel from a synthetic spool in the pack, a feature designed to render the weapon functional in combat without an assistant gunner. "When cover looks that inviting, I should figure it's a trap."

"Shut yours," Hays said, rearing back and firing a quick burst. Two or three wiry little tribesmen who had burst out of the trees armed with single-shot shotguns and steel-tipped spears fell. The other rabbited back into the darkness. "I'm getting you out of here."

"That's a big negative, Mike," Robison said. "I've got cracked ribs, and I think a dislocated hip. Anyway this sucker's got me pinned like a butterfly on a board. You gotta get out of here with the team."

"Screw that, sailor boy. We never leave a man behind."

"Oh, to hell with that burly noise. You can combat loss me or write off you and Sean and still lose me."

Hays had slung the machine gun, ignoring the searing heat radiating from the barrel into his back. He squatted beside the fallen tree, digging his fingers in beneath a gnarl of branch and straining as if trying to deadlift it off his comrade. "Save your breath for screaming, pal," he grunted, "when we pop that leg back in."

Elbow on the ground, Robison fired his double-action revolver twice. A tribesman fell screaming and thrashing, coiled around the searing agony of guts pulped by a 10 mm Black Talon bullet that unfolded like an eagle's claw on contact.

"Don't you get it?" Robison asked as a burst from Reichert's AK-108 assault rifle ripped the woods in the direction of the village they had intended to protect—and whose occupants, it seemed, had betrayed them to their mutual enemies from downriver. "I'm here to stay, unless you got a crane in your pocket."

"Not…listening." Hays's face was dark beneath the brim of his own boonie hat as his blood pressure soared.

"Your call." Robison turned around the five-inch barrel of his S&W and stuck it up under his own bearded jaw. "Remember *Blazing Saddles,* big fella? Back off."

Hays stopped. "You're kidding."

With a sliding multiple click Robison cocked the piece. "Pound and a half of pressure," he said. "That's all it takes now. Think I'm bluffing?"

In the background to all this Marina was calling, trying to find out what was happening to her adopted family. Both men had ignored her, but now her voice took on fresh urgency.

"Phoenix, Phoenix, I have signatures closing in from the southeast. Many signatures—could be company strength. Get out of there now. Please."

"Iron Man here," Weaver replied. "I'll slow them down as much as I can. But if we don't all pull out in the next few minutes they'll surround us."

Robison cocked his head meaningfully. He still had his finger on the now single-action trigger. A slight pressure, even inadvertent, would decapitate him as efficiently as a guillotine, if a deal more messily.

Shaking his head and growling in disgust, Major Mike rose. He unslung his machine gun and fired a long shuddering burst into the night.

"We'll come for you," he told the trapped man. "Bet to that."

"I'll hold you to it," Robison said.

Screams rang from deeper in the woods, along with a hellish blue-white glare. Reichert had popped a white phosphorus grenade in among a fire team of Río Marañón troops. Now they danced, writhing in tendrils of thick white poisonous smoke, flailing uselessly with their hands at the fragments of burning metal that ate their way into their bodies and sent beams of hideous light shining forth from their flesh.

By the light of burning men, Hays ran.

"So," THE VOICE SAID in English. It was feminine. And all too familiar. "The heroes of Team Phoenix are mortal after all."

"Fallible, anyway," Robison said. Around them the sounds of a firefight faded away into the south. He turned and pointed the Smith & Wesson at the short, slight woman who stood by the tree. She seemed all but overwhelmed by the baggy camou utilities she wore, much more by the Kalashnikov slung across her back. She did not flinch. "*Mortal* remains to be proved."

He cocked the handblaster again. "Ladies first?"

She laughed. "Go ahead and kill me, if it will make you feel better, Señor Robison. You will still serve your purpose—luring your friends back to rescue you, so that they can all be dealt with. But I can promise that should you kill me, those who are captured will suffer greatly before they are allowed to die. And you would witness that suffering."

"You're not going to threaten that I'd be shot to pieces by your bodyguards if I killed you?" he asked.

She shook her head. Her long dark hair was tied into a pair of braids that whipped about her shoulders.

Like Marina, the woman who stood over the trapped operator was descended from the local Atshuara tribe, the most powerful—and aggressive—of the Shuara people, the folk once known and feared as Jivaro. Like Marina she had been raised among the European-descended planters of the Río Marañón republic, had learned Spanish as well as English, the latter being an affectation of the upper classes.

Unlike Marina, she had not been a slave. Rather she was the half-breed bastard daughter of a powerful republic politician. She had fled to the bush to make herself a leader in the indigenous fight against Río Marañón encroachment. She had subsequently become an ally of Team Phoenix in a desperate battle against an irruption of monsters genetically engineered by one of Gil Bates's pet mad scientists.

And finally, she had succeeded her late father as military dictator of the republic.

He rumpled his mouth inside his beard in a wry expression. "So you're opting to play upon my basic codependent nature, knowing I'd willingly sacrifice myself if I could take out the leader of our enemies?"

"Many of you *norteamericanos* are that way," she said. "Also, you talk too much."

"I knew that, too." He let in the hammer with his thumb and tossed the handgun onto a soft patch of grass-covered soil. "Careful with that. I'm going to want it back."

She laughed again. Then she whistled. Several soldiers in camouflage appeared. One stooped, collected the handblaster. He started to stuff it in his belt. She held out one smooth hand. With visible reluctance he placed its grip in her palm.

"We've got it figured why you turned on us," Robison said, "not to mention your own people—good old fashioned lust for power."

"Not entirely," Consuelo said. "When I was a girl, raised among the Spanish in Santa Caridad, I acquired tastes for a certain standard of living. Standards not to be met among my beloved Atshuara."

Larry nodded. "Which makes me wonder—since you turned on them, too, once we removed El Liberador from your road—why the Atshuara chose to join you, when you've been trying so hard to conquer them and we've been helping them fight off your downriver thugs?"

Soldiers were moving around them now. They seemed to be examining the tree that pinned Robison with great interest. Consuelo looked at them and fired off some commands in Spanish that flowed faster than Robison's comprehension. Then she looked at her captive again.

"The Atshuara are a warrior people," she said. "They too

understand the lure of conquest. They also understand that, over time, the superior means of the downriver people will prevail, that they and the other native peoples will be pushed back inexorably, eventually wiped out. It is the way of things."

"So they decided to take the long view and sign up with the winning side?"

She nodded.

"What about the other Shuara?"

She shrugged. "They were not so foresightful as my people. So I fear they must be among the first swept into the dustbin of history."

"But what about the Atshuara?" Robison asked, visibly clamping down on a grimace of pain. "Don't they understand your European-descended friends from downriver will never really accept their continued existence? That they're only delaying the inevitable by allying with them?"

"Perhaps they are not so foresightful as they might be, the Atshuara," Consuelo said. "But as you say, the end result is inevitable. The tribal people are an evolutionary dead end, and will pass away. So perhaps the Atshuara have chosen correctly, in that they will at least get to enjoy helping conquer their cousins before they themselves are dealt with."

"You're cold, lady."

She smiled. Coldly. "It is a useful trait in a part of this world where hot-bloodedness is the norm, I find."

She turned to her troops. "Bring the ropes and tackle, and hurry!" she commanded in Spanish, speaking deliberately enough for Robison to follow. "We must get him out so that he can receive proper medical treatment in time.

"And if through clumsiness you kill him, or even let him die, then you shall all stand in for him at a very public execution in Santa Caridad!"

LEANING BACK in a chair in the briefing theater, Kane looked at Grant. "Sounds like our friends the deep-sea vent-forms well and truly screwed the pooch on this one, partner," he said.

"So did we," Grant grumbled, standing behind Kane. Brigid, Domi, Sally Wright and Lakesh were also present for the briefing session.

The big man with the gunslinger mustache down the sides of his long, strong chin crossed his arms. Then he uncrossed them with a grimace. His lower rib cage was too sore for such contact. "We trusted that asshole Bates, too, after all."

"Old Tower did not employ quite so colorful an idiom, friend Kane," Lakesh said. "But I suspect he would endorse your assessment."

"If somebody long, long ago built some gimmick that could switch the universe off like a light bulb," Domi said, "why did the vent bugs tell Gilgamesh Bates about it, of all people?"

Lakesh sighed. "They do not truly understand us and our ways," he said. "And Bates possesses a diabolical skill at manipulation. One that transcends apparently impassable chasms of culture and biochemistry, it would seem."

"This just keeps getting better and better," Grant said. "I should've stayed in New Edo last time."

"As good a place as any to be when the universe quits existing," Kane said with his voice slightly strangled from having chin down on his chest.

"Mebbe you should give us a hint as to how Bates plans to end the universe," Grant said, sipping coffee.

"We don't know for sure that he does," Brigid said.

"What the hell does that mean?" Kane snapped.

Brigid's head jerked back. Her green eyes flared.

"Your tone is quite uncalled-for, Kane," Lakesh said briskly. "Dearest Brigid is doing her best to apprise you of the situation. It is, as a moment's reflection might reveal to you, somewhat involved."

"Yeah," Kane said, looking slowly away from Brigid's green laser-death glare, "well. You know I've never exactly been the reflecting type, Lakesh."

"Yeah, you're a regular black hole, partner," Grant said.

"Sorry, Baptiste. It's just that all this loose talk about the end of the universe is making me a little, you know, testy. Especially since you and Lakesh can't exactly seem to get your story straight on whether it's about to end or not—"

"Kane," Brigid warned in a dangerously throaty voice.

Kane waved a hand. "Sorry, sorry. I'm an asshole."

"Sometimes you display a remarkable gift of understatement, friend Kane," Lakesh murmured. "Now, as to the apparently uncertain status of our universe vis-à-vis imminent destruction, consider this—knowing Bates as we do, do we imagine he would prefer to destroy the universe or rule it?"

"Rule," said Domi, biting into an apple.

Beaming at her, Lakesh nodded. "Quite correct, darlingest Domi!"

"So you reckon he intends to use the device for a little cosmic extortion," Kane said.

"And blow the whole thing to Hell if he can't get his way," Grant added.

"He really got the goods?" Domi asked. "I mean, seems to me, if there was this blaster lying around that could destroy the universe, somebody would have done it by now. Just to see the bang, y'know?"

Lakesh sighed. "We don't know for sure. Apparently the device was created—if indeed it was ever completed—over a million years ago."

Kane squinted. "A million years?"

Grant shrugged. "Why not? Supposedly our Annunaki pals got here upward of three hundred thousand years ago."

"Perhaps we should let Old Tower speak for himself," Bridget said.

"Providing he's going to say something we can understand," Grant said.

It was no foregone conclusion. The deep-sea vent lifeforms were alien, and not just because they never evolved on Earth. They had almost nothing in common with the surface-dwelling humans—far less than the hybrids, or even the overlords. The only reason they could communicate at all was that they had spent aeons as interstellar traders, and acquired third-party technology that enabled them to converse with air breathers at need.

Just not *well*.

"Capital idea, dearest Brigid," Lakesh said. "Let's go to tape."

Five sets of eyes peered blankly at him. The corners of his mouth impressed. "An ancient expression," he said. "Preskydark. Forgive it, please—perhaps I indulge in a hint of nostalgia, in the stress of the moment."

"As if the twentieth century's anything to be nostalgic for," Kane said. Brigid scowled at him; he waved a negligent hand. "Go ahead, Lakesh. Let's see what Puss in Boots has to say."

Lakesh nodded to Sally Wright. She clicked a controller in her hand. The theater lights dimmed to a small amber gleam of footlights along the base of the walls.

The redoubt director stepped to one side. The wall behind him glowed, and on it stood what appeared to be a long-haired white cat, human-sized and standing on its hind legs.

Like all three colonies the Cerberus contingent had "met" in the vent-forms' deep ocean habitat for surface dwellers, the seeming senior, who went by the name Old Tower, manifested as a cartoon. The projected image wore something like seventeenth-century dress in blue satin: a tight vest over a white shirt, roomy pantaloons, leather jackboots with rolled-down tops. It peered at them with immense green eyes that clashed horribly with its ensemble.

"My friends," it said, its inhuman lips moving in an uncomfortably human fashion, "dire news have I to report.

"A million or more cycles of your sun ago, a terrible device was created. Or so legends say. It was so designed that, upon activation, it would bring to an instantaneous end the vacuum fluctuation hypothesized to constitute the universe. Were that to happen, the universe would collapse like a giant bubble. All within it would be destroyed as if had it never been."

"That seems pretty comprehensive," Grant said. Lakesh waved a hand at him for silence.

"This machine was called the Cosmic Eye. Imagine can you, humans, this development not welcomed by all. It began a war that destroyed a galaxy-wide civilization itself megayears old and took many quintillions of sapient lives. In end the race that created the device was exterminated to the last zygote."

"What became of the device, Old Tower, my friend?" came Lakesh's voice from offscreen.

"Lost was it. Knowledge of how it was created lost was, too—or suppressed. But so fearful was the prospect that its memory survives today in fables chemically transmitted to bring alarm to fresh-budding colonies."

At a gesture from Lakesh, Sally froze the giant cat's image on the screen.

"I infer that he speaks of what are in effect the young of his species," Lakesh explained.

"We got that, Lakesh," Kane said. "We all know the vent-forms are colonies of sentient microbes."

"Sapient, Kane," Brigid said. "*Sentient* just means possessing senses, such as sight or smell or even touch. Even paramecia are sentient."

"Well, fuck me, they're that, too, aren't they?" Kane ignored the startled glances that met his outburst. "I didn't mean literally. Just get on with it, okay?"

Sally Wright cleared her throat apologetically. She did most everything apologetically. "If I could make a suggestion," she said, "if nobody minds, that is, perhaps we might just to synopsize, given Old Tower's somewhat circumlocutory style?"

"Good idea, Wright," Kane said. "Even Lakesh gets to the point quicker than Old Smokestack, there." The assistant archivist blushed and looked down at the floor. Even after over a year in Cerberus, she remained timid and withdrawn. Yet somehow she was always most comfortable dealing with Kane, despite his abrupt and anything but gentle manner.

Lakesh cocked an eyebrow. "Did a scrap of praise for me accidentally escape your lips, Kane?" The erstwhile Magistrate shrugged. "Well, then, I shall try to be worthy of your trust. Somehow, Gilgamesh Bates winkled knowledge of the Cosmic Eye from the vent-forms. And somehow, or so Old Tower suspects, he then correlated that knowledge with data that may have revealed to him the location of this ultimate doomsday device."

"How the hell did he manage to get them to tell him that?" Grant asked.

"And why are you telling us all this?" Kane said. "Other than to brighten our day, that is."

"Simple," Domi said. "He wants us to stop him."

Chapter 4

"You have got to be shitting me," Sean Reichert said. Had it not been for the headsets in the helmets they all wore, his words would never have been audible over the growl of the chopper's twin T700-GE-701C turboshaft engines and the roar of the rotors "Why in the wide, wide world of sports would the vent-forms tell Bates about something like this Cosmic Eye?"

"Boy never actually saw *The Wide, Wide World of Sports*," Major Mike Hays said over the intercom. "He picked up the phrase from *Doctor Strangelove*—"

"Stow it," Grant growled from the pilot's left seat up front. "It'll just make our heads explode."

"To answer your question," said Kane, who was outfitted in his shadow suit and sitting on one of the pull-down seats inside the chopper, "they didn't exactly blurt it out to him. Or maybe they did. They mentioned it to him in conversation. Then he evidently found some kind a record of it in their database."

"Their database?" Major Mike demanded in disbelief. Head enclosed by a helmet, dark green aviator-style shooting glasses covering his eyes, he rode behind the 7.62 mm M134 mounted minigun in the open starboard bay, ready for action if they took fire from the wooded hills below. "This just keeps getting better and better."

"You'd have to ask Baptiste for a better explanation of all this," Kane said. "We can only give you the quick-and-dirty synopsis."

He glanced across the compartment to Domi. The albino wild child sat on her own pull-down seats leaning forward eagerly, practically caressing the AK-108 resting across her milky white knees. Which were bare. She had refused to wear anything but khaki cargo shorts, and the ballistic-weave camou blouse she'd been issued from the Fortress of Solecism arsenal was knotted up to leave her pale midriff bare regardless of the fact it robbed some of her most vulnerable vitals of protection. She also wouldn't wear a helmet the way the rest of them did.

After the way he'd been cut off after the last time he cheated Domi of danger, Lakesh hadn't even tried to hold her back from going on this mission. Kane was just as glad, despite certain deep stirrings of misgiving about allowing one so feminine and seemingly frail to put herself in harm's way. The fact was the feral girl had been fully formidable before she ever came to Cobaltville to seek her fortune, in Outland terms, as a contract slut in the Tartarus Pits, and her years of experience and training as an ace field operative for Cerberus redoubt had made her equal to many elite male warrior.

She was craning to look past Hays and the minigun at the ground below. For obscure reasons, Kane preferred not to look out himself. Perhaps it was just that the Black Hawk, as sleek and powerful as it was, seemed like nothing so much as a giant lumbering vulnerable target compared to the Deathbird in which Kane and Grant had spent so much of their lives together.

Sean Reichert, though the best pilot among Team Phoenix, held down the copilot's seat; he had been surprisingly willing to defer to Grant's far superior piloting expertise. The final members of both groups, Iron Man Joe Weaver and Brigid Baptiste, had been dropped off several klicks south of their target to hump their heavy equipment to a vantage point in clear sight of the objective. Good thing that Baptiste's a sturdy girl, Kane thought, and wondered if she was repenting of her bravado in offering to carry as much as she had.

Grant guided them on a course that swung many klicks wide and to the north of the Atshuara ville. The team's redoubt lay almost a hundred klicks away to the east: on general principles, the Team Phoenix had kept the location secret from their indigenous allies. For missions along the river and its surrounding valleys, Reichert or Robison had flown the team in one of the redoubt's utility helicopters with bolted-on gun packs to within ten or so klicks of their goals and they had humped the rest of the way on foot, as they had on the fateful final mission that resulted in Robison's capture.

"See," Kane said, "Bates offered to revamp their database management for them."

"And they went for that?" Major Mike demanded. "I thought the vent-forms and their technology were millions of years old. I mean, I know Gil Bates was a computer genius and all, but seriously."

"Like I said, Baptiste has a better handle on this than I do. To the extent any human can, I guess. The deal is, the vent-forms don't have a lot of contact with the outside world, being that they need to live in environments like the bottom of the ocean and on hell-planets like Venus. Not exactly accessible. While they're pretty conservative—kinda get the impression most of the old star faring races are— they're always looking to improve their chops when opportunity arises. So along comes old Gil, the software god. And the rest is history."

"And so the universe might soon be history, too?" Reichert said. "They must be the most gullible rubes in the universe, these black-smoker beings."

"Bates is nothing if not a master salesman," Grant said. "He sold the Archon Directorate on his damn operating system. Sold you boys a pretty line of goods, too, I seem to remember."

"So how the hell did these native allies of yours know to spoof overhead infrared surveillance, anyway?" Kane asked.

"We taught them," Major Mike said. "Right after we shut down Bates's monster factory in the redoubt, and took up residence there ourselves, we had a honeymoon period with the lighter-skinned folks downriver. After all, we'd kind of greased the skids for our little pal Consuelo to become president of the republic. They claimed they were having some problems with some naughty tribals along down to the southeast. So we provided them some of our UAV drones with the usual sensor suite—the redoubt is full of them, they must've been pretty cheap to produce."

"They're just basically RC model airplanes," Reichert said.

"So you gave your once and future enemies recon drones," Grant said.

A moment of silence. Relative, of course, given the commotion of the chopper's flight.

"That's affirmative," Major Mike said.

"Seems like maybe the vent-forms aren't the only naive ones on the block."

"Dirty Bird, this is Nest," Marina's young voice said crisply over the net. "You are within ten klicks of your objective. Our drones show patrols and lookouts to two klicks north of the village. Suggest you look alive."

"Nest, this is Dirty Bird, descending to nape of the earth," Grant radioed. The sound of the rotors changed as Grant altered their angle of attack. The helicopter slowed. Kane felt it begin to fall away beneath him.

Trouble. Same as always.

"LISTEN TO ME," Larry Robison said to the youthful Atshuara guard. "You need to help me. It's your best bet."

Swatting at a horsefly buzzing around his head inside his cage in the hot, sun-flooded plaza, he repeated his words in what he felt more keenly than ever before was woefully inadequate Spanish. Over the months in-country Team Phoenix had picked up a smattering of Atshuara pidgin; most fluent, if that word even applied, was Joe Weaver. Robison's flimsy grasp of the language was if anything geared to seductions of a different sort—certainly not to convincing someone to betray his own people. Even if, as Larry knew too well, what he was trying to talk the boy into was saving his own people from ultimate betrayal.

Squatting on his heels, the youth wouldn't even look at him. He was dressed in his Sunday best for his important duty: new red loincloth and a spotless white turban with some blue-and-red feathers stuck in it. His right hand kept a relaxed grip on the haft of a spear with a forged steel head; the various Shuara tribes traded feathers and herbs for blasters and other implements to merchants who came from far downstream toward the Amazon basin in steam sternwheelers. The spear was not a terribly high-tech weapon, but if push came to shove it would do the job it was intended to do: kill the captive before his partners could consummate their inevitable rescue attempt.

The boy's fellow tribesmen, meanwhile, needed all the more modern weapons to insure that the attempt ended in the death or capture of Robison's three comrades.

"Listen to me. Please," Robison urged.

While even some of the Indians spoke English, mostly taught by their Río Marañón princess turned guerrilla leader, not all of the Atshuara even spoke Spanish—or, in any event, would admit to it to an outsider. The kid paid his words no mind whatever tongue they came in. Obviously, he wasn't interested in making it easy on his charge.

But hey, Robison told himself, you're the team diplomat. You can make the sale. No pressure—only your life depends upon it.

And the lives of his friends. Consuelo had laid a cunning ambush. If not necessarily a very subtle one. But then, subtlety wasn't necessary when you had staked out a bait you knew the tiger would be drawn to.

Rather than carry their prisoner back to their fortified base camp down on the river itself, or back to Santa Caridad, his captors had put him on display in the center of the ville he and his buddies had imagined they were going to rescue. He was penned in a cage made of saplings lashed together with tough grass, of a size that guaranteed he could neither stand straight nor straighten his legs when he sat or lay down.

He was grateful they given him his clothes back, after they had stripped him down to search him and bind his cracked ribs. Although neither the heat nor the humidity was as brutal as it would have been down in the Amazon proper, up here the sun burned his unprotected skin quicker. Before even searching him, though, about six republic soldiers had sat on him while a team of three more had pulled his right leg until the ball joint snapped back into the hip socket. They wanted him to get around under his own power, since he was a head taller than most of the Río Marañón troopies, let alone the Indians. He reckoned his friends had to have heard his bellow back in the redoubt.

At the moment the small plaza in the ville's center was deserted. Periodically throughout the two days of his captivity groups of people from surrounding villages had been squired through by his captors to gawk at him—mostly children, like school groups on field trips. With the sun now more or less directly overhead, there came a break in the tours. Perhaps the locals had acquired the Spanish habit of the midday siesta.

While the plaza was deserted, Atshuara warriors had been gathering in the village steadily since his capture. Worse, downriver troopers had been streaming in. They were now at least two hundred fighters concealed in the village, as many more in concentric defensive bands around it, both concealed in fighting pits and roving on patrol.

It was a trap, though not a particularly well-concealed trap. Indeed, it stood as a challenge to Team Phoenix: come and get your man. Come if you dare.

Larry Robison knew his mates too well to believe they would fail to pick up the gauntlet. None of them was exactly the sort to back down from a challenge, however steep. And he constituted one-fourth of their effective fighting force.

More, he knew, he constituted one of their last living links to a world long gone to dust.

"You have to believe me, amigo," he said urgently. His guard gazed steadfastly into space, chewing on a blade of grass. "Your leader, Consuelo, she's already betrayed both your people and the Spanish down the river. She's going to betray you again. She's going to get you to help her smash the other tribes, and she's going to wipe you out, too."

No response. The green lizard watching from a flat stone fifteen yards away showed as much responsiveness to Robison's words. He hung his head between his knees.

I've got to get through to these people, he thought desperately. If those idiots come after me, they're going to die. Either quick and easy here, or slow and hard down in the main public square in Santa Caridad.

Then he heard something. Rather, he stopped hearing something. The birds in the trees north of the village had kept up a steady squawking racket from an hour before dawn to deep twilight. Robison knew: he'd been here all along. But now they had gone silent.

He felt it as much as heard it—a soft drumbeat that seemed to rattle in his chest. Then he heard shouts and shots from the north, and the cry, "Helicopter!"

From the doorway of a hootch fifty yards away Consuelo emerged. The little *generalissima* looked seriously pissed.

"*¡Mátalo!*" she cried.

Even Robison's jackass Spanish had no trouble telling him what that meant.

Kill him.

Chapter 5

One hundred yards ahead as the helicopter swept in low over the trees, Grant saw the scrubby little native guy jump up, reverse his spear in his hand and cock it back to stick the captive in his cage.

"Shit!" he exclaimed. "He's gonna chill him!"

The Black Hawk carried rockets in racks under its stub wings, ready to leap forth at the touch of his finger. But they weren't exactly precision weps. Launching one now was as likely to wipe out Robison as it was to deter his would-be murderer.

The mission was about to be over before it properly started. And there was not one damn thing Grant could do about it.

LARRY ROBISON HELD his hands out palm first through the bars of the cage as his guard raised his spear to strike. "No, wait," he said, "can't we talk about this?"

Dang, I thought I'd die with more dignity.

The young Atshuara's wild eyes were wide, showing white around dark irises. He seemed more terrified of failing in his charge than anything else. The muscles of his skinny body writhed like serpents as he tightened them to deliver the death stroke.

Then his rib cage burst open in a dark shower of blood

in chunks as if he'd been harboring an adolescent alien. The tip of his spear went into the dirt. His body fell into a jumble, folding in ways human bodies weren't supposed to.

Robison heard a noise that was a cross between a panther snarl and a dragon's roar. He knew what it meant. He threw himself flat on the barred bottom of his cage and pressed hands over ears as a long-house-style hootch with a thatched roof less than thirty yards away flew to pieces.

"ROCK 'N' ROLL!"

At Mike Hays's exultant cry Kane's cheeks rode up in a grimace. He heard it over a headset, since the aviator helmet he wore had extreme sound dampening properties; otherwise the racket of the chopper's turbine engines rotors would have given him a splitting headache. He was still tempted to press his palms to either side of his head at the jackhammer noise.

The major cut loose with his minigun. It swiveled on a heavy mount that jutted out the side of the chopper, with a strut-braced box girder for main support. He hung on to the hefty spade grips; bungee cords secured him to the aircraft itself.

The chopper managed only one overpass, and couldn't linger. However, Team Phoenix had some aces up their camou sleeves, courtesy of the long-ago designers and builders of the Fortress of Solecism. Among them was a handful of recon UAVs with wingspans bigger than the ones they normally used, mostly transparent synthetic membrane on a lightweight frame. They could stay airborne more or less indefinitely, far too high for the human eye to spot, powered by solar collectors in the upper surfaces of their wings. The team was sparing in their use: they had only a few of the things, and they were painfully vulnerable to the mercurial Upper Amazon weather.

But now with their buddy's life at stake it was time to "smoke 'em if you got 'em." They'd had one of their long-loiter spy planes over the village for the past twenty-seven hours, keeping tabs on the comings and goings from the village.

Mostly coming, as tribal warriors and downriver soldiers converged for the *gran matanza*—great bloodletting—Consuelo had written in her day book.

Grant, Kane and the Phoenix trio had memorized the ville's layout. They knew which huts were filled with soldiers or outside warriors, which meant they were unlikely to harbor too many innocent noncombatants. There was always the chance of chilling a comfort girl or two, but for all their qualms about civilian casualties Team Phoenix tended to regard such as simply support personnel and thus legitimate if low-priority targets. If they got in the line of fire, that was their lookout. It was an attitude that made sense to Kane.

So Hays laid his heavily armored optical sight on the first barracks hootch available and lit off his piece.

Kane felt the Black Hawk start to heel to the left in response to the minigun's awesome recoil. Forewarned by Hays's battlecry, Grant had shoved the collective stick over to counteract the effect. The whole ship rocked.

And roared. The noise was unbelievable despite the sound-deadening helmet. Domi had stuffed little sponge hearing protectors into her ears as they made their final approach. Kane hoped they did the trick, not because he felt a lot of sympathy with her perverse decision to forego a helmet, but because they were going to need everybody operating at a hundred percent when their boots hit the ground; they couldn't afford to have one of their shooters as deaf as a rock, even if only temporarily.

Kane had moved across the compartment to sit beside the albino girl. He wanted to see out.

The show was worth it. The hootch Hays blasted just flew in every direction. It looked as if it were being hit with God's own weed cutter.

The burst ended. Kane could hear—barely—the mosquito whine of the electric motor that kept the M134's six barrels turning, cooling them and keeping them ready for instant action. Spent casings ricocheted all over the inside of the chopper. Domi jumped and cursed as hot brass stung a bare thigh.

A Río Marañón troopie bolted out the door as the structure, or what was left of it, collapsed behind him. He raised his AKM at the chopper. Behind him pale flames, lit by tracer bullets, ran through the wreckage like frightened mice.

Hays shifted the heavy weapon. He thumbed the butterfly trigger again. Dragon flame belched from the minigun.

Kane was never sure if the man simply disintegrated or was just flung into the smoky ruin. One instant the soldier was there; the next there was nothing but a mist of blood hanging pink in the air.

Grant turned the big chopper in a tight circle, ten yards above the cage on the ville commons. The Black Hawk handled as differently from a lithe Deathbird as an Abrams tank did from a Formula One racer. Grant had declined so much as a check ride back at the redoubt, so supremely confident was he of his ability to master any rotary-wing aircraft that was capable of actual flight. And mastery was what he showed.

Activating his monstrous blaster in short pulses, Hays blasted half-naked warriors and bearded men half again their size in camouflage into red clouds and flopping wet rags as they rushed out to repel the invaders. Kane suddenly understood why Hays, a man without a conspicuously low body-fat ratio, had insisted on wearing gauntlets, a jungle-green turtleneck beneath his armor-cloth utilities and a full assault-armor vest with steel-ceramic inserts that would stop even Magnum rifle bullets from penetrating his vitals. Even in the relative cool of the helicopter moving through the high-valley air the visible parts of his skin swam in sweat, and he stank like a goat despite showering that morning. Man-handling the awesome blaster was as much fighting it and firing it. Muzzle-blast and volcanic noise blasted the operator despite the fact the M134 was literally outside the aircraft; freshly emptied casings, each as hot as a branding iron, were blown in clouds back into the open hatch by the swirling currents, along with dust at sandblast velocities.

But the minigun took a toll on would-be ambushers like the Angel of Death's own chromed scythe. Because of the steep firing angle, Hays was able to blast attackers directly and not spray any hootches he didn't want to. Mostly—but there were practical limits to Hays's compassion, as there were for Kane's.

Both men knew their advantage, as breathtaking as it was, couldn't last. There was a whole battalion of bad guys on the ground here, waiting to rip into the expected ground infiltration of would-be rescuers. They could take the Black Hawk apart with just AKs and indig break-open shotguns if they had enough time. And Robison—

Somehow another native had got inside the deadly circle swept by the minigun. He fired his shotgun from the hip at Robison. Past the bottom of the hatch Kane could see the captive, now crouching, duck away with hands held defensively upward as soft lead pellets tore a chunk out of an upper corner of his confining cube. Yelling soundlessly over the hellstorm of noise from above, the tribesman broke open his piece on the run and began stuffing in a fresh shell of greasy brown paper. Kane jumped from the pull-down seat, raising a bullpup Copperhead, hoping to get the angle for a shot, knowing he never would—

The whole right side of the running Atshuara's chest ripped open. Sections of broken rib spun away in a cloud of frothy pink blood as a 20 mm projectile exploded inside his body cavity. His right arm flew away from his body as if jettisoned. He rolled three times when he hit the dirt, fetching up against the base of Robison's cage. He had to have still been alive, from the oceanic surges of red that flowed from him to become dark mud.

That meant Joe Weaver was still on the job with Little Willi, with Brigid Baptiste spotting and pulling security for him—double bonus, in that it gave Iron Man unaccustomed help and gave Kane a plausible excuse to get his *anam-chara,* his soul friend, out of the hurricane's eye. The once mild archivist had become a seasoned special operative, even more deadly in her way than the happily homicidal Domi.

As if on cue her voice poured into his skull like honey,

calm and almost soothing despite the words it spoke: "Kane. Grant. We're spotted. We've got minimum one hundred hostiles closing on us. Please hurry."

"Take us down, Grant. We got to get this show on the road," Kane said.

"Affirmative," Grant's voice came back through his helmet headset. The Black Hawk leveled, wallowed slightly, then settled straight down. Its wheels thunked the tan well-packed earth scant yards from the cage. The rotors slowed and began to droop, sweeping out a steel-and-synthetic umbrella over their heads as Kane peeled off the helmet and leaped out.

He was followed at once by Domi, and a beat later by Sean Reichert, who carried his AK-108 in his left hand using the sling over his shoulder to support the foreend, and his H&K grenade launcher in his right. Domi scuttled to the front end of the bird, crouched and sprayed a hootch fifty yards off from the shade of whose entryway muzzle-flames danced. Reichert ran around to the tail, keeping wary track of the still-spinning tail rotor and bent to avoid the main rotor's deceptively slow and gentle rotation.

Kane turned back. Hays handed him something heavy from within the chopper, then hunkered down again behind his spade grips. Pulling his burden over his right shoulder, Kane ran the few steps to the cage.

Robison squatted inside. "Come to get me out of this damn thing?" he shouted.

"Not exactly," Kane yelled back. The turbines still whined loudly, and there was still a firefight going on—he couldn't help wincing as bullets kicked up dust not a yard from his right boot. "Not yet."

Scrambling up so that his body overhung the top of the five-foot-high cage, he slammed the heavy hook down, made sure it engaged a bar toward the middle.

"Kane!" Hays shouted over the intercom. Kane looked up.

A trio of Río Marañón soldiers in green-and-black jungle camou had appeared from nowhere and were running right at him. They held their Kalashnikovs at their hips but for some reason didn't fire. Maybe they thought they could capture the bird and its crew; maybe they had just fired their magazines empty. One way or another, Kane was right in the major's line of fire, his own hands empty of everything but cage and skyhook.

The men's speed carried them a full step into the rotor circle before the first blade found them.

The man on Kane's right ran hunched forward so that the blade took him in the temple. It tore out his eyes and knocked the top of his skull off, officer's black beret still attached. The next two men had their heads sliced from their necks as neatly as by a guillotine. One ran a few steps more like a decapitated chicken, blood geysering from his neck, before he flopped into the dust and rolled against the cage with a sodden, sorry impact Kane felt through his ribs and belly. The other just dropped in a tangle of uncontrolled limbs.

Then Reichert called out, "RPG!" It was a phrase the young operator and his fellow United States soldiers had first learned to fear in Mogadishu's tangled streets.

A puff of motion had already caught Kane's eye, off to his right as he lay still half-sprawled across the cage trying to attach the hook. A puff of white smoke, an impression of dark object hurtling toward him trailing dense dirty ivory smoke and sparks.

Major Mike fired. The missile was approaching from about forty-five degrees off the Black Hawk's nose, giving the M134 a clear shot—barely. Kane first felt a stinging slap on his rear and the backs of his thighs as the muzzle overpressure wave hit him. That continued to spank him even as the passage vacuum of thirty bullets a second tugged at his boots as if trying to suck them right off his feet.

The rocket-propelled gren had flown far enough to arm when the bullet stream hit it. It went off in a dazzling white flash. Kane closed his eyes and turned his head as an incandescent lance of vaporized copper spiked toward him.

The shaped-charge jet lost both heat and velocity rapidly in air. Kane felt a slap on the back of his right calf, looked down to see a splotch of semicooled copper red on one leg of his shadow suit.

The turbines had already begun singing up the scale, the blades to rise and fade from their deceptive shadow visibility. Dust exploded from the ground around Kane as a hurricane buffeted him from above. Domi and Sean had already rabbited back into the bird. That left Kane—

"Oh," he said, "shit."

Crouched beneath him, staring up with brown eyes the size of saucers, Larry Robison said, "I hope this thing's as well built as it feels."

"Me, too!" Kane called back as the helicopter leaped up into the sky, the winch beneath it yanking the cable taut with a jerk and carrying the cage and its two unwilling occupants up into the cloud-scattered blue sky.

A pair of RPGs stabbed up from the ville like smoke fingers in pursuit. Both missed to explode in futile blots of gray smoke.

LYING COVERED BY ROCKS and screened by light brush, Brigid lined up the AK-108's iron sights on the camou-covered chest of a man emerging from the trees at the bottom on the hill. She squeezed the trigger. The recoil of the 5.56 mm cartridge lighting off in a rifle weighing close to ten pounds was negligible, just a shove against the shoulder against which she held the butt firmly snugged.

The man went down fast and bonelessly, meaning likely dead. Brigid didn't pause to admire the shot, taken at less than a hundred yards; there were too many other enemies emerging from the woods, shooting as they came.

Thunder crashed from her right. It was a token of her intense concentration that she didn't flinch at the sky-breaking report of the 20 mm sniper rifle. Joe Weaver had the blaster set up on its bipod just back from the crest of the hill, so that he could cover the distant ville without exposing himself to too much fire from below. He lay behind it peering through the huge aftermarket 10-power Unertl scope, firing in support of the helicopter's escape over a klick away.

Brigid thumbed her selector to full-auto and raked the line of green-and-black mottled figures emerging from the woods with a long burst. Several fell. It was far from enough. At least twenty of the Río Marañón soldiers were charging in an undeniably valiant attempt to neutralize the massive rifle's long-range death touch.

Brigid ducked back down out of sight to yank her spent magazine and replace it with a full one. At least ammo was in ample supply, though they hadn't brought any survival supplies but water, med kits and a few protein bars. They weren't meant to stay out here long. Weaver had carried both packs containing the broken-down NTW-20 rifle himself, although he had allowed Brigid to carry some backup ammo for it. For her part, Brigid had brought plenty of magazines for her longblaster.

She felt a presence and looked up. A Río Marañón soldier stood over her, faceless against the overhead sun. He raised his rifle to smash her skull with the steel buttplate.

Shots cracked from Brigid's right. Weaver had rolled away from his giant longblaster and drawn a .40-caliber Witness handgun from a flapped hip holster. The enemy soldier jerked to the double tap and toppled backward from view.

Brigid came up onto her haunches. Three or four more soldiers were in view, mostly as floppy-hat-covered heads. She fired a long burst from the hip. A hat flew from a skull in a spray of blood. The others disappeared.

She was sure she had only hit the one. Anyway, there were plenty more behind. Holding the blaster by its pistol grip and sling, she dug in a synthetic pouch on the ground beside her.

Three soldiers loomed up before Weaver. He had rolled to a sitting position. Firing with his arms in an isosceles configuration, he shot each once center of mass, single shot, left to right. He added a double tap for the last, then started working back with a second shot to the sternum of the man in the middle. The first man he had shot didn't even need a second: the high-speed 135-grain Tritons were the most reliable man-killing handblaster slugs available when Team Phoenix had gone to sleep, Reichert had told her.

But enemies kept coming. Another soldier appeared to Weaver's right, on the far side of the hill from Brigid. Weaver dived away from a hip-fired burst that stitched a line of dust spouts across the hilltop. His dive took him beside Little Willi. He grabbed the massive rifle, twisted his torso, fired.

The 20 mm shell hit three fingers beneath the troopie's web belt, blowing his pelvis apart. His legs fell away, and his torso dropped straight down into a tangle of his own flash-cooked intestines.

Brigid's hand came out of her pouch. She quickly armed the three random microgrens she'd brought out, pitched them over the lip of the hill, ducked.

The grens cracked off with a quick savage ripple. Screams ensued.

At least one gren had to have been an incen: the screams rose to demonic, soul-searing intensity and went on and on. The smell of stirred-up dust and blood and heated propellants and gun lubricants was joined by the smell of burning flesh.

Clamping her jaw on the rising column of vomit, Brigid got to her knees shouldering her rifle. She was just in time to see lines of smoke ripple into the trees beyond the foot of the hill.

A series of orange explosions toppled a couple of smaller trees and caught two hapless soldiers. An instant later the Black Hawk swept over the hill, volleying ballistic rockets from beneath its wings at targets behind the besieged pair. Its minigun roared like a dragon, so low Brigid had to duck to avoid being brained by—

"Isn't that your friend Kane hanging on to that cage beneath the helicopter?" Weaver asked with surprising mildness.

Chapter 6

Sean Reichert threw back his black-haired head and caroled, "Bates in space!"

The others gathered in the Cerberus cafeteria—the four Cerberus field operatives, his own three comrades, Marina—stared at him. Kane leaned back in his chair and looked at Domi, who sat nearest him, perched on a counter chewing a pemmican bar traded from Sky Dog's Lakota. He raised an eyebrow.

She shrugged. "Fused out," was her judgment, delivered around an expanding mouthful of meat and berries.

"Muppets reference," Robison said, as if that explained something. He winced; it hurt to talk from his busted ribs, although DeFore had fixed a trickle-charge unit to him, which electronically induced calcium ions to migrate to the site of the fractures to expedite healing. For that pain, as well as the residue from the tissue damage done both by the dislocation of his hip and its rough-and-ready reinsertion, he was flying solo today; he would take no meds stronger than aspirin for fear of clouding his thought processes. Only when it came time to sleep would he let the Cerberus medic dose him with serious analgesics.

Major Mike leaned forward with his elbows on the table. "You say you have evidence that Bates went into orbit when he blew out of the Amazon redoubt?" Literally seconds ahead of retribution in the form of his erstwhile employees, Team Phoenix, and their Cerberus allies, he didn't have to add. They'd all been there.

"I deduced as much," Brigid said, "from his physical condition when we encountered him briefly in the vent-forms' stronghold." She stood to the side looking severe in her white Redoubt Bravo jumpsuit.

"Puffy features, bloating of the upper torso and apparent atrophy of lower limbs." Robison nodded. "That means serious microgravity hang time. We'll accept your deductions, Ms. Baptiste—they've played out pretty well so far."

She smiled, fleetingly and wanly. "Not always," she said, "as my compatriots will no doubt be only too glad to tell you."

"Don't sell yourself short, Baptiste," Kane said. "You're right more often than not. Even if only a little."

Brigid bit her lip and looked at the scuffed synthetic-tile floor. Domi sighed exaggeratedly. Kane looked around, blinking.

"What? What'd I say now?"

"Just stepped on your prick again," Grant rumbled. He sat slumped in a chair like a lounging colossus, big chin sunk to big chest. "No big deal."

Kane shot him an I-thought-you-were-my-friend look. Grant failed to rise.

"I'm afraid we don't have too much insight to offer you folks," Hays said, sipping green tea. The Amazonia contingent was all mad for the stuff. Kane felt a certain surprised relief they weren't all hooked up on some local kind of DMT-laced hallucinogenic brew. "Anything the U.S.

government had going that involved high technology, it's a fair bet Bates had his tentacles in."

"Even the Archon Directorate," Domi said.

"It's got to be some kind of secret space base somewhere," Reichert said around a bite of his fried-fish sandwich. "Stands to reason."

"Given that it seems the U.S. government went on an orgy of building secret facilities toward the end of the 1990s," Robison said, "both inside and outside this Archon Directorate."

Brigid nodded. "The problem, of course, being to identify the particular secret facility."

"How many damn space bases could they have built?" Hays demanded. "The official story back then was they didn't have any presence in space at all beyond a junky international station and the occasional shuttle flight."

"I thought you'd got hold of the location of all those secret facilities," Robison said.

"Jump nodes," Grant said. "The redoubts with gateways built on them."

"What about your records?" Robison asked.

"They primarily document facilities constructed under the aegis of the Archon Directorate," Lakesh said crisply, striding in. "In dear Brigid's absence I have had Sally Wright canvassing our files in an attempt to see if some germane information is to be found within them. Speaking of which, where is she? She was supposed to join us here. It's quite unlike her to be other than punctual."

The Cerberus four shook their heads. Lakesh did likewise—a crisper, irritated gesture. "In any event, we must recall that rival factions and empire builders existed even within the scope of the Archon Directorate—worse perhaps than inside the U.S. government, to the extent the two differed. There was a very great deal of undocumented building. Not even I knew of all the directorate's projects."

"But I thought Dr. Baptiste here—" Hays began.

"Archivist," Brigid said, somehow at once assertively and shyly. "I was never a doctor."

Hays shrugged. From his experience of Sky Dog's clan, Kane wondered if the team leader might have some Kiowa in him. They had that kind of stocky build, not like most of the Plains warriors, who ran to tall and wiry. Couldn't tell from his color, though; Hays was fair, for all that he'd just come from months of bashing bush in the Upper Amazon. Being late-twentieth-century types, and thus paranoid about health, the men of Team Phoenix were avid consumers of sunscreen.

"*Ms*. Baptiste," Hays said, "has a photographic memory. And your records here are pretty comprehensive, aren't they?"

"As complete as a century of assiduous collection by all nine baronies could make them," Lakesh said with unconcealed pride, "to say nothing of the recent contributions of the Manitius Moon base archives, and the intrepid collection efforts of my very good friends here. It is fair to say that our Redoubt Bravo database is entirely without parallel."

"Except Bates's," Reichert said.

Lakesh's face went statue-blank. Domi suppressed a snicker.

"Hearts and minds," Robison murmured.

"Sorry," Reichert said hurriedly. Team Phoenix was privy to the fact of Bates's penetration of the Cerberus computers, of which even most of the redoubt's personnel was unaware. While it was unknown whether the software mogul had siphoned all the data available on the network, the smart money held he'd made a clean sweep. It wasn't Bates's way *not* to grab for all the goodies in sight, unless he saw some compelling contraindication. The whole episode was a still a markedly sore patch on Lakesh's hide.

"I can only remember what I've seen, Major," Brigid said. "To view all the data in our files would be the work of many, many lifetimes."

"Both dear Brigid and her capable assistant Sally have made a priority of trying to ferret out and analyze every scrap of information we possess on Archon Directorate projects. Unfortunately, the documentation for the ones we know about is vast, and must be canvassed for brief and possibly cryptic allusions to unknown endeavors. Such documentation as their noble efforts have uncovered has tended to be tagged with misleading code names and rendered in formats dissimilar to those customarily used by Directorate operations."

"Sort of the purloined-letter-in-a-haystack technique of data security," Robison said.

Lakesh stared at him a quizzical moment, then smiled and nodded. "Just so, friend Larry, a most apt analogy. Hidden in plain sight amid an inordinate mass of unrelated data. Additionally, many of the relevant documents are undoubtedly among the immense quantities of encrypted data we have stored."

"We'll do our best for you, but we can't promise results," Robison said. "It might help us if you could give us a little better idea of just what the problem is."

"We get that Bates might have found the means to destroy the universe," Reichert said.

"For example," Hays added, "what exactly would be a vacuum fluctuation?"

"Think of it as a bubble in reality," Joe Weaver said. He sat back in his chair with his sturdy legs thrust out before him and his jaw sunk to the T-shirt stretched across his powerful chest. His round spectacles caught the light of the overhead fluorescents and turned into shimmers of blankness, hiding his slanted aquamarine eyes. To Kane he seemed to possess the same sort of controlled elemental power Grant did, although he was neither as large nor strong physically.

He also spoke even less than Kane's longtime partner—somewhere between Grant and a bronze statue, say. And like Grant, when he did have something to say, it was usually to the point.

"It can collapse at any time," Weaver said. "Then it's as if it never existed. That's the hypothesis, anyway."

Lakesh nodded. "A more than adequate summation, friend Joseph. Admirable. To expand—"

Kane held up a hand. "No," he said. "Stop."

He looked to the Phoenix four. "What Weaver says is right, and enough," he said. "We know. Because Lakesh and Baptiste can go on for hours about it, long after your brain has shut down entirely and started to smoke. Ask me how I know."

"Iron Man *knows* things," Hays said proudly. "Even if he is an ex-lawyer."

Both Lakesh and Brigid looked a little deflated. "So the universe is a bubble, and you're telling us Bates has the pin?" the major said.

"Not a bubble, exactly," Brigid began hopefully.

"Brigid," Grant growled.

"And we don't know for sure Bates has the pin," Kane said. "Odds are if he did, we'd already be screwed."

"Game over," Reichert said, nodding. "Wanna play again?"

"It's more he may know where to *find* the pin," Kane said.

"Okay," Robison said, drawing the word out, "and given that Bates managed to persuade the vent-forms into letting him suck *their* database dry under pretext of trying to help improve their data management and retrieval. What were they doing with the secret of how to extinguish life, the universe and everything?"

"Apparently they don't possess the secret," Lakesh said. "Not as such. They have knowledge of it—as much in the form of legends as anything else. I might say in passing that the deep-ocean vent life-forms, comprising as they do billions of microorganisms in colony form, do not make much use of external or mechanical data storage or retrieval. Rather their data is stored electrochemically within them, in holographic form—a sort of racial memory, as complete and comprehensive as Brigid's photographic memory, but spanning a million years or more."

Robison let out a long, low whistle.

"So Bates read their minds?" Reichert asked. "That's just nasty."

"Gil's a software kind of guy," Hays said. "How could he help them manage their own memories?"

"Apparently data storage and retrieval on such a scale is problematic, even when the data is in effect part of one's own organism," Brigid said. "The vent-forms have developed techniques for doing so, just as humans have developed techniques to improve their memories. Gilgamesh Bates apparently convinced them to give him access to their memories."

"But how?" Robison said.

"One of the main items the vent-forms have to trade with other sophonts is information," Lakesh said. "They have sophisticated means of interfacing their own innate data storage with external devices, both for output and input."

"Wow," Robison said. His eyes shone with nerd rapture.

Hays pointed a blunt finger at him. "Stow it," he warned. "For now, what exactly is this galactic legend Bates found out about?"

"Apparently," Brigid said, "about half a million years ago, a race in the far arm of the galaxy developed a device they called the Cosmic Eye, which they claimed would close the vacuum fluctuation that is our universe. Now, nobody then, nor now, so far as the vent-forms know, has ever been able to prove or disprove whether the universe truly is a vacuum fluctuation."

"But nobody wants to find out the hard way," Kane said.

"The builders were religious fanatics of some sort. They were also evidently arrogant. They actually bragged about their marvelous device before they actually completed it."

Reichert whistled. "*Big* mistake."

Brigid nodded. "What ensued, as anyone less blinded with zeal might have easily foreseen, was instant war of total extermination waged against the Cosmic Eye's builders. It destroyed not just them but an entire cycle of galactic civilization, which indeed has only recently built back up to near the level it had attained then. A cycle, I might had, that has apparently been repeated in the Milky Way for millions of years—the spread of civilization throughout the galaxy, followed by a cataclysm that shatters it."

"Lovely," Hays said. "But riddle me this—were the Eye's builders so big and bad they were able to wreck the rest of the galaxy all by their lonesomes? It'd seem the Eye was a little bit redundant if they could do that already."

"They didn't," Weaver said. All eyes turned to him. "The other races did. They smashed each other, fighting for exclusive control of the Eye. Or at least the technology behind it."

He looked over the top of his round lenses at Brigid and grinned. "Am I right?"

"Quite."

"Swell," Hays growled, pouring more tea from a little brass pot. "Three hardened special-ops vets get schooled in intrigue by a civilian pogue."

"In my early days as an attorney," Weaver said, "before I learned better, I handled some divorce cases. It gave me a feel for these kinds of transactions."

"So what does this mean for suffering humankind?" Reichert asked.

"From the vent-forms' memories Bates learned of the Eye's supposed existence," Lakesh said. "He also, or so Old Tower and I surmise, may have deduced its supposed location, probably through fragments of Annunaki or Danaan records."

Hays rubbed his forehead. "Why would you and this building surmise that?"

Lakesh stared at him.

"It's a person," Domi said. "Kind of. Old Tower's the name of one of their colonies, like. Their boss."

"He's a cartoon cat," Kane said.

Hays gave him a look. "If you say so. The question remains, what makes everybody think Bates tumbled to this ancient cosmic secret?"

"Because the vent-forms have failed to receive expected communications from him," Brigid said. "Specifically, he has not yet asked for payment."

"Oh," Robison said. "Shit."

Lakesh nodded. "An accurate, if earthy, appraisal of the situation."

"That's why we need to find Bates's new hideout," Grant said. "Yesterday at the latest."

"Roger that," Robison said, sitting up straight in his chair now. "But do you really think there's any danger of Bates actually destroying the universe? Even if he knows where this cosmic dingbat is, and it actually works."

"Which we don't really know, do we?" Reichert asked, looking around. "I mean, they never even tested the damn thing, did they?"

Everybody looked at him. A moment of silence seemed to stretch toward infinity.

Reichert suddenly colored again, gulped and waved his hand. "Oh," he said. "Never mind."

"And provided he can get to it," Hays said, as if Reichert had never spoken, "Far Arm of the Milky Way's a long way to walk."

"Oh, he can get there," Grant said. He had resumed his seat.

"We and Bates did a little job for the vent-forms a while back," Kane said. "Payment we both got was knowledge of how to build an interstellar jump device."

Team Phoenix exchanged looks. Kane knew that little ritual: he, Grant, Domi and Baptiste had performed it often enough, in the years since they had become renegade outcasts from baronial civilization.

"I'm not so sure, here," Robison said. "Bates is a megalomaniac. He's the sort to want to run the universe. Not blow it up. Or put it out—whatever."

"Friend Larry, is the power to destroy not likewise the power to compel?" Lakesh asked.

"In other words, use the Eye for cosmic extortion," Weaver said.

"And if he doesn't get his way," Reichert said, "then poof." He put his fists together and fluttered them apart, opening his fingers, at the same time blowing between them.

Lakesh nodded. "Just so."

"But blackmail whom?" Hays demanded. He took a stub of cigar out of his breast pocket and stuck it in his teeth unlit. "These overlords you told us about seem pretty weak beer, given they haven't even yet managed to take over Earth."

"And why would Bates want Earth," Robison asked, "when he could have—well, everything?"

"We suspect," Lakesh said, "that friend Gilgamesh has set his eye on higher stakes."

"Remember that galactic civilization that's just about rebuilt from the last go-round?" Kane asked.

Weaver barked a laugh. "So whether Gil manages to get his hands on a working end-the-universe gadget or not," he said, "he's going to pull his usual stunt of outsmarting himself. And set off a galactic war in the process."

"Which, if it's like the last one," Robison said, "could wind up just accidentally scouring both us *and* the overlords off this insignificant little mudball."

"Collateral damage," Reichert said.

They sat for a moment and digested that. Kane got up to refill his own coffee cup.

"Gee," Reichert said in a small voice, "I wish we could help you."

Robison tapped his forehead with his fingertips. "There was something," he said. "Remember that time in California, about our sixth week of training? We were doing acceptance tests on our AK-108s out at the URS dry lakebed test facility." URS was Universal Resource Software, Bates's multibillion-dollar megacorporation.

Weaver nodded. "He had just flown back from Los Alamos in his Gulfstream." The Iron Man's last employment before recruitment by Bates had been as a machinist for Los Alamos National Labs.

"He was laughing with some of his cronies about a great boondoggle that was being run on the bureaucrats up there by some of the nerds," Hays said, nodding vigorously. "It was a real big joke. He said once it was done they could really look down on the rest of the solar system."

Kane squinted at him. "What the hell does that mean?"

Hays shrugged an exaggerated shrug. "Me no know."

The door opened. A tall man with thinning blond hair swept straight back sauntered in.

"Ah, friend Brewster," Lakesh said.

Grant's forehead knotted into an even more profound scowl. Kane made a sound low in his throat and sat up straighter. There was no love lost between them and the self-appointed chief of the Manitius refugee scientists. "Have you seen Sally?" Lakesh asked.

Brewster Philboyd blinked around the room from behind his thick black-rimmed glasses. Kane noticed his expression showed no more approval when his myopic eyes swept the members of Team Phoenix than it did when he looked at Kane and Grant.

"Yes," the physicist said. "That's why I'm here. I've been looking all over for you."

"Well, you found us," Kane said. "What's with Wright?"

Philboyd smirked. It was an unusually nasty smirk. Even for Philboyd.

"I suppose you'll all just have to come with me," he said, "and find out."

Chapter 7

"You've got this girl locked in a room?" Reichert demanded. "What did you bring us here for? To bust her out?"

They stood staring at the closed door in the vanadium-steel wall.

"Woman," Brigid corrected.

Philboyd's smirk deepened. "You Phoenix gentlemen are much of a muchness with your opposite numbers within Cerberus," he said in a self-consciously superior tone. "Violence is the court of first and middle resort, as well as last."

"Do you want to break his face as much as I do?" Robison asked Kane in sidelong sotto voce.

"You betcha," Kane answered the same way. "Don't. If we don't get to, you don't, either."

"That's fair."

"Brewster, what is the point of bringing us to this empty corridor?" Lakesh asked testily.

"We have Sally Wright secured inside this compartment," Philboyd said.

"Like Sean says," Hays asked, "is this a hostage situation?"

"Ha, ha," Philboyd said. "I deemed isolation a necessity to avoid distraction. Given you gentlemen's simple but—shall we say, vigorous?—approach to problem solving, I believe my assessment amply justified."

"Brewster," Lakesh said, "why are we all standing here?"

Philboyd sighed a martyr's sigh. "We have been conducting an experiment in remote viewing."

"I'm out of here," Reichert said, turning and starting to walk off.

"Wait," Brigid said. "Sally has displayed certain psychic sensitivities in the past. We should keep our minds open, under these circumstances."

"And you guys just told us you didn't have any better ideas," Grant said.

Reichert drifted back, his plump but handsome face set in mulish lines.

"You gotta admit," Robison told him, "that this isn't any weirder than a lot of stuff we've been through already. Might as well give it a listen."

An intercom unit set into the wall beside the sealed door popped alive. "Dr. Philboyd?" Sally Wright's voice asked tentatively. "I've finished."

"I HOPE I'VE DONE all right," Sally Wright said, slumped in a chair, sipping tea. Because the researcher had seemed so wrung out, they had returned to the cafeteria to get her something to restore herself.

"You did fine." A bit tentative herself, Brigid reached to touch her assistant lightly on the shoulder in encouragement. She had never become truly comfortable with human contact, especially the casual variety.

Kane sat at the table, shuffling through a sheaf of pages torn from a notebook. He frowned. "What are these, pictures of planets?"

Sally opened her mouth to speak. She froze. She was

by nature painfully shy, to a degree that made Brigid seem gregarious. Now terror of incurring disapproval blanched her already pallid features.

"It's the solar system," said Brigid, who had flicked through Sally's notes first, "not drawn to scale, obviously."

"What's this dust-looking stuff here?" Kane asked. "All these specks between the last little circle and the first big one?"

"I believe they're the asteroids, sir," Wright said timorously.

"But we knew that!" Philboyd stated. "We already knew Bates was in space. The entire point of the exercise was to find out *where*, not to tell us what we already knew."

"Jump back, Jack," Major Mike growled. "The lady saw what she saw. The experiment was your idea in the first place, anyway."

Philboyd, who stood at the side of the room, turned and began to pace. "I refuse to be held accountable if the woman won't even try."

"I did try," Sally said. The physicist's response seemed to make her more assertive. "That's what I saw—Jupiter, Saturn, a little red ball that must've been Mars. The stars around. But mostly a sense of looking down at the planets spread out beneath me."

Philboyd emitted a disgusted sound. Seated at the head of the table, Lakesh looked up at him sharply. "If you feel your efforts are wasted here, Brewster, you may be excused."

The Manitius refugee opened and closed his mouth twice, like a beached carp. Sitting at the table across from Sally, Grant laced his fingers together, turned his palms outward and stretched. His joints cracked like gunshots.

Philboyd spun and went out the door.

"Well, that lightens the air in here," Reichert said as the door closed behind him. But it didn't, much. Everyone was slumped in a varying degrees of dejection, no matter how hard they tried to hide their disappointment from Sally Wright.

"I knew Gilgamesh Bates might be hiding in outer space," Sally said, wringing her hands in distress. "But I tried not to let that influence me. Really I did. The target Dr. Philboyd set for me was Bates's location. I tried to blank my mind of everything but focusing on that."

On the walk back to the cafeteria, Philboyd, then in his triumphal-banty-cock phase, had explained he had been conducting minor experiments in remote viewing with the assistant archivist for several weeks. He had bragged of achieving what he termed really striking results. It was as if he were seeing the images himself.

"Strange that Philboyd would be interested in remote viewing, anyway," Kane said. "He's usually got such a ramrod up his ass about scientific stuff."

"Maybe spending your life on the Moon, chased by car-nobots and menaced by an ancient god has a way of shaking up your perceptions," Grant said.

"Good thing he never thought of trying to peek in on the overlords," Domi said.

"Why do you say that?" Kane said.

"Mebbe they look back."

"Now, there's a cheerful thought," Reichert said.

"Is there anything else you can tell us, Sally dear?" Lakesh said. "If you search your recollections for every slightest detail, you might unearth something that would be of immeasurable help to us."

The woman shook her close-cropped head of graying blond hair. "Everything I could put in words is already in the notes, Doctor," she said, close to tears. "What I saw, I tried to draw. I'm sorry I'm such a terrible artist."

"Actually, you're not bad, Ms. Wright," Robison said. "You got the Red Spot on Jupiter and everything."

Kane stood up and stretched. The muscles in his back cracked.

"Well, I don't really know about all this remote viewing stuff," he said. "I'm willing to admit I'm not smart enough to figure out what's so special about this vision Wright had. But I'll say one thing—if she says this is what she saw, it's what she saw."

"That's if there's anything to it," Joe Weaver said. "With all due respect to Ms. Wright, even if remote viewing works, it probably doesn't do so all the time."

"But it seemed so clear to me," Sally said. She was almost pleading. "It was just as if I were looking down at the solar system spread out below my feet—"

Larry Robison sat up as if goosed with a cattle prod. "Wait one," he said. "Isn't that just what Bates said, out there on the firing range? That crack about looking down on the solar system?"

Reichert crossed his arms on the table and laid his chin on them. "'Up above the world so high.'" He shrugged, which made his elbows wing up and down. "But what else would you see from outer space?"

"But how would you see the planets?" Robison said. "If you were just out in orbit, say."

"Been there, done that," Grant said. "Just look pretty much like stars. Mebbe a little brighter."

"Yeah, they don't look anything like Wright drew them," Kane said. "Not without a telescope or something. You think that's important?"

"Not how big they are," Robison said. "The angle."

"Seen from a point on Earth or even on the Moon," Brigid said, "the planets appear to line up."

"Okay. Now, where would you have to be to see them in order? Where you're looking down on them?"

"One would have to be outside the plane of the ecliptic," Lakesh said.

Robison snapped his fingers and pointed a forefinger like a gun. "Exactly. And that's where we'll find Gilgamesh Bates."

"OKAY, LISTEN UP," Grant said. His voice echoed among the racks and crates of weapons of all descriptions in the Cerberus armory. "We're going in with laser pistols as our primary weapons." He held up a shiny metal handblaster. "This way we get minimal chance of breaching the space station's hull integrity."

"Why are we worried about that?" Sean Reichert asked. "We've got to wear these monkey suits." He and his partners were dressed in bulky white pressure suits. Their helmets rested on a table to one side.

"At least they're a lot less clumsy than the ones we always saw on television, back in the day," Robison said.

"Apparently all the real space missions were a load less clumsy than what they showed us on TV," Major Mike said. "That really gives me a rash—I was always a big supporter of our space program. Now I find out it was all just a shuck."

"Just like everything else they told us," Joe Weaver said. He stood by another table examining a bulky longarm.

Grant stood and glared at them. "Do you want me to answer your question, or go off on your own comedy routines?"

"Sorry, sir," Robison said. "We've spent so much time with just one another for company, we've got into some bad habits. We'll listen."

Grant glowered a moment longer. Kane wondered if being called *sir* pissed him off or just befuddled him. "We wear pressure gear because no matter how careful we are, there's a chance the hull might get punctured. We're not going to be the only ones shooting."

"We aren't that lucky," Kane said, sitting on a table swinging his long legs.

"Don't you start in," Grant told him. "But we want to minimize the damage we do to the station. We're going to need to do things there ourselves, and working in a vacuum is always a hassle. Not to mention that what we're going to be breathing, we're gonna pack in ourselves, and it won't last too damn long."

That wasn't strictly true of the shadow suits the Cerberus group would wear, Kane knew. But what Team Phoenix didn't know wouldn't hurt them. Though they had started out as enemies—Team Phoenix had in fact been awakened and dispatched by Bates specifically to kill Kane and Grant and take over Cerberus—they had grown into firm allies and to a degree friends. There was only so far friendship went, though, especially with outsiders.

And as far as Kane, Grant, Brigid and Domi were concerned, everybody who hadn't been with them since their initial flight into exile from Cobaltville was an outsider.

"Also, there may be personnel in the station," Grant continued. "What Brigid and Wright have been able to dig up suggests it's pretty large. We want to keep at least some of them functional. They'll know how to run the equipment lots better than we will, and time counts here, people. Since we're looking to hit the place by surprise, and the crew probably isn't going around in full pressure suits with helmets all the time, a sudden pressure drop isn't going to do them any good."

"That's if they'll agree to cooperate with us," Sean Reichert said.

"If they're all dead," Kane said, "I bet they won't."

"This is true."

"Remember," Grant said, "this is probably just a stage along the way. Since Bates forgot to call the vent-forms back for his check, we have to figure he's already jumped to the Far Arm of the galaxy with his interstellar mat-trans gateway. So once we get to the station, we need to find out where Bates has gone from there."

LAKESH AND BRIGID had gone into overdrive once it was realized Bates's hideout likely lay outside the plane ecliptic, along which the planets circled the Sun. Except for Pluto, the exception to most rules. And even by the end of the 1990s many astronomers argued that Pluto wasn't even properly a planet, but a rogue moon that somehow wandered near enough to Sol to get tangled in the nets of its gravitational attraction.

In short order, once the proper key words were employed, Brigid found records of a top secret proposal in the mid-1990s to build a station well outside the plane ecliptic, ostensibly to keep watch in case unspecified rogue states tried to put their own station out there to manufacture thermonuclear, chemical or even biological weapons.

That gave a good laugh to Team Phoenix. "The only state that could possibly put something out there was us," Robison told the Cerberus crew. "The U.S.A. Not even the USSR had near the capability. Sure, they kept more of a manned presence in space than we did—publicly, anyway. But it was all pretty one-lung stuff, mostly PR."

The bare proposal gave few specifics as to exactly where the station was to be located, nor to its actual design. Elaborate artists' renderings, including computer slide presentations and even animations, showed what such a station might look like. But Brigid knew from long study of the late twentieth century, especially the interface between government and technology, that such things were really just science-fiction entertainments, with no more necessary connection to reality than the *Star Wars* vids. Their usual purpose was to extract grants, no more.

Obviously this one had gone further. But Brigid was on the hunt, and her nose for data was keen. She was able to get key names, especially of the Project Starwatch creator, an Air Force colonel named David Griffith Williams. And she knew how to make use of esoterica of catalog and reference numbers.

In short order she was able to locate sufficient fragments to confirm that Project Starwatch had in fact been built, in total secrecy. Unfortunately, fragments were all that existed, at least in readable form in the Cerberus files.

No blueprints for the facility existed, beyond the fanciful illustrations for the original proposal, which could safely be presumed to be as fictive as the station's ostensible purpose. But with Sally Wright's able assistance Brigid did locate certain tantalizing hints as to where the elusive station might orbit....

Chapter 8

"Kane," Grant said, nodding at his partner.

"Huh?" A moment later, Kane tossed the bulky longarm he was handling to the big man. Grant fielded it deftly—and shot Kane a ferocious glare.

"You don't want to treat these things as casually as my associate here," he said. "He's a point man, and point men are all crazy, as we all know."

"Hey," Reichert piped up. "I resent that remark!" While everybody in Team Phoenix was extensively cross-trained and basically did everything, he was their scouting specialist—their point man of choice.

Grant ignored him. "This is a pulse-plasma rifle. It does what the name says. This is your heavy support weapon. Each team in will have one of them."

"Why not more of them?" Reichert asked.

"First, we don't have many of these things. Second, they're triple powerful. Like the laser pistols, they won't burn through the station's hull in a single hit, but for a different reason—the heat tends to dissipate too widely. But a second hit anywhere near the first and all hell breaks loose."

The four Team Phoenix members looked suitably impressed. It's a good thing we haven't mentioned the rail-gun blasters, Kane thought, or they'd be clamoring like little kids for those. The electromagnetic weapons, while ideally suited for microgravity combat because of lack of recoil, also had way too much penetration to be used inside any enclosed space whose integrity was an issue.

"If you want other blasters, you can bring them," Grant said, "so long as you can hump them yourselves with everything we have to carry for this mission. And so long as you keep any projectile weapons unloaded and do not fire them."

"We can do that," Major Mike said, nodding. "Right, Sean?"

Reichert nodded. "Sure, boss man. I know when to keep it in my pants. Sorry, ladies."

"That's a new development," Joe Weaver said. Neither Brigid nor Marina showed any response. Kane guessed the girl had gotten accustomed to her adoptive family's blend of vulgar horseplay and goofy gallantry.

Hell, if she hasn't fused out and chilled them all over their incessant damn references to vids and TV shows she's never seen, she's lots stronger than she looks.

"Speaking of ladies," Robison said, "where's Domi?"

"She won't be joining us," Lakesh said, striding in.

"You think," Grant muttered.

"I have good news," he said, bouncing up and down on the balls of his feet. "The Keyhole satellite we tasked to look for the extraecliptic station produced these."

He laid several sheets of paper printed with black-and-white images—mostly black—on the table next to where a plasma rifle still lay. The others crowded around to look as he fanned them like a hand of cards.·

"Not the Hubble?" Reichert asked.

"The Hubble optics were faulty," Brigid said, "and never

fully corrected. The imaging software NASA used to massage the images gathered always contained a high level of conjecture."

"Whereas the KH birds had far superior optics," Joe Weaver said. "At least a decade before Hubble went up."

Lakesh nodded. "Precisely."

"I hate to think what kind of pictures the Hubble would take," Kane said, frowning down at the printouts, "if this is all we get out of 'far superior' optics."

"Kinda disappointing little blurs, for sure," Robison said, eyebrows arching over his own round glasses. Kane was endlessly fascinated by the fact that excellent eyesight had not been requisite for membership in Team Phoenix. He supposed it was a natural consequence of needing a combination of elite fighting troops and nerds.

All four wore corrective lenses, although Reichert mostly used soft contacts that had apparently been laid in for them in inexhaustible supply at a series of caches buried across North America. These had been small and concealed cleverly enough to escape discovery by generations of highly motivated scavvies who had unearthed most of the much larger redoubts.

"Angular smudges," Grant said.

"Ah, but the key lies in the angularity, Grant," Lakesh said. He was still practically bubbling over with pride despite the cool reception his picture show had gotten. "No naturally formed objects ever observed within the solar system have ever displayed it. We suspect the station may consist of limbs or lobes arranged around a central hub."

He laid down another image: a startlingly clear picture

of a cruciform structure with a circular center, like an old Celtic cross.

"Please don't take that too literally," Lakesh said. "It's an extrapolation—our good Donald got a bit creative when I asked him to produce a visualization of what analyses of the satellite imaging suggested was a likely shape for our objective, I fear."

Major Mike grunted. "Not bad, though." He tapped the new picture. "Gives us some idea what to expect. Always better than dropping in blind."

"How did your satellite find this thing, Lakesh?" Kane demanded. "Unless it's big enough to park the Great Pyramid in one of those arms, you'd have to be looking in just the right place to spot it no matter how good a telescope you were using. I don't claim to know much about it, but last time I was out there, space was—" he made gestures in air as if molding a globe of clay before him, then threw his hands wide "—big."

Lakesh nodded magnanimously at Brigid. "She provided a list of possible locations based on her researches. I matched them with maps, some derived from the Annunaki, of the magnetic fields of the Sun and solar system. It produced a number of possible nodes that would be able to support a matter-transmission gateway. When we compared the lists, we found a match. And at the indicated location—at a distance from the Sun corresponding to approximately midway between Mars and Jupiter."

"About where the asteroids are?" Reichert asked.

Lakesh scowled. He hated being upstaged. "Indeed, at roughly the middle of the asteroid belt, but rotated upward by forty-five degrees."

He sighed theatrically. "If only I had thought to calculate the likely nodes in outer space earlier, we should have had a great deal less uncertainty. With all the great respect due our intrepid Sally, I admit I had my doubts about the efficacy of her remote viewing."

While Kane goggled slightly at anybody, even Lakesh, describing the mouse-timid former archivist as intrepid, Grant said, "What really chaps my ass is having to admit Philboyd was right."

"Hey, even a broken clock is right twice a day," Hays said. Kane and Grant stared at him. "You know, analog clocks, the kind with hands? Never mind."

"Most encouraging of all," Lakesh said, "is that our own mat-trans system has established protocols with the gateway on the satellite. It's live and functional—"

"Which we knew," Kane said.

"—and ready to receive you when you are ready to depart."

The others all looked at one another. "Couple hours to prepare, max," Major Mike said, after a quick nonverbal poll of his teammates. It included Marina, Kane noticed; the pubescent Atshuara girl seemed to have integrated smoothly into the tight-knit team.

"Same here," Kane said. Grant and Brigid gave the same response.

Lakesh nodded. "Then if you gentlemen and the charming Marina—" the girl hid her mouth with a hand and giggled "—will excuse me, I have other business to attend to." He turned and strode briskly out with his wrists crossed at the small of his back.

"Looks just like Groucho Marx when he does that," Sean Reichert said.

Brigid snorted.

Kane and Grant looked at her in surprise. "Well, it was funny," she said defensively.

"We just keep forgetting you have a sense of humor hidden away under the ice-and-fire exterior, Baptiste," Kane said. "Always takes us by surprise when you trot it out, once a year or so."

"Are you saying I lack a sense of humor, Kane?" the redhead demanded in a dangerous tone.

"Yeah," he said. "Functionally, anyway."

"We need to do a little planning ourselves before we just go barging in," Larry Robison said, a little louder than strictly necessary and shifting to interpose himself as if accidentally between Kane and the now-smoldering Brigid.

"Not our style," Grant said. "Kane just usually dives in headfirst, and I grit my teeth and follow."

"Sure," Hays said. "And since we got nothing more than a cover illustration for an old *Analog* magazine to light our way, there's a limit to how much in-depth tactical planning we're gonna do. But let's figure out what we can."

He stuck the cold cigar half beneath his silvery mustache. "For example, we go in first."

"Negative," Kane said. "I'm the point man."

"Then go in before the rest of your crew. This is our job."

Kane turned to face him squarely. "Listen, Hays," he said, trying to clamp down on the wolf anger that suddenly raged within him, "your rank don't cut no ice in Cerberus. You tell your own people what to do. Not me. Not us."

For a moment their glares held each other like grapplers, winter-sky-blue and wolf-gray. Then Hays laughed. "The rank doesn't mean squat anyway," he said. "I retired a couple centuries back."

"But still," Robison said, "Mike's right."

"How do you reckon?" Grant asked. He had his arms crossed over his chest, making his forearms bulk as large as Popeye's.

"You guys are the specialists. You've got experience in dealing with the matter-transmission technology."

"Enough to know how much jumping sucks."

"Amen," Robison said. "But you have all the experience in dealing with this…level of technology. Whereas our boots are still pretty firmly mired in the shallow mud puddle that we thought was the deep end of high-tech, late-twentieth-century style."

"Mebbe," Kane admitted grudgingly. "But Grant and me are still mostly gunslingers. Unless there's piloting to be done. Which it doesn't look like there's gonna be this time out—it's a little far even for our Manta TAVs."

"The do what you do best—guard the lovely Ms. Baptiste while she does the real work."

Kane stared at the former SEAL. Then he swiveled his gaze to Grant.

Grant shrugged.

"If you look at it without testosterone-tinted glasses," Brigid said, "it does make perfect sense, Kane."

During the confrontation, Grant had drifted up to stand backing up his point man. Kane wondered if it were even conscious. Crossing his own arms, he leaned back against his partner's redwood bulk.

"Mebbe it does. What are you proposing Major?"

"Two waves," Hays said. "Your jump gateway's not that

big anyway. So we jump in first. We secure the facility. Or at least a foothold. You give us five, ten minutes and come in after to do the deed."

"What happens if you get flatlined?" Grant asks.

Hays shrugged an ursine shrug. "Then you boys and girls get to play hero. Again."

"DARLINGEST DOMI," Lakesh said, "why ever are you wearing a shadow suit?" But his heart was already sinking within his chest.

The little albino woman continued striding purposefully toward the armory. Her albinism was only visible in the head, almost shocking with its white skin and plush of white hair, which sprouted from the midnight black of the suit that covered, unusually, the entire rest of her body. It did nothing to conceal the tightly packed curves of that body—quite the opposite—and caused a tightening in Lakesh's throat that had nothing to do with concern for her welfare.

"Don't try to stop me," she warned.

He chuckled. It rang false even in his ears. "But how absurd, Domi. This is an exceedingly dangerous mission. Perhaps the most dangerous we have ever attempted."

"Brigid going," she said tautly. "So that little Indian girl."

Lakesh winced. If her speech was compressing, it meant she was more than a little serious.

"Brigid's going because her expertise is required," he said. "Marina is going for reasons of her own." In fact, he had reservations of his own about that. But the child had made clear she had no intention of being separated from her family.

And it would be hardly fair to try to keep her here. She simply would not fit in.

"You not stopping her."

"She's not mine to stop," he said.

There was a beat before he realized how neatly she'd mousetrapped him.

There was so much more to say. Worlds to say.

She said no more.

As she strode by him, neither, for once, did he.

Chapter 9

"Come on," Kane said, although it felt as if his eyelids were lined with sand and his belly with worms and cold grease. "Got to…get…up. Showtime."

A faceless man-shaped shadow floated just above the floor of the jump chamber: Grant.

Kane was concerned. His jump had been nightmarish. But no more so than usual. Grant reacted strongly to the transitions, though, and might vomit. Kane pushed himself from the nearby lilac-colored armaglass wall and stretched out a hand.

Grant waved him off. "I'm all right," his voice said through Kane's commo implant. Kane also heard him through the shadow suit hood, meaning the space station still held air.

He quickly looked around. Brigid was curled into a ball with her hands to her head. "I'm fine," she croaked. Which was a lie, except insofar as it was meant to signify she was no worse than usual after a jump. Functional. Domi, meanwhile, was checking her own blaster as if nothing out of the ordinary had happened.

The door opened. Kane drew his laser pistol from his belt.

Marina waited just outside the jump chamber with her long black hair in a ponytail floating behind her head like a literal tail. A laser pistol was clutched in a small brown hand. Bulky packs belonging to her and her four males comrades had been lashed to stanchions above the gateway control panels with bungee cords. Team Phoenix had packed along their customary weapons, except for the 20 mm sniper rifle, which was just too monstrous to carry along with much of anything else. Kane wasn't sure whether sentiment or mad optimism lay behind the quartet's packing the blasters. But it had been their call.

"Hi," the girl said cheerfully. "We ran into some problems."

Kane skinned off the hood and let it flop down the back of his suit. The first thing he heard was the crack of a laser ionizing air. The girl's fine Atshuara features didn't twitch.

"What's the situation?" Kane demanded.

He glanced around as he spoke. Grant had his hood off and was massaging his heavy face. It looked gray and glistened with sick sweat. Brigid hovered by him, her own hair and face uncovered and the latter more than a little green. She offered him a water bottle. He waved her off.

"We're in one of the arms of the station," Marina said.

Kane frowned. "Not the hub? I was sure they'd build the thing around the gateway. Hell, we all were."

"The boys said they think the builders put it off as far away from everything else as possible because they feared it might give off dangerous radiation they didn't even know about," she said. "People were real afraid of radiation in their time, they say."

"Just like that bunch," Grant said, "to theorize in the middle of a firefight."

"They had something to be afraid of, you ask me," Kane said. "Go on."

She nodded. More laser shots cracked in the background. Then came an unidentifiable hum, followed closely by the shattering report of a flash-bang. Kane winced as the noise needled his eardrums; the console and bulkhead visible past the young Indian girl's head lit to a brief garish flash of blue-white.

She showed no sign of noticing. "Satellite security has us stalled, halfway down this arm. There's six of 'em, like spokes of a wheel. And, uh, an axle."

Kane nodded. It struck him that this child, barely a teenager, was taking all this quite calmly. Indeed, delivering quite a professional sitrep. Then again, she'd been through plenty of tough times already. Probably knew what it was to resign herself to death. Maybe more than once. Anyway she'd been learning her job as tactical director for the Phoenix mob for months. He joined his companions in quickly making fast their own extra gear as their predecessors had.

"The security guards are normal human beings. They act pretty funny, though. They fight like machines. They don't seem to move well in no gravity. Then there's these others. They're causing most of the hassle."

"What kind of others, Marina?" Brigid asked.

"You'll see."

"That you guys?" Mike Hays's voice demanded in Kane's head. "Get your asses out here!"

Kane looked to his companions. With Lakesh's assistance Robison had modified their own commo sets to broadcast and receive on frequencies used by the Cerberus exiles. Kane's, Brigid's, Grant's and Domi's units were set to exclude them from broadcasts unless specifically sent to them, preserving a measure of privacy for the four.

Grant was checking his plasma-pulse rifle. "Don't know why I bother," he muttered. "Machines never have any trouble with the damn jumps. Just things with brains."

He looked to Kane. "Well, we're loaded and locked."

Kane had his laser pistol out. His Sin Eater was strapped reassuringly to his forearm, even though it had no magazine in the well. Maybe the men of Team Phoenix weren't the only ones who needed security blankets.

"Time to rock," he said.

THE BUZZ BEGAN low in volume but already painful, like a mosquito whine near your ear. It soared quickly to an eye-watering crescendo and culminated in something like a cross between a squib going off and a shrill, ear-tearing tintinnabulation. It reverberated inside Kane's skull long after the actual noise had ceased.

Larry Robison nodded at Kane's scrunched-up expression. "That's how the spuds avoid damaging their home's integrity," he said. "Sonic weapons."

"We don't know what they do if they hit you," Major Mike called from across the passageway. "Fortunately the swoopy little bastards are terrible shots."

"Hard to hit, too," Sean Reichert muttered.

He jackknifed and made a sound like a cat coughing up a hairball. "You shot?" Domi asked from behind Grant, who sheltered behind a flangelike projection that was probably a structural support closer to the end of the arm—and the gateway—than the one Kane was behind.

"Space sick," Robison called back.

"Shit," Grant said. His cheeks had taken on a greenish tint. "All we need is that crap floating over and getting all over us."

Kane risked a three-second look around the stanchion. Several bodies floated at various stages down the passageway, which was a circular tunnel a good ten feet across, sectioned by almost equally large hatches. Apparently, reasonably large objects were intended to move through the gateway; its door had been pretty outsized, too, now that he remembered. He hadn't exactly been noticing such details consciously at first, being first preoccupied with the effects of the jump, and absorbing the tactical situation as relayed by Marina.

At least seven bodies, or parts of them, floated in the passageway. Four of them were mostly blackened and burst, the signature of plasma pulses.

"How'd you manage to blast both legs off three of 'em?" Grant wanted to know.

"I didn't," Hays said. "Wait one."

A figure zipped from an open hatch near the far end of the passage. From the waist up it was a normal, if smallish man, with close-cropped graying hair. It fired some kind of blaster at them. The flange before Kane rang as if struck with a hammer. His cheeks stung as if sprayed by fine grit, the hair rose at his nape, his teeth vibrated as if being drilled. He and Grant both snapped shots after it, which dug little divots out of the bulkhead at the passage's far end. Clean misses.

"No legs?" Domi demanded. "They all amputees up here?"

"We think they grew that way," Weaver said.

"Apparently they don't have much use for legs," Robison said. "They use some kind of little jets worn around the waist. Electrostatic air impellers, most likely."

"How does their blood circulate, without the great muscles of the legs to help the heart?" Brigid asked.

"Pretty freely, from the way they splash when they're hit," Robison said, provoking a fresh round of retching from Reichert. "But remember, their tickers don't have to fight a nasty one g to push the blood through their little arteries."

"Some of the chills have legs," Kane said. Four in fact—all men clad in skintight uniforms of a blue so dark as to seem near-black, and looking normal enough. Except for the dull gray metal skullcap each wore on his shaved head.

"Bates's mercs," Hays said.

"More freezies like you?" Domi asked as one of what Kane now understood why Team Phoenix called spuds leaned out a hatch and popped another sonic blast at them. This one buzzed down the corridor and made a nasty clang on the bulkhead behind them.

The Phoenix members laughed, even Reichert, who had mostly recovered from his fit and wiped his mouth on the back of his hand. He had had self-control enough to puke toward the curved bulkhead, which resulted in most of it sticking in a nasty wad instead of floating around in gobbets waiting to get in everybody's hair, like exceptionally vile flies.

"Not hardly," the young man said. They knew at least one more team of handpicked special operators had been recruited by Bates and put into suspended animation preskydark, as they had been. The new quartet had made an attempt to assassinate Kane and Grant and gotten wiped out some months before. "Basic outlander stonehearts he hired somewhere."

Another spud launched himself side to side, screaming and blasting furiously with sonic blasters held in both hands. Kane jerked back and held his hands over his ears. The beams themselves made only a slight, strange hum, but when they struck metal, the noise they made caused his skin not just to crawl, but seemingly to try to crawl away.

He saw a ruby flash. The terrible clangor stopped. He risked a quick look and saw the spud, still driven by its jets, bounce off the far bulkhead to join the chills floating in air. He had a dark spot just above his wide-open staring eyes, and his head, shorn close like Domi's, had a weird kind of distorted look to it.

"Good shot, Iron Man," Reichert called.

The erstwhile machinist did not look triumphant. Rather his face was set in what looked to Kane like disgust. He shrugged.

"These people are defending their homes from invaders," he said. "I don't feel real good about killing them."

"You rather it was you?" Grant asked.

Weaver's cheeks rode up in a cheerless grin, turning his strange slanted pale green-blue eyes into slits. "If it's them or us," he said, "I pick us. Obviously. But I think it's time to try negotiating again."

Grant looked to Kane, who shrugged. "I'm not much happier about it than he is, come to mention it. Besides, talking's always better than shooting. Less chance of getting shot back."

"Amen, brother," Hays said. "Your play."

Kane stuck his head back out. He kept well clear of the flange he sheltered behind; he was considerably more leery, at this point, of suffering the side effects of a near miss than actually getting hit.

"Hey, you people," he called. "Let's knock this off! We didn't come here to hurt you. We don't mean any harm. We're looking for Bates."

A flurry of shots fired blind made the stanchion Grant hid behind screech. Grant cursed.

"Bates was a false one," a voice called back in English. The accent was peculiar. It sounded a bit like the twentieth-century American English Team Phoenix used. The voice was pitched high; Kane couldn't tell whether it belonged to a man or a woman. "If you seek him, you can go to hell!"

"That's where we want to send him!" Larry Robison called.

A pause. "You claim you come in peace. Why did you kill us?"

"You shot at us, remember?" Hays said.

"Bates's evil ones shot at you."

"Well, you did, too."

"You invaded our home!"

Hays looked at Kane and shrugged. "I don't think logic's playing out real well here."

"We just want Bates," Robison called.

"He has gone!"

"Damn," Grant mouthed. It wasn't really a surprise. Still, Kane felt a sudden hollowness yawn in his own belly. The size of the universe, it felt like…for now.

"Then all we want to do is find out where he went and go after him," Robison called. "We apologize for invading your home. We apologize for killing your people. We'll pay any restitution you ask."

"You sure that's a good idea?" Kane hissed.

"Hush," Brigid said. "He's right."

"Mebbe we can jump 'em fresh food from Cerberus," Domi said. "Lakesh'll work it out. He always leaves us holding the bag. His turn!"

An indecipherable murmur floated down the hall. The surviving spuds were discussing their options.

"If we have to," Hays's voice came over the net as he subvocalized, "we can use stun grenades. Rush 'em, try to overpower them before they recover."

"These probably aren't the only defenders," Kane pointed out, likewise subvocalizing so the station inhabitants could not overhear no matter how keen their ears. "If we have to fight, we might have to clear this whole huge place compartment by compartment."

"We will fight no more," the voice called down the tunnel. "But you must prove yourselves worthy."

Driven by their impeller belts, a half-dozen spuds suddenly swarmed out of compartments all around the passageway. Fingers tightened on firing contacts despite the promise of no further combat. But as quick as hummingbirds the legless humans vanished through the far hatchway.

"Looks like they're good as their word," Robison said.

"So far," Kane said. He pulled himself out from behind his stanchion and pushed off to propel himself like an arrow down the tunnel.

"Hey!" Reichert shouted, and launched himself in pursuit.

"That's Kane," Grant said. "Always the point man."

The others followed. Marina stayed back in the compartment near the jump chamber. Kane wished Brigid and Domi would prove so accommodating about staying behind out of danger. If they just weren't so damn handy in a shooting scrape…

He pushed off the body of one of Bates's mercenaries that drifted into his path. As he reached the passageway's end, a blast panel slammed across it with a bang that seemingly made the entire satellite ring about them.

Chapter 10

Kane jerked back an outstretched hand. Had he gotten any closer, he would have lost fingers, if not his whole hand. Instead he collided with the alloy armor panel.

"That's gotta hurt," Sean Reichert said from right behind.

He rotated deftly to land feet first on the panel, flexing his legs to absorb his momentum. Microgravity seemed to disagree violently with his stomach, but the rest of him seemed to get along with it just fine.

Kane said, "Shut u—"

A voice blared from an intercom panel set in the curved wall of the tunnel. "Intruders! You may be the strangers from the stars for whom this station was set to watch, long ago! If you do not speak the proper word of power, this station will destroy itself!"

While loud and forceful, the words lacked inflection, as if synthesized. "What kind of astronomical observatory has a self-destruct sequence?" Reichert demanded. "How screwed-up is that?"

"About typical for the late twentieth century, I'd say," Hays said, pulling himself to a stop by a stanchion one shy of the blast partition. The others braked themselves around him, all somewhat more gracefully than Kane had done.

"Do you think they mean it?" Robison asked.

"They mean it," Kane said grimly. He hovered by the panel rubbing a bruised cheek and feeling around his teeth with his tongue. None seemed missing or seriously busted, although he tasted the coppery tang of blood. "Lot of these groups survived after Nukecaust, technicians or guards at various secure facilities. Because they tended to be pretty much fortresslike, with provisions stored up against emergencies, and located in remote locations, they were pretty well set up to survive even through skydark. And over time a lot of them sorta degenerated, became cults.

"Okay," Kane continued. "All this is real interesting, but none of it is keeping us from being blown up. How the hell do we figure out this word of power they want? Or should we just pull back to the gateway and jump back to Cerberus?"

"Wouldn't that just be putting off getting blown up, until Bates pushes the button on the whole universe?" Reichert asked.

"Maybe he'll get his way," Hays said, "and get to run the universe. Or at least the galaxy."

"If there was anything that'd make having the whole universe blow up around us look attractive..." Robison said.

"I know," Brigid said. She kicked off a stanchion and floated forward.

"What was that, Baptiste?" Kane said as she floated determinedly past him.

She put out a hand to the bulkhead beneath the intercom and used her arm as a shock absorber to stop. "I know," she said. "I know the word of power."

"Are you sure?" Hays said. "Whatever's talking to us sounds like just the sort to yank the lanyard if they get a fake password."

"If Baptiste says she knows, she knows," Kane said with a hard edge to his voice. He looked to Brigid. "Don't you?"

She pressed the transmit button. "Taliesin," she said.

After a long pause a thud sounded through the arm of the station. Kane felt it through the metal of the hull.

Reichert jumped away from the stanchion he'd been hugging as if it had gone white-hot. "Damn!" he yelped as he tumbled into a position inverted in relation to the others.

Hanging on to another stanchion, Domi reached out and reeled him in by an ankle as he flailed.

More solid-impact-like sounds echoed through the cylindrical passageway. Then a sliding sound.

The armored door panel ground aside. A figure floated just within: a spud, apparently male, with a bald head and bloated gray-green features. His arms were long and seemed wiry-powerful. His legs were no more than scarcely-perceptible round bumps in the gray trunks that, with his belt and a sort of T-shirt, were his only garments.

"I am Teal," he said. "You are the long awaited. Welcome to Starwatch Point."

"How can these be the long awaited," the female spud who floated nearest behind Teal asked, "when a long awaited has already come?"

Kane thought he recognized her voice as the one that had negotiated with them before the blast door closed. Behind in a large passageway crisscrossed by cables of some sort, apparently part of the huge round hub, hovered twenty or more of the legless humans. Teal had led them here down a short passageway after greeting them.

"They are not necessarily *the* long awaited, Carmine,"

Teal said firmly. "The legends said that there might come one, or few, or many, in the fullness of time."

The allies from Earth faced the inhabitants of Starwatch Station in what was apparently a commissary in the greater hub structure. Marina had joined them. Once it became clear hostilities were suspended, Domi and Marina had brought the packs from the gateway compartment. It hadn't required heavy lifting—more like herding.

"Place is effing huge," Reichert said out the side of his mouth. He understated, if anything: as near as Kane could reckon, the hub had to be minimum thirty yards across, the six arms radiating from it, like the legs of a child's jack, a hundred yards or more in length and fifteen wide.

"Not much problem with building materials," he answered the same way, "once they got a gateway out here."

"Shh!" Brigid dug an elbow sharply into his ribs. His shadow suit did way less than it should have to take the sting out of it. He floated away, grabbed by reflex at one of the cables that webbed the compartment interior, discovered it was flexible, like the bungee cords they had used to secure their backpacks.

"They said the word," said an ancient spud. Or at least it looked ancient to Kane's eyes, from the wrinkling and liver-spotting and hair loss. Then again, as far as he knew, the thing might be twenty years old and suffering radiation exposure of some kind. He wasn't even sure what sex it was; all these creatures had high-pitched voices, male and female, bulgy upper torsos and wisps of sparse, almost colorless hair. The only way he knew any of them were female, really, was that there were little floaters who had to be kids, football-sized beings yoked to parents with bungees. They called themselves the Watchers.

"But are they not the evil ones the first chosen warned us against?" asked another.

"What was he if not an evil one himself despite possession of the word of power?" asked another. "The ones he set over us were surely evil."

That produced a rippling rumble of assent. Followed by vociferous argument.

"Whatever Bates did," Grant said aloud to his companions, since they found themselves suddenly ignored by their hosts, "his shave-headed imported blasters didn't exactly endear themselves."

"Given that the spuds are armed," Kane said, "I wonder why they didn't just rise up against 'em?"

"We've seen similar patterns of behavior elsewhere, Kane," Brigid said. "When isolated groups of technicians become in effect self-sustaining sects, they are often so bound by what they regard as ancient prophecy they cannot bring themselves to act in a way that might run counter to it."

A debate was rattling on crisply as a firefight. The spuds weren't so awestruck by ancient prophecies as not to have pretty firm opinions about their true meanings, nor to be noticeably tongue-tied about expressing them. Kane's attention quickly drifted. The spuds had admitted them, and perhaps most important, downed weapons. With an old door-busting Mag's eye for the bottom line, Kane reckoned that meant that the side that won the debate would be, ultimately, the one the Cerberus bunch and Team Phoenix backed.

"What's with these people anyway?" he asked Brigid, floating over toward where she hung by one wall and grabbing one of the bungees strung here and there to serve as handholds. "They muties?"

She glared at him a moment, then shrugged, obviously coming to conclusions similar to those Kane had reached concerning the argument in progress. She shook her head.

"Just adapted to microgravity."

"But, damn," Grant said, likewise drifting over, "they barely got legs."

"Even among astronauts raised on Earth there was substantial lower-body muscular atrophy when protracted periods were spent in orbit," Brigid said. "Also, it's likely a certain amount of load-bearing and repeated impact is necessary to stimulate bone growth in the young, as it is to cause bones to continue to replenish themselves and retain mass among terrestrial adults. The other characteristics, such as the bloated features and upper bodies, result from a migration of body fluids upwards—also characteristic of long stays in orbit."

"Hope we don't stay here long," Reichert said, joining them. His olive complexion still held a distinct green tinge.

He shook his head. "Damn, I hate to say that. All my life I wanted to go to space. Now I'm here, and I can't wait to feel gravity again."

"I don't think it's catching," Hays said. "I suspect they may have been genetically monkeyed with at some point."

"Not the first time that kind of thing happened," Grant grumbled.

"Look on the bright side, kid," Kane said. "We didn't come here to take up residence. We'll be moving on soon. One way or another."

"There may be some degree of inbreeding involved,

here, too," Hays said. "There's thirty-one of the inhabitants in here by my count, including ankle biters."

"If they had ankles," Reichert said.

"Even allowing some of them off doing duties in other parts of the station, and the five we dropped, that's what, fifty? Not much of a breeding population. As it is, I'm a little surprised they don't all have fifteen fingers."

"Some of them do have extras," Joe Weaver said softly. The others looked at him. He had moved to a table by a bulkhead and rested against it. "They display both poly-dactyly and syndactyly, if you look closely."

"And in English those mean…?" Grant prompted.

"Extra digits, as he said, and fused digits," Brigid answered.

"I'm curious about the mercenaries," Weaver said. "Spe-cifically, those thick metal bands around the backs of their skulls. I checked a couple out—they seem to be clamped to the bone itself, right through the scalp."

"That can't be what it's for," Robison said.

"It's a SQUID controller," Brigid said suddenly.

The others looked at her. Robison's expression went studiedly blank.

"It's not a term of derogation for a SEAL, frogman," Hays said. "Means Superconducting Quantum Interphase Device. SQUID, squid."

"Erica van Sloan used a variation of such a system to control her Chinese security troops in the Xian Pyramid," Brigid said. "Those were implants, though, I believe."

"Erica van Nasty," Domi said with venom. She was not appreciative of the mutual interest between the newcomer to Cerberus—their former bitter foe—and her paramour,

Lakesh. Not that any of her companions harbored very congenial thoughts toward the cold, calculating woman.

"You mean Bates was brain controlling these dudes?" Reichert asked, voice getting a bit shrill at question's end. "Jesus. I almost feel sorry for 'em now."

"Be glad," Weaver said with a gravelly chuckle and sardonic grin, "he didn't decide to do it to *us*."

"These guys were just generic coldhearts," Grant said. "He wanted you guys for your initiative, not just to be remote-control drones."

"Why, Grant, that's the nicest thing you ever said about us," Robison said.

"Look how well it turned out for him," Domi said with a wicked grin.

Kane shrugged with his eyebrows. "Look at it this way—it shows us once again that Bates, smart as he is, can make mistakes. Big ones."

"Are you becoming an optimist, Kane?" Brigid asked.

Kane grunted. "Probably a touch of space sickness, like the kid's here," he said. "It'll pass."

"My friends," Teal said. They turned to see him hovering a few yards from them, holding almost negligently to a cable with two fingers. "We have come to a decision."

Kane felt the tension wind up in all of them, as if they were bound by the same tightening wire. He let his right hand drift to the butt of his holstered handblaster.

"We have discerned our duty," the spud leader said, "and it is to serve you as the true foreseen ones. Our home and our services are at your disposal."

Chapter 11

"Doesn't look like much," Reichert said, pressing his nose to the armaglass viewport in the command center in the core of the hub. Outside lay the universe, the stars diamond chips in ultimate blackness, untwinkling and visible despite the lights within.

"What are you talking about?" Larry Robison demanded. "It's the whole Milky Way in all its splendor! Like no view you could ever get from inside Earth's atmosphere."

Reichert shrugged. "But you can't see the planets," he complained. "Or at least they don't look any different from all the other little white lights. No big white-and-yellow Jupiter with a red eye, no Saturn with all gaudy gold rings."

"In other words," Hays said, "you're upset because you don't see the solar system the way the Wright woman did, back at Cerberus."

Reichert turned to look at him. "Well, yeah."

"Scaling problem," Robison said. "The planets are too small to see from here. And if you could see several of them at once—for all I know you can—they'd be way too small to see any detail."

"How'd she do it, then?"

Robison shrugged. "I don't know how remote viewing works."

"If it does," Hays said. "Maybe it was just a lucky guess."

Kane floated between them and a central console where Brigid and Teal had their heads down peering at a screen. Off to another side Marina chirped with delight as she pointed out the faint fuzzy patches of nebulae and distant galaxies to Domi, who hung beside her nodding indulgently. Kane was inordinately amused to see the albino, whom he thought of as little more than a girl herself even though she had to have ten years on the Atshuara, playing the knowing adult.

The control center was a wedge of space set at what seemed to Kane to be the top of the large central hub, right on the rim. He thought of it as the top because the seats and consoles were fastened to the surface nearest the hub's center, which thereby became the floor. Brigid told him they were actually head down toward the plane ecliptic.

Kane noted that the few compartments they'd seen so far tended to feature permanent or semipermanent attachments—consoles, food-preparation areas, table—placed in an orientation consistent with a certain arbitrary *up*. More readily transportable items, such as mechanical units moved into a given area for a given task, tended to be anchored with flexible cables in totally random orientations. He guessed from that that the station had been built in such a way as to minimize spatial confusion among its original crew, who after all had been born and raised on Earth. Their descendants, if that's what the spuds were, had no such attachment to *up* and *down*.

"It appears Bates has encrypted his files," Brigid said from the console.

"What else did you expect, Baptiste?" Kane asked.

"Nothing," she said coolly. "Still, I had to check. It might be vital to find a record of what he has discovered using his interstellar mat-trans."

"Can't we bust the cipher?" Grant asked. "I am transmitting the encrypted files to Cerberus. Lakesh will be able to devote his full attention to cracking them."

"What happens now?" Kane asked.

"Fortunately, we know from the plans the vent-forms provided us that the interstellar gateway is similar to our own mat-trans units in that it retains the last location transmitted to in memory. We should be able to discover the coordinates of wherever Bates has gone."

"Then what?" Reichert asked. "Do we jump after the son of a...gun?"

"No, Mr. Reichert. That's far too risky. We must discover some way of getting information from the other side first. Perhaps a probe. After we examine the gateway itself we can consult with the redoubt—"

A Klaxon began its rising-falling electric cicada song.

"STATION DESTRUCT SEQUENCE initiated," the sexless voice that had first challenged the newcomers announced, seemingly from the air all around them in the command center. "Detonation in two hundred seconds."

"You have *got* to be shitting me," Grant said. The big man sounded more disgusted than anything else.

"What?" Reichert demanded. "What did we do?"

Teal's face had looked greenish-gray before. Now it looked like fresh wood ash on a burned log—only a few shades darker than Domi's skin. "It is the station mind!"

"Evidently Colonel Williams harbored a strong belief

in the possibility hostile aliens might actually enter the system and seize the station," Brigid said. "Unless, of course, he was simply paranoid...."

Kane had already seized the first pack that came to hand and stuffed an arm through the strap. The others did likewise. "That's real fine, Baptiste," he said. "Explain all you want. But run while you do it!"

She pushed off from the console toward her own pack, which hung with most of the others in a small alcove out of the way. Kane turned to Teal, who hung staring at the screen with his small round mouth open.

"You got to get your people out of here," he said. "Jump them back to Earth or come with us. *Fast.*"

"But we have nowhere to go!" the spud leader said. "We cannot survive on a planetary surface!"

Kane's eyes met Brigid's. Her green eyes were wide, her cheeks ashen. He shook his head and headed away from the control center.

There wasn't anything to say.

The stellar gateway the spud techs had built lay at the far end of one of the two arms that sprang from the hub's center like an axle. Kane dived into the corridor toward it from the control center. Startled spuds zipped up and down it on their belt air-jets, calling to one another in high, keening voices.

Kane blanked them out. Hard man that he was, he couldn't bear to hear whatever they found to say.

Can't afford distraction, he told himself as he pushed through a hatchway that led to the arm. He knew it was a rationalization, no matter how true.

Arrays of handholds lined the passageway. It was wider

than the one through which they had entered, a good four yards. Hatches leading to compartments arranged radially around the passage led into the bulkheads at regular intervals. Of more immediate import, lines of handholds ran longitudinally to the bulkhead with a heavy circular hatch in it that closed the far end.

"Use these grips!" he shouted, grabbing the first and propelling himself toward one set about four yards up the circular tunnel. "Don't—"

Domi did what he was about to tell them not to do: she gathered her strong slender legs and pushed off hard from the vestibule. She streaked past him, her bare head a white comet with her shadow-suit-armored body a small black tail.

He swam grimly after. He saw her strike the far bulkhead. A moment later her shrill yip of pain reached his ears.

Spud faces, bloated, big pored and fearful, poked out of opened hatches at him. Their mouths formed questions he would not permit himself to hear.

Had he believed in a benign god, he would have suggested prayer.

Domi thrashed in air a couple yards shy of the bulkhead like a speared catfish, clutching her right shoulder with her left hand. The odd angle of her right arm told him at once she had dislocated her shoulder. Continuing to use the handholds to keep his velocity down, he pushed off five yards short of the hatch, turned his body, touched down with the flexible shadow suit soles beneath his feet slapping the metal.

His legs flexed, absorbing his momentum. He had not quite adequately allowed for the mass of his pack; it peeled itself off his left shoulder, giving it a good wrench in the process, bounced down the backs of his thighs and slammed into the bulkhead with a crunch of impact.

Hope nothing too vital broke, he thought.

"Sixty-five seconds to detonation. One minute…"

Unacknowledged in the depths of his skull and his gut, he had harbored the dread that the entry to the jump chamber would be electronically locked and either require a password they didn't have, unless Baptiste's magic word worked again, or was simply locked against them by the destruct routine.

But from halfway down the passageway he had seen the hatch opened with a wheel. The bulkhead itself seemed a recent addition: he could see rough beads of weld along the juncture of the metal panel and the tubular passage, fancied he could smell the metallic tang that lingers in air when metal is heated to softening. Leaving Domi to twist, he grabbed the wheel and turned.

It didn't budge. His heart plummeted like a Deathbird in a power dive. Moaning with frustration, he tensed his every muscle and heaved.

The wheel now spun so readily only his grip on its cool surface kept him from launching himself into the passage wall. His legs flew out behind him and waved like banners in a brisk wind.

The others came swarming up like hybrids of fish and monkeys as he got his feet back on the bulkhead and hauled the hatch open. So adrenalized was he that he had to jump clear at the last moment to avoid being crushed by the heavy vault door. It clanged against the bulkhead so hard it seemed to make the passageway ring around them.

Kane's escape leap fired him back up the corridor. To

his astonishment Sean Reichert jackknifed and double-kicked him in the hip as he passed. Kane angled toward the far side of the passageway, where Major Mike Hays threaded one arm through a steel handhold and snagged Kane by the hood of his shadow suit with his free hand. Kane bounced off the curved wall.

"Wrong way, big guy," Hays told him, stepping all over Reichert's shouted apology for his rough treatment.

"Damn," Kane said. He had given his forehead another nasty crack and had fireflies behind his eyes. He shook his head to clear it and followed his companions through the hatch he had opened.

The jump chamber stood on a platform braced on what appeared to be longitudinal structural members of the arm itself. It was set at a right angle to the arm's long axis; when Kane swam into the larger-diameter compartment that contained it, he was upside down in relation to it. It looked much like the other mat-trans chambers he had known if not loved. The main difference was that instead of being walled in metal and armaglass it was enclosed by panels of what seemed to be translucent plastic, capped top and bottom with metal.

Grant was up by a wall holding a stanchion with one hand and Domi, thrashing and squalling like an injured cat, clamped to his chest by one arm. Brigid floated by the control console.

"Forty seconds," the voice tolled the time until doom.

"Go, go, go!" Kane shouted. "Get inside now!"

Larry Robison put a hand on the small of Marina's back and launched her unceremoniously through the chamber's open door. She yelped in surprise. The Phoenix four followed with speed, one at a time to avoid getting hung up in the entry with their bulky packs. Grant and Domi came right behind.

Brigid still fidgeted at her control panel, possibly trying to figure out what other coordinates Bates had jumped or sent things to before the last transmission. Kane just grabbed her around the waist, twisted his feet to brace against the panel and jumped.

Before Brigid could finish her outraged demand to let her go, they sailed through the open door of the interstellar mat-trans.

The door shut behind them. The space-twisting effect caught them in midflight. Kane was turned inside out and he felt his soul and hers poured out among stars like sugar spilled on a vast black plain....

Chapter 12

On the main screen in the Cerberus command center, a new star flared white.

The screen showed real-time feed from a Keyhole satellite tasked to watch, not the Earth surface scrolling endlessly beneath it, but an object so distant from the planet that it showed only as hints of dull gray-metal gleam and occluded blurs of distant stars.

And now it was gone. A nova flamed in its place. As the duty crew in the command center watched, too stunned even to gasp, it cooled perceptibly to yellow.

The watchers released their held breath in a low collective moan. "Data transmission from the Starwatch extra-ecliptic orbital facility has been cut off," Donald Bry said from the main panel. His usually pale expanse of forehead was as white as polished marble, and sweat beading his withdrawn hairline sparkled in the uneasy light of the fluorescent tubes overhead. He had never been particularly friendly to the redoubt's star operatives, but his voice trembled with the announcement.

He turned to stare at Lakesh, who stood just behind his chair looking up at the screen. The scientist's own dark face had gone the hue of wood ash.

"There's no doubt," Bry said. "They're gone." As he spoke the new star on-screen faded from view.

Without a word Lakesh turned and strode from the room.

A TINY BLUE SUN SANK toward mountains fringing a vast red plain like the teeth of a barracuda's jaw, casting orange-edged shadows across sand and stone.

Crushing weight pinned Kane facedown in warm sand. It smelled dry but otherwise strange, like some kind of exotic spice with a faint metallic tang. Only by rolling his eyes up in his head was he able to see the sunset.

He realized then that what was squatting like a troll on his shoulders was his own mass. A mere few hours under virtual weightlessness in Starwatch had gotten his body unused to gravity. "Hell, I don't even know what the gravity is on this world. Or whatever the fuck thing I'm lying on.

"Isn't that kind of harsh language to greet a brave new world with?" a voice asked. Kane swiveled his eyeballs in sockets that seemed lined with broken glass. Larry Robison was sitting a few yards away. The slanting sunshine was as garish as a spotlight on his bearded face.

Kane realized he'd spoken his thoughts aloud. He tried to push himself up off the ground. A seismic wave of nausea rolled over him, soles to crown. All he managed to do was roll over with a loud moan.

"Look on the bright side," Sean Reichert's voice said from somewhere out of view. Kane felt an overwhelming desire to smash that plump olive-skinned face with his fist. Or he would have if an earnest desire to throw his guts up wasn't overriding all other sensation right then. "We didn't blow up."

"That's the *bright* side?" Kane heard Grant say. He

sounded the way Kane felt. Kane felt a certain sympathy for his partner. Although Grant was markedly less psychically sensitive than Kane, and so suffered less from certain disturbing jump phenomena, he had a more violent physical reaction to the unnatural stresses of the jumps.

Reichert sniffed loudly. "There's air!" he said brightly.

"You did *not* just quote *Flesh Gordon*," Hays said from somewhere out of Kane's field of vision. "Oh, crap. I've sure felt better."

"Nothing like a trip through the mixmaster of misery to give you perspective," Larry Robison said. "How's Domi?"

"Hurt, you prick!" something like a panther screech responded to him. "Arm all jacked outta socket! Lemme pull yours loose, see how you feel! Pull something else loose for you, had tweezers!"

"At least we know Domi's basically all right," Reichert said. "Hasn't forgotten how to cuss or anything."

Kane sat up. His head felt as if it were filled with viscous liquid that sloshed toward the front of his skull as he arrested his motion, then rebounded queasily. "Great," he said. "I think my brains are finally pureed."

A scrap of memory floated up into his consciousness, from the soul torment of jump. A face beloved, twisted in torture… "Baptiste!"

"Here, Kane." Her voice rasped slightly. "I'm examining Domi. Or I would be if she'd lie still."

Kane looked around. They had landed distributed in a rough circle. Everybody was present and stirring, if not exactly turning handsprings.

"We're all basically intact?" he asked in a voice like forty klicks of bad road. His mouth seemed lined with rancid cotton. It cried for water; his stomach rebelled at the concept.

"Team Phoenix present and accounted for," Major Mike said. He stood up, swaying only slightly, and began stripping out of his white pressure suit.

"What about those poor people," Marina asked, "back on the station?"

Silence answered her.

Brigid crouched by Domi soothing her like she would a frightened horse. Sean Reichert, the Team Phoenix medic, knelt the other side of her, rubbing his chin and studying her.

"So now the question becomes," Robison said, "where are we?"

"We're sure not in Kansas anymore." Hays, Robison and Reichert turned their heads toward Joe Weaver, who had already shucked off his monkey suit and was digging in a pack. He had probably popped upright as if he were spring-loaded after jump, not a micron the worse for wear. Kane tried not to hate him.

"What?" the erstwhile lawyer and machinist asked his comrades. "I thought I should try to hold my own with the movie references."

Groaning, Kane struggled to his feet. It cost him more effort than it should have even allowing for the stresses applied to mind and body of late. He dug in a pouch belted at his waist for his microbinoculars.

"Middle of nowhere," Kane said. "That's for sure. What the hell was Bates thinking of, jumping out here in the middle of the desert?"

A desert it was, he now saw. Like most of the deserts

on Earth, it showed widely scattered but plentiful signs of life: tufted hummocks of some kind of low, bunched ground cover, dark bushes with leaves that clattered like ceramic scales in a brisk westerly wind—if west was the direction the sun set hereabouts. The breeze itself was edged with chill and smelled of the odd spicy dust.

And moisture. A band of clouds the color of lead stretched across the horizon, hiding the sun's fierce, concentrated glare, which sent vivid blue rays reaching across a purple sky. Violet lightning suddenly laced the distant clouds, illuminating them without and within.

From behind he heard a yowl of rage from Domi: "Get your paws off me, you big bastard! Get these—*mmph!*"

Her outcries cut off rather, Kane thought, as if Grant had clamped a hand over her mouth. A moment later he heard a multithroated grunt of effort, followed at once by shrill squeal that seemed to be squeezed out through somebody's nose.

He didn't look around.

Almost at once Domi's mouth was unclamped. She uttered a final peal of fury and then gave over to panting moans, interspersed with obscenities.

"It looks as if a storm's coming," said Joe Weaver, walking up to stand beside Kane. He had a red mark high up on his cheek, and maybe an incipient shiner clouding up his right eye. As if a small flailing heel had caught him one as he knelt to help immobilize an angry young woman's legs, for example. His manner was calm as always.

"More than that," Reichert called from behind them, as Domi's tirade played out into a series of gasps. Kane heard Marina cooing to her. "Got quite a meteor display brewing up back there to the east."

At the same time a star appeared off above the cloud bank, slightly to Kane's right. It seemed an abrupt appearance for an evening star, but he was no astronomer.

The star grew brighter. And brighter. And bigger, until it almost seemed to show a disk.

Then it went out.

"Shit!" Kane exclaimed, spinning. "Those aren't meteors!"

"No, I think they're actually meteori—" Robison began.

"That's a space battle!" Kane shouted over him.

For a moment there was silence. Only the thin whistle of the wind, freshening now, disturbed it, and the rustle and clatter of the sere vegetation.

Silence seemed strange to Kane. Far overhead, as the sky darkened through deep purple toward indigo above eastern mountain peaks, he could see the rippling starbursts and flashes of what seemed to be the world's largest fireworks display. But it made not a whisper of sound.

He could even see tiny points of light moving around up there, between the unmoving stars they superficially resembled. As he watched one simply winked out.

"Bates!" Hays exclaimed in disgust. From the breast pocket of the camou blouse he had worn beneath his spacesuit he took half a cigar, which he stuck in his mouth and lit from a lighter with a defiant flourish. "He's been here, all right. Only that son of a bitch could piss off so many people that badly in so short a time."

"Do you think they're really people?" Grant asked. He loomed like a protective stone statue above Domi, who now knelt clutching her resocketed shoulder, rocking to and fro and moaning as Marina stroked her short-haired head and dabbed her face with a scrap of cloth wet from a water bottle. Kane noticed consciously for the first time that the Atshuara girl was even smaller than the albino.

Robison shrugged. "Given a sufficiently broad definition of 'people,'" he said. "Not humans, for sure."

"Baptiste," Kane said, turning to where Brigid stood. A wisp of her hair, which she had wound up in a tight bun to fit inside her shadow-suit hood, had slipped free and now fluttered about her face like an unconsuming flame. Its orange-red filaments glowed as if incandescent in the vicious glare of the sun, which had finally slipped between clouds and mountains on its way to day's end.

She laughed. "I don't have all the answers, Kane. Not even my memory can tell me something I don't know— such as where in creation we are."

"Do you think Bates really is here, sir?" Reichert asked Hays. Kane couldn't remember hearing him use the honorific before to their boss, couldn't remember any team member doing so.

"No." Hays gestured with his cigar at the sky. Its end was a red bead of light. "I think he's up there. Up above the world so high."

"Like an asshole in the sky," Robison murmured.

The sky above lived with twinkling that wasn't stars. A glow Kane had first thought a rising moon had rolled up into full view from behind the eastern mountains. It was a gauzy patch of yellow.

Elsewhere lights streaked, flared, vanished. To the north a trickle of red sparks ran briefly down a narrow arc of sky. Off to the west something burned a slanting line across the heavens, passed behind the thunderclouds, vanished behind the far mountains. A low dome of white light briefly appeared in the place where the streak would have ended.

"Whoa," Reichert said.

"I was never really a fleet guy," Robison said in a voice seemingly too small to come out of his big body. "And anyway ours was an earthbound kind of Navy, so I don't hold myself up as any kind of authority on space battles. But still I have to say, that is one big fight."

"Nor have we any way of knowing how far out it reaches," Brigid said.

Kane felt his mouth compress and stretch into a long, thin line.

"Okay, listen up," he said. "What's our situation here? We got water for mebbe a day, ration packs for a week if we eat regular and mebbe a month if we tighten belts. Dunno what you Phoenix guys have in your rucks, but I'm guessing we'd likely burn up all the ammo and energy packs we brought in one good firefight. And we're out here all alone in the middle of nowhere, somewhere at the ass end of the galaxy. Fair enough appraisal?"

"Yes," Joe Weaver said. "Except for one thing."

Kane turned a frown to him. "What thing is that?"

In the last rays of the miniature sun's vanishing Weaver's spectacles were disks of blue fire above an evil grin. He pointed.

Out across the red plain, small with distance, a pink dust-cloud was rising. It seemed to move toward them. Out before it Kane saw a last beam of sunlight glint in eye-stinging splinters off polished surfaces of polished metal.

"We are not alone."

Chapter 13

Kane snapped microbinocular to his eyes. Four vehicles of some sort approached at good clip across the desert floor with the sun at their backs. They seemed made of polished metal, aluminum for all he knew. Their shapes suggested old-style irons, the sort used to press clothes, but lacking handles.

He looked around. On Earth very few locales were actually flat, in the tabletop sense. This place was no different: aside from rising gradually to the east, becoming steep hills and ridges a mile or so behind them on the way to sprouting into mountains, the land was broken by rolls and swells, and outcrops of what looked like sandstone slabs with brush around their bases and sprouting from the interstices.

"That's the place we'll fort up to await events," he said, pointing to a lopsided hill that rose a hundred yards to their right and slightly behind. A pile of boulders dotted the landscape, big rounded slabs looking like carelessly discarded building materials.

"We'll take perimeter," Hays said. "You keep the ladies safe."

For a moment his pale blue eyes held Kane's gray ones. In the blue sun's electric light they seemed to burn with an eerie light. Kane nodded briskly.

"Right," he said. He turned to the others. "People, let's move like we got a purpose."

"Are we sure they're hostile?" Brigid demanded.

"Ms. Baptiste," Robison said, hoisting his ruck to his shoulder, "we're out here because some of these people, or their racial ancestors, made a good-faith effort to blow up the entire universe. I don't think we can afford to assume they're friendly."

They disposed themselves as if they'd rehearsed this all day. The Phoenix four spread out in a diamond shape around the outcrop Kane had picked as a makeshift fort. They had brought along enormous rucksacks stuffed so they could barely stand up beneath their mass; the mat-trans didn't care, and naturally they'd simply left them behind on the assault of Starwatch.

Not even Joe Weaver had been able to shag Little Willi, the huge bolt-action 20 mm sniper rifle, along. He had two longblasters strapped on his pack, though: a more conventional sniper rifle, a scoped bolt gun in 7.62 mm NATO he'd built himself on a Winchester 54 action, and a strange stubby bolt-action carbine with a box magazine and a shrouded barrel.

Taking Marina with him, he moved up to the top of a higher, steeper hillock about forty yards southeast of the position Kane had chosen. The Indian girl carried Weaver's enormous field glasses, which had once belonged to some World War II German field marshal, and an AK-108 hung on a long sling. She would be his spotter and security while he lost himself in his glass to snipe the putative bad guys.

Despite the fact that she seemed altogether dwarfed by her utilities and boonie hat, both made for someone twice her size, and the Kalashnikov longblaster was almost as long as she was, Marina moved with solid confidence that belied her years and almost elfin appearance. She seemed not the least bit fearful or intimidated by setting or situation.

Grant paused a moment atop the hill. His gaze followed Kane's. "Guess they breed 'em pretty tough in the Upper Amazon."

"Seems like. In terms of looking out for herself she reminds me of Domi."

"Lot sweeter disposition, though."

"I heard that!" came an outraged cry from behind them. "Pig bastards."

The other three Phoenix members spread themselves out in an arc between the boulders atop the hill and the oncoming unknowns, digging into the sandy soil using natural depressions, rocks and clumps of ground cover to provide themselves both cover and concealment. Reichert and Robison, out on the wings, carried standard AK-108s as primary blasters. Hays had his chopped-and-channeled FN-MAG set up on a bipod ready to rock and roll.

"Wonder if the bad guys have sensors that can pick 'em out," Grant said, helping the sulking Domi up into concealment among the rocks. She tried to shake off his helping hand, but then gasped with the pain it caused and gave in with ill grace.

Kane shrugged. He found himself a spot where boulders tumbled together had made a sort of triangular window that would serve fine as a firing port.

"Who knows if they won't just vaporize the whole area? Who knows if our blasters will even touch them?" Although he had a rail pistol and Grant a pulse-plasma rifle, and Phoenix had one of the latter, as well as laser pistols. They might help if the bullet launchers didn't.

Or they won't, and we'll all just die, Kane thought.

He pushed the rail pistol experimentally into the opening. The ground was soft from wind-deposited sand and pleasantly warm from the day's sun. I deserve a break right about now, Kane told himself. Unless I get so comfortable I nod off.

A glance out across the desert where the shiny flat-iron shapes were now clearly visible and coming fast through the twilight put paid to any chances of his nodding off. There was a weird musty smell down there, and a scatter of little pellets at the bottom of the space that looked suspiciously like animal droppings. Kane winced; he didn't mind getting crap on his hands. But he'd object to getting bitten or stung by some kind of unfriendly local wildlife. He took a moment to stuff a magazine into the Sin Eater he'd carried strapped to his forearm all along. He had noticed Grant taking his Sin Eater from his own pack and strapping it on.

Grant and Brigid propped themselves behind different slabs, Grant with the pulse-plasma rifle, Brigid with a Copperhead. Crouched behind one of the slabs that concealed Kane, Domi also held a Copperhead with her good hand; her left arm was still too sore for her to hold anything. She'd be their reserve, such as it was.

Kane put his microbinoculars back before his eyes. He realized with a shock that the strange vehicles were within half a klick. In this landing, sizzling light, he could see them quite clearly where long shadows pointed each out like an arrow. But there wasn't much to see: they had contours, but no other discernible features. Neither sensors nor obvious weapons broke the smooth molded planes of their shapes. He couldn't see any telltale outlines of hatches. Not even anything that looked like a windscreen or viewport.

"How do these things see?" Grant muttered. He had his own microbinoculars out now.

"Better than we do, no doubt," Brigid said grimly. She relied solely upon her own green eyes.

"I hope these Phoenix boys have sense enough to maintain radio silence with those things around," Grant said.

"I hope they can't RDF emissions from our comm gear, even when we're not transmitting," Kane said.

"I hope they can't detect the sound of our voices or the carbon dioxide of our breathing or our personal magnetic fields," Brigid said sharply. "Let's not go borrowing trouble."

Grant emitted the rumble of a mirthless chuckle. "She's got you there, partner."

The four silvery flat-irons slowed to a stop a 100 yards from where the Terrans had entered this world, 120 or so from where Team Phoenix lay hidden and 150 from the rocks beyond them where Kane and his comrades lay. Three vehicles stayed in place. A fourth nosed forward, sliding soundlessly over sand and sparse vegetation.

Kane realized he could see ground beneath the object's flat bottom. "Ground effect?" Grant asked.

"Mebbe not," Kane said. "You see anything blowing out from under it?"

"Hush, you triple stupes!" Domi hissed. "They hear us!"

Kane bit his lip. As violently volatile as she could be, Domi was usually rock steady in action. The pain of the dislocated and summarily reinserted shoulder, two jumps in a short period of time and all that had happened sur-

·rounding them, had to have tumbled her gyros more than a bit. Nonetheless she had a point.

Deliberately the alien craft approached the place where they had materialized. It slowed even further. Something about it seemed tentative; Kane had the peculiar sensation that what he was seeing was not a crewed craft or even a machine. He had the weirdest trickling sensation in his gut that it was somehow alive.

It seemed to be sniffing for them.

It was also getting dangerously close to Hays's position. Kane heard Hays subvocalize, "How do we play it if they stumble into us. Kane? Your call."

Kane grimaced. Thanks, he thought, even as he realized Hays was showing both good sense and respect for Kane's leadership by calling. The thought of Hays breaking silence made his guts twist like a rag inside him. Yet he didn't see the ex-Marine had any choice.

Wincing, he subvocalized back, "Hold tight. Shoot if your gut tells you to. But hold off long as you can." Which he knew was something of a cop-out.

"Kane, Mechanic," a crisp female voice said in Kane's skull. It was a beat before he recognized Marina from her high pitch and accent. "We have riders approaching rapidly from the east, behind us. At least a dozen, fifty yards out."

"Riders?" Kane repeated. He didn't sound as if he knew what the word meant. Even to himself.

He shouldn't have been too surprised, he realized. Back in the Outlands horses were a common mode of transport. If anybody, the Team Phoenix guys were the ones who should be taken aback, coming as they did from a time and place where riding horses were rich girls' and boys' toys.

But somehow here on an alien world on the far end of the galaxy he expected something a little higher tech.

"Everybody hold tight," he said desperately. He twisted, no easy feat when lying supine with his head stuck in a hole in some boulders.

For a moment he saw nothing except peaks and sheer cliff faces turned the color of blood by an alien sunset. The desert beneath had become a lake of shadow. Then lighter shadows against shadows: great, galloping shapes, like bulked-up giraffes, approaching with long rockinghorse strides across the packed sand and bunchgrass. They bore riders, for a fact. He could see that they had hoods pulled up over their heads. Or whatever they had atop their bodies—he could tell even in the failing light, the flash glimpse, and billowing cloaks that these things weren't human.

He didn't even think they were all alike.

"What we do?" Domi barked. She sat with her back pressed to the rock beside Kane, knees and the muzzle of the Copperhead she gripped in one hand up.

He glared at her. "Hold on!" he said. It was the only thing on this or any world he could find to say.

Parting like an incoming tide, the riders split to flow around the clump of boulders where the Cerberus operatives hid.

Chapter 14

The response wasn't long in coming.

A cyan pulse spit from the scout vehicle. A loping, slope-backed shape swerved aside. A bush flared green in what had been its path, then burned in reassuringly normal yellow-and-orange flames.

Another blue-green pulse answered the shot, this far larger and so bright it left a great big magenta streak of afterimage pulsing in Kane's retinas. It struck the silvery front of the lead craft, and yellow sparks and a great white billow of steam and sparks erupted.

A second explosion flared big and white from the direction of the trailing machines. Kane couldn't tell if any of the craft were hit.

A beam stabbed from one of the strangely shaped hovering craft, a white so intensely bright Kane's eyes seemed to see a dark core within before he looked away and threw up a hand to shield his face. He felt the heat on his checks and flanks. A scream ripped out, too gusty and prolonged to have come from human lungs. When he looked around, blinking at a pulsating pink afterimage, eyes tearing, he saw a line of brush burning to the left of their fort in the clump of rocks.

"Who the hell are the good guys?" Kane demanded. The

smoke stung his nostrils. It smelled a little of sage and a little of soap.

"I didn't get a program when they passed them out," Hays's voice came back over the comm net.

The Sun had gone now, leaving only greenish glare between storm clouds and far mountains. Streaks of light passed near overhead, coming from behind. Screams tore the sky. More explosions blossomed to the west.

Kane could hear little for the cacophony of cracks and booms and cackling flames. But he felt impacts through his thighs and elbows, realized they were the drumming of hooves—of heavy feet, at any rate. He turned and rose.

The riders were among their boulders. He thrust his arm at a colossal misshapen shape looming against the sky, flexed his hand. His Sin Eater sighed from its forearm holster.

Brigid struck his arm up. His triburst went toward the alien stars.

"Don't you see they're not attacking us?" she shouted, clinging to his elevated arm with both hands. He read her lips more than heard her.

The rider loomed above them both as if one of the peaks to the west had come to call on them. Kane had the impression that the rider was swaddled in robes, as well as hooded. It also looked to be larger than him and Grant rolled together.

It pointed to him with a great blunt finger. "You," it said blurrily but unmistakably. "Must come. Now."

Flashes tugged at Kane's peripheral vision as blasts assailed his ears. He smelled hot metal and a strange, almost sweetish smell he intuited had to be alien bodies burning. Brigid's body was almost pressed to his. He could see

Grant and Domi both staring at him. He felt as if he were all alone at the center of a universe of threat and chaos.

Only because it was true.

"Everybody, listen," he directed over the comm net. "We pull out with these people right now." He was far from sure they were people—he was mortally sure they *weren't*—but no was no time to chop semantics.

"Roger that," Hays replied at once.

Kane thrust Brigid at the gigantic rider. Its tree-trunk arm swept her off the ground and behind its high-cantled saddle as if she were a little girl, depositing her astride a beast that, in the pulsating light of flames and explosions, looked to Kane more like a miniature caricature of a Brach-iosaurus than a horse.

The beast whirled with startling alacrity and galloped away, shaking the whole rock pile. Another approached, smaller and slimmer but otherwise looking like the same species as the first mount. This one's rider seemed no less tall than the first, but impossibly thin even in the hooded robe that concealed its form and face, always assuming it had one. It stretched out to Kane a handful of fingers like crab legs, palm up.

Avoiding the hand, Kane sprang forward, sort of belly flopped across the riding beast's croup. The air whoofed out of him as the weight of his well-stuffed pack came down on his rib cage. He swung a leg astride, was momentarily pleased and grateful he'd had presence of mind to do so in such a way that he faced forward.

He immediately found himself slipping down the sloped haunches of the creature he was on. He grabbed at the saddle's high back, which had a figure-eight shape to it, more like a chair back, he thought, than a saddle. It was obviously meant to keep the rider from sliding off the creature's butt.

Without much choice he threw both arms around the rider's midsection and clamped hand on wrist. Its narrow torso felt like a metal pipe. Kane felt a stab of gladness the hood hid the rider's features from him.

Yellow light lances stabbed past. For an instant Kane had an impression of dazzling yellow beads strung on yellow threads. One of the shiny metal craft unmistakably blew up, sending a geyser of blue-cored white flame twenty yards straight up.

A number of the curious slope-backed mounts came loping back, away from the flat-iron machines. Kane realized the Phoenix members who had been dug in at the base of the hill clung to the backs of three of them.

"We never fired a shot!" young Reichert called out, in something like despair.

"Do you think we had anything that could hurt one of those things?" Kane called back. He doubted a rail pistol or pulse-plasma rifle would do more than scratch the finish.

The rider before Kane booted heels into its mount's sides. The beast tottered into a run. Its back-and-forth gait was like instant whiplash, snapping Kane's head forward and backward with every stride.

He looked to the right. A riding beast, fleeter than his or just more lightly burdened, passed. Its rider was another tall, skinny, cowled and robed figure. Behind it crouched a figure like a cross between an exceptionally fat toad and a bald lemur, clinging with pad-tipped fingers and toes. It turned its outsized head to peer at Kane with great eyes like orbs of black glass that showed him flame reflections. Its expression seemed to be one of sheer terror—of him, not the energy-weapon battle slamming and roaring behind. As his gaze locked with the toad thing's, Kane felt an impact bchind his eyes that made him reel in the saddle.

"Kane," he heard Brigid over the comm net, "are you all right?"

No. "Yeah," he said. "What about everybody else?"

Unbelievably everybody quickly checked in: Grant, Domi, the Team Phoenix quartet, Marina, who—with Joe Weaver—had just been scooped up by the strange riders.

"What just happened?" Major Mike wanted to know.

"Well," Kane said, "either we just been rescued or kidnapped. One of the two."

"How about both?" Larry Robison asked grimly.

Pounding Kane's tailbone and sloshing his brains in his skull, the bizarre beast fled into the night. Behind them, the desert burned.

"Look," Kane said, "who are you people? What do you want from us?"

Out on the plains below, three hulks of wrecked craft burned, sending smoke vines twining up the starry sky, their bases illuminated by yellow flames.

The striding figure Kane accosted was robed. Everybody in the camp in the sharp tall hills wore robes with the cowls pulled up over their heads: variegated shadows. Except the bald lemur-toads, like the one that squatted in the dust five or six yards away staring at him in apparent dismay. They wore nothing at all, neither clothing nor harness.

The tall being turned its hood briefly toward Kane. Inside was blank blackness; Kane imagined he saw a glint of starlight, or fugitive flame from the battle that raged unabated in orbit, reflecting on a surface other than skin.

The being rasped a noise at him like a file across granite and strode on.

"Son of a bitch," he said, kicking at a rock. "I should kick your robed ass."

"That wouldn't do any good, Kane," Brigid said, materializing out of darkness.

"Sure, it would. It'd make me feel better."

She turned away. The rebel—or bandit, or whatever—camp lay up in the serious hills that served as prelude to the even more serious mountains to the east. Specifically it rested on the top of an outthrust about seventy yards by fifty, and flat on top. A sheer fifty-yard cliff of windscooped sandstone, pale in the light of a small moon that had just emerged over the eastern peaks and pocked with small holes, backed it. To front and sides it was sporadically palisaded by boulders like elongated sandstone eggs set on end.

They had been dumped here with a few grunts by way of explanation. Hays and Weaver reported hearing riders address them in simple English, too, so if that was Kane hallucinating he wasn't the only one.

And now they seemed to be ignored.

Brigid stood a few paces away, back to Kane, staring out over the plain. In the sky different-colored dots of light still arced and veered. Sometimes they came together. Sometimes they expanded rapidly. Sometimes they just went out.

She turned and walked back toward him, hugging herself beneath the breasts, although it was cool rather than cold even in the breeze sweeping across the exposed height, and her shadow suit provided a great deal of insulation.

"Kane," she said quietly, as if not wishing the others to hear, "I'm worried." She moved herself between him and the other, subtly crowding as if to herd him away.

He stood his ground. "Join the crowd," he growled.

"No. It's not the danger. You know that."

He looked at her a moment. Then he nodded. "Yeah. I know that, Baptiste."

"It's the uncertainty," she said, her voice low and husky. Part of him thrilled: it would have been altogether erotic, had he permitted it to be. But...that door seemed forever closed to them. At least in this life.

"Why are we here? Why would Bates come to a desolate place such as this?" Brigid asked.

Kane shrugged. "We didn't have much choice of destination, you might remember." As he said it he was almost shocked to realize they had jumped little more than an hour ago by his wrist chron. A whole lot's happened since then, he thought, even by our standards. "And the device said this was the last destination Bates accessed."

"What if that was a trick?"

Kane looked at her upturned face—not far upturned, because he wasn't that much taller than she. It was strained and pale, and the gem-green eyes had dark thumb smudges beneath them.

"I don't know any better than you do," he said, in a voice that sounded broken to his ears.

"If I'm not intruding too much," a voice said from behind him, "I think I do."

Kane turned, frowning. Mike Hays stood behind him with his cigar in his mouth.

Hays took out the cigar and waved it, drawing a red arc through the night air. "Gil Bates is capable of any kind of trickery you want to name. Treachery? That's his middle name. But as funny as he would no doubt find it, I don't think he set us up to maroon ourselves out here on the ass end of the galaxy."

"Why not?" asked Grant, who had moved to join what had subtly become a group discussion from a private conversation.

"He wants an audience," Larry Robison said. "He wants somebody to see how clever he is. And not just a bunch of ETs. Humans."

"Us," Weaver said. "You folks from Cerberus, us four, Marina, here."

Thunder split the sky. But it wasn't normal thunder, not a distant grumble, nor even a sharp, hard crack like a giant door slamming. This was threaten-your-eardrums, heavy-artillery-barrage thunder.

As the crack reverberated in Kane's eardrums, Reichert yelled, "Incoming!" and hit the dirt. Everybody else just ducked.

Something made Kane look up. A large ovoid shape hurtled across the star field, northeast to southwest and already past the zenith, its form partially masked by a glaring yellow bow wave of atmosphere heated incandescent by friction and shock compression. Behind it came two smaller shapes, arrowheads veiled by air made almost plasma by their own violent passage.

Lines of violet darted from them and struck the fleeing

greater ship. They flared in brief white coruscations, faded. The ovoid spit back a blob of pink radiance. It struck the lead pursuer. The arrowhead blew up; its residue chased the pursued and surviving pursuer out of sight beyond the horizon like meteors.

"If you want a sign telling us where Bates is," Weaver shouted through the ringing in everybody's ears.

They looked at him. From the corner of his eye Kane saw Reichert picking himself up off the ground, dusting off his camou blouse and trousers and looking sheepish, as well as grateful not to be the center of attention.

Like an Old Testament prophet Weaver raised an arm to the torn sky. "How about a sign from Heaven?"

"What do you mean?" Grant asked.

"Do you think it's just a coincidence that Bates happened to land on a planet just beneath a colossal space battle? Isn't that stretching the laws of probability just a bit?"

"When we first landed, Robison said only Bates could piss people off that much," Domi said. "Mebbe he's right."

"So this—" Brigid flipped a hand toward the stars and the ongoing space battle, silent again.

"Is all over Gilgamesh Bates," a strange voice said. "And the terrible knowledge he possesses. Yes."

Chapter 15

It was, Gilgamesh Bates realized, all the fault of his naive belief in progress.

As the guards, their metallic pincers digging cruelly into biceps left bare by the white T-shirt he wore, dragged Gilgamesh Bates into the orbiting throne room of a monster queen, he drew a deep breath, mentally recited the mantra he'd received during a brief flirtation with Transcendental Meditation in his thirties and tried to assess the situation.

It sucked, the teenaged hacker buried deep within him told him succinctly.

The enormous arched hall was metal polished to a gleam by legions of octopedal slaves. They applied some manner of soap or polish with their foremost pair of limbs, dried and polished with their hind set, and with the two pairs in between managed somehow to cling to an apparently solid metal surface, even sheer walls or upside down, despite a gravity Bates felt with acute discomfort to be at least approximating that of Earth. For muscles and bones grown unaccustomed to gravity, it was a painful, bowing burden.

Note to self, Bates thought. Add to list of grievances for which I will make these barbarians eat shit in exchange for being allowed to live, once I rule the galaxy.

Across the chamber rose a huge metal honeycomb. It reminded Bates of a wall of Japanese sleeping tubes.

The queen's head and enormous torso protruded from a hex-shaped cell in the great honeycombed wall, into which her RV-sized white bloat of an abdomen was stuffed. She was a sight to strike the strongest man mute with terror.

How fortunate for Bates, then, that he was not strong, but mad.

And also pissed. "Your Majesty," he proclaimed when he was dragged close enough to the curved talons with which she was polishing the horizontal, insectile portion of her mandibular array to be heard by whatever aural apparatus her long, unlovely head might possess, "I must protest. These are hardly the terms on which I agreed to treat with the Circle of Life!"

The chamber itself seemed vaguely domed, although the honeycomb was as flat as a motherboard. Curving flanges and stanchions of mirror-polished alloy, structural, ornamental or both, suggested Gothic flying buttresses soaring to meet far overhead in a great groined vault. Several dozen other beings occupied the chamber, as well, ranging in size from small dog to Japanese economy car, and of at least half a dozen exceedingly variegated shapes.

The queen studied Bates with an insultingly small number of her multiple eyes. She had, so far as he could count and allowing for a certain factor of uncertainty as to what in her case might constitute eyes, to have eighteen of them, distributed mostly along and across the top front quadrant of her five-foot-long, overturned-boat-shaped head. In general she appeared to combine the characteristics of a rat, a soldier ant and possibly a dragon, if those odd leathery excrescensces projecting from her back were the vestigial wings they resembled.

To Bates, even under duress, she possessed a certain beauty. There was unquestionably a purity to the terrible queen.

He still felt bubbling outrage but little fear. The idea that he might himself suffer consequence was one that came slowly to him, and left quickly.

But it came as she clashed her compound mouth at him, the gleaming black tips of her larger mandibles clacking within a handspan on his nose. Saliva or some similar fluid drooled from her mouth, to be sponged quickly away by one or another of the host of small attendants like arthropod opossums with nasty white spider-fur who swarmed about her. Her breath, which emanated from pink lined vents in her thorax armor, frilled with a very attractive and slightly iridescent royal blue, stank of rotting hopes.

"You are in my power now," she said. Or rather she emitted a series of wheezes, whistles and joint pops. A disk of some hard substance he'd never gotten a good look at had been attached to the mastoid bone behind his right ear, and it translated her vocalizations into feminine American English, perfectly clear and colloquial if on the sibilant side. "Which is of course the power of the Circle of Life, which naturally encompasses the true will of the all of sacred life within the galaxy. Therefore you are mine to dispose of, small soft thing. As a mere individual you are of no more consequence than a single cell. Do cells presume to negotiate with the bodies of which they form microscopically insignificant parts, much less dictate?"

"Yes," he answered forthrightly. "When a cell possesses a secret as potent as I do. Your Majesty."

The creatures, or robots, who still held his arms, hissed in outrage and cruelly pinched his arms with their attenuated lobster claws. He frowned.

ON ARRIVAL ON THE PLANET that he presumed still lay some distance beneath the six-mile-long dreadnought belonging to the so-called Circle faction of the Grand Council, he had been met as arranged by a shuttle in the shape of a great purple crystal. Unfortunately, and contrary to his clear prior understanding, he had been seized by beings like Shetland-pony-sized spiders with five legs and, after a certain brisk unpleasantness that left him somewhat bespattered, hustled unceremoniously aboard the craft. As it lifted skyward on some silent propulsion system he had glimpsed on a screen some kind of dogfight twisting in air overhead, where similar green bell-shaped craft dueled with golden spindles with lances and dazzles of pink-and-violet light. Then he had been half dragged, half carried into a compartment with amethyst walls tantalizingly translucent but in fact revealing nothing, and sealed within so completely he could not even make out the outline of a door.

No doubt the gem shuttle carried out some violent evasive maneuvers at the least; he doubted it would voluntarily engage in combat with such invaluable cargo as himself inboard. As a congenital nerd, born and raised in the weird and dustily sterile suburb-without-an-urb of Los Alamos, dropped more or less at random in the midst of New Mexico's Jemez Mountains, he was a lifelong science-fiction fan. Therefore he understood that these aliens had to possess some form of truly wizard inertialess drive—antigravity plus a whole lot more—that would allow a craft not simply to defeat the miserable one g or so pull of the pink-sand planet, but to allow its contents, including fragile protoplasm passengers, to survive both momentary and sustained g loadings that would otherwise reduce them to russet paste.

Despite the fact that he was restrained and undergoing a strip and search as thorough and impersonal as if carried out by automobile-assembly robots, that made him smile. What power I will soon have at my command! he exulted. Despite the humiliation of his current predicament—and the burning shame at this cruel surprise, this horrid, unjust, evil cheat—that filled his cheeks with a warm prickling rush like a megadose of niacin, made his lips smile and his cock stir within the boxer-style underwear his handlers yanked back onto him after an authentic, but mercifully brief, alien anal probe.

THE VERTICAL INNER components of the great queen's mouth worked in what seemed agitation. "Is this impertinence? I have little direct experience of your kind, man of the Orion Arm. Although you are ubiquitous as lice in the space that the council controls. What did you anticipate you might find here, small soft thing?"

Inside Gil Bates seethed with righteous rage. Fortunately he was accustomed to keeping inside all those feelings he did not suppress altogether. Consequently he had a great deal of experience in hiding rage. It had been a skill necessary to that ability to deal with powerful dolts who had formed both foundation and structure of his enormous fortune.

As it forms the basis now of my vault to ultimate power, he reminded himself. But first I've got to survive this interview with this jumped-up fifties movie monster.

The thought of the Circle of Life queen as a puppet, a simple marionette like Mothra or Rodan, made him smile within his gray-edged pink beard and feel much more in control of the situation. He held his head a little higher.

"I hoped I might find beings with whom I might do business!"

For a moment the chamber rang with silence. All the sound was the echo of his words chasing themselves around the gleaming steel nooks and crannies of the audience hall. The various creatures that crawled and stilted and scuttled within froze into place.

Bates plunged ahead. "I don't mind that your minions killed the men of my escort, Uvaluvu. Such misunderstandings tend to happen, and anyway they were expendable. What I find unforgivable is the way I have been manhandled, mistreated and sequestered since."

The silver-crustacean guards who stood to either side of the queen clashed their pincers in agitation. The queen's abdomen began to pulsate, bulging out of its cell. Ripples of greenish light chased one another, just discernible within the harsh blue-edged illumination that filled the chamber, across it as if just beneath a layer of translucent dermis. Then the furred and armored torso shook, and the hard-shelled limbs of various sizes and apparent function. The little winglike things on her back spasmed and clattered. And finally all the parts of her odd mouth performed a compound dance as she nodded her huge, gray-tufted, many-eyed head.

It came to Gil Bates that the Circle queen was laughing at him. You bitch! he thought. Wait and see! First I shall see you crawl, then I shall have you boiled to monster Stroganoff!

"You amuse, little thing," she said. Motion returned to the chamber, except for the guards who held Bates's arms and the dozen or so similar beings standing guard in the royal chamber. "Be glad. Be very glad."

He held up his head. "Your Majesty," he said, unable now to keep a bit of nasty nasal whine out of his voice— as he sometimes could not, even with all his skill at dissimulation, when faced with fools too great to suffer no matter what the upside, "please don't insult my intelligence. You need me. And if you could get what you want from me without my cooperation, you'd have already wrung me dry and discarded me like a used Kleenex. Wouldn't you?"

He used the ancient Earth trademark name with malice aforethought, in hopes of giving the alien translation software hiccups. As a matter of long experience, not to mention extremely sophisticated technical expertise, he knew full well that no matter how badly you chopped logic with a computer, you could never actually get it to spark and smoke and shut down the way you always could on the popular science-fiction television shows he'd watched as a boy in the sixties. But hope springs eternal.

The queen's spines and limbs and fur bristled. She emitted a noise like a stepped-on bagpipe, with such vehemence that the pressure of expelled air or maybe sheer sound forced both Bates and his captors back a step.

"Arrogant louse of a space rat! You shall suffer until you

learn to how proper humility before the living embodiment of all of sacred life! Away!"

As the metallized guards wheeled him about and frog-marched him with quite unnecessary *brio* back to the great sliding door that shimmered as it slid aside, Gil Bates sighed a martyr's sigh.

"I presumed," he called back over his shoulder as he was hustled into a poorly lit vaulted corridor outside, "that surely the races of the Far Arm would have matured beyond the excitability that had caused that galaxy-wide genocide a million years ago. Evidently I was—"

The door slid shut across the word *wrong*. Which in its way was a pity. It completed a phrase seldom heard by human or alien from the pink-bearded lips of Gilgamesh Bates.

Manifestly, the voice of the inner observer said within his head, this great interstellar civilization has matured as much as it was going to, long since.

That'll teach me to trust.

THE TERRANS TURNED as if all their skulls were joined with thin glass rods. A robed figure approached from the direction of the tall dark peaks. At first it looked little different from the rest in the darkness, though granted there was broad leeway. It was shorter than any other alien Kane had yet seen except the crouching naked toad-things, two of which now squatted staring at the Terrans from nearby. He felt an urge to skip over to one of the things and give it a good swift kick.

As it drew near, the newcomer swept the hood back off its head. Kane stared. The face was oval, framed in short, dark hair. An undeniably human face.

A *woman's* face. As well as voice.

"What the…?" Reichert began.

"How the hell do you speak English?" Kane demanded.

"For the same reason you are here," she said. "The man called Gilgamesh Bates."

"Whoa," Larry Robison said.

"That's my line," Reichert stated.

"Hush," Brigid said like a stern schoolmistress. "I want to hear what this young lady has to say, even if you don't."

The newcomer was a most attractive young woman, Kane was just noticing, and seemingly just a few years older than Marina: no more than eighteen terrestrial years. Provided also, he reminded himself, that she was fully human—or human at all and not a simulacrum. And that humans aged the same way here, tens of thousands of light-years from their ostensible home, as they did back on it.

"Who are you?" Kane asked. It was a remarkably lame question, he realized, but in its way inevitable.

"I am P'narvayrot," she said, the final glottalized *t* being followed with a sort of pock from somewhere at the back of her slim throat.

"Say what?" Grant said.

"One of those hyphenated foreign names," Reichert offered cheerfully.

"The translation software," Brigid said. "It's explaining itself over an ambiguity."

"Let's call you Pine," Larry Robison said. "Spare our throats some."

The young woman paused, possibly listening to the translation, then smiled and nodded. She had a very winning smile. "That would be fine," she said.

"I'm Kane," Kane said, then pointed to his comrades. "This is Grant, Brigid Baptiste and Domi."

Pine smiled and nodded as if it all made sense. She was either a pretty fair diplomat or the translation software understood Kane better than he himself usually did.

Major Mike stepped forward, took Pine's hand, raised it to his lips and kissed it. She looked for a flash as if she were going to yank it back and run. Then she positively twinkled. Kane felt a transient urge to kick him.

Hays introduced his teammates, including Marina. Then everybody from Earth started talking at once.

Pine blinked and wilted slightly under the barrage of questions. She had to be overwhelmed, Kane reckoned. She might run with a pack of hard-core bandits or freedom fighters—whatever they were, they were stoneheart enough to take on some kind of hovertanks from the backs of sawed-off giraffes or shrunk-down Brontosaurs or whatever the raiders used instead of horses—but she was still no more than a late adolescent, and more than a bit vulnerable.

"Baptiste," he said from the corner of his mouth, "you're good at the order-out-of-chaos thing."

She was already stepping forward. "Let's not overwhelm our new friend," she said with more diplomacy than was usual for her. "I'll present questions, one at a time."

Pine looked grateful and nodded.

Kane took a look around, just to keep on top of the situation. No good getting complacent, stuck deep into hostile territory with a fleet action going on a few thousand klicks over our heads, he thought. The only noise came in the form of grunts from the riding animals, all bunched together grazing back toward where the promontory widened to join with a ridge, as if constrained by an invisible fence of some sort. Alien shapes moved with quiet purpose all around the outsiders. In the gloom, even with the moon fully risen, Kane couldn't tell what most of the hooded figures were up to. Some were obviously checking gear, including weapons that consisted primarily of stubby launch-tube-looking things and stocked longblasters like ultraskinny rifles at least five feet long.

The outlanders' own gear, stacked near where they stood clumped, the aliens ignored scrupulously. Either they're disciplined enough to sit hard on their curiosity, Kane thought, or they just can't be bothered with a bunch of primitive trash. He decided he didn't want to ask.

Pine was holding up what looked like a sizable gold pendant hung around her neck and talking animatedly to Brigid while everybody else stared with interest. Except Domi, who had gotten bored and wandered off to grub through her own backpack, no doubt looking for something to eat. Kane had consciously tuned the conversation out while he did his quick 360 scan to make sure the bandits weren't all sneaking up on the Terrans while they were distracted, to truss them up and boil them in big pots for supper.

He caught up quick enough when Robison said, "Good thing you have this cool universal translator software. Otherwise we'd have to communicate like a bunch of bad mimes."

"And there ain't any good ones," Hays added.

"How come the device speaks English, though?" Grant asked. "You sure don't. And you can't tell me anybody else out here does, either."

"Oh, but one does," Pine said. "As I told you, we learned from Gil Bates."

Everybody got real silent and still. She had said that right off, Kane belatedly remembered. Apparently everyone else had spaced the fact for the general wonderment of finding an apparently human being out here, the same way he had. He caught himself with his hand formed up in a half fist ready to trigger his power holster to slam his Sin Eater into it. In the corner of his eye he caught Grant deliberately opening his own right hand.

"So was it you who negotiated with Gil Bates?" Brigid asked, suddenly in the studiedly neutral tones of a lifelong archivist. "Your people?"

Before Pine could respond, a retina-searing light beam speared a blazing yellow transverse down the sky. A tall figure striding past not twenty yards from Kane emitted a terrible shriek and fell to the ground with its robes blazing blue.

Chapter 16

Blinking at a pulsating purple streak of afterimage and gagging on stinking smoke, Kane looked up into the night sky. The descending figures were approximately man-sized and visible only as shadows drifting across the stars they apparently were dropping from. Until they fired beam weapons from their hips, which illuminated the fronts of vaguely humanoid figures with snouted helmets.

Yellow-and-blue-green beams stabbed back at them from the ground. A tumult of hisses and shouts surrounded Kane.

He wheeled, drawing his laser pistol. The promontory was bare, as well as flat—no cover there. He ran to the front of the projecting bluff. Behind him he heard the snarling crack of an energy beam, felt pebbles thrown from its blast pelt the sole of his right foot.

At the brink he stopped short. Three low, flat vehicles scuttled across the plain toward him. In the dark it was impossible to make out details, although they moved as if on multiple sets of wheels. In the dark their sinister intent seemed unmistakable.

"Kane!" He heard Brigid cry from behind him.

He spun, bringing up the laser. One of the humanoids dropped right toward him. He fired the laser pistol. It sparked white on the being's chest. Showing no ill effect, it raised its own stubby blaster.

A shatter of noise, a shuddering flare of light from Kane's left, then the creature suddenly pitched forward. Pinwheeling about the axis of its own waist, it spun past Kane to slam on its back against a boulder at the bluff's edge with spine-snapping force. As it whirled by, Kane noticed it had a thick tapered tail, also apparently encased in armor.

He looked quickly back. Major Mike Hays stood with legs braced, one hand holding up his FN-MAG machine gun, the other with an ammunition belt trailed across the palm. "If I can't shoot through their armor," he shouted, "I can at least hose them off their lift-columns."

Noise rasping through the tumult snapped Kane's attention back to the fallen alien. It stirred, tried to rise with a scraping of metal or possibly ceramic on rock. Its snouted head was flung back; to Kane it looked as if the flexible armor beneath the long jaw was vulnerable. He took up the slack on the laser pistol's trigger, brought the pink targeting dot to the joint of throat and jaw, squeezed off to send a pulse of killing energy down the redline to the tiny circle.

Metal sublimated to instant incandescence spiked away in a white jet. It was instantly followed by a gout of steam and flash-heated fluids. The creature's body arched upward from the rock on which it lay. In its convulsion of agony it threw its blaster away from itself. Its armored heels clacked against the stone. It slumped, clawed twice against the rock beneath it, went still.

Kane holstered his laser pistol, then ran the several yards to where the alien's discarded blaster had fetched up against a stone. He picked it up. It was bulky, a little larger

than the head of the creature that had wielded it. The back
of it was scooped out; trusting to his shadow-suit armor to
protect them from any booby traps that might lie in wait
for anyone but the rightful user who attempted to fire it,
he thrust his hand into the hollow. Instead of the expected
bite, sting or flash of searing heat, his black-gloved hand
closed around a firm, padded grip. It felt strange to his
hand, but nothing he couldn't handle.

Until the blaster discharged, blasting a dazzling yellow
bolt into the ground two yards from his feet. Little globs
of molten glass arced away like miniature yellow volcanic
bombs. Apparently the blaster fired through simple pressure on the grip.

Triple-stupe way to set it, Kane thought. Mebbe these
things got a different startle reflex than we do. To his surprise equal to the shot itself was the fact that the gun produced a marked kick, more like a standard handblaster.

He looked around. Everywhere was confusion: figures
running, backlit by explosions and flares of violent, satu-
rated color. He saw one of the armored tailed humanoids
standing behind Brigid, not ten yards away. She seemed
unaware of his presence. Kane aimed the stolen blaster at
the center of the creature's mass and fired. He hit; the shot
produced an admirable spray of red sparks and white
smoke and steam. The alien fell as Brigid spun, clutching
her own laser pistol.

"Everybody," he called over the comm net, "grab blasters from the deaders."

Not everybody had to. He saw one descending alien
flare into blue-cored orange flame from a plasma pulse
from Grant's big blaster. When the flare dissipated Kane

could see the charred armor suit had a great gape cratered in its chest as it dropped, trailing smoke tendrils, to land out of sight behind struggling and running figures.

"Can't go over the edge," he heard Reichert report. "Got more bad guys coming in vehicles."

Kane felt a stab of guilt; he should have reported seeing the surface craft approach. It as just that immediate survival got in the way. "We got to get back up in the hills, then," he said. "We can't stay out here. Everybody intact?"

He got back a ripple of reports. All nine Terrans accounted for themselves.

"Whatever kind of night-vision gear the kangaroo aliens have," Robison said, "they don't seem to be able to pick us up."

"Mebbe they're too busy staying alive themselves," Kane said.

"Screw mebbes," Grant's gravel growl came. "Just run."

Seeing wisdom in that, Kane obeyed. He snatched up his heavy pack, not noticing the mass at all, slung it over one shoulder. Then he ran for Brigid, who had her pack on already and stood near the edge of the drop-off, laser clutched in both hands and staring around with green eyes wide.

Hell's own flames were mirrored in them. "Let's go," Kane shouted as he came up to her. "In all this confusion we got a chance."

It seemed true. Aliens continued to fall from somewhere in the sky; Kane wondered if they were doing the grav-belt equivalent of a HALO drop, from an aircraft invisibly high overhead. The bandits or guerrillas or whatever were fighting enthusiastically, shooting or even wrestling with the invaders. He saw one of the outsized ones such as the one who had taken Brigid off the hilltop, half again as tall as Grant, rip the arm off an armored interloper.

Nobody paid any attention to the humans. "It's as if we're too insignificant to notice," Brigid said, with her head near his.

He shrugged. "Hope it stays that way."

They headed toward the bluff's eastern end, where boulders clustered like hard fruit reared high, and a ridge rose higher just beyond. Domi and Grant moved to join them; thirty yards away he saw Team Phoenix, forming a loose circle around Marina. Reichert had their pulse-plasma rifle; Hays still hung on to his machine gun.

"Wait!" a voice cried. "You must ride out of here! You will never get clear otherwise."

It was Pine, running toward them with her hood down. If she was armed, Kane couldn't see it.

"One problem with that," Grant told her. "We can't ride those things."

"They're well-trained," she said. "They know how to keep riders aboard. Hurry!"

She led them off along the north edge of the promontory. Not running—that would attract attention, as Kane knew well, quite possibly even provoke some kind of predator chase reflex among the attackers. Or mebbe even our guys, Kane thought grimly.

The melee was concentrated more on the southern side right now. Team Phoenix joined up with Pine and their fellow Terrans. They stationed themselves on the inland side, as if pulling flank security. Kane caught Grant's eye; the big man shrugged. Neither of them felt like arguing about who would be closest to danger right now.

For the moment danger seemed eerily, almost surreally absent. Mostly what the Terrans had to contend with were huge swirls of dust and smoke that stank brutally. They had to duck stray beams periodically, but the two alien factions were so engrossed in trying to kill each other they really did seem to have little attention to spare the Terrans. There seemed to be more of the robed defenders battling with the attackers from the sky than Kane could remember seeing before. Maybe some of them had been out on the plain pulling perimeter security and pulled back to fight the most immediate threat. Whatever, he thought, they're keeping the bad guys off us.

Robison and Weaver had picked up alien weapons, Robison a bulky space-kangaroo handblaster like the one Kane had, Weaver characteristically one of the longblasters their rescuers, or whatever, tended to favor. Looked at up close, it seemed to be made out of some kind of glass that glinted purplish in the light of death beams. It was exceedingly skinny and had strange nodes like swellings at seemingly random intervals.

As Kane watched, Weaver stopped, snugged the weapon's butt—conventional enough, if widely flared—to his shoulder, triggered a quick yellow pulsation. A figure standing away off high on the rocks above where the riding beasts were milling and tossing their heads flared and fell, a blaster of some kind falling from its hands.

They reached the animals. Kane thought he felt a sense like passing through a very thin, weak membrane as they approached. Maybe it was a field of some kind that kept them constrained. Mebbe it's just my imagination.

Some of the animals were still saddled. Kane didn't

need Pine's direction to see the rigging straps behind its high backboard. He swung off his heavy pack, threw it over and lashed it down. He did need the girl's help, momentary, with the fastening: simply pressing the ends, which were capped in what seemed black plastic, against patches of similar material on the back skirt-flap of the saddle itself. They fused at once and took up slack.

"Nifty," he said as she moved on to help the others. He swung aboard his chosen mount. It tossed its big head and made constipated-sounding moans, sidestepped a little, but did not fight him.

Domi forked another creature not three yards away. She held a sort of foot-long bar in the middle of what seemed to be a conventional set of reins. Kane saw a similar arrangement looped over the neck of his own mount.

"Can't be this easy," the albino girl cried. "Never this easy!"

"Where do we go from here?" Major Mike Hays called out from his own prancing, jittering beast. He still, incongruously, held his FN-MAG by the rear pistol grip, with a cartridge belt looped over his arm. It made him look like Lawrence of Hell.

"Damned if I know," Kane said.

"That way!" shouted Pine, who had materialized beside him. She pointed for the rocks off which Weaver had picked the enemy sniper, now forty yards distant. They were more big elongated chunks, which looked more jagged than the smooth sandstone boulders that palisaded the end of the bluff. Maybe granite—Kane was no geologist.

"They're just rocks, lady," Sean Reichert called.

"Just go!"

"Look!" Brigid pointed toward the rocks. A rider was there, right at their base, gesturing unmistakably for the humans to hurry.

Kane looked to Grant, who had mounted up next to Domi. "Your call, point man," Grant said.

Kane tipped an extended forefinger of his brow. "Classic one-percenter," he said.

When he picked up the bar the beast suddenly quit dancing and seemed poised. A slight twist one way brought its head around. Holding back an urge to boot the thing massively in the slats—which he suspected might provoke it to launch him up into the hills headfirst—he nudged its sides gently with his heels.

Like a rocking-horse responding to a rider's weight shift, it began to lope toward the cliff. Kane heard shouts and whistles from his companions as they got their mounts likewise moving and headed in the right direction.

The lone rider awaited them. Its mount stood calmly, head up, as if watching the proceedings with active but mild interest. The rider raised an arm and loosed a ripple of yellow beads toward the southwest. Kane didn't bother looking around to see what he was shooting at. There were plenty of targets, and Kane was unlikely to pick his specific mark out of the shouting, shooting, dying scrum behind. Plus he was afraid of losing his seat if he got too creative twisting in the saddle. The beast's gait was unlike any horse's he had ever ridden, pitching up and down in an exaggerated motion at every stride.

"Kane!"

Brigid's cry made him turn despite his fear of falling.

A surface craft had appeared at the promontory's far

end. Although the manner of its coming made him wonder if *surface* was quite the right word: it seemed to rise straight up on an even keel, above a jut of boulders, and slide smoothly forward with no sign of jets or for that matter the dust-cloud of ground effect. Another appeared at once to its left. They looked nothing like the weird shiny-silver steam irons that had chased them earlier: these were low flat arrowheads, sinister and angular.

But that, he quickly saw, was not what Brigid was trying to call his attention to. Pine writhed in the grip of a pair of the tailed aliens Robison had dubbed "space kangaroos."

And Sean Reichert, whose call sign Loverboy was most appropriate, rode hell-bent to her rescue.

Light flashed from the lead craft. An explosion erupted right under the forefeet of Reichert's mount. It smashed beast and rider savagely to the ground.

Chapter 17

The short-haired young woman made frantic efforts to struggle clear of her captors. It did her no direct good. They had her well and truly overpowered, and even as Kane approached at a fast gallop in darkness shot through with energies, it was pretty clear she'd never break free. But she was doing an ace job of keeping their attention.

That couldn't last. The one on Kane's left noticed him. Even in this commotion, wrestling with a highly motivated human girl, there was only so long you could *not* notice a twelve-foot-tall two-ton creature bearing down on you at speed. Keeping a grip on a slim wrist with his left gauntlet, the alien pivoted away, bringing up his blaster.

Kane was all over him. His own blaster was already extended alongside the beast's sweaty leather-skinned neck. He triggered a bolt that had to have struck something explosive strapped, not too wisely in Kane's view, to the being's chest. There came a huge flash and bang and the thing flew back in a flail of limbs whose very looseness told Kane that death was instant.

Unprotected, Pine screamed as armor frags and hot organic debris pelted her. Instead of bolting or fighting more effectively with her newly freed arm she covered up. A natural response, but thoroughly unhelpful.

To Kane. Not to her remaining captor. He reeled her right up against his chest as a human shield and hunkered down, aiming his blaster toward Kane over her shoulder.

"There was no way Kane could blast the monster without chilling Pine, even laying aside the fact he knew nothing of what hellacious radiations the yellow particle beams emitted. His best shot was to get in close and try either for a shot or club at that round-skulled long-nosed head.

But the alien wasn't going to give him that much slack, of course. It fired a bolt that cracked like lightning past Kane's left ear and made his head buzz and his vision momentarily swim. He ducked behind his mount's thick neck and hoped like hell that it would stop the alien's next blast— and that the beast's decapitated corpse might bowl the thing over and give Kane a crack at finishing his adversary.

Instead, a quick spurt of beads of a different yellow pulsed back past Kane on a heading reciprocating the alien's bolt. Its head disappeared in a big white flare. In the process Pine's hood had been yanked up over her head; it seemed to protect her from the splash and scatter, but Kane didn't get much of a look as she fell like a pile of discarded laundry.

He pulled back on the rein bar. To his amazement the creature put down its haunches and braked to a stop in such short order that he was slammed against the back of its neck. Good thing this saddle doesn't have much of a horn, he thought.

He had to neither think nor look back to know who had fired the shot that killed the hostage taker. Iron Man Joe Weaver had slipped from his own mount to put a shot where it would do the most good, as if placing it with his own blunt, powerful fingers.

Kane slid to the ground. Nobody else was near. Thought of the strange arrowhead wags that had blasted the hapless young Reichert gnawed at his mind. But only two were in sight, and everybody, bandits and sky kangaroos alike, seemed to be shooting at them. The one on the right, which had first appeared, now sat on the ground unmoving. Kane caught a few glints of red glaring out through slit openings. Back on Earth that usually meant a crew was roasting alive inside a buttoned-up steel crematorium.

Most everybody was shooting at the float tanks. A yellow beam cracked over Kane's head as he knelt over Pine. A team of four tailed aliens trotted toward the rear of the promontory, as if looking to secure Kane and Pine, as well as the incapacitated Reichert.

Yellow beams lanced to either side of the huddled humans. An alien went down with what Kane could only guess was a scream swallowed by its full-head helmet, throwing both arms up in the air so that its blaster catapulted backward into the night. Another folded around a shot to the groin that made Kane wince even though he had no way of knowing if these things were male, or for that matter wore their reproductive gear between their hind legs.

Robison was rolling up toward the prone Reichert on a riding beast, firing captured handblasters with both hands. Kane helped out by pausing to put two shots into the alien nearest him. The last one threw up its hands, too, this time as if to seek the head that had suddenly gone missing as the methodical Weaver found the range for another target.

Pine was already sitting up. Her hood half covered her short hair. Kane saw an angry dark splotch on her right cheek.

"I am fine," she said as he reached toward her head. He

instead grabbed a handful of robe and helped her to her feet. The fabric was thicker and heavier than he imagined. He wondered if it might serve as some kind of armor.

Although she protested briefly, he boosted her into the big animal's saddle. "You know how to drive this thing," he said, clambering up to an uncomfortable and uncertain perch aside his own pack; he'd have jettisoned the damn thing if he knew how, but there was no time to screw with that now.

To her credit the girl didn't argue, just turned the beast and sent it galloping back for the boulders where their comrades waited. Kane saw Robison helping a dazed but not totally unconscious Reichert onto the back of his own mount.

Covering fire stabbed from the back of the promontory as they rode fast for it. The hooded guide was still there, its mount sidestepping and tossing its head. Kane couldn't see the alien's face for its cowl, but it looked impatient at all this delay.

Kane couldn't really blame it.

The rider whirled its mount as Pine and Kane rode up. The girl called something to it that her translator didn't bother to translate for Kane. It sounded like a combination of gargling, choking to death and nasal humming. The rider didn't respond.

The other Terrans were mounting up. "Just where are we going, anyway?" Kane asked his driver. "Those rocks are big, but don't look like they'd hide more than one or two people mounted on creatures this size."

She flashed a quick, shy smile over her shoulder. The animal she had slowed to a trot. "Wait," she said.

"Oh, a cave," Kane said. "I see." He didn't, exactly. No matter how big a cave it was, it wasn't going to stop the space kangaroos from coming in after them for long. Maybe there was some kind of extensive subterranean catacomb system.

What do you want? his brain chided him. Safety? Security? Should've stayed in bed.

A colossal blast overrode the clamor of battle. Kane looked back.

The remaining arrowhead float tank erupted in violet-tinged white fire thirty yards into the night sky. High above it a strange shimmer of light was visible in the night sky like the trail of sunlight on water.

A green beam stabbed down. A green fireball erupted from the ground where it struck. Kane could see bodies tossed away, ragged robed or tailed silhouettes black against the blaze. A half-visible craft floated over the promontory. And it seemed to be blasting everybody there—the rebels, the kangaroo creatures and whatever was in those float tanks.

"Come on, big fella," Mike Hays called. He had his machine gun slung, and he urged his mount to a fast trot toward the rocks.

Kane saw Domi's mount disappear into a gap he hadn't noticed before between two tall standing stones. Hays followed.

Pine, with Kane along for the ride, came right behind; she hadn't been in any danger of getting stuck gawping at this new, exciting menace from the stars. Damn, Kane thought. I wonder if this shit goes on all the time.

Blackness swallowed them as they passed between tall rocks. He smelled cool stone. A cave for true, just like Earth.

He couldn't hear any of his companions, though, not even the noises of their big animals panting.

He was still wondering about that when a twisting dislocation seized him and turned him inside out in an all-too-familiar way.

IT SEEMED AS IF a glass tube with thick walls had been shoved into Gilgamesh Bates's face, covering his nose and mouth. Even as suction was applied, pulling all the breath from his lungs and threatening to rip his tongue out right across his teeth, he could see nothing.

The compartment was dark but not totally black. There was nothing material touching Bates's face at all. But the force threatening to suck his guts out his mouth was as tangible as anything he'd felt in this life.

The strange asymmetric black shape hunkered over a squat mechanism in the spill of dim amber light that was the chamber's main illumination emitted a very human-sounding cackle. Of course, it wasn't the being at all: it was a translator unit it wore, or perhaps was part of the great Paa space-dreadnought *Compassion* itself, flagship of the Circle of Life fleet.

What wonderful toys these aliens have! The thought that he would soon possess them all—and wonders as yet unimagined—thrilled him despite the extreme discomfort of being suspended in midair, naked and spread-eagled, while some awful force sucked all the breath from his body until it felt his very cells would collapse.

"It is a simple trick," the creature said in tones of crisp self-satisfaction. "Employing positive and negative gravitic effects—tractor and pressor beams. I form the repulsion field in a tube, and then use the attractor to apply pseudosuction."

The shape stirred in what for all Bates knew might have been an adjustment of the gravitic projector, an alien shrug, or just a tic. It had to have been the former: the terrible combination of pressure vanished instantly.

Bates hung limp in the silvery alloy restraint cuffs joined to the gleaming ovoid ring of the torture frame by faint, wavering beams of pale green light. He sucked in an immense shuddering breath, shook his head, gasped.

"You won't get anything useful out of me using these crude means," he said. He was unable to keep an edge of chiding out of his high-pitched voice. For all that he'd schooled himself to take the measure and account of his fellow beings' emotions, almost as if they mattered, there were times he could simply no longer control himself. He hated to see a thing badly done.

The creature cackled again. As far as Bates could tell in the uncertain and inadequate light, it had five limbs: bipedal hind legs and three tentacular arms, with some sort of face at the top of its torso hump.

"Oh, it's not intended to," it said. "No indeed. This is therapy. It is intended to induce a state of willing compliance, and surrender to the will of the duly anointed representative of all of holy life—our own queen, Uvaluvu of the Paa."

"You're torturing me to make me love you?"

"Of course," it said. "How better?"

Bates had to think about that. He'd been known to try employing a variation or two of that. He'd learned well from his father.

"I don't think it's working," he said.

"Well, you know what we in the service of the Grand

Council always say," the pentapod said in an avuncular chuckle. "When force doesn't work, apply more force."

It straightened somewhat; it appeared to have a permanently hunched posture. Its right-hand tentacle tip probed itself beneath the speech mouth, in a gesture entirely reminiscent of a fat man scratching his double chin.

"Let us see." It picked up a small pad whose face glowed to bluish life. "I gather that these—" a green laser pencil stabbed from somewhere in its shadowy bulk to run a lascivious dot over Bates's exposed genitalia "—according to our expert xenologists, these constitute your organs of generation. My, my, what a ridiculously exposed place to put them.

"Now, don't they look sensitive? It seems to me that a certain amount of both positive and negative pressure, applied right here—"

The green dot came to rest on the hole in the tip of Bates's dick, which had shrunk up to scarcely more than a nub. He opened his mouth to explain that that very sort of positive and negative pressure, if in sparing doses, actually provided some of his life's more beguiling pressures.

The chamber flooded with light. It exploded into the room from a sudden circle, over two yards in diameter, which had blinked into being to Bates's right and somewhat behind his torturer. The five-limbed alien turned, throwing up a tentacle to shield its face from the blinding glare.

"What is the meaning of this?" it demanded.

A white dazzle was its answer. The alien tormentor screamed and fell in a heap across its mechanism, smoking and stinking.

A figure stepped through into the room from the shining circle. It was tall, almost as tall as Bates itself, bipedal.

It had a furred, snouted face and big triangular ears. It looked like some kind of man-sized dog dressed up in a severely tailored uniform of midnight-blue jodhpurs and stiff-looking tunic.

"Secure the compartment," it commanded as a squad of other beings, none similar to it or to one another, came through. Each bore a stubby two-hand weapon and wore a midnight-blue uniform as close to the others as divergent body types allowed. "Then see to releasing the noble Bates."

The aliens moved swiftly to obey. With its gun-toters safely across, it holstered its own side arm and stepped forward. "I am Olfamor of the Zuri, knight commander of the Triangle of Force. I have come to liberate you from these totalitarian monsters. You are well, I trust, noble Bates?"

Bates smiled. "What took you so long?" he asked.

Chapter 18

"Okay," Kane said, "so now where are we?"

It was night. The Terrans had dismounted in a valley nestled among soaring peaks. It felt like the same night and looked like the same sky. It had the same stars that sometimes moved and sometimes went fast-motion nova and sometimes just went out. The air smelled roughly similar, if you added some cool mountain smells and subtracted ozone, alkali dust and sundry burning organics. But they could have been off at the back end of the Andromeda galaxy for all Kane actually knew.

"About the same as you were before," a new voice said. "Just a few miles away. The exact number I won't disclose—what you don't know you can't blurt out when the Grand Council torturers get their hooks in you."

"I love you, too," Kane said to the small hooded form approaching on foot. Around them a camp bustled with several hundred beings. Some went in and out of shelters either scooped from rocks or cunningly designed to look like them. A few fires burned, which seemed to compromise their security from overhead surveillance. "What's wrong with you people? It's like the planet of the jolt-walkers."

"It is the Grand Council," Pine said softly. "They touch everything with violence. With their madness."

Suddenly Kane was very, very tired. The jump from inside the cave in the rocks had been relatively mild as such things went, but they had been through a lot—since leaving Cerberus early that morning.

Domi walked over, hugging herself tightly beneath her breasts. Like Brigid she had skinned out of her shadow suit. She wore a vaguely blue tank top and cutoff jeans faded near white. Despite the fact that the oddly scented air had a chill bite to it up here in the mountains, her posture did not seem a reaction to the temperature.

"Sean's in a bad way," she said. About fifteen yards away Brigid, Marina and the three mostly intact Team Phoenix guys huddled around Reichert, who lay stretched out on a pallet on the ground.

He lifted his head. "Can we do anything for him?"

Domi shook her close-cropped head and sniffled. She had a soft spot for the Phoenix crew, and its youngest member in particular. "He's busted up inside. There's internal bleeding, big time. Major Mike's talking about hitting him with a morphine overdose and letting him go out easy."

Kane's upper lip skinned back off his teeth. "Shit. That's rough."

"We can do something for him, young man," the hooded figure said. "And I'm not used to being ignored like part of the furniture. Although most races of what you call the Far Arm look for nothing but uncouth behavior from humans. I look for better. But perhaps I'm spoiled by association with P'narvayrot, hey?"

It took him a moment to recognize the real name of the young woman he had rescued. She was already fixed as

Pine in his mind. Evidently the translator units could be manipulated so as not to translate every syllable automatically.

"Okay, lady," he said, for the voice the translator produced was that of a middle-aged woman. "I apologize all to hell for my manners. I'm Kane. Who're you?"

Pine, who stood nearby, gasped, apparently at his rudeness.

"I am Ma'ot," she said.

"Ma'at? Like the Egyptian goddess?"

"Ma-*ot*," she corrected firmly. "An *oh* sound. Even your rudimentary vocal apparatus can handle that sound. But don't trouble yourself. You will call me Bug Mama—everybody else does."

And she raised small hands and swept back her hood. Sure enough, Kane found himself looking into the great glabrous eyes of a giant insect.

Giant relative to insects he had known if not loved, anyway; she'd make maybe four-feet if she stood real straight, he guessed. Domi towered over her.

It wasn't a real threatening head, giant bug or not. It wasn't even ugly. It reminded Kane of the head of a praying mantis, more or less triangular, perched on a neck he couldn't see for the robe and hood. Several pair of jointed antennae bobbed between the big eyes. The various-sized parts of a compound mouth worked constantly at the lower end of the triangle. Kane couldn't watch them long; he found their restless motion not disturbing so much as hypnotic.

So were the eyes, which had a fascinating quality of shifting hue according to the angle from which they were observed, like a tiger's-eye opal. Like a mantis's eye, each had a little dark spot in it, which also moved with Kane.

He couldn't tell whether it was a trick of light or whether they actually indicated where the creature was looking.

"Yes, yes. Go ahead and stare. You endoskeletal types are so parochial. Honestly."

"Who are you?" he asked. Pine bit her lip and started to shift her weight in agitation.

"We're the good guys."

She seemed to smile. At least, he felt as if she were smiling. Hell, he was just filling up with warm, syrupy feelings toward her, big-ass bug or not....

He shook his head. "Are you pulling some kind of mind-control trick on me?" he demanded.

"Not at all. I am not gifted in psi, as some of our people so very fortunately are. But if I were it would do little good. Interspecies psi is a rare and abstruse talent, and you humans are notoriously resistant to all but your own sensitives."

Pine cleared her throat. "He saved my life, Mistress Ma'ot," she said. "He deserves candor."

"Candor! Child, do you dare to impugn—"

"About the pheromones—"

"A trivial detail. One which slipped my mind, really."

"Pheromones?" Kane narrowed his eyes. His body was starting to feel the floating sensation of advanced fatigue, but suddenly his mind was focused to a glass-shard edge. "Why would alien pheromones work on me?"

"A little gift from evolution," the insectoid said, throwing her hands up in a gesture that could only be the equivalent of a shrug. Those hands were startlingly humanoid, though covered in chitin. "I assure you growing up on our home world was no picnic, speaking as a species. You notice that in addition to the ability to generate little insignificant wafts of pheromones based on what we learn about other species' biochemistry through our scent receptors, we had to develop intelligence. Highly advanced intelligence, as you've no doubt noticed."

Grant approached. The creature looked up at him with a happy curious waving of its antennae, not at all fazed by the fact the human was one and a half times her height and easily three times her mass, unless her chitin were stiffened by iridium or some other heavy metal the way calcium put starch in human bones. "Greetings, sapient Grant."

Grant shook his head, more as if he had water in his ears than in negation, and furrowed his brow at her. "What's she saying to you?" he asked his partner.

"I have no idea."

The sound of violent expostulation roused him. Over by a fire Major Mike was red-faced and shouting at a humanoid hooded shape even taller than Grant. Robison held him back by one arm, and Brigid was trying to interpose her not inconsiderable mass between them.

"Oh, dear," Bug Mama said. "It appears that Thand is being high-handed again." She had turned her head to look; now the two black dots in her eyes moved as if to focus on Kane. "Heroes are like that, I fear."

She started off at a short-legged busybody bustle. "Wait," Kane called after her. "I've got a few questions here."

The eye spots rolled over the top of her protruding eyes to focus on him again from the back of her head, which came close to creeping him out utterly. "Your mind won't hold the answers until you get some sleep, boy," she said crisply. "P'narvayrot, child, be a dear and see them to some comfortable quarters."

"The way she goes from all mother-warm to senior Mag on inspection mode," Grant said musingly, "she should've been a ward nurse."

Kane stood up. It was quite an effort. "Look," he said to Pine, "can't you at least tell us what's going on here?"

He held up a finger to still her protest. "The short form, okay? I promise I won't ask any real detailed questions until we've slept. The answers'd probably make my brain smoke, anyway. Your boss lady's right about that, anyway."

Pine sighed. "Your arrival was detected, of course. The anomaly that sent you produced quite a great noise across the electromagnetic, psi and probability spectrums."

"Probability spectrums," Grant echoed, his deep voice somewhat hollow.

Kane crossed his arms and leaned back against his friend's comforting bulk. He affected not to notice Grant's slight unwonted sway; the big man had to be as dead on his feet as Kane himself.

"One of our bands was watching the spot. They rescued you. They defeated the mechanical remotes, as you saw. Unfortunately, there were Subatip and Zeduvol forces overhead who weren't too closely engaged to send units down to the surface to investigate."

"That'd be the kangaroo dudes and the weird flat tanks?" Grant asked. She nodded. "What about those guys at the end? The shiny spaceship that was zapping everybody?"

"I was unable to see who they were; I will inquire of a Grok as to their psychic emanations if you desire."

Grant waved a hand. "Just be one more meaningless jumble of syllables to me."

"So how'd Thand and his boys manage to pop through

the gateway in time to haul our chestnuts out of that particular fire?" As fuzzy as his brain was, he was alert enough to use Earth-specific metaphors, just to poke their hosts' translator software. It was the most defiance he seemed able to muster.

"Oh, the Groks alerted us," Pine said, sounding surprised he didn't know.

"Seems a bit risky using commo gear with all kinds of enemies right overhead," Grant said.

"Oh, but the Groks communicate by direct thought transfer. The dominant races of the Triangle and Circle hate and fear psi. They use mechanical detectors for it."

She grinned, and looked for the first time like what she had to be: a healthy teenaged girl. "They aren't very good at it."

Over by the fire hooded forms were loading Reichert's limp form onto a stretcher. Hays stood to one side glowering over folded arms. Marina stood beside him, hand on his arm, obviously gentling him like a truculent horse. Bug Mama stood looking up at the tall shape of Thand.

"Somebody's getting a righteous ass-chewing," Grant remarked.

"I wonder if she's making him like it," Kane said.

The stretcher rose as of its own volition and floated off toward a boulder-shaped shelter with several attendants trotting alongside. Hays sat down abruptly, slumping as if his bones had dissolved.

Kane stretched and yawned. "I know the feeling," he said. "Pine, the bug lady said something about you finding us some beds for the night?"

"Oh, certainly." She drooped her eyes. Kane wondered

if she were blushing, decided it was just a trick of light and shadow.

"Heads up," Grant said out the side of his mouth. "Big bastard heading this way."

Thand himself strode toward them with long strides. Kane sighed. "Christ, is he pissed because we haven't thanked him yet for saving our asses?"

But Thand ignored both the Terrans. Instead he strode straight up to Pine. She did not seem to want to look at him.

He reached out and with a gigantic, very humanoid hand gripped Pine's chin gently and turned her face around and up toward his.

"No words for me, little one?" he asked in a voice like a cannonball rolling around inside a steel drum.

He swept off his hood. Long backswept blond hair and a beard framed a craggy, handsome, entirely human face.

"I am sorry, Thand," she said, not sounding too happy. "It's the strain. The fighting…"

He nodded briskly and turned to Kane. His eyes were blue. His nose had obviously been broken once. Instead of disfiguring his face, the slight hump redeemed it from what otherwise might almost have been prettiness.

Kane could just tell this guy was the kind things broke that way for: all the luck. He decided he hated him.

"I thank you, sapient," he said. "I saw how you rescued my beloved Pine from the cruel Subatip. The coalition and I are in your debt."

"Uh, yeah," Kane said. He extended a hand. Kane eyed it dubiously; it looked like a rock crusher with knuckles. Even one of Grant's mighty meat hooks would be lost in that paw.

Damned if I'll back down to this bastard, he thought.

He crushes my hand to paste, I'll just knee him in the balls and let events take their natural course.

Instead Thand gripped his hand with a firm grip, then let him go. Kane hated him even harder.

"You must rest now," the blond man said. "In the morning we will talk about how you can help us triumph over the evil ones. We will talk strategy."

"Uh," Kane said, "sure."

Thand turned to Pine and bent down. He had to bring his torso down almost vertical. She presented a cheek for a kiss.

"You rest, child," he said. "You have been through much, and the worry for your brother must wear upon you." He wheeled and walked back toward a clump of other hooded warrior jocks.

"I hate heroes," Grant murmured as the big man strode away as if he were rolling the world beneath his feet. "They tend to draw fire."

"Affirmative," Kane said.

Brigid and Bug Mama were walking back toward them, heads together in conversation. "Those two hook up," Grant said, "life won't be worth living."

"I hear you," Kane said. "What did that mean, Pine? What he said about your brother?"

Her eyes had been fixed on his face. Now they dropped away. Her cheeks unmistakably colored this time.

"Her brother's been captured by Grand Council slavers," Bug Mama called, "and they'll kill him in a flash if they so much as suspect he's a potent human psi. What, Kane, do you have a talent for rubbing salt in raw wounds?"

"Yes," Brigid said. "But he doesn't mean to this time, I'm sure."

"Sorry," Kane said, glancing at Pine. "I didn't know. "

"You could not," she whispered.

Bug Mama stopped before her acolyte and put her hands on her hips. Or about where her hips would be if she happened to have hips. "So that's how it is. Oh, my, we might be in for melodrama, here—"

Away over the peaks a red shaft stabbed down from above. *Look away!* Bug Mama screeched.

Fortunately Kane's reflex had caused him to snap his head aside. It didn't save him from having a giant bar of cyan afterimage pulsating behind his eyelids. He suspected that it hadn't really saved him much of anything; if the terrible energy beam was powerful enough to damage his eyes at this distance, the damage had been done instantly.

Fortunately, as the afterimage died away, his sight seemed unimpaired. Around them, the whole camp had gone still. Hooded heads turned slowly back toward where the awful beacon had shone. Wisps of ghost light seemed to twine and drift through the path it had taken—air turned to plasma by the beam's incredible power.

He thought he saw a pink glow silhouetting the peaks in that direction. "It seems some of our friends from the Grand Council have decided to settle all disputes back at our former observation post for good and all," Bug Mama said brightly. "And now to bed, gentle sapients. Nothing more to see here."

Chapter 19

The yard dispatcher's office was as hot as a kiln. What had apparently been a few sheets of plastic, possibly documents, lay on a desk and on the floor. They had half melted into the surfaces they rested on in the heat of the high-desert town. Dust lay in pink ripples on the drab synthetic floor, and occasionally skittered about like small creatures, when the breezes sneaked in through the broken windows. The room smelled of alien dust.

Ignoring the heat, Joe Weaver settled the crosshairs of his sight on the juncture of the stalklike yellow neck and slump-shouldered body of the sentry walking his post across the street that ran alongside the yard's high concrete wall. Weaver thought of the sentry as "he," even though he knew the Talladora, of a minor Grand Council race that made a great show of professing neutrality between Triangle and Circle, were neither wholly plant nor animal and reproduced asexually, budding out their young following direct transmission of plasm between two or more adults. Unlike some Far Arm sophonts, they did have centralized brains and certain vital organs.

Which he knew well how to reach out and touch. The Terrans' allies had provided him plastic cards displaying rotatable 3-D images and all relevant data concerning every race that made up the Grand Council Peacekeeping Force on Sidra. He had not brought them but had simply committed them to memory through intense study the night before. He had no further need of them.

Sidra itself, Bug Mama's lieutenant Servillon had told them, was of little intrinsic importance to the Grand Council, which ruled the Far Arm. That was why the coalition had been so active before the arrival of Bates—and almost immediately thereafter, half the battle fleets in the Far Arm. They felt they had a good chance of prying the planet out of the council's talons, lying as it did on the galaxy's far outer fringes.

The council's peacekeeping force, though a trillion or so strong overall, was a sideshow, an afterthought. The major races kept it up for appearance sake, but for the most part declined to lower themselves to having anything to do with it. It was occupied, as here, with paperwork and protocol that were in fact meaningless.

Except of course to the residents of the planets on whose necks fell the burden of the Grand Council's yoke. But no one of consequence cared about them.

"Magic Voice to Iron Man," words came into his skull. "Everyone reports they're in position."

"Roger that, Magic Voice," he subvocalized.

He snugged his short and stocky weapon's buttplate to his shoulder, welded his cheek to the stock, took up slack on the trigger. He had dragged a table beneath the big window overlooking the satellite uplink station across the packed-dirt street. The table allowed him to prop his elbows on it for a stable firing position without actually hanging out the busted-out window himself. As long as the blue Sun didn't glint off the object lens of his four-power scope, he was unlikely to be seen in the gloom of the dispatch office for a long-defunct surface-transport company. And both an extended lens shroud and the angle of the morning Sun, hanging off out of sight over his left shoulder halfway up a mauve sky, militated against any traitor reflection.

He drew a breath deep into his abdomen. The sentry reached the end of his short route along the side of the blocky relay building and paused to turn. Weaver had the rifle waiting.

The crosshair centered right between the two fleshy inch-wide stalks on which the peacekeeper's eyes were mounted, right below the brim of his helmet. Weaver let out some of the air he held captive within his lungs and squeezed the trigger.

Nothing at all happened. Apparently.

"WHAT IS THIS STUFF?" Kane asked, warily eyeing the breakfast he had been handed.

"Looks like roast rat on a stick," Larry Robison said, and bit off a chunk. Grease ran down into his beard. "Yum."

"I like roast rat," Domi said. "Roast coyote—now *that's* nasty."

The Sun wasn't even over the mountains to the east. The sky had turned a pale turquoise, silhouetting the nearest peaks. But down where they were twilight still held sway.

That was the bitch about being well up in the mountains; daylight was abbreviated. They had all observed that often enough outside in the Bitterroots, where Cerberus lay. But nobody spent enough time out in the open to mind it much. And in Cerberus it was always daylight. Sort of.

"I should hope to frig a three-toed sloth," Robison said.

Grant froze with his own food poised before his open mouth. "Jesus Christ," he said, lowering the stick with a small roasted animal. "This stuff's bad enough without your humor for seasoning."

"What?" Robison demanded. "I was just absently quoting an H. Allen Smith book I read a couple centuries ago."

A tall figure stilted up to them. Kane recognized it for its robes as what Pine described as a *tlin-tlan*, one of the indigenous creatures: a six-foot tall stick figure with a knobby purple exoskeleton and a kind of beak. The creature was hidden beneath the robes currently. The robes shielded the wearer from various forms of detection, Pine had said.

"When you done," it said, and its language was obviously alien enough that the small autotranslators they'd all been given for their very own had trouble rendering it into English on the fly, "you come."

"Say please," Robison said to its retreating back.

Kane bit off a mouthful. It mostly tasted hot and greasy. He set the stick with his half-devoured creature on it on a rock beside him.

"Let's go," he said. "I'm done."

THE DELISLE CARBINE was a highly successfully but little known weapon of World War II. It was one of the very few truly silenced—as opposed to sound suppressed—firearms ever deployed.

Joe Weaver had built this clone on a rebarreled and re-mounted action for an Ishapore MkIV, a license-built model of the old British Enfield on which the original De-Lisle was based. Because a .45ACP cartridge had the same base dimensions as the British .303 caliber in which the rifle was chambered originally, it was easy to adapt so that it fired the short, fat pistol rounds.

The .45ACP had two sterling qualities: it was already subsonic, meaning it didn't have to be loaded down in power so that it wouldn't betray its firing with a mini-sonic boom the way a higher velocity projectile such as a 9 mm would. And its heavy slug was plenty potent even traveling at less than the speed of sound.

Weaver used special ammunition, delivering 180-grain Triton slugs with hollow tips. Although they moved a bit slow to expand reliably, they still did somewhat more damage than standard jacketed .45 ball.

The limitations of the system were that it was bolt action, not semiauto—to Weaver's mind not a limitation at all, since by definition *any* decent sniper rifle was bolt action. Also, even with the somewhat higher—though still slower than sound—velocity imparted by extra barrel length over the usual pistol, and by the lighter slug, the .45 had a trajectory not a lot different from a thrown baseball.

Weaver had of course personally and exhaustively tested the combination of cartridge and weapon, firing thousands of rounds under a variety conditions of weather, light and wind, and meticulously tabulating the results. He could form in his mind a reliable three-dimensional projection of the whole trajectory each shot would follow. Even so he would not try for a head shot at more than 150 yards. Outside of two hundred yards he wouldn't take a shot at all except under direst emergency.

The alien peacekeeper poised on its heel just a hair under seventy yards away. Weaver hadn't had to risk using a laser rangefinder to confirm that. His eye measured the distance precisely enough.

Launched with literally no sound beyond a whisper—not even the clack of a bolt reciprocating—the bullet flew to the locus of the sniper's intent. So slow was its flight and mild its recoil that Weaver had the scope back down in time to see a hole appear between the entity's eye stalks.

A mist of green fluid puffed out behind it. It fell like a suddenly emptied suit of clothes.

"Phoenix," he subvocalized, "Iron Man. Eyeball down. I say again, Eyeball is down."

"HERE'S THE DEAL," Bug Mama said. After breakfast she had gathered the Terrans with Pine, Thand and her chief lieutenant, a small, scaly party named Servillon, inside one of the boulder shelters. Kane couldn't decide if it was some kind of camouflaged prefab structure or really a big hollowed-out rock, since the interior was covered in some kind of poofy-looking insulation and badly lit by orange light pouring upward from what looked like little pots around the bases of the walls. Probably for effect, he judged. "The Far Arm is run by the Grand Council, which in turn is dominated by a thousand so-called major races, give or take. That might seem like a lot of races. Believe me it's not. They're a minority in the arm they claim to rule.

"Real power in the council is split between two giant factions, calling themselves the Circle of Life and the Triangle of Force, respectively. The Circle is dominated by a race called the Paa, the Triangle by the Zuri. One claims to represent the spirit of the community of sophonts, the others the firm guiding hand of authority. I'll let you guess which is which. Not that it matters, because basically the platform of each is that all us humble sophonts should get our lives run by our betters and wisers, and get it good and hard.

"They are, if you're us, the bad guys."

Through this Thand, sitting cross-legged next to Pine, seemed to be mostly interested in trying to scoot closer to her. She paid no attention, but kept inching away, as if subconsciously. Servillon, who looked like nothing so much as a snake with arms and an outsized chest, sat coiled back on his tail, which served in lieu of hind legs, with taloned hands hidden within the capacious sleeves of his own robes and nodding sagely. Or perhaps it was a tic.

Bug Mama stuck the stem of the long skinny pipe into her compound mouth and drew. The herb she'd tamped down and was smoking smelled vaguely sagelike. It was pleasant to Kane's nostrils, although he noticed Reichert, who'd been brought in on an antigrav stretcher that currently propped up the upper half of him like a hospital bed, twitching his nose and sniffling as if in allergic reaction.

"We're the Coalition of Nonaligned Races," Bug Mama went on. "It's what it sounds like—an assembly of minor races disenfranchised or outright oppressed by the current deal and taking a proactive approach to keeping themselves from being swallowed whole. We are, if you're them, the bad guys."

She puffed her pipe. "In other words, misfits, rebels, outcasts, malcontents—the whole foul brew. We're the forces of anarchy."

"Oh," Servillon interjected hastily, "of course we're not

actually anarchists. We believe in order, in the establishment of a just order, equitable to all."

Bug Mama took a pull from her pipe. Blue smoke wafted from her neck spiracles. "Sez you."

"But," Reichert said, "if you're nonaligned races, how can you have a coalition?"

"It's really very simple," Servillon began earnestly. He had, via translator at least, a not displeasing tenor voice. And, quite improbably, a palpably British accent. "We constitute a community, you see, of like-minded—"

Bug Mama waved him to silence. Kane could see that she was laughing again. "Let's just say we're folks who've noticed that this concept of one giant galactic government has brought us a couple million years of the very evil it's supposed to be protecting us from—near-constant interstellar war, punctuated by arm-wide blowouts that leave most everybody dead and most of the survivors grubbing around in their respective Stone Ages. We would like to break this spasm."

She shrugged. "Of course, that's been tried a few thousand times before. But hope springs eternal—and all that happy crap."

COVERED BY HAYS behind a pulse-plasma rifle, Larry Robison moved out toward the uplink station. He saw the body of the sentry lying on its face, yellow limbs twitching.

The door of the station opened. Another vaguely humanoid creature, this one with a long blue head and protuberant band eyes like wraparound sunglasses and likewise dressed in peacekeeper camou, strolled out. It stopped, did a doubletake and scrabbled for the side arm holstered on its right hip with a six-fingered hand.

Robison had moved out with the .40-caliber MP-5 shouldered. He lined up and fired a quick 3-round burst into the center of the elongated head. It came apart in a curiously dry fashion, like a partially dry-rotted squash. Pieces fell to the ground. The creature followed.

Drawn by the multiple blats of the suppressed gunfire, another sentry came around the corner of the cubical station building. This one was like the first Weaver had dropped: yellow skin, eyes on stalks. It aimed a longblaster at Robison.

From behind the hulk of what appeared to be a tracked vehicle with its tread long since removed, rusting just inside the open gate of the deserted yard, Mike Hays fired his plasma blaster. A miniature sun appeared on the alien's thin chest. Its upper torso exploded as yellow-and-blue flames wrapped it. A terrible scream pealed forth. The creature was dead already; the sound was superheated air venting from its lungs.

"So much for stealth," Robison heard Major Mike say in his head. "Sorry. Couldn't resist."

Robison moved quickly to the open door of the station, dared a three-second look inside. It was empty.

"Clear," he reported, by reflex. Holding the MP-5 at the ready with his right hand, he unslung a heavy satchel from his back. He dropped it against the outside wall by the door, then knelt briefly to grasp a small handle protruding from it and yank it away.

"No worries, Mechanic," he added, using Hays's actual call sign as he straightened up and backed rapidly away. "There's gonna be a lot more noise in a couple minutes anyway."

Chapter 20

"—that we noble Clays be thwarted by mere organic efflorescence, far less a space rat! Defy us at your certain peril! Your soul energy shall vitalize our crystalline structures with vibration—your organic detritus shall nourish our stuff!"

It's strange, Bates thought, listening to the seamless translation into English of a tirade directed against him by what was to all appearances a six-foot tub of red dirt. To think a space battle of unprecedented proportions is taking place outside while this debate goes on.

"Do not be alarmed, sapient Bates," a small, sleek, furred being sitting beside him said in the great echoing amphitheater. "All of this is simply posturing."

Bates chuckled mirthlessly. Teach your grandmother to suck eggs, Ximado. He was tempted to tell the Liitan just that to test the limits of the translation software.

"I know that," he said, forcing himself to be patient. The living soil sample continued to rave and rage. He tuned it out. Once he had ascertained that the rhetoric would remain just that, inasmuch as no matter how militant the Clay ambassador got, his other captors would never permit harm to befall him when he still held the great secret they all desired above all else in the universe, it had no further meaning to him. Although he did muse idly how he would make the Clays suffer for daring to threaten him once he had achieved his aim."

The venue was a battle planetoid that belonged, once, to some race of humanoids whose name Bates wasn't bothering to retain, inasmuch as they weren't a very significant player. Their main distinction was that they had the huge armored sphere relatively near to Sidra when word of the great discovery spread across the Far Arm. They had been among the first to arrive.

Which was their downfall: not being the very first. That had been the Paa, the first race Bates had managed to contact from his extraecliptic space station. Although they had not succeeded in keeping the secret to themselves—in part because Bates had contrived to contact a freighter owned by a Triangle race, likewise orbiting Sidra, shortly after first remote contact with the Circle powerhouse—they had not omitted to take measures to try to maintain what they thought was their monopoly on knowledge of the secret's discovery. The alien planetoid had, upon materializing a couple of astronomical units out from Sidra, run smack into some kind of unspeakable double-threat psi-improbability mine, which had shaved off about an eighth of the planetoid's unbelievable mass, leaving edges and surfaces all mirror bright and vaporizing every living entity in the ship, down to microbes.

Bates could only revel in the prospect of that kind of power.

Since it was untenanted and abandoned—even the monstrous Paa, it seemed, were somewhat creeped out by the effects of their own superweapon—the armored planetoid had made an ideal no-being's land in which those competing for possession of Bates, and the knowledge he held, could contest for that knowledge in the only way available to them: negotiating with the man himself.

Which of course entailed hammering out terms with one another. The fighting outside the collapsed matter-plated hull, with its ridiculously promiscuous waste of treasure and life, was about bargaining position, no more. The real action was right in here.

Bates let his eye fall on the Zuri representative. Chaufat had somewhat puffy brown fur and a supercilious manner. He wore a severely cut silver-chased black tunic and trousers. The spokesbeing for the Triangle of Force was, however, scrupulously deferential to Bates.

Bates had convinced the Zuri that if the other races thought they would get a monopoly on Bates, and hence the secret all to themselves, they'd simply take whatever horrific reality-warping steps might be necessary to destroy both the doglike sophonts and their honored guest. Privately he doubted that. Indeed, he was counting on the same cupidity that had led to galaxy-ravaging war an aeon before coming into play here.

He studied the Zuri, who was reproving the Clay representative for its intemperance. They're really not that doglike, Bates thought, nor wolflike. But they had descended from muzzled, furry, tailed predators—from their demeanor, no doubt pack predators.

I can deal with them, he reflected. For now, of course, he had to show no favor.

But when he had cemented his position—after he had reluctantly accepted the position of dictator of the arm, when the major races decided, inevitably, to press it upon him—he would make the Zuri his chief enforcers. As pack predators, they were natural fascists; and as the dominant form of political animal on twentieth-century Earth where he had grown to manhood and the height of his powers, fascists were creatures he felt greatly comfortable dealing with. They understood *obedience*. More, they made a fetish of it, a very religion.

The members of the Circle were useful, in their way. He would use them masterfully.

Ah, but the Paa, he thought, and their vile vassal races, most particularly the unspeakable Uvaluvu. The Paa as a species might or might not be spared, if they proved themselves properly useful, and amenable; likewise their slaves. But the proud Circle queen and her direct lackeys were destined for the wood chipper of history.

The thought made him smile as he sat listening, with one leg folded above the other and his huge hands knit upon his knee, while monstrous beings raved to see his blood.

After all, he knew that however much they might want to, they didn't really mean it.

SLAVERY WAS OFFICIALLY illegal in the Far Arm.

The Grand Council did, however, allow for administrative detention of antisocial persons. These persons, naturally, were compelled to serve the common good, despite any inclinations they may have felt to the contrary. To reduce the burden on the benevolent state, their services were contracted out. Those who took over their indentures licensed their labor from the state. As a natural consequence, the contractees were empowered to do what was necessary to compel the obedience of the detainees to the will of the state, and to take whatever steps proved necessary to recover them when the selfish shirkers attempted to flee their just obligations.

It wasn't a bit like slavery. You just had to work for somebody else for no pay. And you could never quit.

Vartan the Venerated, as he liked to style himself, or Vartan the Venomous, as the denizens of Sidra unfortunate enough to have crossed his path called him—when they didn't call him something worse—was the planet's leading contractor for administrative-detention labor. He regarded himself as a subcontractor, renting out the services of his clients, as they were legally known, on a temporary basis when applicable, and in cases where it was desired and the fee offered high enough, selling their indenture outright to those in need of more permanent help. Despite the slanders of seditious detractors, this had nothing to do with selling their persons. That would be slavery. And slavery was illegal.

Personal service was a hallmark of Vartan's business, which was why he rode along to the noontide auction of long-term contracts scheduled for the public square in the depressed and squalid village called Khaduli. He had picked the place for the headquarters of his planet-wide operation precisely because its isolation and insignificant population made it difficult for relatives of his clients, and other ingrates who failed to appreciate the vital service he performed for the body politic to get close to him. Strangers tended to stand out, and since the ville was located on the bend of a grim stream across a generally featureless pink plain, they could be seen coming a long way off.

A flatbed grav-crawler, loaded down to within twelve inches of the street by a pile of scorched parts salvaged from a recently crashed spacecraft, backed suddenly out of an alley in defiance of all sense and traffic regulations. Vartan's own grav-sled, despite his high-pitched bellow of alarm to his driver, promptly smacked into the flatbed.

Suppressing an urge to belabor his driver, Vartan opened his door of the cab and dropped to the street. Though the sled had not yet grounded and he had a good yard to fall to the cracked and sun-hot pavement, he felt as if he floated down with featherlike grace. His own planet of origin had a surface gravity of over five gs. This place, which couldn't even muster one g of pull, was the next thing to orbit to him.

It tended to reinforce his sense of superiority. Indeed, invulnerability.

The driver's door of the salvage floater banged open, adding some dents to its already impressive collection. The driver hopped out: a female human, not much taller than Vartan himself, wearing a battered billed cap, a gray short-sleeved shirt with a dark line of sweat down the belly, baggy mauve cargo pants. Her eyes were obscured by dark sunglasses against the primary's ultraviolet-rich glare.

"What's the matter with you, you big ugly bastard?" she yelped.

Vartan felt an urge to smash the impertinent being's misshapen face with a tentacle. He only recognized it as a female of its species because of his experience in dealing in antisocial detainees, throughout the Far Arm the space rats made up a disproportionate percentage of the indentured laborers.

He had to remind himself that this specimen was not one of his clients. It actually had rights.

I had best settle this, he thought, irked, especially since the thing continued to screech its half-translatable imprecations at him. I don't want to be delayed to the auction. It's poor form to keep the paying customers waiting.

And later, he would see to remedying the legal fluke by which this pale, paper-skinned, obscenely binary being was able to abuse him, a respected servant of the council's will!

His aural sensors, like every other organ of consequence arrayed in sextuplicate around his circumference, detected the comforting sound of his enforcer, Urd, getting out of the other side of the vehicle. Had his six lipless ingestion-mouths been capable of smiling, they would have.

"Here now," he said, forcing himself to use the tones that the translator device he wore would render conciliatory, "we are both reasonable beings. What can I do to assuage your loss anger?"

His radio-frequency sense tickled, then, briefly.

The creature's whole demeanor changed. The previously unbroken stream of obscenities issuing from its unnatural single maw ceased. Instead it produced that distortion of its grotesque features Vartan knew constituted an expression of pleasure.

"Die," it said.

And before his giant Slump bodyguard could even find his away around the long grav-sled—whose snout was inextricably locked with the bed of the other floater, and had a ton or so of twisted metal plate toppled over on it like a grapnel—the unspeakable space rat had drawn a short concealed blaster and fired a bright yellow particle beam straight into the wide dome of Vartan's skull.

THESE REBELS GOT some ace tech, Kane thought as the electrically sealed rear hatches of the seventy-foot-long slave wagon popped open in response to the defeater bar that had just bonded itself to its adamantine armor plate.

Inside two guards stared out in the dismay of complete surprise. Like the boss slaver himself they were off-worlders: Bug Mama had told the Terrans it was common practice for slavers to be of races other than those dominant in the area they worked, lest fellow feelings tempt them to give species members a break.

The guard to Kane's left was a humanoid with yellow, damp-looking skin and eyes on stalks: a Talladora, from a star system not far from Sidra along a major faster-than-light transit route, which Kane understood dimly wasn't the same as being near in normal space. The Talladora were commonly used as muscle by the council and its contractors, since they were loyal, once bought, and their loyalty went cheap to anyone they feared.

What they weren't was particularly elite. This one goggled a moment, its eyes literally standing out like a character of a twentieth-century cartoon vid. They did that anyway, of course, but now they seemed to reach like little supplicating arms toward the bearded, tan-visaged human who stood outside in the Sun's blue glare.

The alien grabbed for its side arm. Unfortunately, the holster was covered by a heavy flap, doubtless to discourage a quick snatch by one of the "clients." It wouldn't have made much difference. Kane already had the pressor pistol the coalition had given him up and ready.

He squeezed the firing stud once. It made a weird *poit*

sound, not loud but penetrating. A ripple of distortion appeared at the end of its barrel, which to Kane's eye was just a piece of some kind of shiny silver alloy bar stock, either solid or tubular with a sealed end. The distortion flowed swiftly to a spot between the stalked eyes, where as if by magic a circular indentation appeared between them.

It was as if an invisible glass rod a half inch in diameter had been hammered into the Talladora's skull. The eyes stood out at forty-five-degree angles as the skull deformed, bulged and then exploded from the sudden drastic fluid overpressure the pressor-pulse induced in its brain. Purple juice with green chunks squirted out seams along the sides of the thing's head. It fell twitching, and from the sudden sulfurous stink, fouling itself.

Its partner was a vaguely humanoid object that wore nothing but harness and was covered crown to sole with spiny gray-edged black and brown bristles. They reminded Kane unpleasantly, in the flash glimpse he got, of the hairs on a tarantula, not mammalian fur. No features whatever showed through the bristles but a triangle of small black convex eyes in the midst of its head.

With better presence of mind than its now writhing and reeking companion, it made no attempt for its purposely hard-to-draw side arm. Instead it lunged straight for Kane with the shockstick it carried in a hand with two pairs of opposed digits.

Its speed made a rattlesnake seem slow. Not even Kane's panther reflexes were up to the challenge. He tried to switch aim, but felt as if he were moving through mud.

A rippling polychromatic flash lit the inside of the long compartment, illuminating stunned expressions and postures among the clients within. A score of microlasers each fired three-millisecond pulses in a random primary color from the short, stubby two-hand blaster Brigid Baptiste held at the level of her slim waist.

The laser shotgun was designed to defeat any kind of armor keyed to reflect or absorb a single wavelength of coherent light, as well as to cause maximal damage to the target, with each successive discharge of each cell burning deeper into the target. It was tunable and set currently to fan its discharges to the breadth of a human palm at five yards, which was the distance from which Baptiste fired.

It was overkill here. The spider-ape guard flew backward into the compartment trailing streamers of smoke and orange-and-blue flames, propelled by the sudden explosion of body fluids in its chest cavity into steam. It bounced off knobbly knees and fetched up on the floor of the compartment, where it ignited the skirts of several twittering females of some avian species with fur instead of feathers.

Letting the laser weapon snap back to her waist on its retractable sling, Brigid clambered quickly past Kane into the compartment to comfort the slaves and make sure the three captives she'd inadvertently ignited were safely extinguished. Which they were, as clients seated to either side of the now-hysterical bird-creatures beat the flames out themselves with horny purple hands, driven by urgent self-interest if nothing else.

"Ladies and gentlemen," Kane said, "step outside. Your contracts have been canceled."

A huge three-fingered gray hand reached over his shoulder and plucked his pressor pistol from his grasp. Then another hand clamped down on his left shoulder and tossed him like a toy five yards down the street.

Chapter 21

"Now might be a good time," Kane had said to his coalition hosts, "to tell us just how it is you come to know so much about our pal Gilgamesh Bates and his cosmic doomsday device."

His smile had been wolfish in the gloom of the shelter, and anything but friendly. "A real good time."

Bug Mama's chief aide turned a worried look and a flickering tongue toward the slight robed figure. "Elder—"

She waved a tiny, chitinous brown hand at him. "Hold your fudge, Servillon. We need these people and they need us. And there's no time for games. Barely enough time for subtlety. But then, there's always time for subtlety."

"There's always room for Jell-O," Reichert echoed.

Robison leaned forward and felt the young man's cheek. "He's a bit feverish," he explained.

Bug Mama waved away both interruption and explanation, "Your answer is simple, Kane—spies and psis."

"What the hell does that mean?" Grant asked. "All respect, here."

Thand glowered at the big black man. Kane thought it might be amusing to watch a stare-down between the two: the rebel chieftain was even bigger and bulkier than Grant, and well equipped for glowering by reason of exceptionally ferocious eyebrows. But Kane's money would be on Grant. He always bet on Grant.

"What it says," Bug Mama said. "Clear out the ear wax, junior."

"We have moles within the major council factions," Pine said hurriedly. "People from afflicted races or in fear of repression. Defectors disgusted by the acts of other members of their own species—"

"And, of course, the normal numbers of purchased or blackmailed traitors and foolish fellow travelers," Bug Mama said.

"Don't look so pained, child," she added to Pine, with what Kane thought was remarkable skill at reading facial expressions totally dissimilar to her own. He made a mental note to be very, very careful around the diminutive alien. "We have scruples—in that we differ from our foes on the council and their lackeys. But survival forces us to be highly selective about even the scruples we allow ourselves. Or at least adroit at rationalization."

"And changing the subject," Brigid said crisply. "How do you know about Bates?"

"And mebbe more," Domi added, "how much do you know?"

Brigid raised an eyebrow at her. Even after spending so much time she had a tendency to underestimate the albino feral woman.

"Several weeks ago," Bug Mama said, "Bates made contact with a Paa corvette in orbit around Sidra. Why exactly he made contact inside this system we don't know— and if our enemies have learned, they've grown damn cagier about hiding secrets from us. But he did.

"The Paa rule the Circle of Life faction within the Grand Council. Their gift for diplomacy isn't why they have so much power. Indeed, their notion of wielding power is, if at first you don't succeed, beat the burden-beast harder. That creates compliance through fear, as they have been demonstrating for about twenty thousand years, and races before them for a couple million years of patchily known history. But it creates damn little loyalty. Paa clients are some of our likeliest allies."

"And that accounts for how you were able to program your translators to handle English," Brigid said.

Kane looked at her, nodding. "Not bad, Baptiste."

"Correct," Bug Mama said. "The council races analyzed Bates's speech and created software for the translator system. We availed ourselves of it."

"How'd all these other folks get word of the party?" Major Mike Hays said, waving a hand toward the ceiling.

The alien waggled her antennae in amusement. "There were other council craft on the surface or in orbit who might have intercepted some of the communications," she said. "Also, we aren't the only ones who know how to suborn spies. Especially among Paa clients."

Pine had been sitting quietly through this. She had never looked once at Thand, whose skull seemed to have finally been penetrated by the realization she wasn't in a touchy-feely frame of mind. He now sat back, great arms crossed, beard down, glowering.

Kane hoped he didn't notice the way the girl's eyes kept flicking toward Kane. It wasn't that Kane feared the big bastard, but their asses were hanging way out here in the middle of nowhere. The last thing any of them needed was any sort of complication.

Now Pine leaned toward Bug Mama, who seemed to be her personal mentor or guru, and spoke so softly Kane couldn't hear. Bug Mama nodded.

"Yes, dear," the alien said. "I fear my love of digression has got the better of me again. But our new friends did ask."

She turned toward Kane and Brigid. "You and we have a common interest," she said.

"All life in the universe has a common interest," Servillon said.

"Stopping Bates," Brigid declared.

"Precisely."

"Stopping," Mike Hays asked deliberately. "Or maybe…taking his place?"

Bug Mama clacked her mandibles in amusement. "Do I look like I want to rule the universe? I got troubles enough riding herd on this motley assortment of outcasts, misfits and individualists."

"How do you propose we go about stopping this clown?" Grant asked.

"Only one way I can see," Bug Mama said. "Find the location of the device called the Cosmic Eye—" tension ran around the group of displaced Terrans like a shock wave "—and neutralize it. As in, blow the damn thing to Hell for good and all!"

"Why not," Grant asked, "just chill Bates?"

"Oh, no, no." Servillon shook his flat-skulled head. Kane began to wonder if certain "human" gestures were universal. Or whether, like so much else, they had been brought along to Earth by the Annunaki from the stars millennia ago. "The council races fighting over him would simply slap his head into a stasis field and proceed with their contest. The winner would unspool his memory chains at its leisure."

"Unless we vaporized him," Reichert said.

"You're still feverish," Bug Mama said. "He's in the middle of the biggest concentration of collapsed-matter and firepower the Far Arm has seen in fifty thousand years or more."

"Then, what?" Kane asked.

"Only a psi can extract the secret from his living brain," Bug Mama said. "Only the most powerful human psi on the planet."

"My brother," Pine said with quiet emphasis.

"Who is held as a slave," Bug Mama added, "by the biggest dealer in sophont flesh on Sidra!"

"MAGIC VOICE!" Kane shouted as he skidded backward along the street on his rump, away from the slave wagon. His eyes still watered from the painful impact of landing on his tailbone. "Tell Phoenix to light the candle now!"

Grinning off a lantern jaw, the giant gray-skinned humanoid dropped Kane's pistol and lumbered toward him. They were known as Slumps, as least to the translator software. They came from a system not far from Sidra along the hyperspace transit net. They were fairly prevalent in this part of space, though not as widely dispersed as humans. They were prized for obvious reasons as soldiers and enforcers; Kane had seen at least one last night, its vast form swathed in robe and hood, among the initial rescue riders.

The creature's skin had a thick, leathery quality that reminded Kane of rhinoceros hide. It wore only a pair of short trunks and a harness holding various unidentifiable items of equipment. Kane saw nothing that looked unmistakably like a wep.

But then, it might not feel the need for one.

Beyond it Brigid appeared in the back of the wag with her laser shotgun. She hesitated. Kane realized she feared hitting him with the spreading spray of multicolored beams.

"Baptiste!" he shouted. "Get the slaves out! I got this."

I hope. Sitting at rest now, he stretched out his right arm. His Sin Eater ripped through the baggy sleeve of his white natural-fabric blouse and slammed, blasting, into his hand.

A LITTLE OVER A MILE away, now perched on a small volcanic tit of hill overlooking the ville from the east, Major Mike Hays thumbed open a cover on the small device he held in his right hand and pressed the red button.

Down in the ville itself, two hundred yards from the position he and his two functional teammates had pulled back to, the satchel charge went off with a glass-edged crack.

Had they wanted to destroy the uplink shack they would have tossed the charge into the open door. Instead they wanted to draw maximum attention to the event. So they left it leaning against the wall outside.

Somewhere in the town an alien siren began to keen a strange, skirling, three-note progression.

Without hanging around to view their handiwork, the three teammates pulled back down the backslope. A squadron of coalition cavalry was already on the way with riding beasts for a low-tech extraction.

KANE'S TRIBURST slammed home in the center of the Slump's broad bare chest. He saw the depressions ripple against the thick hide.

The creature's grin widened. "Damn," Kane said. "Natural Kevlar skin. Figures."

Can't be armored everywhere, bastard! Kane exulted.

The creature inclined its head slightly and bullets bounced off the brow shelf as from a slab of granite. Kane fired another triburst, then another. To no greater effect.

The slump raised its head again. The bullet strikes to the skull had had some slight effect: rivulets of blood ran black down craggy, distorted features. It smiled, showing yellow teeth stained with green like moss on the stones of a waterfall.

Behind the Slump Brigid and Domi were helping confused slaves of several species from the back of the vehicle.

"Best snap it up," Marina's voice said in Kane's head. "Our local pals report their sensors detect a pair of peacekeeper monitors headed your way."

Kane got to his feet, a little more gingerly than he would have liked. All we need, he thought. The monitors were the real weight of the generally ineffectual peacekeepers, dressed in half a metric ton each of power armor with the firepower of a twentieth-century armored battalion. It had been hoped that they, along with the ville's civic patrol and standard peacekeepers, would be drawn to the diversion created by Team Phoenix.

And when did you ever know a plan to come off like it was supposed to?

The Slump stopped three yards from Kane. Raising a huge hand, it tapped two of its three fingers on the black-bloody abraded patch above its eyes.

"You want my best shot?" Kane asked. "You got it."

The Sin Eater slammed back into its holster. He took two rapid steps and launched himself in a dive between the widespread legs of the behemoth.

With surprising speed the creature bent. Reflexively it also twisted its vast torso to its right, anticipating Kane would try to pop up behind it. As he belly flopped painfully on the silvery pavement, with only his shadow suit protecting his elbows and knees from nasty contusions, Kane sensed the creature's center of balance shifting forward.

He jumped to his feet again. He straightened, head bent forward, until the monster's crotch and legs came down on the line of his shoulders like a yoke. At the same time he flung both arms around its pillarlike left thigh. It was like hugging a concrete structural column.

Sucking in a breath and tightening his every muscle, Kane drove upward with all the force of his back, belly and thighs. It was in effect a dead lift, and while he feared the Slump might weigh as much as half a ton itself, he didn't have to heft anywhere near that.

Just keep the thing's immense mass going the way it was already headed…

The Slump planted its blunt unlovely face in the concrete with a shock that bounced Kane a half inch in the air. Or maybe that was just spring effect from having its alien weight no longer pressing him down toward the core of Sidra. The muscles of his lower back and along the lower right side of his rib cage burned as if aflame. He ignored the pain, whirling like a catamount. Then he leaped like one to bestride the vast sloping shoulders as the monster heaved its upper torso up off the street.

Roaring, the giant alien raised its head and began to turn to its left as if to look at its pesky tormentor. Kane enfolded it with his arms, locking hands on the lantern slab of jaw. Then he flung himself off to the right.

The creature's head turned with him. Too far. Its body spasmed as its neck broke with a sound like a great tree branch snapping.

The Slump's final convulsion hurled Kane off to the side. He managed to get a shoulder down and bounced painfully off the pavement four or five times before coming to a stop. If he broke anything, it wasn't of consequence.

The monstrous body lay twenty feet away. Its head was lolled, its face turned away from Kane. Its rump kept jumping upward into the air as its neurons fired their last electrochemical charges, giving it the impression of trying to hump the street.

A ruby laser beam stabbed the pavement beside Kane. Molten debris sprayed his right hip. He smelled burning: vaporized pavement. It had set the baggy khaki trousers he wore over the shadow armor to smoldering.

He looked around. Two squat armored shapes lumbered down the street a hundred yards away, approaching with a rolling gait. A fire team of four unarmored peacekeepers winged out to either side. Another of these fired its laser longblaster at Kane, who threw himself backward and rolled away as the red beam cracked overhead.

"Kane!"

He looked back. Brigid was herding the last of the bewildered slaves around the other side of the parts-floater Domi had used to crash the slave wagon, out of the line of fire. Her laser shotgun would be ineffective at this range.

Domi stood ten yards back from the antigrav wagon's open gate. She lobbed his pressure pistol underhand at him.

Her aim was true. He had to lunge only a foot to catch it in his right hand.

He rolled, half sat up. Overly emboldened by their armored backup, the peacekeepers had trotted past their ponderous allies. Not trusting his handblaster to penetrate that armor, Kane lined up the sights of his pistol on the chest of the closest peacekeeper and squeezed the firing stud.

Recoil kicked the blaster upward over his head even though he hung on with both hands. The peacekeeper farthest to Kane's right fell over backward with pink blood foam squirting from his nose and mouth, pistoned out by the sudden dramatic overpressure of having an invisible cylinder a half inch wide stamped a finger length into his keel-shaped sternum.

Light sparkled white on the front glacis of one of the monitor's armor suits. It rocked slightly back on its heels. Domi had tried her luck with her own grav-gun against the armor. Apparently the power suits had some kind of force screens.

"Grant!" Kane shouted. "Get here ten seconds ago!"

"On the way, point man," Grant replied from the rescue aircraft. "Take a little while, though."

While the various enemy races were going still at it overhead—the coalition had reported more fleets kept arriving and instantly flinging themselves into the fray—they were too busy to pay much attention to events on the surface. But the attempts to seize Kane and his companions after their arrival showed that some at least of the battling council species were aware others had followed Bates from his home world, and thought they might be able to win some advantage by snagging them. Or insuring somebody else didn't.

There were also purely planetary enforcers to contend with, both occupying peacekeepers and those belonging to the quisling planetary government, who though corrupt, demoralized and badly armed could still interfere lethally. So the small flying disk Grant now piloted to the rescue had been compelled to hide out some miles away from Khaduli.

And speaking of badly armed but potentially lethal, Kane quickly blasted the other unarmored peacekeeper to his right and dropped one to his left as Domi chilled the last. Then he had to roll aside as one of the armor suits sent a yellow beam of destruction probing toward him. The blast rolled him along the pavement.

"Kane!" He wasn't sure if he heard Domi's voice through the comm net or the somewhat thin, dusty air of the planet. "Run! *Now.*"

He did. For all the doubts he might entertain about the little albino in other aspects of life, she was lethally reliable in combat. He hopped up and sprinted away at an angle toward some top-heavy ville structures leaning together like drunkards alongside the broad street.

He heard something clunk twice off the pavement behind him. He launched himself into a prickly man-high growth that seemed to be sprouting like a weed from between a couple of slabs of sidewalk.

A powerful gren cracked off behind him. Unprotected face and hands lacerated by sharp, stiff blue leaves, he twisted his head to look behind him.

A virtual sea anemone of white smoke tendrils was shooting away from a dense central cloud. Each tendril was tipped by a tiny blue-white star. He felt something strike the back of his left calf. It felt like being flicked with a finger.

He looked down. A tiny white light glowed there, gouting dense white smoke. "White phosphorus!" he yelped. Team Phoenix had shared some of its supply of the devilish bombs with the Cerberus crew for this mission.

Already he felt warmth on the back of his calf as the phosphorus flake, unquenchably burning at a heat sufficient to melt steel, began to eat its way through even his shadow suit. He gouged at it with the muzzle of his pressor pistol: better have a hole burned through the wep than him. The vicious little star fragment came away, glowing on the tip of the rod-like barrel. He scraped it quickly off on the pavement.

Through the central smoke cloud the gren had left, already breaking up into a sort of plant with many waving fronds, the two armored suits emerged. They were apparently unscathed by the blast.

But each was covered in a constellation of tiny, bright, smoke-bleeding stars....

One turned toward Kane. He rolled again. The bushy weed he had dived through burst into orange flame and oily black smoke. He jumped up and darted between buildings. He heard a loud bang and the rumble of a concrete facade, beam blasted, collapsing into the street.

"Domi, run for it!" he shouted. He darted along the rear of the building he had sheltered behind, peered around the wall.

A rocket flashed along the street, obviously fired from a boxy launcher mounted on the shoulder of one of the power suits. It exploded beneath the open rear of the slaver's grav-sled. The heavy vehicle was tossed into the air, rolling over to the left. It went right over the head of a fleeing Domi, wreathed in smoke and dust, to smash a trio of storefronts alongside the street.

Kane's lips peeled back from his teeth in a grimace of fury and frustration. Domi darted behind the salvage floater where Brigid and the freed slaves sheltered. But another such missile would strip that protection away and leave the two women and the helpless captives totally exposed to the fearful firepower of the powered armor. Including Pine's brother, without whose gifts, Bug Mama assured them, they had less than no chance of stymieing Gilgamesh Bates.

Kane dashed forward with his pressor-pistol held at full extension in both hands, fired a blast at the side of the head of the nearer suit, then another. Both sparkled into futility on the force shield.

"Come *on*, Grant," he muttered through clenched teeth, more to himself than his partner, whom he knew was straining the unfamiliar alien craft to do just that. He waved his arms and shouted.

"Hey! Over here, you big bastards! Whoa!" He fired again at the power suits simply to distract them.

Suddenly the farther suit stopped dead. Then it began to totter in a small circle. The other suit flung up its thick arms, throwing away some kind of squat blaster it gripped in a mittenlike metal gauntlet as it did so, and walked with choppy slow steps toward the buildings on the far side of the street.

Kane realized he could no longer see the little stars of phosphorus clinging to the outsides of the armored shells.

Instead, white smoke now poured out of dozens of tiny holes through the thick metal plate.

"Shit," he said. It was a tough way to go, even for such a pair of ruthless alien bastards.

A flurry of blue-green bolts slanting down from above struck the figure fleeing in slow motion from Kane. The armor shell split open like an egg struck with a hammer. Whatever was burning inside was vaporized or blasted apart by the energy bolts. A second burst shattered the other power suit and its occupant.

A shadow stole across Kane. He looked up. A silver disk twenty yards across floated no more than its diameter overhead, blotting the violet sky.

"If you're done screwing around down there, Kane," Grant's amplified voice boomed down like thunder, "gather up the captives and hustle your ass aboard! The bastards upstairs have noticed us. Our friends report that small craft are busting out of orbit and coming down to investigate."

Chapter 22

"My friends," Bates said, and such were Grand Council acoustics that he had the pleasure of hearing his voice, amplified, ringing out to the ranks of delegates from a hundred alien races gathered about him in the vast amphitheater without risk of feedback spoiling the effect. Which was fully as splendid as his most megalomaniac fantasies might have wished.

"My friends," he said again, though he knew the odds were pretty good that behind each and every alien visage, or equivalent, pulsed a burning desire to see him, Gilgamesh Bates, in Hell with his back broke, as his grandmother used so charmingly to express it, "I thank you for the trust you have chosen to repose in me.

"From this day forth begins a new era of peace and plenty! Not just for our Far Arm—for I know you are all much too noble and selfless to try to hoard the benefits of this new order for yourselves. But for the Milky Way galaxy as a whole. And who knows—tomorrow the universe itself might be brought under our benevolent sway!"

That got them. The wave of exaltation washed over him. They may hate him, hate even worse the dire necessity that had led them to this pass: the hideous yet inescapable logic that they could trust him, an outsider, long before they could trust any one or any combination of their own factions or races or even individuals within their own species.

To exercise ultimate power.

The prize was his.

And all that remained was to negotiate the protocols necessary to secure the source of that power: the universal doomsday device known to legend as the Cosmic Eye.

"THEY'RE ALL AROUND US!" Kane shouted, hauling back the rein bar of his outsized mount. "Ride for it! Ride like hell!"

The raid on the grounded Paa longboat was ambitious. The coalition needed some means to reach orbit, to launch a smash-and-grab raid to get Kane into proximity with the man whom he and his companions had pursued for tens of thousands of light-years.

But they had ridden into the claws of a trap.

Death beams cracked from the gray granite boulders around them. Their mounts reared and screamed as ozone filled their sensitive wide-flared nostrils. Pebbles and sand, some molten and glowing yellow, flung up by near misses scourged their legs and flanks.

The small birdlike alien who had led them into this narrow defile in the mountains above the pocket valley where the grounded Circle of Life ship lay hidden might have been a prime suspect for treason. But even as Kane fought his frantic mount for control at least a trio of yellow beams from the surrounding boulders intersected on its slight hooded figure. A single screech of despair and agony escaped its scarlet beak. Or maybe just air heated to near-plasma venting from its flash-cooked lungs.

As it fell burning, the holographic sight above Kane's

grav-handblaster flashed yellow. A figure like an erect lobster wearing a gray mane like a wig on its head, or at the least the top of its spindle-shaped torso, was highlighted in the act of firing its own two-handed blaster at the supine, flaming figure of the guide. The blaster bucked in Kane's hand. He was rewarded by the sight of the arthropod falling backward, green juice spurting from a punched-in carapace.

Around him coalition raiders fell smoking from rearing mounts as sizzling or cracking energy beams blasted them. Kane's own mount bucked and screamed as a beam seared its shoulder. Fighting to control it, without any very good idea how, his eyes were drawn to a high point on a ridge overlooking the boulder-lined dry stream the raiding party had been following when the Paa warriors and their vassals hit them.

A solitary figure stood against the sky. There was no mistaking the silhouette of Thand, Pine's jilted suitor, on his mount, with the hood of his antidetection robe thrown back. Kane thought he saw a glint of gold in his beard. Then Thand turned his mount and rode, down away out of sight of the massacre of his comrades.

Kane had the satisfaction of seeing two more crustacean Paa warriors go down to his shots from the back of the crow-hopping, rearing beast. Then he caught sight of a squat red creature that seemed to be mostly belly and mouth, perched on a boulder aiming a bell-mouthed blaster of some sort at him. As Kane spun to try to get a shot off first, the cavernous muzzle gouted golden coruscation.

Kane shouted as what appeared to be a glowing gob of molten metal darted for his face. He fired, saw blood spurt from the squat entity, black in the arc-welder sunlight. The

molten glow spun, expanding into a circular net of glowing golden filaments. Kane tried to avoid it by throwing
himself backward over the saddle's high cantle and down
his beast's slanting croup.

But it struck him, enfolded him, entangled him in sizzling
discharges that filled his brain and nerves with yellow fire.

Then darkness.

"LORD GILGAMESH." It was Chaufat himself, approaching
Bates's high seat in the amphitheater. The Zuri noble,
though high both by birth and military rank, seemed to embrace subservience to Bates. Even though Bates had yet to
be acclaimed dictator...a small matter of delivering on his
promise of leading his new peoples to the Cosmic Eye.

Around them fresh debate raged in a cacophony that
would have come close to deafening Bates had he not been
able to surround his chair with a hush-field. The sound
damper was instructed to pass oral communications addressed to him directly, and those only from parties he speci-
fied. Chaufat was among those so permitted to speak to him.

I should have expected this, Bates thought wearily, not for
the first time. They have agreed in principle to declare me
dictator. Now they wrangle endlessly over protocols. He
knew that he would have to indulge his subjects—for a while.

It would give him time to perfect his plans.

Chaufat halted the ten feet away his culture demanded
as a gesture of respect and bowed. "Forgive me this intru-
sion, I beg you, Lord."

It could only make Bates smile behind his beard. "By
all means, good Chaufat. I know you would never dare do
so without ample justification."

Chaufat practically wiggled at the implicit whip-crack. Authoritarians were so easy to manipulate; once you held the whip hand, it almost wasn't fun lording it over them. They craved submission so. Not like the damn totalitarians of the Circle of Life, who wanted to emote endlessly, whether before clamping down or caving in. And it was a bonus that he'd drawn the Zuri with their cavalier courtesy as dominant race of the Triangle, a position they had attained a scant ten thousand years ago. Hard-edged authoritarians, such as the twentieth-century military officers he'd spent so much time dealing with, were boring and officious.

"The Paa report they have captured one of the humans you alerted us to be watchful for, from your very planet of origin. A male, if they can be believed." The translator software was so sophisticated that his skeptical intonations, that the archenemy Paa were to be trusted in anything, rang through clearly. "He is being brought to this battle-planetoid straightaway, as you have ordered."

"Very good, Chaufat. Very good indeed. You have done well." Actually the Paa had done well. But Bates knew no authoritarian would dream of contradicting a superior who praised him. And frankly Bates would rather praise a good Zuri without cause than the most extravagant success from the Paa, who enjoyed everlasting pride of place on Gilgamesh Bates's list of enemies. Of all the many enemies he had made, and he had made a great many indeed, none had actually gone so far as to torture him before.

"I will interrogate the creature privately when he arrives." He looked around. Even with the sound damper up he could tell the thousand-voiced argument blatted on as cacophonously as ever. If he was any judge of these matters, they could play this out for years. Possibly millennia, while keeping up the space battle outside without interruption the while. These aliens took the long view.

He did not. When he judged they'd had enough fun, he'd give them the toe of his boot in the spot where it would do the most good.

"I will retire to my chambers to await the captive," he announced. "I need a rest anyway."

Chaufat touched the moist tip of his snout to the deck plating. "He shall be brought to you straightaway on arrival, Excellency."

Bates only hoped he'd have the self-discipline to wait until he caught some more of his old tormentors from Terra before exacting punishment. It would be so much more rewarding to have an audience, both to empathize with their comrade's pain and anticipate their own.

Bates stood and actually rubbed his great pallid hands together. This is going to be fun, he thought.

WITH SHINY PINCERS CLAMPED on either biceps, Kane was frog-marched down the echoing alloy corridors of the alien battle planetoid. His guards were two six-foot-tall crayfish with big grasshopper-like hind legs, a pair of two-foot pincers and two central set of arms with more conventional hands sprouting from the thorax. They were shiny metallic silver all over; he couldn't tell if they wore armor over their carapaces, if they had plated their exoskeletons, or if they actually had metallic shells.

It didn't matter either way. Their claws might as well have been welded to his bare arms. He felt a trickle of blood run down the left one from a stinging cut in skin.

You're a long way from home, point man, he thought. The words echoed in his brain like his own booted footsteps in the high arched corridors of alloy steel.

Like a bell tolling his doom.

"WELCOME TO MY HEADQUARTERS, Mr. Kane," Gilgamesh Bates called out grandly as the door hissed shut behind Kane and his inhuman guards. "I must admit I'm surprised to see you. I would have thought one of my erstwhile employees would be first captured. They appear to have acquired quite a case of monomania concerning my humble person."

"You have a gift for making people hate your guts, Bates," Kane said.

The pair of heavily armed Zuri bodyguards who stood flanking Bates's formfitting easy chair growled at his insouciance. The fur of their neck ruffs was already bristling from the proximity of a pair of silver Paa warrior elites. Clawed hands fingered the triggers of weapons and the hilts of pain sticks.

"I won't ask how you managed to follow me here," Bates said. He sat at ease, his long legs crossed. A cigar smoldered between two of his long spider-leg fingers. The battle planetoid's HVAC system sucked up most of the smoke, but a waft that reached Kane's nostrils didn't smell quite right, somehow.

"The fact is," Bates said, pausing to draw on the stogie and savor his mouthful of smoke, "that I left a trail wide and clear enough even for you and the ever-unimaginative Team Phoenix to follow."

"What are you talking about?" Kane asked.

"Show respect for the honored life-form," one of the Paa warriors rasped.

Bates waved a negligent hand, drawing a short-lived line of blue smoke. "He won't. Don't concern yourselves. It matters hardly at all right now. And before long, it won't matter at all."

He leaned forward and his eyes gleamed in his long, pale face. "It's important to me that you realize your friends are trapped, Kane. All of them. Just as surely as you are. I've trapped you all. I drew you here across half the galaxy so that I could deal with you once and for all. And I shall. The only question is how long it will take to scoop up the rest of your motley band.

"I only hope the rest are rounded up before one of my new allies gets impatient and decides to vaporize that arid, cheerless little world. I'd hate to be cheated of the pleasure of watching each and every one of you die at length."

"The feeling's mutual. They'd all hate to be cheated of the pleasure of watching you die, too. Bates."

Briefly Bates scowled. Then he laughed and sat back. His smart-gel chair bobbed slightly. "Where can I lay my hands on your compatriots, Mr. Kane? If you tell me their whereabouts, I promise that Brigid Baptiste will be granted a quick, clean death."

Some of the emotions that suddenly seethed inside Kane had to have bubbled to his face, because Bates laughed again.

"It surprises you I know how you feel toward the woman? Remember, I enjoyed access to the computer files of Cerberus redoubt. I was able to read not just personnel files, but even personal diaries. Fascinating reading, in parts."

"I didn't keep a diary."

"Ah, but others did. What do you say? Remember that the best you can hope to achieve by not telling me is to prolong the inevitable."

Kane jerked his head toward the glittering silver-shelled creature who held his right arm. "Tell these chrome-plated lobsters to let me go. I don't think too good with blood circulation cut off to my hands. Just the kind of guy I am."

"I could order them to snip off both your arms with their pincers. They could do it, you know." He snapped his fingers. Kane winced as the painful pressure increased on both arms. "Quick as a flash. Except I already know that you're an iron-jawed stoic type. Which is why I didn't bother offering you a less…exacting death. So I will humor you. For the moment."

"Lord Gilgamesh!" one of his Zuri guards exclaimed in protest.

"Don't question me!" Bates snapped. The guard cringed. "Besides, he has his hands restrained before him. There's nothing he can do."

He gestured. The painful pressure on Kane's biceps suddenly released. His forearms and fingers burned and tingled as blood flowed freely back into them.

"And now, Mr. Kane, quid pro quo. Your answer?"

"Wait for 'em in Hell!"

In three quick steps Kane crossed the distance between himself and Bates. Before any of the alien guards could react, he grabbed Bates by the throat with both hands and dragged him up out of the chair.

Bates gobbled in panic. Spittle flew from his bearded lips, already starting to turn blue under the killing pressure of Kane's hands. From the corner of his eye Kane saw the wolflike guard closing in on him. He side kicked one, felt a rib or some such bone snap.

The other dug his pain stick in beneath Kane's short ribs. Nova pain shot up through his chest, driving air from his lungs, and plunged a white spike of agony through his brain.

And then the darkness washed in over him like the infinite sea and he knew no more.

GILGAMESH BATES FELL back into his chair. He clutched at his throat, gagging and wheezing.

For a moment he feared his trachea might have been crushed. He had never experienced such strength from a human being before. Although, granted, his near-superhuman bodyguard Enkidu had never dared lay violent hands upon his master.

His fear turned at once to consuming rage that threatened to overwhelm his vision. "Wake him," he commanded. "He's going to pay now for touching me. The *bastard!*"

One of his Zuri bodyguards knelt over Kane, who lay on his face on the colorful carpet. The creature looked up at Bates with despairing liquid eyes.

"We cannot, Lord Gilgamesh," he said. "He is dead."

Chapter 23

"Did he have a hollow tooth?" Bates demanded, pacing the floor of his opulent compartment. "Intolerable! He might have breathed poison gas in my face!"

"Excellency," the Halmi physician said, bowing in its pale robes of blue with a hint of green, "do not concern yourself. He was clearly under a neural compulsion to die. No doubt he was programmed to self-destruct once he assassinated you. Likewise, when it became clear the attempt had failed."

"Neural compulsion? What do you mean?"

"A form of hypnosis, backed by subtle adjustments to his brain chemistry. It instructed his brain, under certain circumstances, to shut itself, and the body systems which support it, off."

Bates scowled. "So the guards' pain sticks didn't kill him, either, then?"

"No, milord."

Ah, well. The Zuri bodyguards and the Paa escort who had brought him still deserved the instant execution he had ordered for their failure to protect him. The thought that one of his enemies might actually lay hands on him, here in his stronghold, at the very moment of his greatest triumph, was so intolerable it made him quivering weak with rage.

"Could we revive him?" At least the scumbag could get a taste of what was coming to him.

But the Halmi waved its slightly webbed hands in a gesture of negation. "I regret not, milord. His very brain chemistry would fight such a resurrection. Indeed, the neural reprogramming he received before being sent here almost certainly included a mind-virus that has already blanked all memories that could prove detrimental to the rebels, even though we employ chemical unspooling."

Bates scowled. He hated disappointment. He glanced around at his fresh set of guards, thinking about ordering the Halmi gunned down to assuage his miffed feelings. Then he thought better of it.

"Very well," he said. "I'll take that much more payment in pain from his friends, then."

The new set of security troops who had responded to his command were heavy-tailed, thick-haunched bipedal beings called Subatip, of a nominally independent Circle race—although membership in the Circle of Life, Bates had quickly discerned, amounted to subjugation by the Paa. Likewise all members of the Triangle of Force were de facto vassals of the Zuri. The actual intricacies of Grand Council law and politics were far beyond both his understanding and his interest. All he cared about was the way things really worked.

And that he'd doped out before he ever made the jump to barren Sidra, now a few hundred million miles distant. Because things here worked just the same as they did back home.

"What shall we do with this detritus, Lord?" asked one of the Subatip in its rasping voice. In full space armor they resembled kangaroos; with its helmet off the creature, with its feathery head-frills constituting olfactory organs, as well as sonic receptors, and its set of pink-fringed nostrils running along each side of its pebble-skinned snout, resembled nothing remotely terrestrial.

Bates shrugged. "Dispose of it with the rest of the trash, I suppose."

EXPLOSIVE DECOMPRESSION is a myth. Unlike traditional myths, about easily pissed-off gods who lived on mountaintops and chucked thunderbolts at mortals to see them sizzle, it's falsifiable.

Unlike those myths it has no basis in reality at all.

If your skin won't stand a lousy one-atmosphere pressure drop, you've got problems without ever having to leave the ground. Such as the skin over your knees and elbows splitting wide open when you try to bend them.

Similarly, a vacuum is bad for you. Leaving aside the minor details such as nothing to breathe, simultaneously baking and freezing and so on, while your skin should hold up pretty well to the pressure differential, your cells will try to equalize and rupture. You'll get red eyes, and petechiae just like somebody who caught a sublethal dose of hard radiation—little blossomlike bruises from subcutaneous capillaries bursting. Eventually, of course, all the moisture will migrate out of your body: but the effect is more that of a freeze-dried raisin than a water balloon.

Not much of which matters if you're dead. Like Kane, say.

One thing the custodial force brought aboard the battle planetoid to clean up after the disputants was efficient at was getting rid of corpses before they started challenging the hulk's not-altogether-reconstituted life-support system. Given the levels of emotion being taken out for rides in the amphitheater, not to mention the back corridors, Kane's wasn't the first chill that needed disposing of before it started to bloat and reek and get all runny. Nor was it likely to be the last.

So it was that Kane's limbs had not yet begun to stiffen in rigor mortis when the trash lock opened and a jet of air— the standard pressure within the station, about twenty percent over that at Earth's sea level—pushed it out to mingle with the stars that long ago gave it rise.

In a graceless sprawl Kane's corpse cartwheeled into infinite night. From out there Sidra was just a purplish dot, and even the nearer ringed gas giants were just oval blobs of lights. Even the participants in the gigantic space battle showed as no more than point-sources, unless they ballooned into temporary nebulae: no combatant was allowed by rough consensus within a light-minute of the planetoid. Its life-support systems weren't all that had largely survived the brush with the improbability-mine. So had enough of its weapon-systems to vaporize any lesser space-war craft, and indeed an unprotected terrestroid planet should one of those happen by.

But craft, either unarmed or with weapons ports sealed and monitored by mixed security parties from both major factions, who boarded from sentry ships patrolling just outside the instant-destruction radius, shuttled delegates constantly to and from the battle planetoid. A much larger current of vessels flowed between it and Sidra, bringing supplies. These ships were not boarded, but merely subjected to a contemptuously cursory neutrino-emissions detection screenings by patrol craft, on the far-off chance somebody was trying to smuggle a hundred-megaton negotiating chip aboard the planetoid. While many carried not strictly legal armor and ship's weaponry to protect them against pirates—or to allow them to indulge in a little piracy themselves—none could possibly carry the firepower to dent the planetoid's collapsed-matter hull plating, or even blast through the internal bulkheads of a landing bay.

The artificial intelligence monitoring traffic near the planetoid noted the presence of the clapped-out freighter near the trash lock, picking its way through the constellation of crap that had already been ejected through that particular port.

It was far from the only ship grubbing through the trash fields orbiting with the station. The AI was programmed explicitly not to care. Like the rest of the junk floating in belts and blobs around the planetoid, the scavengers' only potential military significance was that they might accidentally collide with and neutralize incoming missiles, in case negotiations *really* broke down.

That a little measly tractor beam reached out and snagged the tumbling body of a dead space rat didn't register with the sentry AI at all. Space rats were beneath notice when alive.

"THIS IS SO COOL," Sean Reichert crowed. "A tractor beam! Far out."

"It shows how much we love you that we're letting you play with it," remarked Larry Robison, lounging in one of the seats on the bridge. The battered space freighter had had a bridge-module designed for humans dropped right into it: plenty of swaybacked, junk freighters had space rat crews, throughout the Far Arm. Crewing such ships was precisely the sort of half menial, half technical labor the Grand Council major races deemed the ubiquitous humans most suitable for.

"Especially since he won't let us drive," remarked Major Mike Hays, who had accompanied the youngster into the bowels of the battle planetoid, which now filled the whole starboard side viewscreens like a wall across the cosmos. The planetoid wasn't actually as big as Earth, but here within a mile of its hull it didn't look much different than Earth did from a thousand yards up. If Earth were made of metalloid collapsed matter, that was, with a dull green-gray sheen.

"No way," the pilot remarked without heat. Grant sat in the main pilot seat. He controlled the freighter by selecting menu choices with his eyes and moving his hands through magnetic fields projected from the arms of his command chair. The piloting display was projected in such a way that only his eyes could see it, as aural impulses were tight-beamed directly to his ears. For a hot combat pilot of his accomplishments the control interface had been ludicrously easy to learn, since it was designed to let even a half-educated space rat operate with only a few hours' instruction. Or pretend to operate while the AI actually ran things. But coalition techs had showed Grant how to override the AI: he was actually driving this junker, even as he insisted.

The ship which, for a number of reasons, Team Phoenix had dubbed the *Rolling Stone*. Grant didn't care what it was called, so long as he got to drive.

"Too bad," Robison remarked, taking a drink of bracing purple fluid from a synthetic bulb. It didn't taste half bad, he reflected, even though it looked like something that might drip onto your driveway. "It's gotta be way cool to pay a ship the way you would a Theremin."

"Whatever you say," Grant said distractedly. Larry figured he didn't know what a Theremin was.

Fortunately, the big guy knows what piloting is. Things could get very, very tricky here in extremely short order....

"Got him," Sean said, waving his hands as he sat next to Grant. The setup whereby he controlled the ship's tractor beam was virtually identical to the one whereby Grant piloted.

The youngest team member showed no visible ill effects from the injury that had nearly killed him but a couple of days before. One thing about Far Arm medical technology: if you weren't killed outright, it could generally bring you back, as good as new and in pretty short order.

Indeed, even if you were killed you could be quickly and efficiently restored, provided that your brain was mostly intact, or that you weren't vaporized. Which after all wasn't a particularly rare occurrence, given the energy levels at which social disputes were carried out in this culture.

"Bringing him to the lock—*now.*" Reichert made a little flourish of his hands.

Robison couldn't help but wince for fear the kid might accidentally activate the wrong choice on a menu only he could see. But then, *he can see them,* he thought, *and I can't.* Although Robison could theoretically summon up a repeater display, without the capability of issuing commands to the ship himself.

But Team Phoenix had been carefully chosen, trained and also seasoned into one another's company. Give the devil his due, Bates and his human resources trolls had done their job well. The team worked together with the smooth unspoken efficiency of a jazz quartet. And one habit they had all conditioned themselves to, no matter how contrary to each man's personal inclinations—and each was in his own way inclined to micromanage, intrinsically unwilling to relinquish control over any given situation—was to let a man do his job without peering over his shoulder.

"Confirm package retrieved," Grant said, deadpan.

"You don't sound as sweet as Magic Voice," Reichert said, standing up and stretching. Robison heard the cracking of his neckbones from three yards away.

"She's prettier, too," Grant said as matter-of-factly as he said most things.

"Enough comedy," Hays growled. He overrode Reichert who began to protest there was no such thing. "Let's get down to the lock and see what we got."

From the set of Grant's massive shoulders Robison judged the man wanted nothing more urgently than to run down and see firsthand to his partner's condition. But his sense of duty and vanadium-steel self-discipline kept him at the controls as he rotated the ship away from the armored planetoid and pointed its stubby, barely streamlined prow back toward the faint violet speck of Sidra. Which only assists from the ship's AI could pick out from the vast jewel field of the Far Arm glittering in the big wraparound screens.

Robison felt a gentle sense of rotation, then of acceleration. The first was an illusion, produced by the ship's internal gravity controls to alert its passengers it was maneuvering. The second was in effect permitted to be felt, a fraction of the actual acceleration delivered by antimatter drives and reaction mass consisting of hydrogen atoms and micrometeorites sucked in by big invisible scoop fields that winged out before the ship, clearing the ship's path, as well as propelling it. The real acceleration was about seventy gs. Roughly what you'd experience free-falling from an aircraft at altitude.

Only not falling, but smacking the planet at terminal velocity. It's always the landing that kills you, the aviator in him reminded himself, not too smugly, as he followed his friends aft.

IT WAS TOO BAD he turned at just that moment. Because no sooner had he looked away from the huge display screens curving across the front of the semicircular bridge than all hell broke loose across them.

Chapter 24

Brigid opened her eyes. Briefly she saw, not her present surroundings, but the terrible scene that had filled her mind only an instant ago, by her perception.

"*Anam-chara*," she breathed.

She felt a pressure on her right hand. She turned her eyes blindly that way. In a moment the image of Marina's concerned young face resolved out of blur.

The background, the bulkheads of a compartment aboard the coalition blockade runner, stayed dingy yellow.

Now she was back to herself, all cool archivist again, and her first thoughts were of duty: "Did he get the information? The boy—" Her words wandered, mirroring her mind, and she chastised herself for weakness. Focus! What's happened to your discipline?

"Take it easy, Ms. Brigid," Marina said. "That had to be hard on you."

"And to answer your question," came another voice, likewise feminine but brassy and self-assured, "yes. Even though it was, as your cohort Major Michael pithily put it, a 'psychic Rube Goldberg device.'"

With an assurance beyond her years the Atshuara girl helped Brigid sit up. Before she could force another word out through throat and lips she realized suddenly were parched, and a mouth that seemed packed with cotton, she felt a cool bulb being pressed into her hands. Marina guided Brigid's hands upward to her mouth. On proximity the bulb extruded a drinking nipple, and Brigid gratefully sucked down cool water.

"An appropriate characterization," she said, and managed to get close to her customary professional crispness. In fact she only just barely recognized the reference, by dint of expertise gained in literally years of study and analysis of twentieth-century culture and technology as a Historical Division archivist in the barony of Cobaltville. "It hardly seems possible, though—such abstruse data, transmitted through so tenuous a link, in so short an period of time."

"Your psychic bond with Kane is extremely powerful," Bug Mama said. She still wore the antidetection robe the coalition resistance had worn planetside, with hood thrown back to reveal her outsized head and huge gleaming eyes. "Far more powerful, actually, than either of you is consciously aware of. Or admits to yourself, maybe. I can't pretend any direct knowledge myself. I have the psi capability of a basalt slab, and not even our Groks, with some of the highest psi potential and skill indices of any races known to our history, can make much sense of human thoughts anyway. Probably one of the reasons we keep you around. Anyway, we did get the coordinates, Svarri did get the coordinates—loud and clear. He's a wonder, that kid, and no mistake. But the truth is, he hardly needed to."

"The Devil's Eye," Pine's voice said.

Brigid turned her head the other way to see the young woman standing on the other side of the couch with her hand on the shoulder of her brother who stood beside her. He was a slight lad with sandy blond hair and a freckled face. Despite having just been rescued, against all probabilities, from alien slavery, and knowing as well as everybody else aboard the *Forlorn Hope* that they were about to run the gauntlet of a potential concentration of firepower approximating the output-over-time of a supernova, he looked, well, normal. Or what some instinct or atavism buried deeply in Brigid's skull, told her *normal* was like: a friendly, open innocence, curiosity, acceptance. So unlike the pinched tension never absent from the faces and frames of children in a baronial Enclave, or the fear and want always mirrored by outlander youngsters, the wariness they always showed even at their most apparently abandoned play.

He was an extraordinary child, she realized as he grinned shyly at her. And not just because of his psychic gifts.

"Who would have expected it?" the young nonterrestrial human woman said. "It seems almost too…obvious for a cosmic secret."

"The Devil's Asshole," Bug Mama said. Brigid sensed her grin. "Pine's polite. I'm not. Although 'Eye' may be more appropriate in one way, it's not so much, in another. It's a naked-eye object from Sidra, a black hole binary not thirty light-years away."

"What's that mean?" asked Domi, who had been uncharacteristically quiet these last few minutes. "In plain English. Or, well, bug."

Pine looked distressed. Bug Mama's laugh was translated duly by her device, a rich contralto bubble of amusement, with a hint of gravel-road rasp, just like the usual speaking voice it gave her. "Plain bug it is, then. You know black holes, child?"

Domi shrugged. "Sorta."

Bug Mama chuckled again. "That's all anybody understands black holes, even after a million years of studying them. They're like God—nobody can really know anything about them, theorize as we might. And you're wrong."

The last she said turning her huge eyes with their weird black darting eye-spots to Brigid, who indeed had been about to interject. "You may think your scientists have a good theoretical model of what black holes are really like. No doubt your draggle-tail Annunaki, who think they're so important bullying a backward, backwater planet think they have one too. But you're wrong. Every theoretical model we've concocted, some observed fact has come along in a thousand years or a hundred thousand and knocked on its kiester."

At that word Brigid cocked an eyebrow. She didn't know what surprised her more: that Bug Mama would use an word analogous to that slang term, or that the translator software knew it. Had it come from Bates? From one of Team Phoenix, more likely, she thought; the software was highorder hermeneutic and learned quickly from experience.

"Anyway," Bug Mama went on, "a few million years ago, long before even the cycle of Arm civilization the War of the Eye knocked to bits got started, a couple blue supergiants formed a fairly close binary system, each rotating around each other. They were so evenly matched in size that they sucked matter out of each other, causing big blazing trails of cooler yellow gas to swirl around 'em. And, yeah, you Earthers might have some kind of cockamamie theory why that can't happen, either. Wrongo. We actually have artifact records—vids—of the whole thing. The ancients thought it was pretty noteworthy, too.

"Especially when one of the big bastards blew up, as supergiants will. It naturally caused the other one to go off right away. The resulting radiation wave wiped all life in nearby systems. It scoured Sidra of everything but deep-ocean life-forms—Sidra had deeper oceans then, before UV from its sun had cracked so much water into its component hydrogen and oxygen. Life came back on Sidra, of course. Fortunately or not, your call.

"So the remnants of the twin supernovae were, naturally, two black holes. Likewise orbiting each other, and *really* sucking down mass. Not just the double-lobed nebula they ejected from themselves—scarfed that long ago—but they've pulled in at least two neighboring stars and are even now in the process of ripping another one apart with their monstrous tidal effects like a couple big carnivores fighting over prey. Hell of a sight, between that and the accretion disk proper. Even from a long way off. You spent a little more time on Sidra, you'd have seen it yourselves— big weird blue glow. Scary even if you don't know what it is. Scarier if you do."

She shook her head. "And *real* scary now that we know what that rascal's been hiding all these aeons."

"Didn't have a lot of time for stargazing," Marina said, sweeping her heavy blue-black hair back from her face. Brigid saw a sheen of perspiration on her dark face in the sourceless yellow light that half illuminated the compartment.

Bug Mama checked a small display inset in the chitin of her skinny right wrist that served among other things as a chron. "We better get to the bridge. One of the biggest light shows since the big twin blues blew is due to bust loose in about forty seconds. It'll be the show of a lifetime, kids. And since the odds aren't half bad it'll be the last thing we ever see, we better get our money's worth."

And now not even duty or intellectual curiosity could bottle up the question in Brigid's heart any longer. "And Kane?" she asked, her attempt to keep desperation from her voice not altogether successful. "He is—?"

"Well, his condition's stable, just as we set up it was going to be." The insectile alien raised arms from her sides in a shrug.

"After all, you can't get more stable than 'dead.'"

THE SELF-CONTRADICTORILY named Coalition of Non-aligned Races was weak. By Far Arm standards, by the standards of the gigantic Triangle and Circle factions. Even by the standards of the major races who dominated them, the Zuri and Paa and their stronger ally and vassal races, they were few.

But trillions of sophonts gave allegiance to the resistance. And they were what their opponents were not: infinitely resourceful, infinitely flexible. They studied and practiced the arcane principles of asymmetric warfare with a master's touch.

And like vast centralized empires over a million years of thoroughly documented Far Arm history, and for mega-years known through fragmentary records before that, neither the Council nor its perpetually warring main parties was institutionally able to adjust to it.

One of the greatest tools the weak had versus the strong was the ability to manipulate that very strength to their own advantage.

The Circle and the Triangle had their counterintelligence officers and dedicated mole-hunters, of course. Millions of sophonts suffered and died at their palps and tentacles and claws each year. Of these many were plain unlucky innocents, arrested by mistake. Many were operators from rival Grand Council factions. And a very great many indeed were in fact loyal servitors of the very power that tortured them to death for imagined treason, set up by authentic enemy infiltrators.

Some were even coalition agents. But, like the coalition itself, relatively few.

Like any vast, centralized organization, the Council and its prime components were a very great deal better at being big than smart.

So it was that, by a seemingly random twist of the fortunes of battle and the intrigue that swirled around all like unseen nebular gases, a million combatant warships suddenly broke off their twisting internecine dogfight and formed a huge wedge that drove like an arrow straight toward the nameless battle planetoid. Renegades from Circle and Triangle and even Paa and Zuri had made secret common cause to seize for themselves the cosmic treasure held inextricably in the brain of Gilgamesh Bates.

Or vaporize that brain and deny its vast and horrid secret to all.

It was an effort doomed to fail. As the coalition moles and provocateurs who had carefully engineered it knew from the inception. As they knew that the odds were vanishingly small that any of them, as individuals, would survive.

But it would succeed smashingly as a diversion for the breakaway from Sidra and its solar system of the tiny ragtag rebel fleet bearing the very treasure such an unimaginable amount of sapient life had been and would continue to be squandered over: the true location of the Cosmic Eye.

As space exploded into an outpouring of energies across far more spectra than the electromagnetic alone, and a populous planet's worth of combatants died in its first minute, the coalition ships lined out in the opposite direction, bound for the relative safety of hyperspace.

Of course, for a single, small, battered freighter dubbed by its passengers the *Rolling Stone*, the odds of survival—here at the interstellar hellstorm's very eye—were slight.

But the occupants all knew the job was risky when they took it. And though men of two drastically different eras and worldviews, all had this in common: none ever expected to get out of this life alive.

Chapter 25

"Caspar van Dien," Sean Reichert was saying when the man came onto the bridge behind him. "Was he ever in anything that didn't blow?"

"No," Larry Robison said. "Because the lights went out all over the world not that long after we went beddy-bye. Poor boy didn't get much chance."

"How are you doing?" Grant asked from the helm without turning. Only the sweat glittering along the line of his short crinkled hair showed the tension he was experiencing as he tried to guide the little, virtually unprotected ship through the bowels of the Hell being created outside its flimsy hull.

Ignoring the way Weaver came just a step behind him to steady him if he swayed, Kane took a sip of the warm broth in the bulb he carried in his right hand. It tasted like a swamper's armpit smelled. He reckoned that meant it was all full of those hydrolytes and nutrients his body craved.

"Like death warmed over," he said. "What else?"

"'Live fast, die young, leave a beautiful corpse,'" Reichert quoted without taking his eyes from the fireworks display filling the wide screens. "Unlike most of us, though, you get another chance to make good on that last one. Which, whoa, respect, you need."

Kane knew he looked the way he felt. He had checked himself in the mirror of the *Stone*'s sickbay as soon as he was steady enough to rise from the examination table. On the third attempt. Even for a man burdened with as little vanity as Kane was, he was conscious of looking like what Joe Weaver once termed "hammered dogshit."

"Look, can we just skip the rest of the living-dead humor?" he said. "I know you guys got a million jokes."

"The poor man's heard most of them by now, anyway," Joe Weaver said.

He stopped then and stared at the surging, blazing light swirls on the displays. His blue-green eyes got as big and round as the rimless lenses before them.

"Holy shit," he said.

"You said a mouthful," Reichert said brightly.

"Jesus," Grant said in disgust.

"I can truthfully say I was better off dead," Kane said. "Why'd you wake me up, anyway? You coulda kept me in the stasis locker till we hooked up with the rest of our little fleet."

"Ever the optimist, are you, Kane?" Hays asked, cocking an eye at him.

"Not so you'd notice, usually. Call it post-postmortem giddiness."

"What's all that?" Kane asked, gesturing at the displays. "Some kind of screen saver?"

"Oh, you know," Major Mike said. "Just a space battle. Biggest one in the Milky Way Galaxy in a million years or so."

"Like I always say, Kane," said Grant, "you got a unique talent for pissing people off."

"I did this? Fill in my memory. Turns out you miss stuff when you're dead."

"You guys're into all this SF crap," Grant said, eyes forward again. "You explain it to him. I got a ship to fly."

"The story to here," Reichert said, after a quick glance around showed none of his buddies wanted to do the honors. "Our hero, the brave, self-sacrificing but maybe not so bright warrior-hero-jock named Kane agreed to let himself get captured by bad aliens on the pesthole planet of Sidra. Sundry spear-carriers bravely lost their lives to prop up the deception—so sad, the lot of indigenous forces. In other words, same-old same-old."

"More succinctly," Kane said in a warning growl, propping his rump against the back of an unoccupied chair.

Reichert pouted and folded his arms across his chest.

"Okay, my turn," Robison said. "You got taken to the big ball of malice out there, where everybody's favorite megalomaniac multibillionaire is getting himself proclaimed Lord of All Creation. He, being the thoroughgoing megalomaniac nutbag that he is, immediately had you escorted into his presence so he could gloat."

"Just the way we knew he would," Reichert said smugly.

"This is 'succinct'?" Grant demanded. "What do you call 'verbose'?"

"Pray you don't find out," Joe Weaver said, deadpan.

Kane waved a hand. "No worse than Lakesh. Not much, anyway. And shitloads better than that dickless wonder Philboyd. Go on."

"So you, hero that you unquestionably are, Kane," Robison went on, with only traces of irony in his tone, "contrived to lay hands on Bates's blessed person."

A slow smile spread across Kane's bearded, still somewhat gray features. "Got both hands around the bastard's throat," he said with satisfaction. "I remember."

"And then a whole lot of things went down, psychically speaking," Hays said, taking up the narrative thread. "Augmented by the remarkable and unplumbed powers of young Svarri, Brigid Baptiste's mind was *en rapport* with yours. There's a remarkable connection between you two you're generally aware of, so that gifted young man tells us. Through that channel between you two, Svarri was able somehow to draw forth from Bates's big brain the coordinates for the Cosmic Eye that's the occasion for all these fireworks. Which our friends tell us have reached such a level that, in a couple years, people in neighboring star systems will be able to see with the naked eye...."

"You guys formed a real, live Psychic Friends Network," Reichert said cheerily.

"They don't get the gag, kid," Hays said.

"I'll save it for Brigid. She will."

"Like we'll live so long."

Kane thought about it for a moment. "That," he said, "is undoubtedly the biggest crock of shit I've heard in my entire life."

"Worked, though," Hays said smugly.

"And then," Reichert said to Kane, "you died."

"Svarri set up some kind of psi compulsion in your deep subconscious," Hays said. "Like a posthypnotic suggestion on steroids."

"With a thermonuclear payload," Robison said. "Okay, mixed-metaphor mode off."

Kane frowned. His memory wasn't clear on everything

that happened after the fierce hot joy of grabbing Bates by the throat. He did remember the rush of exultation, and then a strange sort of serial explosion in his mind, like a string of firecrackers going off, but in weird pulsations instead of bangs.

Then…nothing. The *big* nothing.

"But it was, like, some kind of coma. Narcolepsy, whatever they call it?" he asked hopefully.

"Ah…no," Robison said. "You died. Were dead."

"But we resurrected you," Weaver said. "You didn't even have to wait the customary three days."

"Some great medical tech in this culture, anyway, even if the rest of it is kind of totally fucked," Reichert said.

"Okay, I was dead kind of, ah, a long time," Kane said, frowning. "Doesn't that cause, you know, irreversible brain damage?"

"Well," Robison said, "yes."

"Usually," Reichert said. "But what you got percolating in your brain right now is your basic brew of busy little nanotech assemblers, who are reconnecting the broken connections in your neural circuits and repairing any organic damage, and in general, you know, keeping your brain from turning into mush."

The thought made Kane's skin creep. "I so don't want to know," he said.

"That's cool," Reichert said with a shrug.

"And out there?" Kane gestured toward the screens that were making the interior of the bridge flash.

"Coalition moles, basically, have caused a major mutiny," Robison said. "Big chunk of the warships in nearby space have suddenly clumped into a wedge and are driving hard for the big round bastard back there. And we're stuck right here on ground zero."

"What about the big cosmic secret? Where *is* this thing, anyway?"

Robison shrugged. "*We* don't know."

"No need to know." Weaver said with a malicious grin.

"Mushrooms," Hays pronounced.

"Kept in the dark…" Robison began.

"Fed only horseshit," Reichert finished.

"But the others—Svarri, Pine—shit, Baptiste!" Panic stabbed through Kane like an abrupt ice pick. "Where are they?"

"They busted loose about a minute before you turned up," Grant said, "from the far side of Sidra and headed the other way from all of this."

"Making a clean getaway while the diversion our hidden allies in the enemy camp created draws all eyes and other relevant sense organs," Robison said. "Not that it takes much to set this bunch off. They're worse than a libertarian chat room."

"But with bigger guns," Reicher said. "And they're a lot less worried about who they point 'em at."

Kane sat and tried to digest all the information. "So what do we do now?"

Team Phoenix passed a look around. "We're your basic wrecking crew, guy," Hays said, taking his eternal unlit cigar stub from the breast pocket of the grimy shipman's coveralls he still wore from his stint aboard the planetoid as a spacegoing scavvie. "We break things and kill people."

"Then put everything back together," Weaver said, "given half a chance."

"But policy," Robison said, "is made above us in the chain of command."

"You're weaseling?"

Hays snapped to attention and saluted. "Affirmative, *sir!*"

"Grant?"

"I'm busy trying to dodge out from between a hammer the size of the barony of Spearfishville and an anvil as big as all outdoors. You're always the flight commander, remember? You point—I fly."

Slowly Kane nodded. "Way I see it," he said, trying to make sense of the great flaring sheets and blazes and lightning discharges rippling across the screen, "this amounts to your basic ambush situation for us, even if we're not the guests of honor. And when you get stuck in an ambush, there's only one thing to do—assault right down the throat."

"I knew you were going to say that," Larry Robison and Grant said in unison.

"What can I say?" Kane shrugged.

"Classic one-percenter?" Grant asked.

"Less, most likely," Kane said. "But it'll do for getting along with, as the Irish say." He tipped a forefinger of an eyebrow in the private gesture he and Grant had shared for so long.

"Then here goes nothing." The big man made mystic passes in the air with his hands. The deck seemed to tilt beneath them as the pseudograv produced an illusion of banking and accelerating—a pale shadow of the real maneuver, which would have left them all a thin pink paste on the bulkheads.

"Right...down...the throat."

"Can I at least man a weapons turret?" Reichert asked, dark eyes agleam. "If I'm gonna die, at least I want to get to play Luke in the *Millennium Falcon* first."

"Kid," Kane said, half amused, half disgusted, "these aren't little bitty space fighters out there. They're dreadnoughts. The ones the length of a city block are the babies. Gnats. So if you want to man one of the popguns this spaceborne trash can carries, or if you want to jerk the gherkin, knock yourself out. Either one's gonna come to about the same."

Chapter 26

Into the valley of death rode the intrepid six aboard their ignoble steed.

"Whoa!" Sean Reichert exclaimed, as right ahead of them the whole port side of a mile-long battlewagon shaped like a blunt-ended cigar suddenly erupted with yellow flames. But not fire, although little wisps of blue-and-orange fire did dance around the edges of the greater explosion, where some kind of combustibles combined energetically with the oxygen in the atmosphere being vented. Rather the flames were an outpouring of metal and synthetics and sophont flesh turned in an instant to incandescent gas and stripped ions.

"Hold on," Grant murmured. And steered them straight into the erupting plasma inferno.

The AI-controlled artificial gravity only produced or allowed faint shadows of the violent g-forces of their maneuvering to be felt. But so extreme were Grant's maneuvers through all three axes that what little motion they felt made Kane's stomach do some slow rolls of its own.

Or maybe it was the display. The way the exploding Leviathan seemed to swoop all around them: left, right, up, down, corkscrewing, as Grant strove to throw off any weapons systems trying to track them.

Throughout the oncoming fleet a thousand alarms

shrilled and flashed and buzzed for the attention of bipeds and octopods; things with feathers, things covered in slime; tubs of living clay. A thousand sensor systems locked up the vessel accelerating straight toward the onrushing mutineer fleet. A thousand battle computers tentatively identified a firing pass. A thousand fingers and claws and remote-controlled waldoes tensed on firing contacts.

Then everybody's battle software, running in quantum architectures at a speed to make the finest supercomputer Gil Bates had ever encountered seem like an elderly snail on Quaaludes, revised its conclusions. The intruder's trajectory did not match a firing pass on any specific ship of the rebelling fleet. Nor did neutrino detectors or probability sweeps show signs the small craft carried any weaponry capable of doing more than scratching the paint of a lesser auxiliary battle wagon.

At contact range.

Nor was the blocky salvage ship, unlovely by any esthetic canons of any of the many species now laying the hairy eyeball and whatnot upon its fleeing form, on any kind of kamikaze trajectory. Whoever was driving seemed to be trying to avoid getting any closer than necessary to any of the approaching warships—while, insanely, plunging right through the midst of them.

What saved the Cerberus heroes and their chronically displaced allies in the end, though, was their complete and crushing insignificance.

Nobody wanted to waste the ergs blasting a microbe with thousands of the gigantic warships of the Council fleet protecting Gil Bates and his secret swarming to meet the attackers with blood in their eyes.

SOME GUNNERS SHOT at them anyway. There was always somebody who didn't get the word. And some people were just that way.

But the *Rolling Stone* had a secret, if not a very big or unexpected one: it was a smuggler's ship. Faster than it looked, it also sported one of the less alarming of the myriad forms of faster-than-light drives the ancient alien races of the Far Arm used.

That wasn't the secret. Nor was the popgun weaponry, which all such ships carried against the depredations of, frankly, other ships such as this one crewed by guys a lot like the *Stone*'s usual bunch, who might think to spy the main chance. Sitting in the dorsal turret behind a pair of antimatter machine guns, while city-sized metal machines raved and gibbered and puked and generally acted out with quantities of energy like all of the Nukecaust in each and every dazzling flash, Reichert had to admit that his blasters felt every bit as wimpily irrelevant as Kane predicted.

But as a smuggling ship and blockade runner, the tubby bitch had an absolutely wizard sensor and ECM suite.

And, of course, she had master pilot Grant at the helm.

"MAJESTY." THE MESSENGER prostrated itself on its fleshy pallid abdomen before its huge and terrible ruler in her hexagon honeycomb of gleaming alloy.

"What news, drone?" the queen asked. Such creatures were not graced with names. It was especially so with tech drones of the higher-skill categories, who had a fatal tendency to get above themselves, believing that their skills and knowledge made them somehow special. As tendencies went, it was, when manifested, literally fatal. "Do we defeat the traitors and heretics who dare try to steal away the secret of the Eye?"

"I bring no news of the battle, Great Mother," the creature buzzed and popped. "Of course the great race shall be victorious imminently. Rather I bring word of a communication."

"Delay no longer, wretch, or writhe long on the pain racks, stung with the venom of a hundred correctors!" she hissed.

Perhaps I should have gone to them directly with that vile space rat Bates, she thought. Of course, he was unlikely to have survived, puny and soft as he is. But we'd have spared ourselves all this....

She took stern control of her thoughts. No—the race was fated to seize possession of the final secret, and absorb the Far Arm, the galaxy and the universe as a whole, until all was brought into full harmony with the Circle of Life.

Subsumed within the genes and intellect and very flesh of the Paa, of course. The only race truly capable, or worthy, of sapience. For the time being she had to indulge the charade going on within the battle planetoid, which still hung near her own flagship in space. But she knew the truth.

The drone writhed on the floor mats in such a delicious ecstasy of terror and mental agony. It exuded fear pheromones in such quantities that they oozed down its heaving flanks to puddle on the dark synthetic mat and filled the queen's scent receptors with such delicious perfume that she decided to forgo subjecting it to neurochemical torture. A sign of softness, she knew.

"It is a communication from one of the ships that has fled the Sidra system," it said. "They lifted off from the planet, spacing from its far side, when the attack on the battle planetoid began."

"What are you saying?" the queen both roared and hissed. Her vestigial wings rattled on her furry back.

"The attack is apparently a diversion, O Mother of the Universe," said the tech, sweating rivers of shiny, reeking exudate now. "The escaping fleet consists of members of the renegade Coalition of Nonaligned Races, who, our communicant believes, have come into possession of the secret of the location of the Cosmic Eye."

So great was the eruption of rage and fear phero-mones from the queen's huge body that the silver-shelled immortals who flanked her throne cell instantly lowered their fire lances and pierced the tech-drone's body with eye-hurting spears of energy. Its puffy abdomen exploded in a cloud of flash-heated steam and scalding bodily juices.

Sensitive membranes stung by the energy discharges, her oculars dancing with painful afterimages, the queen squalled greater rage still. From the fur of her thorax beneath either wing snapped long multijointed arms, tipped with pincers like shears. These snipped the heads off the shiny torpedo-torsos of the two bodyguards standing nearest her, who had fired their weapons to reduce the tech into a pile of steaming, smoking, stinking organic refuse in the midst of her throne room. Green ichor gouted once from each body. Then both toppled, their various limbs twitching.

Small furred servitor-beings, her own daughters although scarcely sapient, scuttled from nests within the hexagonal cells to remove the corpses and begin sopping up the mess. A fresh pair of the immortals stationed around the throne compartment shifted to stand flanking the mass of the queen, now quivering with a complex of emotions.

So great was the queen's agitation that she deigned to call upon the flagship's communications AI herself instead of waiting for an underling to do it. All her body servants who were more intelligent than mere animals had darted to comparative, if temporary, safety in the great metal honeycomb.

"Tell the grand fleet," she ordered her ship mind, "to break off this futile charade! Tune sensors to maximum sensitivity! The renegades must not be allowed to beat us to the holy Eye!

"And subject yourself to twenty microseconds of pain-analogue stimulation," she added, to make herself feel better.

"Twenty *micro*seconds?" The artificial voice seemed to quaver.

"Thirty! Now do as I command, or I shall teach you the true meaning of the word *suffering!*"

"It shall be done, Queen of All Life," the ship replied.

"MY FRIENDS." Translated into myriad languages, Gilgamesh Bates's words echoed up the terraces of the great metal dome. Minus the irony he felt, of course—he had naturally learned to command his personal-translation software to suppress that when he desired. "We, the responsible and caring sophonts of the Far Arm, face tonight, together, the greatest challenge in the history of all our races."

And now, Gilgamesh Bates thought as he stood in the focal point of the battle planetoid's immense amphitheater, now we tell these monsters how the cow ate the cabbage.

The population of a small prenukecaust North American city had gathered in the station over the past few days.

Now pretty much all—from so many different species Bates had long since given up trying to keep track—were assembled in the ranks of metal boxes, some containing and maintaining pretty divergent microenvironments, though the vast majority of beings here assembled were oxygen breathers. Or at least did not find oxygen environments too toxic in brief doses.

Inside he seethed with fury. He didn't know whom he was more pissed off at, his incompetent allies, who thought themselves fit to rule the universe but couldn't keep track of a handful of bandits and backwoods savages. Or those savages themselves, his fellow humans from far-off Earth, which he had now decided he would see one last time, from orbit, before having it blown to an asteroid belt.

They're like cockroaches, he thought, Kane and Grant and those idiot ex-employees of mine. You can't kill them, and they won't go away.

Except they *had*—and all indications were, they had somehow, impossibly, stolen the secret of the location of the Cosmic Eye.

From *him*.

A tumult of a lot more noises than Bates was sure he could name settled down as he spread his hands in a gesture commanding silence. He had quickly taught his hearers to respect his gestures. There was an advantage to having enthusiastic authoritarians as his greatest allies. They could be counted on to punish slow learners enthusiastically and rapidly—even as Bates plied his expertise at manipulation to marginalize the offenders getting chastised, and so strengthen the loyalty of the others.

"As you may know by now," he declared, "the secret of

the location of the great and terrible artifact known as the Cosmic Eye has been stolen."

That brought a hush like the vacuum of deep space to the whole enormous hall, for the first time since Bates had set foot inside it.

"Stolen, I say—" he allowed his voice to rise and ring with outrage that was not at all contrived "—by bandit renegades and terrorists. Some who tracked me from my own home world in the distant Orion Arm with the very purpose of stealing that ultimate secret for their own evil, antisocial, chaotic ends."

He turned, holding his arms outstretched as if to embrace every creepy, crawly, fuzzy, chitinous one of his listeners. "My friends, our holy community of life, our sacred principle of order, are threatened now as never before.

"But this I promise you. The forces of individualism, of mere anarchy, will not prevail. I lead you now in a holy crusade, uniting all the races of the Far Arm, in the last and greatest battle of all time—the final confrontation of good and evil. And I lead you to a victory that shall endure...*forevermore!*"

The amphitheater erupted in thunderous noise. The battle planetoid's AI clamped a damper field around him to prevent his fragile tissues from damage by a volume of noise like a hundred jet engines arrayed around him, not to mention the effects of certain unusual high-frequency harmonics, including enough microwaves to fry him to a cinder where he stood. Indeed he saw a couple of gushes of juice and organic goo from boxes occupied by delegates whose own microenvironmental controls were insufficient to similarly protect them.

Meanwhile his translation routine repeated mindlessly to

him in the soft-voice monotone it used to convey concepts that weren't literally translatable: "Wild applause…wild applause…wild applause…wild applause…"

And then from the enthusiastic and perilous din arouse a single strain of chanting: "Lead us! Lead us! *Lead us!*"

Bless my Zuri friends, he thought. I didn't even need to prep them—they're natural shills. And their vassal races and allies, of course, whom the evolved pack predators' abrupt ways with discipline had long taught on which side their bread was buttered.

The chant was taken up, and Bates saw that the Circle of Life delegates had taken up the chant more lustily than any, as if to drown their Triangle rivals and so co-opt the idea.

The idea that the alliance of great races, of factions that had fought as bitter rivals for hundreds of millennia, should be united and led by one…lowly…space rat.

It took all his iron will to keep himself standing upright. Hell, he thought, from dissolving into a mass of undifferentiated protoplasm.

Because he had had the absolute whip hand—and lost it.

There was no reason for these monstrous beings, the weakest of whom commanded power to blot Earth and its reborn alien overlords from the cosmos as casually as wiping their sphincters, to leave him alive. His great bargaining chip was lost beyond hope of recovery.

But in the greatest act of salesmanship in his entire life, he had convinced this collection of monsters that not only should he be allowed to live, but he had to continue to rule over them all. That he and only he could recoup what could still win for them ultimate power.

There remained to him but one final, sublime sacrifice—and risk.

"I thank you, my friends," he said, once more raising hands above his head and bringing them down as if calling creation into being. "And now I will share with you, the representatives of all life and the stewards of order, the secret our enemies have stolen, that the evil individualists may not hoard it for their own selfish ends."

And he spoke aloud the location of the Cosmic Eye.

Chapter 27

"The Paa possess the ability to adapt their genetic coding to that of other species they absorb."

Outside the disk-shaped frigate that served the ragtag coalition fleet as a flagship the Far Arm blazed like a city of stars. It was a modest vessel, not much larger than a prenukecaust sports stadium. The humans gathered on her semicircular bridge, whose design struck Kane as oddly familiar somehow, had gotten blasé about the terrific light show shown on the huge wraparound screens that mimicked viewports. A lot more fearful wonders occupied their minds just now.

"You mean DNA?" Kane asked Bug Mama. Having escaped the space melee that covered the flight of the coalition ships and their cosmic secret, the *Rolling Stone* had made rendezvous in orbit around a sullen red giant several parsecs from Sidra's Sun, as prearranged on the off chance they got away. Bug Mama had waved off all objections that that might prove poor security. If the earthlings didn't get away, she claimed, they'd be vaporized, if not edited right out of reality's fabric by probability weapons, leaving nothing of their memories for even the most abstruse science to reconstruct.

Kane suspected, privately, that the *Stone*'s AI was instructed to vaporize itself and its occupants if it came into danger of capture. Bug Mama had been solicitous, even friendly, as she proposed the desperate plan in their hideout on Sidra, once Svarri was back with his loving sister Pine and her insurgent playmates. But the little insectoid was never more congenial than when she was sending her allied sophonts to face certain death: whether the coalition volunteers, their memories scrubbed of inconvenient detail by a devil's concoction of neurochemicals and Grok mind manipulation, or Kane himself who, like them, had died.

He shuddered. Then shook it off. *I'm alive now*, he thought. *And I intend to keep it that way.*

Bug Mama shrugged in response to his question. "I mean genetic sequencing in whatever form. Although there are surprisingly few systems of such, among which DNA is one—the fact has led certain susceptible souls to postulate that all species within the galaxy arose from the acts of some unknown and possibly unknowable creator race.

"Mother-caste Paa can absorb the tissues of other beings. They eat it, not to put too fine a point on it. Only they divert it to a special chemanalysis organ instead of letting it slide off down the alimentary canal. They can read genetic information from the ingested tissue, select characteristics they deem desirable and assume these characteristics themselves. Or store the gene codes for editing together with others to create highly specialized offspring."

"So they play cute little recombinant-DNA games," Grant rumbled. "Like the Annunaki."

Bug Mama's eyes danced. "Ah, the Annunaki," said the small figure, nodding. "I remember them."

"You met them yourself?" Grant asked.

The big-eyed head shook in a very Earth-human gesture. "Oh, no, not even I'm *that* old, thank you very much, youngster. Read about 'em, is all. They haven't been seen in this part of the galaxy in a good hundred thousand years, that I know of, anyway. Although it's a big arm, to beggar the blazingly obvious, so who knows if they still come skulking out this way every now and then?"

"What happened to 'em?" asked Domi, sitting on a counter eating steaming stew from a bowl. It appeared to be sausage and rice, very earthly fare. It may have simply been a human constant dish, and the kitchen software programmed to account for the tastes of the ubiquitous if disesteemed space rats. The alternative, given the current trend of conversation, Kane decided he didn't even want to think about.

He had to eat too, sometime. Even though the appetite he'd felt coming on had mysteriously vanished....

"In effect, exile," Bug Mama said. "They were too annoying to be tolerated, and too persistent—and powerful in their own sneaky way—to be exterminated. So off they took themselves off to the howling wilderness of what you call the Orion Arm—and also home."

"'Howling wilderness'?" Robison asked.

"Comparatively. In the very far past various galactic civilizations have risen and fallen. The last fall came about, as we told you, with the War of the Eye. Since then no civilization has yet aspired to extend beyond an arm. And your arm has for whatever reasons remained rather backward, in terms of developing true interstellar civilization."

"For which," Pine said in a small, apologetic voice, "you should be grateful."

Servillon looked at her, golden eyes wide with outrage. "How can you say that? Arm civilization has brought the blessings of peace and plenty to octillions of sapient beings!"

"Yeah, Major Mike said. "Like those poor bastards dying by the million back in the Sidra system."

"Over a billion by now," Bug Mama said. "Although combat has mostly ended in that system, and only a few especially conspiracy-minded groups remain behind, suspecting plots. The bulk of the component fleets now follow us."

"Good to be wanted, huh, Grant?" Kane asked.

"You keep it. There are trillions and trillions of beings wanting my black ass who I didn't know existed a week ago. They didn't know I existed, either. I can't think of much I'd like more than to go back to that state of affairs."

"Something I don't quite understand," Brigid began.

Bug Mama twitched her feathery antennae in amusement. "Only something?"

Brigid flashed a rare smile. "Okay, something that particularly puzzles me. Given the Paa ability to assimilate other species' genetic traits—"

"Lamarck gone wild," Robison murmured.

"—or Lysenko," Brigid said without skipping a beat. Hays pulled an appreciative mouth and nodded, as did Weaver and Robison. Reichert looked as blank as Kane felt. "Given that, why would they as a species ever evolve intelligence? Usually, or so we believe—and so such knowledge as the Annunaki shared with their human puppets seems to support— organisms evolve intelligence in response to severe environmental challenges to which they cannot otherwise adapt quickly enough, such as by evolving armor or natural offensive armament or even superior strength and speed."

"Generally true," Servillon said. "Then again, in a galaxy as big as this one, many things are true."

"You can say that again," Grant breathed, "though please don't."

"But the Paa didn't evolve intelligence," Bug Mama said.

"Now you're talking out your...whatever," Kane said.

"Hearts and minds, Kane," Robison murmured. "This ain't our spaceship, and it's a long walk to solid ground. At least with air wrapped around it."

"But she's telling us the most powerful race of all those weird monsters chasing after us in warships the size of Mount Everest aren't intelligent?"

"No, I'm not," Bug Mama said. "I said the Paa didn't evolve intelligence. They stole it."

It became very quiet on the bridge.

"Say what?" Grant said at last.

"The Paa originally evolved as microbes. Bacteria. For whatever reason, they managed to parlay the ability some such organisms have, to exchange gene plasm among individuals of their own species, into something bigger. And, if you ever happened to wander within range of them, far more sinister."

"They stole intelligence?" Hays exploded. "Jesus Christ."

"He didn't have nothin' to do with it," Reichert murmured.

"This is no time to be quoting Steven Seagal movies," Robison said mock-severely. "If it ever is."

"Precisely," the insectoid said. "Some other species, rodentoids, did evolve intelligence. And the Paa, infecting them, obtained it. And used it first of all, of course, to absorb them."

"That's creepy," Domi said.

"Indeed."

"And they can do this to…creatures from other star systems?" Brigid asked.

"Do. Have done." Bug Mama shrugged. "Will do."

"Well, that makes me feel all warm and fuzzy about the universe," Reichert said.

"So what about this rival bunch that runs the Triangle, the Zuri?" Kane asked. "What's creepy and horrible about them?"

"Nothing quite as elaborately grotesque. They're just pack predators with a hypertrophied sense of hierarchy. Bates and they seem to've warmed to each other, from what our spies tell us. They can be quite charming to you if they think you might be superior to them."

"So why don't we just try to hook with them?" Domi asked. "They sound better than these weird germ-things."

"Better is relative, little miss," said Bug Mama, who along with Svarri was the only being on the bridge smaller than the albino girl. The boy sat silently in a corner building three-dimensional projections with waves of his small hands, multicolored lights from the display illuminating a look of keen concentration with just the tip of his tongue protruding from his mouth. "They show a very different side to anyone they perceive as inferior, as individuals or as species. Not to mention those they regard as prey."

"You're saying," Grant said, "they engage in cannibalism?"

"Not since they got civilized, mostly," Bug Mama said. "But unless I want a refund on my translation software, what you're really wondering is if they eat sophonts of other species. Yes, indeed they do."

Robison cocked an eyebrow at her. "Maybe you should get some kind of rebate on that software anyway," he said.

"Nope," she said. "It mirrors my speech just peachy keen. I actually said that, 'peachy keen.' I've been studying your language, in my copious free time. Not too often we come across a lingo utterly unknown to our jaded arm lore. Fascinating, in a primitive way."

Robison looked to the other earthlings and shook his head.

"What about the factions, then?" Hays asked. "This Circle of Life and Triangle of Force jazz. They sound like tree-huggers versus engineers."

"That sums it up pretty neatly," Bug Mama said. "Or they'd like to think it does. The Circle of Life represents the will of the community of all sapient beings—of the universe itself. Of course, that will can only truly be manifest by certain beings of superior mental and moral attainment."

"Like, I'm guessing, the Paa queen," said Kane.

The triangular head nodded, its feathery antennae waving gently. "You got it. Although strictly speaking—and you don't actually need to care about this—she's not the Paa queen. There are a number of queen-caste breeders. There is a Paa queen—the Circle queen is the boss of her, and by extension all Paa. And everybody else, of course, if she gets her way."

"Charming," Robison said. "And the Zuri?"

"They represent the principle of authority," Bug Mama said, "which of course can only manifest itself in certain superior beings who show themselves fit to rule."

"You don't," Kane observed, "make 'em sound a lot different."

"That's because they aren't."

Servillon reared up with a hiss of outrage. A neck ruff of skin none of the earthlings had noticed before flared from his neck, yellow fringed with scarlet. "But that's insane, elder sister! They are altogether different. The Circle represents the consensus, the Triangle order imposed—"

"And both of them crush the individual," Bug Mama said, "and by inevitable extension screw the masses. And all of what they preach comes down to rule by force, naked, pure and simple. You can split hairs all you want. All I know is that I've dedicated my life to fighting both sides."

"Looks like," Kane said, "we all have. At least for the moment."

IN THE DARK OF INFINITE NIGHT, a man sat alone.

It appeared to be a dome extruded through the hull of *Forlorn Hope*, as Bug Mama dubbed her flagship. It was no such thing: such features would offer aimpoints to enemy weapons, and weaknesses in the battleworthiness of its hull; even its weapons were hidden away under armor in pop-up casements and turrets, which poked out briefly to fire and then retreated behind the sleekness of the saucer hull once more. It was a half bubble of space, about eight yards in diameter, somewhere in the guts of the craft abaft her combat information center.

But the walls either sported huge video display, or were the displays themselves: the Far Arm stars in their millions, so close together only the brightest or the nearest could be seen as discrete points of light, blazed forth like a shout of divine triumph made light. To the man who sat cross-legged on the padded deck in the middle of the space it appeared as if he sat, not even in an external observation dome, but suspended in space itself, with nothing but the miraculously maintained atmosphere between his skin and stars.

The door to the chamber opened behind him with a discreet hiss designed to prevent its occupants being taken by surprise—for serenity's sake more likely than to avoid a dagger in the back, he reckoned, though in this messed-up culture you could sure never tell.

"I hope I'm not intruding," a woman's contralto voice said, both soft and husky.

"If you are, it's already done," the man said, "so don't get your clout in a twist about it, Baptiste."

She walked forward, her footsteps silent on the sound-absorbent mat that covered the deck. Her arms were crossed tightly beneath her full breasts. She stopped a pace behind him, just close enough for his keen senses to register her feel without triggering alarms in his subconscious through violating his space.

"The arm races maintain such sanctuaries on many of their vessels," Brigid said softly. "Even warships. 'Chamber of reveries,' the name translates to." She raised her head to look at the splendor revealed in the false viewports.

"It seems a civilized idea."

"Yeah," Kane said. "Everybody's entitled to miss one now and then."

"You don't much like our hosts, do you, Kane? Even though they've a civilization hundreds of thousands of years old, and records of prior civilizations stretching back a billion years or more?"

"What's not to like?" Kane said, his voice a rasp. "Their dominant races are packs of genocidal nutbags who since we got here have thrown themselves a space battle with enough casualties for a rerun of the nukecaust, and that's if they haven't decided to blow away Sidra on general principles, or kinda whacked it by accident. The main redeeming feature for our hosts, here, so far as we can see, anyway, is that they *aren't* those other people."

"Be fair, Kane. They have treated us well. Considering."

"I'm not in the mood for fair. I'm pissed. And 'considering'? Considering what? They set up a bunch of their own people to die and even blanked their memories so they wouldn't, when the shithammer fell, even have the comfort of knowing they were doing it for a purpose. If thàt's a comfort."

He turned and looked at her. His cheeks were drawn, his eyes retreated into his skull. "And I died, Baptiste. Even knowing I had a chance to come back. I *died*."

"I know." Her voice cracked. He turned full to face her. "I...felt it."

"You did?" He shook his head. "Shit. I'm sorry."

Her smile was wan. "It wasn't exactly your fault, Kane."

He shook his head; his shaggy silver-shot hair slapped his bearded cheeks. "But I never even thought about it. About what it'd do to you. I—that doesn't feel right."

"Would you have done any differently?" she asked. "No. *Could* you?"

He looked back forward, to the bright smear of stars across the curved wall of the compartment. "Reckon not," he said so quietly she had to strain her ears to hear.

"And don't think for a minute I'm comparing my sacrifice to yours," she said. "For me it was emotional discomfort. For you it was literally dying. Even if there was a small chance it was temporary."

"I care about how you feel, Baptiste." The words came out as if they demanded to be spoken despite his volition. "Mebbe I wish I didn't. But I can't change."

She came to stand full beside him in the eyes of a billion stars. "Nor can I," she said. "We are linked, *anam-chara*."

She laid a hand on his shoulder. He raised a big hand to cover hers. In the stark star light it was pale, almost self-luminous; writhing scars stood out boldly, a dead, smooth white in comparison to the undamaged skin. The hairs of his hand looked dark, and cast shadows.

Just for a moment the contact held. Then he dropped his hand, and she hers.

And together in silence they stood and sat and confronted the infinite alone.

Chapter 28

The great warship shuddered as torpedoes tipped with anti-matter warheads launched. The screens of a Paa battle cruiser sparkled as a thousand decoys hurled themselves against them. At least one actual missile threaded the needle of its counterbattery fire and found a weak point where the capacitors had discharged under the assault of dud missiles. A section just forward of the real-space propulsion array flared white.

Sitting in the combat-control center in the bowels of his flagship, Gilgamesh Bates smiled. The glare spread through the great warship like some kind of organic blight seen in fast-motion: white brilliance vented through seams previously invisible, running forward along its bulk and then suddenly blazed forth in patches. These quickly spread to grow together as the whole latter half of the battle cruiser consumed itself.

All was not going the way of his New Order forces however. Off to the right he could see where a swarm of tiny craft, each little more than ten feet long and visible only because his own ship's battle-AI augmented them for visibility on the display, beset a second Paa battle cruiser. Ripples ran suddenly through the stuff of space itself, spreading from the enemy vessel. Where they passed, the sparks the AI used to represent the tiny attack craft simply went out.

With each the life of a sophont no larger than a terrestrial beaver, formerly of a Circle race forcibly subservient to the Paa, was likewise snuffed out. The fact made no more impression upon Bates than had he been playing a video game.

"Probability weapons," said Chaufat with distaste. "The Paa revel in the filthy things. But they turn to bite them, often as not."

Bates looked to the other alien who stood beside him. Others in the hemispherical compartment sat or crouched, according to their body styles, at consoles facing outward along the bulkhead.

"Does your ship carry probability weapons, Vice Captain Yeinos?" he asked.

"We do, Leader." The alien nodded its elongated head. The Kelm were a mildly humanoid Circle race. The Kelm executive officer sported an outsized cranial bulge above a long, harsh-boned face, all planes and masses. Its skin was pink and yellow mottled in brown that increased toward the rear of its skull, as well as its long, splay-fingered hands. It lacked external hair.

Chaufat growled low in his throat and his ruff rose impressively. But he kept his peace. He knew his place. That was the beauty of the Zuri: they all did.

The ship that had devastated the swarm of microcraft came under attack from a pair of Zuri saucer cruisers. The screen flared with energies, many of which, like the presence of the now-vanished Mitsai fighters, were only visible to organic senses because the AI helpfully mapped them on the screen: not just beams, but sheets and spheres and fields of swirling brilliant force lines.

Marvelous, Bates exulted. All that power.

And it was all going to be his. Soon and soon. Because the vile Paa had screwed the pooch.

Big time.

SOMETHING—PROBABLY A SPY—had warned the grotesque monsters who ruled the Circle of a breakout from Sidra's surface by rebel forces. Evidently Uvaluvu had leaped to the conclusion that the small fleet was bound for the system that held the Cosmic Eye. She had therefore broken her remaining loyal forces out of the action defending the neutral-ground battle planetoid and hurled them into hyperspace pursuit, either tracking the fugitives by the probability-distortions of their hyperspace wakes or simply informed by spies of her own.

Bates knew all this because of *his* spies.

The Grand Council system that had ruled the Far Arm, after a fashion, for almost a thousand millennia, wasn't so much rotten with spies as permeated with them. Bates had perceived this smart quick, even before jumping from the safety of his extraecliptic space station into the furred, chitinous, treacherous arms of Uvaluvu. Indeed, it had been his saving from her torturers, since the discovery had led him to make other arrangements with the Paa's blood rivals, the furred bipedal Zuri.

Once liberated he had, all the while cultivating the Zuri's combination of mad cavalier vanity and inborn desire to lick the boots of a truly strong leader, also begun sending out feelers for the disaffected. They weren't few. The Paa were as monstrous to their own underlings as they were to foes, and as for the pack predator Zuri, they brutalized those weaker as enthusiastically as they toadied to higher authority. And so he had quickly built up his own intelligence network, and used it to drive his own intrigues.

It was fortuitous, and damn helpful, that the Zuri and therefore the powerful Triangle of Force faction had declared outright for his plan to unite under his own selfless command. It hadn't been necessary. He had cold-decked the ad hoc parliament meeting in the moon-sized hulk like an old-time card sharp.

So he had gone about subverting the arm's power structure even as he sought to bend it to his own ends.

It was still in its way a shame about the Paa; they were capable monsters, he had to give them that. To seize and hold the dominant position in one of the Grand Council's two main factions for a hundred centuries and more required both ruthlessness and ability. He would of course have settled accounts with the unspeakable Uvaluvu. But he intended to make use of the Paa as lieutenants, as he did the Zuri—playing one off against the other.

But the Paa had broken away and acted on their own. Which had given Bates and his agents a chance to turn the bulk of the Paa's vassals and bullied allies against them. Under the very rubric of the Circle of Life, which Bates's agents proclaimed the Paa had betrayed by their selfish act of unilaterally pursuing the secret of the Eye.

It was a shuck, of course. The Paa break constituted a grab no more naked than the whole space battle around Sidra and its vicious blue-dwarf Sun. As an act of treachery it lacked distinction even by day-to-day Grand Council standards. But perception was everything, in politics if not all of life—and among aliens at least as much as among

Bates's fellow humans. He claimed the Paa had committed a treachery unforgivable. For reasons of their own, most of the forces gathered around Sidra were eager to believe it.

And so, still using possession of the cosmic hammer of the Eye as driving force and prize, Bates had forged his new and improved order. They even sallied forth beneath a logo he had cunningly designed: an equilateral triangle within a circle defined by its apices. Already debates raged among its adherents as to which position was dominant, enfolding Circle or the Triangle which defined all; his agents had been assiduous in starting them. It gave the various component races and individuals something better to think about than the whole shadow show Gilgamesh Bates, a friendless space rat from a backward planet half a galaxy away, had pulled on the greatest civilization in the Milky Way....

"IT DOES LOOK like an Eye," Brigid said in hushed tones.

"The Devil's own eye," Grant added.

Domi took a bite from a piece of oval orange fruit brought from Sidra. "More like a butterfly," she said.

"It's all in the perspective," Major Mike Hays said.

It was not the first time they had seen it, of course. The coalition fleet employed the form of FTL drive in most common use in the Far Arm. Its ships advanced in a series of many quantum "microjumps," each covering a fraction of a light-year. Because the jumps had literally no duration, in common with transferences between mat-trans gateways, most of the voyage's length was spent between jumps, in real time/space, while sidereal observations were taken and the next jump calculated. Which caused their destination to swell in the viewscreens in a series of stages.

The leading players in the binary Eye system were of course invisible, though their presence was clearly marked by two accretion disks. The system's most obvious feature, a gigantic cosmic beacon glaring forth like a hundred suns from between those disks, was itself nothing substantial.

"This system is unique in observed space," Servillon, Bug Mama's chief lieutenant, said, "a binary pair of supermassive black holes, sucking in matter from circumambient space. And between them, at the focus of the system, the flux of electromagnetic and probability energies creates a bizarre multidimensional discontinuity whose true nature is as unfathomable to our best instruments as to our theorizing. That is what produces the great glow like the two-lobed pupil of an eye, in the midst of a transparent glowing nebula of gases being drawn into the black holes' respective accretion disks, which are themselves distorted by mutual proximity. Yet there are many other equally enigmatic objects known to arm science. None has ever attracted particular attention to itself as possible location of the doomsday device known as the Cosmic Eye."

"Forgive me all to hell for being all ignorant and everything," Reichert said as they stood on the bridge of the *Forlorn Hope* staring at the glowing strangeness through the great false port of the viewscreen, "but why didn't somebody just vaporize the damn thing when they had a chance, and put an end to the whole issue once and for all?"

Bug Mama's robed arms rose and fell and her neck spiracles fluttered in a sigh. "That would have been best, youngling," she said. "Truly, from the mouth parts of grubs... The truth, sorry as it is to report, is that no one involved, so far as we can ascertain, had the moral strength to resist the allure of ultimate power. Nor even the basic grasp of rational self-interest to see that their surest salvation lay in making sure the device was never used—that if they couldn't have it, no one could. Instead, at the end, their lust for power rose to an unprecedented pitch. Or so we infer, for none survived. Instead in their madness they destroyed each other, so that all that remained, ironically, was the bone of contention itself—the Cosmic Eye."

"All were weighed in the balance," Joe Weaver said, "and found wanting."

The bronze-sheened mantis head nodded. "Just so."

"Why would anybody build something like that in the first damn place?" Grant asked, his tone laced with disgust.

Bug Mama uttered a chittering sound that the translator relayed as a rich amber laugh. "A kind of twisted cosmic Gnosticism, son. Its creators belonged to a sect that believed the material universe was an evil aberration of true creation. They believed if they could turn off the gigantic vacuum fluctuation that constitutes our physical universe, they could purge the true creation of the corruption of matter, and restore all to its unsullied state as pure spiritual essence."

"Whoa," Domi breathed. "That's fused-out big time."

"Like every big evil, in other words," Joe Weaver said, "they wanted to do it for everybody's good."

Bug Mama nodded. "The same old story."

"What about you," Kane asked, "this Coalition of Nonaligned Races? What do you want to ram down everybody else's throats?"

"I can only speak for myself," the insectoid alien said, "but I think most of us are with me, that all we want to ram down anybody's throat is a good, solid distaste for trying to ram anything down *ours*. We're united mainly by our over-riding desire to be left alone to go to hell in our own way."

"Hear, hear," Major Mike said around his unlit cigar. It was unlit by habit: the climate control in this place sucked smoke and smell right out of the air as if it teleported the molecules away. Which so far as Kane knew, it did.

Bug Mama hesitated. "I hope most of us are with me on that. Not all of us are for sure."

"It seems a somewhat irresponsible position to take," Brigid said.

"We're interested in taking responsibility for ourselves," the alien said. "You get too wound up taking responsibility for what other folks do, then you get into taking responsibility for what they believe, sure as pee runs downhill. And sooner or later you get—"

She waved a hand at the baleful blue image glowing on the great screen.

An image appeared in midair: Thand, huge and scowling, with vast-muscled bare arms crossed over a vest of gray fur. He looked every inch the barbarian chieftain. Though Kane knew perfectly well the huge human in fact stood on the bridge of his own corvette, *Sons of Vengeance*, commanding the *Hope*'s small security escort.

"Elder," his 3-D projection said, "our screening force reports multiple emergences in-system, at a distance of just over half a light-year from our present positions."

"How can you detect something half a light-year away in less than half a year?" Brigid and Larry Robison asked simultaneously.

Kane stared at the projection. He'd seen moving holograms: this wasn't one, or so far as he could tell. This gave the sense of *solidity* like no projection he'd encountered, the feeling that, if you swung at that lantern clean-shaved jaw, you'd bust your knuckles on it.

The giant apparently heard. He laughed. "Have you Earthers paid attention to nothing since you arrived in the arm?"

"Lots of ways," Bug Mama said. "Most likely probability perturbation—although there's plenty of probability static from that improbable monster out there."

"Tachyon signatures indicate exclusively Paa vessels," Thand said. "They are fools to employ their probability drives so close to such an object."

Kane leaned his head near Grant's. "For a fur-covered barbarian," he said under his breath, "do you get the uncomfortable feeling this big bastard has forgotten more science than Baptiste and Lakesh together ever knew?"

"Why is that foolish?" asked Brigid, whose brow had furrowed enough to indicate she had overheard Kane's rhetorical query.

"The terrific probability-distortion caused by the black-hole binary," said Servillon. "Probability-drives are inherently unstable and dangerous—frightening things. To use them in such proximity to the Eye indicates rash arrogance unusual even for the Paa."

"Sadly, it looks like they made it," Reichert said.

"Some did," Domi said succinctly.

"Too many," Thand said. "They will shortly detect us and come this way."

"Do your best to stand them off as long as you can, if it comes to that, Thand," Bug Mama said. "For our part we'll do our best to be quick."

Offering what seemed to Kane a somewhat ironic smile,

Thand touched his sternum and brow with his fingertips and winked out of existence.

"Elder," a technician said from one of the consoles, "we have calculated a jump node within the nearer Eye control station, near the curious artifact." The curious artifact was a needle of some unimaginably dense material a hundred miles long, whose presence the *Hope*'s instruments detected. It couldn't be seen with the unaided eye.

Bug Mama rubbed her hands together. "Well, let's go all see what the fuss is all about," she said. "Who's with me?"

Chapter 29

"Excellency," the senior technician said. It kept all its various eyes averted from the person of its terrible queen, "a traitor fleet has entered the system. They outmass us by over two to one, outnumber us in hulls by three to two."

She could smell the fear pheromones that swarmed from it like agitated gnats. She found them good. Which the strictly rational part of her large and complex brain knew perfectly well was the point of such fear pheromones: to appease the wrath of a superior with an overwhelming biochemical message of submission. That didn't stop her savoring it, though.

The pleasure induced by the pheromone-cloud united with a rising sense of triumphal rage. "Let them come!" she screamed, agitating her vestigial wings with a rattling sound that made the drone cringe. "We hold the advantage. Ours is the destiny! The Eye shall be ours—our enemies shall be destroyed.

"And the Paa alone shall rule the cosmos!"

The body-servant forms huddling in the cells and the ant-like cleaning forms crawling across the great metallic honeycombs and the domed walls and floor of the chamber set up a chittering in echo of their mistress's jubilant screech. The drone performed the most complicated gesture of self-abasement it knew with its various limbs and sensors.

"May it be so, Greatest Mother."

Uvaluvu waved a lesser manipulator benignly. "So it shall. You may leave." The creature turned and scuttled away.

"Senior Marshal," the queen commanded next.

A creature stepped from the wall. Like the immortals it possessed eight major limbs, using four currently for locomotion, leaving two pairs for manipulation. In contrast to the bodyguards with their shiny metallic carapaces, its chitin gleamed dully in the same shades of gray iron and brushed steel as the royal chamber and great honeycomb, and highlights from the illumination ran like silver bands across it. Its subtly shifted hue as the being moved.

It was also almost twice the size of the immortals, who themselves were over a foot taller than standard warriors. Size and rank were proportional among the Paa, except for certain nonsapient prime-mover and gross-labor forms. No life-forms larger than the microscopic were suffered to exist on worlds claimed by the Paa, except Paa daughter-strains. Leaving aside the odd member of a slave race and representative of an alien species, who shared a similar status and were seldom permitted to forget it.

The marshal performed a genuflection. It was barely polite, which Uvaluvu failed to notice. Even had she felt less exalted she would have taken no offense: the marshal had no more chance of supplanting the queen than a space rat did. While a degree of upward mobility was granted among both servant and warrior castes, with promotion in rank accompanying infusions of new genetic material, the only way to be a queen was to be born one.

Besides, a degree of arrogance was not just desirable but necessary in a commander of exalted rank. A self-effacing battle leader was of no more use than a timid one. Still, in the past this particular daughter of Uvaluvu's had skirted the edge of unacceptable impertinence.

She did not now. Uvaluvu could smell her daughter's pleasure in the bold and masterful move they were making. Like her queen mother, the marshal could smell conquest. First the Far Arm, and then…who knew?

"Senior Marshal," Uvaluvu said; only queens had names among the Paa. "I understand we have located the renegades."

"It is so," her daughter said. "Several of their vessels cluster near a pair of unfamiliar artifacts, one apparently a space station, one of natural materials as yet beyond our capacity to analyze."

"The Eye control station!" Uvaluvu's joints popped with the thrill she felt. "Can we jump in a commando unit to seize it now? Before the traitors can contest us for it?"

"Negative, Majesty." The use of the honorific indicated that not even the bold and powerful marshal failed to feel a certain trepidation at saying no to her sovereign. She was, after all, no less a slave than the lowliest recycler-mucking drone. "The dimensional dislocations caused by the proximity of two such sizable singularities, to say nothing of the unknowable effects of the irregularity at the binary's focus, render conventional matter transmitters nonfunctional beyond a hundred miles, if even so far."

"Then use our probability transmitters to place a boarding party aboard the station!"

"It will be most dangerous, Queen."

Uvaluvu produced a hiss and clatter indicating amusement, contempt and a touch of disappointment. "Have you grown soft-hearted, Marshal? If our first party vanishes into improbability, send another. And another, and another. We have trillions of warriors—there is only one Eye!"

For two beats of the queen's giant compound heart the marshal hesitated. Then she bowed again.

"It shall be as you command," she said. But troubled pheromones tickled her mother's chemoreceptors.

Afraid, my daughter? she thought as the marshal turned away to issue the necessary commands. Could some genetic flaw be coming to the surface, in this our moment of glory?

It could be, my dear child, that you will not survive the coming triumph.

"QUITE A FIGHT GOING ON out there," Bug Mama said, waving vaguely at the viewport that dominated the ancient satellite's control compartment. Unlike the screens on most contemporary spaceships it apparently was a real viewport, of some unimaginably strong metallic crystal.

There was nothing to see beyond the fearful glory of the Eye itself, except, off at an edge, part of an orange smear where a giant Sun, still light-years distant, was being drawn in and pulled apart by the black holes. As Brigid and Robison had protested, the actual light of the battle that had broken out between the two fleets would not arrive for half a year. But the forces employed that were not bound by the local limitations of relativity were unmistakable. Nor did they even require instruments: Kane could feel a thrill of unease like a dancing in his nerves from the psi weapons being employed, for while the Grand Council races eschewed use of psi for sensing, there seemed nothing they were the least bit reluctant to weaponize.

Or mebbe it's just this place, he thought.

They stood in what the coalition scientists believed to be the main control room of the space station, where they could control the ultimate weapon known as the Cosmic Eye. The Cerberus quartet was joined by Team Phoenix with Marina, Pine and her younger brother, Svarri, both staring silent awe at the image splashed across the viewport, and Bug Mama and her chief aide, Servillon. The control room was surprisingly spacious, ten yards across and twenty long, with the bulk of the station beyond a hatch aft of them.

The Earth humans had not explored after jumping there from the *Forlorn Hope*. They were normally an inquisitive bunch, not to mention paranoid enough to want to know everything knowable about any surroundings in which they found themselves. Perhaps they shared the creepiness that the pervasive sense of age—and unimaginably terrible purpose—engendered in Kane. Despite the fact that the air was comfortably cool, almost neutrally free of smells, and the physical surroundings were as clean and dust free as if they were maintained daily.

Busy technicians of several species swarmed around, examining consoles clearly built for no creature similar to any among those gathered there, trying to discern the secrets of operating the Eye. They seemed unperturbed by the design, indeed oblivious to any inconvenience. Kane realized there was a certain advantage in coming up in a culture in which, outside of enclaves peculiar to one's own race, one had no expectation of encountering anything specifically designed to serve one's comfort or capabilities.

The six-foot stick figure of a Sidran native approached. Gold highlights skittered across its reddish-purple carapace as it stood, storklike, on one leg before Bug Mama.

"Elder," it said in its sibilant, voiceless wheeze, "we have created a heuristic translation routine for the station's information system."

"Incredible," Brigid breathed. "To be able to figure out at all how to decipher a language a million years dead, much less in such a short time…"

"Don't be too impressed, sweetie," Bug Mama said. "While most of the knowledge of the day got wiped out along with Far Arm civilization and all those octillions of hapless sophonts, dozens of whom were surely innocent, an awful lot was left over to become the seeds for our current technology."

She broke open a small gray bud with a horny thumb and passed it beneath her olfactory sensors. "Happens our universal translation routines are known to have derived from the prewar concordance."

"Still pretty impressive, if you ask me," Hays said.

"Suit yourself." She turned to her subordinate. "Have we learned anything useful yet? Or just how to ask questions?"

The creature swayed on its single planted leg. Though the creature looked a lot like a very attenuated human—granted, with hard purple skin and weirdly distorted features—the pose made it look as insectile as Bug Mama herself.

"Spit it out, Wix," she said. "Bad news is news, too."

"While the theoretical explanations of the workings of the Eye are so abstruse as to remain beyond the capabilities of our software as yet," the tech said, "the builders saw fit to provide both an overview of the device's functions and operating instructions in a form I can only call childishly simple."

"Makes sense," Grant said, "if the bastards were that eager to have the universe blown up."

"Almost as if," Brigid said, "they foresaw they might be stymied. And wanted to make it as easy as possible for anyone who found this station to do their dirty work for them."

A cold wind blew right down Kane's spine. "What if the bastard's booby-trapped?"

"Don't worry," Bug Mama said. "We'd have set it off already. No, these religious nutcakes seem to have wanted volition involved in destroying the universe—somebody making a moral choice to wipe out all of everybody and everything as if they'd never been."

"You seem to know a lot about how these loonies thought," Major Mike said.

"It's a gift. So what has been learned, and what revealed? Sooner or later somebody's gonna bust out of the scrum out there and come barreling down on us like a billion years of bad luck."

"First, we do believe that the apparatus can be duplicated," the technician said. "Even though we do not yet understand it. The manual, if you will, indicates the basic principle is so painfully simple as to be self-apparent, once the basic possibility of building such a device is grasped."

"Seems pretty damn far-fetched to me," Kane said. "Why didn't everybody work it out?"

"You'd be surprised, Kane," Brigid said. "Earth's history is full of technological innovations which, in retrospect, seem painfully obvious."

"Think how stupid everybody felt the day *after* the wheel was invented," Joe Weaver said.

"Apparently this binary system is unique in the known galaxy," Wix said. "The instructions claim that once the builders saw the implications, the Eye almost built itself."

For a moment silence filled the compartment. "Oh," Reichert said, "shit."

"Triple shit," Domi added.

"So what does it mean for suffering humankind," Robison asked, "not to mention everybody else?"

"To prevent the Cosmic Eye from being employed to destroy the universe," the technician said, "the system itself must be destroyed."

A hatch at the rear of the control compartment hissed open. "Elder," another technician cried, "we are invade—"

A blast of white energy silhouetted it from behind.

Chapter 30

The technician fell, blackened and smoking and stinking so horrifically Kane could smell the burned-hair odor despite the superpowered ventilation system.

A silvery shape appeared in the hatchway: a Paa commando too tall to pass through a passageway that would readily admit Grant. It clutched a bulky energy weapon in two of its manipulators. Its adaptive camouflage made its outlines indistinct though it stood scant yards away.

Major Mike Hays pivoted. The pulse-plasma rifle he had been carrying slung over his back was in his hands. Its spit an eye-hurting stream. The Paa commando exploded in flame and fell backward steaming.

Reichert turned and hurled a flash-bang gren through the hatchway. It cracked off with a dazzling pulse of blue-white radiance that cast hellish glare and strange attenuated shadows across the control chamber deck. Holding a stubby two-hand particle-beamer he followed it through, stepping to his left once inside the compartment beyond.

A beat later Larry Robison ducked through, crouched and stepped right. He held a Far Arm handblaster in either hand.

Similarly armed, and with his Sin Eater strapped to his forearm, Kane jumped through next before anyone else could move. Like the others from Cerberus he wore only shadow-suit armor. He hoped it worked as advertised against alien supertechnology.

The after compartment was larger than even the control chamber. To either side the bulkheads were lined with mounded, sealed compartments, their shape reminiscent of conformal fuel tanks from a twentieth-century fighter jet, curving upward from the decks to meet the walls higher than Grant's head. Several objects around four feet high and two feet wide stood fixed to the deck apparently at random. Whether they were furniture or instruments Kane had no clue. No one had figured out what the purpose of the compartment, its containers—which had resisted the desultory attempts to open them—or the strange metal fixtures might be.

Not that anybody'd given the matter much thought. Not with the Eye device itself at hand.

A dozen lobster shapes fought with coalition techs and sec men. The latter were five hard-core desert raiders who seemed to all owe fealty to Thand. They had been ordered aboard by Bug Mama despite the presence of eight well-armed and battleseasoned Terrans. Not to mention the seeming unlikelihood of encountering threats aboard a space station abandoned for a million years. The insectoid alien's paranoia had paid off in spades.

The Paa commandos showed as strange shifting shapes as they wrestled with the coalition forces. Through gene manipulation or external technology their carapaces changed colors to match the backdrop. Against the compartment's dark yellow metal their shells gleamed as if they had been extruded from the walls themselves, like antibodies generated by the station itself.

The alien attackers all walked on four legs and used their forelimbs in two pairs, upper and lower, to brandish two two-hand blasters. Each set of frontal members sported disparate manipulators, one "hand" of two fingers and two opposed thumbs, one a fighting pincers a foot long. The lower of the two blasters each enemy carried fired a yellow pulse of some kind that seemed to have no great penetrative capability; as he came through the door Kane saw a fighter hit in the chest with one. His robe flamed up instantly. Beneath it both an armor vest and his own thoracic chitin had been cratered, as Kane saw in a flash. Despite the wound, and its hard-shelled face being wreathed in flames, the stricken warrior fought to raise a handblaster.

The intruder's upper weapon pulsed what appeared to be a cyan laser into the same hole. The coalition fighter was propelled backward against the bulkhead beside Robison by a jet of its own flash-boiled bodily fluids.

Robison ducked, then went to a knee as the creature's smoldering, flopping corpse slumped onto him. Kane raised his twin handblasters, sighted down the right one—surprisingly standard notch and post-iron combat sights—and triggered both.

Like a Terran crustacean the Paa commando had a pair of eyes that jutted on stubby armored stalks from the pointed tip of its carapace and moved independently. One of Kane's searing yellow particle beams blew one off. The other struck between stalks and blasted open the gleaming shell. Dark fluids boiled out.

The headless, eyeless creature fired its weapons simultaneously. Point man's reflex sent Kane facedown on the deck. The energy blasts passed through the door behind him. He had no time to concern himself with what hell they might have rung loose on the other side.

He struggled to get his blasters to bear as the creature, ruptured upper torso still erupting steaming goo like a flesh volcano, blasted bolts left and right at the level of where Kane's waist had been a moment before. Then two more particle blasts reached out and touched it amidships. One of the upper pair of arms, clutching the beam weapon's actuator, was blown away. The other clung stubbornly and uselessly to the blaster's fore end.

Another pair of beams struck it; then another. The creature's frontal armor was shattered. With ropy green-and-brown organs, well-cooked and smoking, slopping out of the cracked open shell, the being fell over backward with a clatter.

"Thanks," Kane said sidelong to Larry Robison, who lay behind outthrust handblasters.

Respecting the commandos' superior firepower, and perhaps wisely fearing the effects of too many stray energy bursts blasted around an enclosed space with the all-important scientists in the command compartment, not to mention possibly delicate equipment, the pair of coalition fighters still on their feet closed with a Paa raider each and wrestled with them. To Kane's amazement, so did the coalition techs.

The whitecoats outnumbered the raiders, at least in this compartment, better than two to one. Hell knew how many others might be aboard elsewhere in the sizable station. But the techs simply had no chance against monsters genetically optimized for battle. When they could not struggle their stubby two-hand blasters around to target their attackers, the Paa dropped weapons to rip with claws and limb spurs.

Kane saw a human fighter eviscerated by a lightning series of savage kicks from a pair of a commando's hind limbs. As he sank to his knees with purple-and-green ropes of his own intestines slopping down his thighs in a welter of blood, he brandished an energy gren with his right hand. Pressing it against the creature's abdomen between her two hind-limb pairs he hugged himself to her and laughed blood as a yellow flare devoured both his upper torso and the alien monster's lower half, and set fire to the robes of two techs who lay dead nearby.

Kane saw what had to be the head snipped off a shrieking coalition tech. As its limbs thrashed in death, the head and upper thorax of the commando that had killed it was engulfed in a ball of yellow-and-blue flame as Grant fired a pulse-plasma blaster from inside the control center.

Even as the techs were torn to pieces they did their work: the Terrans systematically blasted the preoccupied commandos with energy guns. Kane, Robison and Reichert worked from within the chamber, while Grant and Hays crouched in the control compartment firing their heavier plasma weps when they had clear targets—such as when a Paa commando literally tore a soft-skinned humanoid tech in two vertically and tossed the halves away. Weaver stood in the opening behind them, firing single aimed blasts from a heavy laser pistol as coolly and precisely as if taking untimed shots on a firing range.

In moments all the Paa commando were down. So were most of the coalition techs and all the sec men.

"Damn," Reichert said, straightening from behind one of the inexplicable metal fixtures as Grant came into the compartment. "HVAC in here's really something. Hardly any smoke, and the smell's lessening by the second."

Picking himself up, Kane realized it was true. With all the burning fabric and flesh the compartment, as large as it was, should be filled from knee height to above head level by a fog bank of smoke that, he knew from bitter experience, should smell, and feel, like a cross between a tear-gas attack and a barbecue gone horribly wrong. Yet the smoke and stench hardly stung his throat and eyes at all, and indeed the smell, as terrible as it was, was going away.

Light flared from the hatch at the compartment's aft end. An alien voice screamed in a bubbling agony that needed no translation.

"Apparently pain's the universal language," Robison said quietly, standing and replacing the power packs in his weapons as Hays and then Weaver came cautiously into the compartment, hastily stepping aside out of the entrance-way's fatal funnel.

Kane shook his head. An explosion, muffled by bulk-heads, sounded from astern. "We better move out," he said.

"That's a big negative, Kane," Hays said. "This is our specialty. You and Grant stay here and watch the babes."

Domi grinned. Brigid started to bristle.

"Why, Major Hays," Bug Mama said across the redhead's fiery outburst before it could properly get going, "how sweet of you."

To Kane's amazement the burly commando leaned forward to kiss her chitinous "cheek" between bulbous eye and complex mandibles. She slapped his biceps playfully.

"Let's go," he said, straightening, with a twinkle in his blue eyes.

"Not another bug hunt," Reichert muttered.

"We've never been on a bug hunt," Robison said. "And don't tell me what you're quoting—I'm way ahead of you."

Grinning, Reichert moved to the rear of the compartment and took up station by the hatch as Robison lobbed a flash-bang through underhand. It cracked off. With Hays and Weaver covering from the hatchway coaming, their companions moved back into the depths of the ancient station.

As energy crashed and flared from astern, Kane met Grant's eye. The big man shrugged.

"The others all right in there?" Kane called forward with an edge to his voice. He craned his head to peer through into the control chamber.

Brigid and Pine came into the compartment. "I'm fine," Brigid said with a nod to Kane. She and the younger woman began checking the wounded.

"We're fine in here, too," Bug Mama called from the control center, where she remained with Svarri and the techs.

"What, uh, about the machinery?" Kane asked, almost afraid to hear the answer. It wasn't that he cared more for equipment than for his friends. But if the wrong thing had been blasted, this whole trip was wasted.

And so was the universe likely to be, as soon as Bates and his alien fanatics got here.

Hunkered over the body of a human technician, Brigid looked up at Kane. She shook her head. It appeared that none of the downed technicians had survived grappling with the armored, inhumanly fast Paa marauders. Not that that was any big surprise.

"Pretty hard-core for whitecoats," Grant said.

"Our people may not all be fighters by training or inclination," Bug Mama said, "but we all braved the same dangers on the surface. We all faced up to raids from the Grand Council's forces. Besides, if they lacked courage, would they be here?"

Followed by Grant, Kane returned to the control center. "So before we were so rudely interrupted," he said, "I think you were giving us some bad news."

Bug Mama called the coalition scientist who had explained that the Eye system had to be destroyed away from his console. "Explain yourself, Wix," she ordered "Why do you think we have to destroy a black hole binary?"

"And what in hell makes you think we can?" Grant asked. He kept an eye on the hatch leading back from the far compartment through the command center's open entrance.

"As I said, Elder," the whitecoat explained, its manner displaying no more emotion than its immobile red-purple features, "once the enemy analyzes the structure of the Cosmic Eye they will be able to rebuild it from scratch if necessary."

"Shit," Kane said.

"Roger that," Grant said.

"Crudely put, Kane," Brigid said, coming into the room. She had a smudge of blood and charcoal on her right cheek. "But I'm forced to concur with the sentiment."

"What can we do, Elder?" Pine asked.

Bug Mama's black eye spots moved toward the chief tech. "We can destroy the system," she said with flat persistence.

Several people started talking at once. Kane held up a hand. "How?" he asked as the others piped down.

"We must trigger it," Wix said.

Chapter 31

"But first," Wix said, "we must make certain adjustments."

"Mebbe," Grant said slowly, "you better explain how this bastard works."

"The mathematics are far too advanced for the layperson," the scientist protested.

"Shove that, Wix," Bug Mama said. "Say it in words of one syllable or less."

Now the alien displayed agitation, stepping from one bare digitigrade foot to the other. "Well—very well. Although I must protest that it will be far from an exhaustive, or even particularly accurate, description."

"Quick and dirty'll do fine," Bug Mama said.

"If I must. Essentially the Cosmic Eye consists of two identical stations arranged on opposite sides of the irregularity in the center, between the orbiting black holes. The inconceivable tidal and gravitic forces of the paired black holes distorts reality between them, producing the effect you see."

"That's the big glowing thing in the middle," Domi said, waving a white hand at the viewport. "Looks like a butterfly."

"I am unfamiliar with the term," Wix said, peevish at the interruption.

"Big-winged bug," Kane said. "Uh, no offense, Bug Mama."

"None taken," she replied.

"Yes," Wix said. "It glows because it draws in more material, even faster, than the accretion disks of the black holes. Indeed, it is somehow sucking matter from beyond the event horizons of the very singularities themselves."

"I thought that was impossible," Brigid said.

The creature's lips were actually a flat chitinous beak, incapable of doing more than opening and closing. Still, the chief whitecoat seemed to smirk as he said, "Near a phenomenon such as this irregularity, very little can be said to be impossible. It is, so far as we know, unique in the universe. Certainly in this galaxy, or any galaxy within the supergroup."

"Get on with it, here, Wix," Bug Mama said, folding her voluminously sleeved arms. "The Paa and Bates's evil crew are in a hurry, even if you aren't."

"I am explaining abstruse concepts in *entirely* unsuitable layman's terms, as you insisted—"

"Wix." She didn't raise her voice. Nonetheless the word stream shut off as if a hundred-ton blast door had slammed shut on it. The tall, gaunt alien drew a breath.

"Each of the two stations controls a single self-powered projectile: a hundred-mile-long artifact of ultradense material orbiting nearby. Each carries a small mass of antineutronium as a warhead. Each is meant to be fired simultaneously toward one another at superluminal velocity."

"'Superluminal'?" Kane asked.

"Faster than light," Brigid said. "I thought the concept of simultaneity was invalid over relativistic distances, such as the two light-years distance the stations orbit from one another."

"But then," Big Mama said, "faster-than-light travel's impossible, too, under your primitive conception of relativity as anything but a special condition, applicable only at certain energy levels. But still, here you are."

"If that stuff was true," Kane said, "our mat-trans gateways wouldn't work, either, would they, Baptiste?"

Her cheeks colored beneath the smudge that still showed on one. "You're right, Kane." She smiled wanly and swept back a stray lock of flame-colored hair from her face. "I must be too wound up to think clearly."

"You're not the only one, Baptiste."

"So what happens when you fire these big antimatter-tipped rockets?" Grant asked.

"They collide at the mathematical center of the irregularity," Wix said, "creating a reaction of an energy level, and indeed a nature, unprecedented since the beginning of the universe."

"And then?" Kane prompted.

Wix shrugged. "If the builders' calculations were correct," he said, "the end of everything."

"The collapse of the vacuum bubble that theoretically constitutes our universe," Brigid said.

"Simultaneously," Bug Mama added with gloomy satisfaction. She snapped her fingers. Since they were covered in ceramic-hard chitin, they made a noise like a small handblaster going off. "The whole shebang, gone at once."

"Well, that would certainly suck," Kane said. "But we knew all that. How can we destroy something like…that… without blowing up the whole universe?"

"All clear," Major Mike called voice from astern.

Kane and Grant spun, hands coming up to ready the blasters they both still gripped. Kane felt a hot flush of embarrassment and plain fear flood through him: What if Team Phoenix lost, or let one of those crawdaddy bastards by?

But they hadn't. The four were all on their hind legs and walking steady, though half of young Reichert's hair was burned off, and the right side of Larry Robison's camou ballistic-fabric blouse hung in shreds dyed in shades of brown by drying blood, showing the beige of a coalition med patch on his rib cage below.

"We had another half dozen of 'em loose back there," Reichert said, grinning, though Kane now saw half his olive-complected face glowed angry red, as if he'd been out too long in the sun. "You know those sumbitches can fire their weapons, *aimed* fire, in different directions at the same time? Like something out of the movies." He spoke with evident satisfaction.

"Good job," Kane said. Domi moved forward and hugged each man in turn; they were friends from way back. Marina followed her, showing a tendency to cling and shake. "This whitecoat here was just explaining to us how we had to destroy a pair of black holes and that big glowing thing out there to make sure the Cosmic Eye could never be rebuilt."

"Oh, goody," Robison said.

"At least we got here in time for the interesting part," Hays said.

"Enough suspense already," Bug Mama said to Wix. "Give."

"Ancient artificial intelligences control the trajectory

of the superluminal missiles," the whitecoat said. "They must be aimed with a precision unthinkable even to our current measurement capabilities. If they do not strike precisely head-on, to the diameter of a hydrogen atom, they cannot produce the desired result."

"If you're the sort of sicko," Reichert said, "who desires the end of the universe."

Wix nodded. "Precisely. But, ah, even should the impact be off by more than the very small margin of error allowed, an unprecedentedly destructive event will ensue."

"Just not big enough," Kane said, "to turn off the whole universe."

"Again, very good. You show quick comprehension for space ra—for layfolk. If the projectiles strike head to head but nanoscopically outside the parameters of optimum performance, a dislocation will occur that, through probability-distortion and raw energy release, will simply destroy everything within a radius of three parsecs. Including both black holes, and these stations."

Kane and the other humans looked at one another.

"Whoa," Reichert breathed.

"I second that Keanu impression," Larry Robison said.

"What are they talking about?" Bug Mama asked.

"You don't want to know," Kane said. "Trust me."

"Can you jimmy this ancient AI so it misses by just the right amount?" Bug Mama asked.

Once again the alien whitecoat's body language showed unmistakable smugness. "It is done already." He bowed slightly toward her.

"So, great," Hays said. "The deal is, we set up some kind of relay or timer here, flit off to the other station, set it to fire simultaneously and warp to safety while the whole thing goes off like the Second of July."

"I thought it was the Fourth," Grant said.

"Should've been the Second," Robison said. "Don't get us started."

Bug Mama's feathery antennae drooped, then waggled disconsolately. "Not exactly," she said.

"WE HAVE WON CLEAR of the traitor battle fleet," the courier said. It was a Halmi with glabrous mauve skin, one of the foremost of the Paa's vassal races, not one of her innumerable daughters.

Uvaluvu had access through instruments in her honeycomb cell by which she could monitor the course of battle and events within her fleet and her flagship. She disdained to use them, as she disdained to have her sacred person sullied by implants. It was for slaves to tend to her, to inform her and serve her and in general wait upon her pleasures.

And soon, she thought, my slaves will comprise all the sophonts of the Far Arm. And beyond…

"But," the Halmi continued.

It failed to quail at the warning way the stiff gray bristles rose about the Circle queen's eighteen variously sized black eyes; she did not desire to hear such a word as *but*. The amphibious Halmi were either immune to fear or a little bit slow. Even Uvaluvu did not know which. Their bricklike lack of imagination made them useful tools, even though it also meant there was no sport in tormenting them. They just didn't get it.

"Even as we head toward the nearer of the ancient

space stations, our enemy streams in hot pursuit," the creature continued.

She clattered some lesser spare limbs in annoyance. "We will win the prize. We must! It is our destiny. We represent the will of all life—impossible we should fail!"

The Halmi bowed. "As you say, Your Majesty." The obeisance was too bland to be gratifying. But, she consoled herself, she had plenty of eminently satisfactory minions to take her dudgeon out upon. Even if sheer practicality dictated that she couldn't actually kill many of them or even subject them to physical torture. Fortunately, she was equipped to enjoy psychological cruelty, as well.

"Shape course for the station." It would take time to get there. Not even the Paa dared make jumps of more than a few light-hours at a time in this place. They had to travel for hours in real space, with the vile little space rat Bates and his renegades nipping at their heels the whole time.

But still they had the advantage. And no one lived to become a full queen among the Paa, far less queen of the Circle of Life, without knowing how to wring the last picogram from each and every advantage.

Besides, she had an ace up her sleeve. Had she a sleeve. "Withdraw."

The Halmi bowed again. It left.

"Senior Marshal," the queen said. Her daughter stepped from her position by the honeycomb on the queen's right. Her own genuflection crossed the boundary to insult. Uvaluvu showed no sign of noticing.

"Your wish?" the marshal asked.

"Have our commandos seized the station yet?"

"Negative, Majesty. I have just received confirmation

that all communication with the commando unit has been lost. They have failed."

"Failed? *Failed?*"

"The word is simple enough."

"Not for me! Not for a Paa! How is it possible they failed?"

"All things are possible. Perhaps it was the influence of the irregularity."

Her daughter's voice and manner were as bland as the Halmi's. Uvaluvu knew full well the marshal no more believed that than she had. The unpalatable truth was, their enemies were most resourceful. Vermin, but resourceful.

"Send twice as many," she commanded. "Five times as many. Ten!"

The marshal hesitated. "It is risky, our scientists inform us, to attempt to interfere so much mass in such proximity to the irregularity. We took a substantial risk last time, as it was."

"Do you fear?" the queen asked in a tone of silken menace.

"Only that we shall betray the destiny of the Paa race," she said, "by taking unnecessary risks and so incurring failure."

The queen swelled with fury. Limbs and thick fur bristled. "You dare accuse me—"

Her daughter stood her ground. "Not yet," she said simply.

"Go and do as you are commanded! I am the queen."

The marshal stood a moment, her pair of eye stalks fixed on her mother's mass of eyes. "I obey."

She turned and stalked from chamber. And surely she did not imagine her mother would fail to hear when, as she stepped through the door that slid open, obedient to her approach, she said in a low voice, "For now."

"MY GROK HERE," Bug Mama said, gesturing toward the toadlike creature who now squatted mutely beside her, tugging the hem of her robe, "tells me the bad guys are on their way here. Still shooting at each other, and not even the Paa are stupid enough to take big steps this near the Eye. But they're on their way."

Kane shrugged. "So what? We knew they'd come. Sooner or later."

"Unfortunately, it's sooner. We're going to need to leave a screening force here to make sure they don't get hold of the station and foul things up. That's a one-way ticket to heaven, as they say."

"We knew we'd have to do that, though," Grant said.

"Perhaps the screening ships can risk a jump out of the system once the projectiles are launched," Brigid said. "Even if it's highly risky, it would offer better odds than staying."

"Perhaps," Bug Mama said. "But there's something else—the Paa might try inserting more raider-forms into this station. Someone has to stay here. On the station. To secure it."

Kane leaned his head first left, then right, stretching his neck with alarmingly loud cracks. "Well, it's too long a walk home anyway."

"Just you and me, point man," Grant said, nodding. "Brigid and Domi can find some way home. Or make lives for yourselves out here."

"That's a big negative, big guy," Major Mike said.

"How so?" Grant said, his scowl deepening.

"This is our job," Robison said quietly. "We secure the station. You go. Make sure everything else comes off on schedule."

"How do you reckon that?" Kane asked, feeling irrational anger surge within him.

"You guys are the ones at the center of the struggle to save Earth from the overlords," Sean Reichert said. "We're way out on the periphery."

"But we're not getting home," Grant said.

"You don't know that," Hays said. "Anyway, somebody's got to go pull security on the other station while things get set up there. This ain't over yet—fat lady's only just doing her throat warm-ups."

Kane shook his head at the blazing non sequitur.

Joe Weaver stepped forward. "Remember," he said, "we agreed to be put to sleep in the first place because we didn't have any connections holding us back in the twentieth century. What kind of connections do we have back on Earth now?"

Kane stood staring at them.

"Listen, boys," Bug Mama said, "I hate to sacrifice any of you, but I'm not getting my druthers here. Rather than getting into a testosterone-level contest, couldn't you just draw straws or something?"

Kane shook his head. "No," he said. "They're right."

"And anyway it's only a difference between a real slim chance," Grant said, "and none."

"Roger that, big fella," Hays said.

Kane and Grant stepped forward, shook hands with each of their opposite numbers. Domi embraced and kissed each man in turn. So, to Kane's surprise, did Brigid, although not quite as vigorously as the small albino woman.

"Let's get this show on the road," Bug Mama said. "We got a universe to save by destroying a big old chunk of it!"

"So THIS IS IT," Larry Robison said, gazing out at the twin-lobed Eye.

"Belay that crap, Navy boy," Hays growled. "It ain't over till it's over."

"Do you really think I take that old chestnut seriously?" Robison said. But the words came out without force. He felt drained. Not resigned—never that. But at loose ends.

He laughed and shrugged. "You're right. While there's life, there's hope."

"No call to turn this into a cliché bee," Hays warned.

"Hey, guys," Reichert called from behind. "Look what Joe and I found."

The two older Phoenix men turned to see their partners walk in, followed by a familiar looming but human shape and several aliens.

"Thand," Hays said, frowning slightly. "Thought you were commanding the screening fleet. What are you doing here?"

The huge blond-bearded man gestured brusquely.

Team Phoenix found themselves staring down the gaping maws of half a dozen energy weapons.

Chapter 32

"The commandos have assembled in the beam-cast chambers," the senior marshal reported. "They await your word."

The queen lay in an attitude of blissful satisfaction as tiny four-eyed pseudoprimates crawled over her body, grooming and cosseting her with agile little hands.

"Send them."

The marshal stood immobile for an instant. Unlike her mother, she wore an implant that made it possible for her to communicate directly with the ship mind, and through it, the rest of the crew and fleet.

"It is done," she said.

"Excellent!" the queen cawed, spittle flying from her ingestive-mouth. The grooming slaves scuttled in fear for the safety of their cells. "Now go and destroy yourself for your presumption, wretched pup!"

"I shall not."

For a moment silence reigned in the royal chamber. All the servants and attendants froze in attitudes of terrified anticipation. Only the mindless cleaning drones continued their endless rounds, scouring the walls and ceilings and floor of the great chamber and the inside of the cells in the great honeycomb wall.

Without command the pair of immortals flanking the

queen's agitated bulk stepped forward, leveling spearlike energy lances. A pair of small plasma cannon mounted on the marshal's carapace to either side of her bullet head swiveled up and forward. They destroyed the silver bodyguards with a single orange pulse each.

As the scorched and shattered bodies fell kicking their spurred limbs with frantic scratching noises upon the metal deck, other immortals along the outer wall dropped their weapons to firing positions. With a whir of servos, the shoulder cannons turned to focus their aim upon the eye mass of the Circle queen.

"Shoot if you wish." The marshal's voice echoed in the vast space of the chamber. "Do you think a marshal fears to die? But my dying impulse will blast this unworthy cull to smoking ruin, be assured."

"Unworthy cull?" The queen swelled until her already bloated abdomen pressed against the walls of its cell with dangerous pressure. The pale membrane bulged precariously around the hexagonal edges of the cell. "*Unworthy cull?* How dare you?"

"For the good of the race," the marshal said calmly, as uncaring of her mother's rage as for the score of weapons poised to send streams of hellfire darting through her body.

"You cannot aspire to be queen! It is not biologically possible."

"Even you might be surprised by what our gene-transfer philosophers have devised," her daughter said. "But it matters not at all whether I succeed you. A new queen can always be grown—and others, of course, lie ready to slither into your place. But supplanted you must be."

That issue, Uvaluvu thought, remains far from decided, O my daughter. Maintaining the appearance of unbearable agitation, she said, "But why?"

IN THE GREAT BATTLESHIP'S transmission chambers a party of sixty commando forms stood waiting. An orange light flashed warning. And then the matter-transmission process whisked them into simultaneous nonbeing.

Instead of being transmitted directly to a destination, though, the signal that encoded and contained their beings was split and duplicated. It was then transmitted, without intervening time passage, to the mat-trans gateway of another Paa battle wagon ten light-days away on the far extremity of the fleet bearing down upon the ancient Eye station.

They were then broadcast as probability waves. The spreading wave fronts interfered with one another, forming nodes of probability. On the first and strongest of these lay the interior of the builders' long-abandoned station.

But unlike the first time, they did not resolve back into being inside the station, ready to sweep away all resistance and seize control of the Cosmic Eye.

Whether it was proximity to the total unreality manifest within the Eye itself or whether the second probability-wave attack triggered a backlash from the irregularity, not even the most advanced science of the Far Arm could ever afterward establish. But after all, no light of the event survived to be picked up by sensors and resolved into images, nor were any probability-ripples caused in the fabric of the universe by the events themselves.

What was certain was that the interference transmission went horribly, catastrophically wrong.

And produced reaction.

A SMALL, SOFT PALPUS at the end of a minor limb, tucked out of sight beneath her thorax, was poised above the contact that would surround the Circle queen in a hemisphere of impenetrable force—impenetrable, at least, to her daughter's pitiable miniature plasma cannon. At the same moment it would trigger a pulse of energy that would scramble the neural biocircuitry of every organism in the room—except Uvaluvu herself—incapacitating them instantly. It might kill some of her lesser, weaker servitors, but they were nothing. Neither, for that matter, were the silver immortals whom the marshal hadn't blasted; their lives were forfeit for permitting harm to threaten their queen.

The important thing was that the marshal herself survive. For her mother intended to make her passing…memorable.

"Tell me," she said, proud of the quaver of feigned fear she allowed to tremble, ever so slightly, through her voice, "why are you doing this?"

Her daughter turned into a flowering bush.

The chamber became a seascape.

Became the center of a blazing nova, and the queen shrieked through all her spiracles as her flesh and eyes began to melt and run.

Became the center of a nursery for bipedal beings with gigantic heads and triple eyes, a species billion years dead.

Became everything.

And then—nothing.

"WHAT DID I JUST SEE?" asked Gilgamesh Bates, staring at the great screens in his combat-control center.

Chaufat had his brown-furred head tipped to the side, indicating he was attending to his implant. "Something has happened within the Paa fleet. A probability weapon, perhaps. Although one of enormous power."

The screens showed images assembled by the flagship's AI from sensors not constrained by relativistic limits, so that they need not wait for tardy photons lagging a light-day or so behind. A wave of something had passed through the Paa fleet. Bates had seen—he shook his head and blinked. He had seen things he could not have; and he cared to remember no more.

But now he saw far fewer images than he had before.

"The Circle flagship is gone, Excellency!" the Zuri yipped. "So is half their fleet. We receive their submission signal now…the surviving Paa petition for admittance into our New Order!"

Cheers rang through the compartment. Bates waved a negligent hand. "Grant it," he said. "Promise them plenary amnesty."

The predator's big eyes, chocolate-colored and set on the front of his head, widened in outrage. "Excellency!"

Bates smiled indulgently. "We can always revoke it later, Chaufat," he said, "after we've got them safely in custody. Some nice public show trials, followed by equally public executions, will serve nicely to introduce our glorious new day to the citizens of the arm."

The Zuri dropped to all fours and pressed a furry jaw to the deck. "I abase myself before your genius, master! Truly are you the leader of the pack."

Bates waved a hand. "Oh, get up." But the gesture pleased him immoderately.

I could get to enjoy this, he thought. As a matter of fact, I believe I shall.

"Tell off a squadron to secure the prisoners—that is, our new allies," he commanded. "Then pass the word throughout the Grand United Fleet—onward, to glory and eternal triumph!"

And the cheers and jubilant howls of his battle-bridge crew warmed him like the rays of a springtime sun.

"IT'S DONE," Wix reported.

Bug Mama seemed to sigh. She looked at the Cerberus four, and Pine and Svarri, all assembled with the techs, Servillon and a quartet of coalition bodyguards in the control center of the antipodal satellite. It was twin of the one they had fled some hours before. Marina remained aboard *Forlorn Hope*, where she had locked herself in her cabin and refused to see anyone.

The *Forlorn Hope* and the few coalition ships escorting it had taken a one-light-year jump out of the Eye system, then several more. Then they jumped back in, close to the second station. The outbound and inbound jumps were fantastically dangerous maneuvers, the insectile alien said, although she refused to elaborate on what the risks might be. None of the Terrans chose to press. The important thing was this roundabout route was still vastly less dangerous than trying to make one long direct jump this near the Eye, and much quicker than a series of safely small jumps would be.

Brigid asked why their Grand Council enemies didn't do the same thing.

Bug Mama had cocked her big, big-eyed head. "First, the council major races aren't particularly subtle." She made no attempt to hide bitterness from the translation routine. "They don't have to be, with such a preponderance of force on their side. But by the same token we must be infinitely flexible, and resourceful, even to survive.

"Second—" she drew a deep breath "—they're too blinded with greed to seize the Eye for themselves to bring themselves to fly away from it. They're too damn afraid someone else'll get there first!"

"What was that about absolute power?" Kane asked.

"Makes assholes of everybody," Grant replied.

"Very well," Bug Mama said. "Good work, boys and girls. We can jump out of here to relative safety. Got thought-box relays set up in either station so we can fire this bad boy psionically, through our Groks."

"I fear, Elder," Servillon said with soft sibilance, "that will not be possible."

"What?" She waved her antennae in annoyance. "What's that?"

Feeling a stab of point-man alarm, Kane started bringing up his right arm, curling his hand into a half fist to invoke his Sin Eater. It wasn't a fancy-dancy alien energy blaster, but it would splatter Servillon's brains all over the image of the Eye glaring through the viewport if he was trying to pull something.

Arms like steel pipes closed around Kane from behind. He fought with all his strength, but his arms were driven down to his sides and pinioned as though by steel rings. His Sin Eater pointed impotently at the deck.

He looked right to where Grant stood. But a Slump

bodyguard held him up from behind in a bear hug, with Grant's feet kicking futilely in the air.

The other two coalition fighters stood with their chitinous purple arms encircling Brigid's and Domi's throats from behind. Each held a blaster pressed against a captive woman's ear.

Chapter 33

"Servillon," Bug Mama said sharply, "what on Earth do you think you're doing?"

Even in his current plight Kane felt a stab of wondering just what the alien had said that the translation-AI rendered as *Earth*.

"Saving us all," the half-serpent alien said, "from our own folly. And achieving the ends of the glorious Coalition of Nonaligned Races. Which you seem, sadly, to have forgotten, Elder."

The mantis-headed alien stared in disdain at the huge-mouthed stubby hideout blaster the serpent-being pointed at her. "And just how do you propose to do that?"

Servillon waved a free hand at the strange two-lobed image smeared across the viewport. "All that power out there," he said. "Ultimate power. Do you seriously contemplate destroying it—robbing our cause of it?"

"No," Bug Mama said calmly. "I am totally resolved to destroy it. No contemplation involved at all."

Kane meanwhile tried going limp, planning to lull his captor into relaxing his grip and then bust free. Instead the bodyguard holding him from behind tightened his grip like a constrictor with weakening prey, making it hard for Kane to draw breath.

"Are you looking to sell us out to the council?" he managed to wheeze. "Is that your dirty little game?"

"Say rather that I choose to negotiate from a position of strength."

"And gain power for yourself, perhaps?" Brigid asked.

"Would that be wrong? I who have the vision to see what is necessary, the courage to act upon it? But you cannot be expected to understand—you come from far away. I do not disdain you humans as some do. But you know nothing of our history, of suffering, oppression, frustration!"

"Servillon, you're pathetic," Bug Mama said. "The Paa will eat you like a processed snack."

"You know the Paa well, don't you, Elder?" The serpent alien turned to the Terrans. "You were not aware, I think, that our elder is herself Paa? It's true. And more—she's a daughter of the Circle queen herself!"

Bug Mama shrugged. "The queen has lots of daughters."

"Ah, but not like you! Not like you, Elder. You were the special creation, the superadministrator, the analyst! Your genes were assembled specifically so that you might hold power second only to the queen."

"Yeah. Well. Everybody makes mistakes. Including my mother. She made me a little too independent, I guess."

"See, humans! You cannot trust her. What makes you think she does not plan to sell us all to the Paa?"

"Mebbe the fact that she's in the middle of wiring this whole damn solar system to blow," Grant grunted, "and you're pointing guns at us."

"Servillon," a tech said nervously from the board, "a small ship approaches rapidly."

"What? What's that?" His slit-pupiled yellow eyes darted aside.

Searing yellow glare lit the control compartment.

Looking for the main chance, Kane had never taken his wolf-gray eyes off the traitor. He saw a pencil of yellow light stab into the creature's serpent mouth as it opened to say something. The yellow-amber eyes went wide, then melted like a snowflake on a hot plate. For a tiny sliver of a second yellow beams shot out the eye sockets like searchlights.

The beam lanced out through the back of the flat skull and dissipated harmlessly on the viewscreen. A spray of cooked brains and blood splashed across the image of the Cosmic Eye.

The snake alien crumpled. Apparently the shot had pithed its medulla or equivalent.

Kane's eyes flicked to Bug Mama. The front of her robe had been flung open, revealing two set of arms. Each hand held a stubby hideout beamer.

The traitor's handpicked compatriots stood as if hit with paralysis rays, their brains unable to process the turn of events. The hands holding blasters moved independently. Kane's eyes widened as he stared down a muzzle that yawned as wide as a train-tunnel mouth.

It novaed into yellow glare.

It felt as if a red-hot branding iron were pressed to Kane's left cheek. He smelled the hairs of his beard burning.

Scalding fluids cascaded down the back of his neck as his ears rang from a crack he had never consciously heard.

The iron-band grip released. He heard the clatter of a heavy hard-shelled body hitting the deck behind him.

He crouched, bringing up his right hand with Sin Eater still clutched in his fist, took a quick look around.

It was over. All over.

Domi stood beside Brigid, helping the taller woman bat out blue flames that ran like vermin through her thick red hair. A swatch of the albino's own white plush had been burned black along the top right of her own head, and a line of burn-reddened skin showed through. Past the two Terran women Pine huddled by a console with her arms protectively around her brother. She had a hand pressed over Svarri's face to shield his eyes from the sight. Being a human kid he had writhed so he could see through her fingers with wide blue eyes.

Kane turned his head the other way. The giant gray-skinned alien lay sprawled on its front. A dark puddle spread slowly from beneath its face.

"Grant?" Kane said.

He heard a grunt. Then the massive deadweight of the alien's corpse was raised up off the padded deck to the accompaniment of a growl rising steadily in volume. It became a shout of rage and triumph as the vast carcass slid aside and Grant reared upright on his knees.

"Most impressive," Bug Mama said. "You Terrans got some unlooked-for traits."

"So do you, Bug Mama," Kane said dryly as he straightened. He gingerly raised his left hand to brush at his cheek. His beard hadn't caught fire the way Brigid's glorious mane had, but rather crisped and melted in a swatch where the beam passed.

"I thought you were a pacifist," Brigid said, fending off Domi, who, tending as always to overdo things, batted at the archivist's now-extinguished hair as if fighting a swarm of soldier ants in a frenzy of helpfulness. Despite her recent experiences her voice was level and fully under control. Once again, not for the first time, nor the hundredth, Kane was impressed by her coolness under pressure.

The sneaky blasters went back into snug little holsters strapped to Bug Mama's beetle carapace. Then the little auxiliary arms crossed, the hands grabbed the hems of the robe and pulled it to again. It sealed itself as seamlessly.

"What gave you that impression, hon?" the alien said. "I command a whole network of freedom fighters—or terrorists, from my dear mother's point of view. You've seen them kill plenty of people. Hell, you helped."

The mouth parts worked to form a smile. "It's just not efficient for me to run around waving blasters like a warrior. Most of the time. I really was born to be the executive type, just like my treacherous assistant said."

"I notice you can shoot in different directions, too," Grant said. He was dusting his gloved hands against each other. "Just like those Paa commandos could."

She shrugged. "Well, I guess Mama wanted her special little girl to be able to take care of herself. If you think Grand Council politics is a full-contact sport, you should see Paa in-nest intrigue. Hoo, baby!"

She turned to the technicians, who all stood ignoring their consoles and staring at her as if she'd turned into a human before their eyes.

"What?" she demanded. "Show's over. We got a universe to save, two black holes to destroy and a loudly ticking clock."

"What about the vessel that was approaching us?" Brigid asked.

"Right," Bug Mama said. She didn't turn her head, but the little black eye spots moved to the tech who had announced the fact. He or she or it—Kane realized he had no idea what the Sidran sexes looked like, or even if they had them—turned back to the board.

"It has been intercepted by the *Longshot*," he said, naming one of the three vessels of their small escort squadron that had accompanied *Forlorn Hope* to this end of the Eye system. "It's calling us now."

He looked up at Bug Mama with eyes wide. "The IFF code identifies it as a longboat from the *Guardian!*"

"Thand's ship!" Pine breathed. She had let go of her little brother and stood up. Svarri was peering with interest at the bodies scattered around the control room.

"Well, what're you waiting for?" Bug Mama said. "Put 'em on."

A solid-looking but miniature image of a compact ship's bridge materialized in midair. A sturdy figure with silver hair and mustache and startling blue eyes and clad in somewhat ragged camou sat in the central chair of command flanked by three other similarly attired humans.

"Greetings, earthlings," said Major Mike Hays. "Take us to your leader."

"I wanted to say that!" Sean Reichert protested from his left.

"Why you alive?" Domi flared. Kane was startled to see her white cheeks gleaming with tears. "Thought you throw lives away in big macho sacrifice!"

"The sacrifice isn't scheduled to have happened yet, remember?" Larry Robison said.

"We got jacked up," Reichert said, "by our pal Thand and his goons."

Pine gasped.

"Don't tell me he's trying to grab the Eye, too!" Bug Mama said. For the first time in their brief acquaintance Kane heard agitation in her translated voice.

"'Too'?" Hays asked. He leaned forward and squinted. "That must explain the bodies strewn around the deck, there. Thought they were decorative."

Kane realized they had to be seeing a similar projection of the station's command compartment.

"Negative to Thand grabbing for power," Robison said. "Just glory. They got the drop on us. Embarrassing as all hell."

"Anticlimactic, too," Hays said, "after we were all primed to go out in a blaze of glory ourselves."

"The glory?" Grant said. "What the hell are you talking about?"

Reichert shrugged. "Ask him yourself. He's dying to talk to you."

"Not even our communications will punch through that monstrosity out there," Bug Mama said.

"I can talk this way," a deep familiar voice said.

All eyes turned to Svarri, who had stopped ogling the chills and stepped away from his sister's embrace to stand upright with a strange fixed look in his eyes. The voice was not the giant human warrior's—not exactly. But its intonation and inflection and pacing were Thand's, and what emerged was amazingly deep and loud to be emerging from such a slight preadolescent chest and pharynx.

"Can you hear me, Thand?" Bug Mama demanded, speaking loudly as if that would help her war chief hear her across two light-years and a great big hole in the fabric of the cosmos. "What the hell do you think you're up to?"

"Doing my job," Thand-Svarri said.

"You're not thinking of using the Eye yourself?" Bug Mama said.

Svarri laughed. The laugh boomed like a huge bass drum. It was way too big for the kid's slight frame.

"Now, that's just creepy," Robison said. Kane realized Team Phoenix was still on-line and watching the whole show.

"Do you know me so little, Elder? I have fought the Grand Council and its hateful major races since their slavers devastated my village when I was but a child younger than the one I speak through now. Do you know that most of the fleets that warred over Sidra have entered the fringes of this system now? Even as we speak they fly toward this station as fast as they dare, to claim their prize. The completion of their great goal—the subjugation of all life to their evil will!"

"We've been a little preoccupied by local events, Thand," Bug Mama said. She turned her eye spots toward Wix, who now bent over some other kind of instrument Kane didn't savvy any more than any of the others. The alien whitecoat nodded confirmation. "You still haven't explained what you're up to."

"I sent the outlanders away. This privilege is mine! I have earned it, and I claim it!"

"The right to throw your life away?" Brigid asked.

"Yeah," Reichert said ironically. "That's our job."

"Stupid gestures 'R' us," Robison said, "or we wouldn't even be here."

Again the eerie giant's laugh. Kane realized the kid was going to have a sore throat when this was over with.

If he even still had a throat.

Pine found her voice. "Thand!" she cried. "It's Pine! Please, do not do this thing!"

Her brother chuckled with someone else's possibly forced mirth. "Do you think I act rashly because you scorn me for the outworlder? It's not that you are not worth it, dear child. But I fear that has little to do with my determination."

"Which is what?" Bug Mama asked. "I'm still waiting to hear that part, Thand."

"To win us success," Thand said, "and strike the greatest blow in history against our ancient oppressors. I have sent the rest of the fleet scurrying out of the system, as well— they would fall like flies in a furnace before the fleet that approaches. I alone remain. And I have one thing to ask."

Silence stretched. Bug Mama played the fingers of one hand on the face of a console. Kane hoped she knew enough about its operation not to do anything like light off the Eye prematurely.

"Shoot," she said.

"I think," Major Mike said from the projection, "that's exactly what he's going to ask for."

Chapter 34

"Excellency," Chaufat reported, "we close in upon the orbital control station. The rebel scum have fled. The way such undisciplined rabble always will. We will take possession of it within mere moments."

Bates could see the image of the station on the viewscreens as well as his furry aide-de-camp could, although Zuri was getting a data feed through implants Bates lacked. He was not exactly cherry enough to trust his new found allies to do brain surgery on him just yet. Come to think of it, he doubted he would ever get such implants: better to make flunkies wait upon him with data, as in all other things, as the unlamented Uvaluvu had her slaves.

Despite the fact he already knew what was going on, Bates felt a thrill at the alien's words. *Thrill* hardly sufficed. It was like a jolt overdose and a million orgasms all rolled together. It was like having the entire energy output of this colossal battle cruiser switched through his body.

I win!

It was all his.

He leaned forward in the command seat that was his throne, and reached out his hand, as if to grasp the Eye like the scepter to rule the universe.

The screen flared white, dazzling him with brilliance.

KANE HEARD A LOW WHISTLE as white radiance expanded to fill the screen. Maybe it came from one of the Phoenix four, gathered on the *Forlorn Hope* bridge with the rest.

Maybe it came from him.

This particular image was cast via some kind of conventional communication—as conventional as faster-than-light communication could be—from the second Eye station. Despite the risk, the *Hope*'s skipper had jumped them a full light-day away on the first go, then put several more behind them.

The flare came from the propulsion system of the great enigmatic needle poised in space a light-second or two away from the station as it accelerated instantly to multiples of the velocity of light. And not just one or two, or dozens: thousands.

"And no, my Terran friends," Bug Mama remarked, as somebody made oohing noises over the figures displayed in midair—translation routines in *Hope*'s computers having the capability to transcribe text and numbers into English, as well as speech. "We can't do that, either. Not close."

The view switched. The bilobed Eye glared forth in terrible splendor.

In the midst of the strange shifting glare, a spot of blue-white appeared. It was so bright against even the unreal shine of the strange attractor that Kane started to raise a hand to shield his eyes, though his mind knew full well that the starship's viewscreens were incapable of transmitting dangerous wavelengths or levels of radiation to the viewer.

From his peripheral vision he realized he wasn't the only onlooker to give into that reflex.

The glare grew larger. Not in a standard propagation sphere: instead it flashed like flame through the lobes of gas and states of matter indescribable even by arm physics, already burning with an energy as far beyond matter-antimatter annihilation as hydrogen fusion was beyond a campfire.

The butterfly wings glowed with a strange, sparkling light. Began to twist. *Change.*

Kane screamed.

"EXCELLENCY! The rebels have destroyed the station!"

"Nonsense, Chaufat," Bates declared. His voice rang with exultation. "It's still there, can't you see?"

He stood up and raised his hands in the air. "I've won!" he screamed. "The universe is mine!"

The universe turned inside out, and tore Gilgamesh Bates and the battle fleets of the Grand Council into pieces in a million dimensions at once.

And each was full of agony a million times greater than flesh could feel. Or the strongest spirit bear.

Protracted to infinity.

"WHAT DID WE JUST SEE?" Sean Reichert asked in a still, small voice.

"I'm not telling," Larry Robison said.

"That's affirmative," Grant said.

Pine wept openly. Svarri stood patting her in a soothing, automatic way. He still stared at the screen.

Which showed…nothing.

Not even stars.

"I'll go ahead and ask," Kane said. "Did we just blow up the universe anyway?"

"No," Wix said, and even he sounded shaken. "It must be some local effect. Look at the other screens."

The center screen showed the black blankness of what heartbeats before had been the Eye. Others flanking it showed the space surrounding the *Forlorn Hope* filled with stars.

"Are the stars as they should be?" Brigid asked. "Might we have been thrown through time?"

"Or to some alternate dimension?" Robison asked.

"The stars are configured as they should be for our location. Which means in time and space, of course," Wix said, checking a display. "As to whether we might have been dislocated to another universe, our instruments are not up to measuring that."

"How about—?" Reichert began.

Bug Mama held up her two visible hands. "Enough, already. Let's not go borrowing trouble. Grok, is Sidra still there?"

She asked the latter question to the small creature with bumpy gray skin that squatted toadlike at her feet. It slowly blinked its huge gelatinous-looking eyes, then nodded.

"And—how do I even ask this question? Is everything, what, normal?"

The creature was already nodding. "That's right. You can read my mind. Silly me."

"Speaking of that," Domi said, "why didn't they read that bastard Servillon's mind, see what he was planning?"

"They only read thoughts by specific intent," Pine said. "Otherwise the thoughts of others would drive them mad."

"You learn to shut the voices out when you're real young," her brother said. "Otherwise it's just too much. Must be the same for them."

Kane watched the Grok. It showed no reaction to the fact the boy was speaking. Evidently it had never evolved external ears, possessing psi. It was deaf to his thoughts.

"Also Servillon wore a portable mind shield," Bug Mama said.

"I thought both the Circle and Triangle hated and feared psi," Hays said, "and wouldn't use it?"

"Well, nobody ever stayed alive long in the insurrection business by taking things like that for granted, boy. And anyway, remember we're cranky individualists, even if we do call ourselves coalition. Lots of us dislike the idea of having somebody being able to read our thoughts at will, even somebody on our own side. And as Servillon showed, 'our side' can be pretty nominal sometimes. You saw how far from monolithic the Grand Council major races are? We're that times ten."

"Why aren't there stars?" Domi asked, waving a white hand at the central display.

Bug Mama looked to Wix. The chief whitecoat looked unmistakably helpless to Kane despite his alien body language.

"As far as I can describe it," the science said, "or even comprehend it, where the Eye black-hole binary was now remains a hole in the fabric of reality."

"Is it spreading?" Brigid asked.

"No. Our probability-wave detectors, which were how we were able to watch the explosion in what we might vulgarly describe as 'real time,' show a seemingly stable shell of chaos—a boundary layer of probability turbulence—

roughly five light-years in diameter. Starlight clearly doesn't penetrate it, as you can see."

"What happens to it?" Hays asked. "Is it sucked in the way a black hole would?"

"I don't believe so. If I may hazard a totally unscientific surmise—"

"We call it a SWAG," Joe Weaver said, "for 'scientific wild-ass guess.'"

The purple humanoid nodded. 'My scientific wild-ass guess is that photons that impinge upon the chaos shell simply unhappen. Please don't quote me on that."

"Your secret's safe with us, big guy," Robison said.

"Still, to publish the first scientific observations of a phenomenon that has almost without question never been seen in the whole history of our universe—"

He turned away, making chuckling sounds in his throat, which the translator routine didn't try to render.

"Wow," Reichert said, "it's a scientific bliss-out!"

"What about the giant damn alien battle fleet?" Grant asked.

"Gone," Wix said. "Every last vessel."

Team Phoenix went crazy: hooting, hollering, high-fiving and embracing one another.

Bug Mama looked to Kane. "They're your people," she said.

He shrugged. "They're happy to be alive." He felt little more than drained. Given what he had been through. Not to mention just witnessed—and felt—and experienced in ways that could only be compared to jump nightmares, but magnified a million times…

"Ding dong, the Bates is dead!" Sean Reichert caroled.

"Which old Bates?" Robison sang.

"The Master Bates!" all four shouted.

Domi shook her head. "Fused."

"I dunno," Kane said. "Now that I know what they're going on about, I kinda second the emotion."

"Yeah," Grant said laconically.

"And so are your enemies, I guess," Kane said to Bug Mama.

"Not hardly, boy," the alien said. "Oh, that's the guts torn out of both the Circle and Triangle factions, which means the best—or worst—the Grand Council had. But none of the players is gone. Well, maybe one or two of the minor allies or so-called independents had their whole fleets thrown into this piss pot. And had things gone on a few more weeks, yeah, basically every interstellar-capable warcraft would've been drawn like flies to a fresh turd, given how high the stakes were.

"As it was—" she shook her great brass-colored head "—the Zuri and the Paa are probably down to their garrison forces, and whatever fraction of their fleets were in transit but hadn't arrived yet. But they've easy lost half their fleets, and it was the best half. Same with the vassals and allies.

"The Grand Council is crippled. But that won't last."

"So now what?" Kane said to Bug Mama.

"Well, we go back to Sidra to see what we can do about picking up the pieces," the diminutive alien said, "and keeping the council from doing the same."

"Does this mean you won?" Reichert asked.

"A battle, boy. Not the war." She stood a little bit straighter. "But a big battle. Bigger than any we've won in ten thousand years. The final outcome's parsecs from being decided, but let's just say that now for the first time in our history we've got a fighting chance."

"But what about us?' Brigid asked.

Bug Mama's antennae drooped. "Um," she said. "Well. Sorry, kids. But one thing Bates never provided the council races was enough data to locate your home world in the Orion Arm. Or at least not that our moles and spies and collaborators—bless their spirits, wherever they are now—were able to steal from the big boys."

Kane looked at Brigid. Tears glittered at the edges of her emerald eyes.

"Kane," she said, "we can never go home."

"Yeah," he said past a lump in his throat. Grant stood as immobile as a statue. But Kane thought he saw the big man's lips move, ever so slightly. And though no sound came out, Kane knew he had said "Shizuka."

"Never say never, kiddo," Bug Mama said. "Eternity's a damn long time.

"In the meantime—you boys and girls want a job? Fighting malevolent alien technology, overwhelming odds—hell, it's right up your alley!"

Epilogue

Kane came awake with a blaster in his hand. A real blaster, too, not his Sin Eater. Fond as he was of the piece, on this world you needed something that spoke with a sterner voice to stay alive.

A small figure, its species concealed by the usual coalition hooded robes, recoiled from the stubby energy weapon. "I said, please come at once, Kane! Bug Mama's asking for you."

He sighed. "All right. Tell her I'm coming."

The wind off the mauve desert buffeted the walls of the tent. Inside it was pleasantly cool: one thing these aliens did right was climate control. And they all think they're roughing it out here in the foothills....

He got up off the field cot that had held his body a foot off the tent floor as he slept and started to get dressed. The aliens didn't have anything that would do that for you; or at least the raggedy-ass coalition fighters didn't.

He was just as glad.

He took his time about it. Not that there was no prospect of emergency: attack was a possibility at any time. But if the bad guys were coming over the wire, Bug Mama would have made sure the messenger told him just that. Whatever else she was, the old insect was a pro.

I still don't know what I expected, he thought, pulling up his pants. He had decided not to bother with the shadow-suit armor in a footlocker near the cot. But it sure wasn't this.

HE AND THE OTHERS had reckoned that they'd wind up in some kind of city while Bug Mama administered the world of Sidra, newly liberated from Grand Council tyranny. But no such thing.

"I'm a freedom fighter, boy," she said as *Forlorn Hope* approached Sidra orbit, "the real deal. The last thing I want to do is set myself up as a government." She spoke the word as if it were an obscenity, as the translation-software made loud and clear.

"But won't there be anarchy?" Brigid asked. They had held the discussion sitting in the commissary aboard *Forlorn Hope* as the vessel bashed its way down through the desert world's atmosphere. The acceleration-damping antigrav permitted only a hint of motion to be felt. Enough to give the passengers a sense they were having an adventure, but not make them seasick or upset any crockery or anything.

"You say that as if it's a bad thing," Larry Robison murmured.

The former archivist's fine brow knit as she looked around the table from one Phoenix teammate to another. "But you were soldiers—"

"Smile when you say that," Robison said. He did, though.

"Well, three of you served in the United States armed forces. Mr. Weaver was a government employee."

"And who better to know what a crock government is?" Joe Weaver asked with a grin.

She shook her head.

"If you're finished with your comedy routine," Bug Mama said, "the real answer is, not my problem. Sidra has a civil administration—the council has traditionally maintained at least the appearance of autonomy for its member systems. What the hell? They get to rule the arm while the locals bear the brunt of enforcement costs. So there's the usual layers of local government. Which, absent council encouragement, isn't too obtrusive. Yet."

She sipped nectar from a bulb. "They have just about enough power to save some of the peacekeepers from being torn to pieces by angry mobs."

"So that's what your supporters are like?" asked Grant, leaning his elbows on the table sipping. The Far Arm sported a mild stimulant brew, usually imbibed hot, that had the texture and kick of strong coffee but tasted mildly peppery, like some kind of tea, and mostly indescribable. The Terrans all found it anywhere from not bad to very good. As far as Kane was concerned it would never replace fresh coffee. Had it all over the freeze-dried shit from the Cerberus caches, though.

"No," Bug Mama said. "That's what the unwashed masses who never took a stand before are like. I don't say some of the mobs don't contain coalition supporters, or at least sympathizers. Like Pine said, we're not monolithic."

The girl and her brother were absent, most likely locked away in the compartment they shared. She had taken Thand's death hard, even if she hadn't shown much patience with his delayed-adolescent jock advances while he was alive.

"For us," Bug Mama said, "we'll do what we've done before—try to stay clear of local politics. Do what we can to make sure Grand Council tyranny goes away and stays gone. Which at best won't be easy, even now."

"But what about the arm itself?" Brigid asked. "Won't the power vacuum cause civil wars?"

"Implicit in your question is the supposition that the council as formerly constituted maintained some kind of peace and order," she said. "What they were really about was exercising power and collecting spoils. Whether we'll see more strife and devastation with the Grand Council crippled is a very open question. And maybe that's what the Coalition's big job is now—to see if we can establish some kind of new and freer way."

"That ever happened before?" Grant asked.

"Nope," Bug Mama said, and Kane knew she was giving the equivalent of a grin. "But that never stopped us before."

"Bet the whole bad-guy battle fleet never all blew up at once before, either," said Domi, who was gnawing on some kind of Arm ration bar. Kane had tried them. They made him homesick: they tasted exactly like pressboard, just like the ones stored back in Redoubt Bravo.

"Not since what I guess we have to start calling the First Eye War," Bug Mama said. "Only this time the effect was localized, instead of taking down civilization throughout the whole damn galaxy."

"But do you know something like this didn't happen back then?" Reichert asked.

"Well, as far as our technicians, ably assisted by the talents of your own Brigid Baptiste, can determine, either through surviving records or modern observation, nothing remotely like the destruction of the Eye binary system has ever happened in our universe, period. But in terms of the relevant, no, we don't know exactly how the big collapse happened, son.

"Nor, in all honesty, do we know the same thing won't happen now. It's what you'd call a whole new bald game."

"Ball game," Hays corrected reflexively.

"Glitch in your software?" Robison asked.

"No. Me trying to use your weird Terran idiom, damnit! Anyway, we don't know what's going to happen. All we can do…is all we can do."

"Amen to that," Major Mike said.

THE SUN HADN'T CLEARED the peaks behind the camp when Kane stepped out into the cool breeze of morning, although the desert stretching to the west was a sea of rose dazzle. He stretched as he walked over to the campfire where the others were already gathered. Apparently the aliens just liked campfires, just as humans did. They sure didn't need them for heat, light or even cooking.

"So what's up, Bug Mama?" he called. "As far as I'm concerned, I still haven't made up my mind about your job offer."

"Same for the rest of us," Grant said.

"But something's happened, Kane," Brigid said. Something in her tone made him tip his head to the side as he accepted a mug of steaming local brew from Domi.

"We received an object," Wix said. It was the first time Kane had seen the chief whitecoat since they'd landed, just out of sight over a hill from the big coalition camp, where the *Forlorn Hope* still lay beneath spoofer screens to hide it from overhead detection. The alien scientist had been busy in some underground lab, gleefully analyzing the data from events in the Eye system. Before making planet-fall he had come up for air long enough to make clear that, once he started publishing, a sizable proportion of the Far Arm's cosmologists and high-end physicists were going to combust spontaneously.

Maybe literally.

"An object," Kane echoed.

Wix gestured. On a folding table sat a metallic object, a pyramid about eight inches in height and along each base.

"It looks like an interphaser, kinda," Domi said.

"Except for the red button," Grant said. "And the note above it with the arrow pointing down, that says, 'Press me.'"

"It would appear that some of your friends," Bug Mama said, "are either exceptionally waggish or exceptionally literal-minded."

"Philboyd," Grant grumbled. "He thinks we're retards."

The aliens, Bug Mama, Wix and a dozen or so random spectators stood waiting expectantly.

"What?" Kane said.

"Well," Bug Mama said. "Aren't you?"

"Aren't I what?"

"Going to press it?"

"Oh. Mebbe Philboyd has a point."

"That bastard," Domi said.

Kane stepped up, paused, pressed the button.

A column of radiance shot out the top of the pyramid. It took the form, three feet tall, of—

"Lakesh?" Kane said, incredulous.

"Friend Kane, my good Grant," the hologram said unctuously, "Brigid dear, darlingest Domi, and our esteemed friends and allies of Team Phoenix. You no doubt wonder how we managed to locate you, since an explosion, apparently initiated by an AI security routine, destroyed the Starwatch extraecliptic orbital station approximately 1.5 milliseconds after you jumped out, according to some quite brilliant calculations by Dr. Philboyd reconciling orbital-telescope observation with our own mat-trans monitors' recording of the outbound transmission. Unfortunately, not even Cerberus redoubt's jump network monitoring capabilities were able to discern where you had jumped *to*. Indeed it strained our capabilities to receive even the crudest telemetry from the station."

The figure sighed. "All academic now, of course. Another crime against science must be added to Bates's tally—"

"Not to mention those poor people," Robison said under his breath.

"By the way, I trust that by this time you have achieved some resolution of the Bates situation. I assure you·I am most eager to hear the details."

"Get to the goddam point," Kane gritted.

"In any event, our rather remarkably gifted Sally Wright appears to have located you by remote viewing," the hologram said. "Several days ago, by our reckoning, she perceived some kind of upheaval in the Far Arm. One of a truly cataclysmic nature and scale."

Hays pointed a stubby finger at Reichert and switched it to Robison. "If either of you quotes *Star Wars* about that," he growled, "I'll shoot you myself."

"Hush," Brigid said.

"Her comment was, it had to be you, my friends, because, and I quote, 'only they can cause trouble like that.'"

"Your friends know you well," Bug Mama murmured.

"That enabled her to home in on your psychic emanations," the recorded Lakesh went on. "Apparently the bond between Kane and dear Brigid creates a feedback loop that broadcasts quite clearly, in psychic terms. You form a sort of beacon, at least to one of Ms. Wright's esoteric gifts. So to make a long story short—"

"That's a change," Grant said sotto voce.

"—we are ready to bring you home. If you will repair to the following location, you and our friends from Team Phoenix will be transported back here to Cerberus."

"SAY WHAT?" Kane asked.

They stood on a hilltop overlooking the coalition camp. The recording and transponder device, or whatever it was, sat on the ground in the midst of the Cerberus four, per instructions.

"I said," Major Mike Hays said, "we're not going."

Kane looked from one of the four to the other. Each man nodded.

Marina stood among them, looking small but standing upright. She nodded, too.

"You boys know this is likely the only train out," he said. "We do."

The breeze kicked the fabric of Kane's trousers around his calves. The pants and shirt were looser than what he was used to from home, but nothing too unusual. His comrades were dressed similarly; Domi, characteristically, had her shirt tied up to bare her flat white midriff. Their shadow suits were folded surprisingly small in the rucksacks resting beside them on the dusty blue ground cover.

"But why won't you come back to Earth with us?" Brigid asked.

Larry Robison laughed. "A better question might be, why are *you* going back?"

"We got a fight back there," Kane said. He glanced at Grant. "Some of us got more than that."

"Well, we don't have anything," Hays said around the stump of a cigar. "Nothing tying us to good old Earth at all."

"The world we knew is gone," Joe Weaver said quietly. "Blew away on the wind two centuries ago."

"The planet we left behind," Robison said, "is just another place to us."

"And you saw our last gig there didn't turn out so well."

"What about fighting the overlords?" Grant asked.

Hays shrugged. "What about 'em?" He shook his head. "They're not real to us, Kane. Nothing on Earth has seemed really real to us since we woke up."

"And the struggle for the Shuara tribesfolk was a whole lot more real to us than the whole battle against the barons or the Annunaki," Weaver said. He chuckled softly, if without much humor. "And as Sean said, it turned out we cared a lot more for them than they did for us."

"I thought you were supposed to rebuild the world," Domi said. "Or even just America." She seemed on the verge of tears again, and fighting hard not to show it.

Robison sighed and shook his head. "That's what Bates hired us to do. What he *told* us he hired us to do."

"Another one of his damnable lies," Weaver said. "You folks should know that if anybody does."

It was Kane's turn to shrug. "Yeah, turned out the job he woke you back up for was to hit us and take over Cerberus."

"That contract is invalid, if I might revert to a previous incarnation—for what I have to say I hope is the last time ever," Weaver said.

"That's the long and the short of it, kids," Hays said. "Earth's turned her back on us—we're just returning the favor. And if that makes you think we're running away from a fight, so be it."

"No," Kane said, surprising himself more than anyone. "I don't think that at all. Any more than you people could say we're running out on this fight here. Hell, mebbe we should be glad that this time we get to pick our battle."

"Yeah," Grant said, after a moment. "Even if we don't really have much choice."

"What about you, Marina?" Brigid asked. "Do you want to go home."

"I ran away from my home," the girl said. She put her arms around Hays's waist and hugged him fiercely. "I want to stay with my family."

"You could stay," Pine said, stepping forward to take hold of both Kane's hands. Her grip was surprisingly strong. "You could help us fight the remnants of the Grand Council. And then perhaps we could come aid you in your fight!"

Bug Mama stepped up and laid a gentle hand on the girl's robed shoulder. "Sweetheart," she said, "we got a long hard slog ahead of us. Our battle won't be done soon. If it ever is."

"And I dunno if that's such a good idea," Kane said. He turned over his hands to take the girl's in his, and looked over her shoulder at the diminutive alien.

"We've seen how politics play out here in the Far Arm,

Pine," Brigid said. "Perhaps it's a blessing that the council never learned of Earth's location from Gilgamesh Bates."

"Yeah," Reichert said. "They came within a whisker of vaporizing Sidra as collateral damage. We may not be too fond of what Earth's become, but I don't think any of us want to see it blown away."

"But we'd help," Pine said. But she wept openly, and shook her head in a gesture that meant the same for her as it did the Terrans.

"We would, maybe," Bug Mama said gently. "You, me. Some of the beings standing here. But we don't even speak for the whole coalition, child. You know that. And we'd never keep the planet's location secret if we started up traffic between the worlds. Even the Paa and the Zuri have a lot of clout left. And enough malice for the whole galactic group."

She shook her huge-eyed head. "Not to name names, my people are more than capable of turning Earth to charcoal just for vengeance. Even if they've lost their dominance over the Circle of Life. Maybe more if they have—we have a vengeful streak, if you haven't noticed.

"No. I think Kane and his friends are right. Best to let sleeping frogs lie."

Brigid opened her mouth.

"It's okay," Kane told her. "Leave it."

Pine wrapped her arms around his neck and planted a moist kiss on his beard. He winced by pure reflex, although the burned skin had been totally healed in minutes by Arm med tech. The beard still had a mighty sparse patch on that side, though.

Hays stepped up to Kane and held out a hand. They gripped forearm to forearm. The silver-haired man stepped back.

"*Vayan con Dios,*" Reichert said. The Phoenix four saluted.

Reality twisted.

Somehow it didn't seem like a big deal to Kane.